HEROES OF HAVENSONG
DRAGONBOY

HEROES OF HAVENSONG
DRAGONBOY

BOOK 1

MEGAN REYES

LR LABYRINTH ROAD | NEW YORK

Text copyright © 2023 by Megan Reyes
Jacket art copyright © 2023 by Ilse Gort
Map art copyright © Megan Reyes

All rights reserved. Published in the United States by Labyrinth Road,
an imprint of Random House Children's Books,
a division of Penguin Random House LLC, New York.

Labyrinth Road and the colophon are trademarks of Penguin Random House LLC.

Visit us on the Web! rhcbooks.com

Educators and librarians, for a variety of teaching tools, visit us at
RHTeachersLibrarians.com

Library of Congress Cataloging-in-Publication Data
Name: Reyes, Megan, author.
Title: Dragonboy / Megan Reyes.
Description: First edition. | New York: Labyrinth Road, [2023] | Series: Heroes of
Havensong; book 1 | Audience: Ages 8–12. | Audience: Grades 4–6. | Summary: An
ancient prophecy has put a boy-turned-dragon, his reluctant dragon rider, a runaway
witch, and a young soldier on a collision course with destiny—and with each
other—in a mission to heal the fractured realm once known as Haven.
Identifiers: LCCN 2022036980 (print) | LCCN 2022036981 (ebook) |
ISBN 978-0-593-48237-7 (trade) | ISBN 978-0-593-48238-4 (lib. bdg.) |
ISBN 978-0-593-48239-1 (ebook)
Subjects: CYAC: Magic—Fiction. | Dragons—Fiction. | Prophecies—Fiction. |
Fantasy. | LCGFT: Fantasy fiction. | Novels.
Classification: LCC PZ7.1.R4824 Dr 2023 (print) | LCC PZ7.1.R4824 (ebook) |
DDC [Fic]—dc23

The text of this book is set in 10-point Warnock Pro.
Interior design by Jen Valero
Map design by Svetlana Dorosheva

Printed in the United States of America
10 9 8 7 6 5 4 3 2 1
First Edition

For Ric—

You are, quite simply, the absolute best.

Je t'aime, mon petit fromage.

PART 1

GROWING
DRAGONS

1.

*E*very twenty-five years, the king of Gerbera is eaten by a dragon.

It is tradition.

What's that, young one? No, I imagine it isn't very pleasant, but what else is the human king to do? He has his honor to uphold, after all. And a deal's a deal. One king every quarter century, and in exchange, the dragons leave the villages of Gerbera well enough alone.

That's the way it's always been. For nearly a thousand years.

No, I am not that old. You mind your tongue, kit. Before I toss you to the shadow bears for breakfast.

Of course I'm joking.

Your mother would be furious with me.

Why do the dragons want kings? How should I know? Maybe they taste better than ordinary humans. Leave it to dragons to be so particular. And, no, I don't know why they wait twenty-five years. Maybe that's when a human is ripe? I don't care to think about it too much, if you don't mind. Now hold still while I get this twig untangled from your fur.

Ah, well, the humans have no choice, you see. They must keep the peace with the fire beasts. They've nowhere else to go. Beyond their forest is Dragon Mountain, and that's where the world ends.

Everyone knows that.

Besides, humans are not as clever as foxes, dear. But don't hold that against them. They do their best. Oof, stop squirming about, would you? I've almost got the blasted twig free.

What's that? Where do they get the new king? Perhaps they grow kings like carrots. My whiskers, you ask so many questions. You are giving me a headache.

Fine. Fine. You may ask one more. If you must.

What would happen if a king didn't present himself to the dragons?

Whiskers of mercy! I pale to think of it. Our forest stretches to the base of Dragon Mountain, after all. The fury of the dragonfire would surely be the end of everyone.

No, youngling. Do not fret. You have nothing to fear. Don't you see? The human king always comes, just as he should. It has forever been thus.

He gives his life to save us all.

Now sleep, little one. If you're quiet enough, you can hear the moon rise.

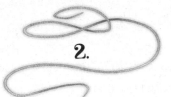

2.

IN WHICH SOME MAGIC GETS THE HICCUPS

THREE HUNDRED YEARS BEFORE THE FOURTH WAR

Many years ago, and half a world away, Madam Seer Madera Starling let out a yelp. Her violet eyes popped open, the pools of midnight darkness pressing in on her, trying to keep her in bed.

The smell of rain and sage flower wafted through the open windows, promising her that all was well. But the old woman knew how flowers spun their untruths when it suited them. She cast the sage petals a look through the window. All was well *indeed*.

Madera slowly swung her legs over the side of the bed, her silver-white hair falling to her waist in twisty braids. She grasped the cane leaning against the wall, drawing in breath slowly, committing each detail of her dream to memory. The moonlight fell across her dark brown hands in a soft glow.

"That *was* you, wasn't it?" she asked the rising wisp of violet smoke hovering over her nightstand.

Madera's Magic hummed its agreement, swirling in a slow circle, drifting toward the woman's outstretched hand. "You haven't given me dreams in ages. Not since—" She shuddered and shook the memory away. Her Magic floated toward her, now a purple tornado. Madera rolled her eyes.

"There's no need to be *dramatic*," she scolded as she pushed herself to stand. The tornado let out an audible huff and then slowed to form a cumulus cloud.

"Haru!" Madera called, knowing the Scribe would hear. The boy slept lighter than a pile of feathers.

A crash rang from the hallway, just outside Madera's bedroom. A few moments later, the door creaked open and Haru stumbled forward, his thin raven hair sticking up like a sea urchin. His firequill glowed in one hand, lighting up his tan face, with a scroll of parchment tucked under his other arm.

"You . . . called?" said Haru, blinking sleep from his eyes. They were brown with little specks of teal—starting to match the color of his Magic, which now sat on his shoulder.

"I need you to record a prophecy, Haru."

The purple smoke growled.

"Now, you *hush*," Madera snapped. "We're doing this *properly*, and that's final."

Her Magic sighed rather theatrically.

"A *prophecy*, Madam Madera?" Haru repeated, his eyes stealing a hesitant glance at the purple smoke. Still a new Scribe, Haru Tanaka was eager to prove himself. The most he'd ever recorded was Elder Myrtle's *Theory on Magical Propriety*. And that was nothing like a prophecy—more of a yawn-inducing ramble.

"You'll do just fine, child, as long as you pay attention," Madera assured him with the same encouraging smile she'd used on new Scribes for the last half millennium. Haru gulped, readying his parchment. He held his hand steady, sparks of red fire shooting from the tip of his quill.

"Help me remember," Madera told her Magic as it settled on the top of her head. She closed her eyes. "I see a newborn child. A boy. The mother is sobbing, but I cannot see her face. The baby is wrapped hastily in a tattered gray blanket. A filthy old thing." She frowned as the next part of the dream bubbled into focus. "There's a full moon and it's snowing. Who carried him—the father, perhaps? The child is left on a doorstep. He . . . does not cry." Her eyebrows scrunched together. "Why isn't he crying? He's so cold."

The Seer searched her memories as her Magic danced lightly at her temples. There was something about a door with the head of a lion for a knocker. She could sense the child's breathing, his quivering gums in the biting cold. His tiny heart raced in sheer terror, and still he did not cry.

"This child is of great significance," said Madera, beads of sweat now trickling down her neck. "But I cannot See how."

"He must be remarkable!" breathed Haru, scribbling furiously across the page, red sparks flying.

Madera shook her head. "No, but that's just it. He is, in fact, utterly *ordinary*. No trace of heroic lineage. And when I try to See his future, there is only . . . vast *nothingness*." Her frown deepened as she searched for more. There was great beauty in this boy. But there was something else too. Something . . . hidden in darkness.

A loud squeak rang through the room.

Haru's scribbling ceased. "Was that . . . a hiccup?" he asked, his eyes fixed on Madera's hovering Magic.

Madera shifted her weight on the cane, convincing herself they'd heard wrong. It was something outside. A beach bat or a river toad. Her Magic squeaked again, and she winced.

No, no, no.

Magic hiccups meant only one thing.

Something dreadful was coming.

"I cannot understand it. An ordinary boy. Destined for greatness and plagued by such darkness," Madera whispered. "But his future is kept from me. Something or someone doesn't want me to See properly." And then a realization hit Madera so suddenly she nearly fell over onto the bed. "It's . . . *him*."

Her Magic bounced up and down.

"Him?" repeated Haru.

"The Awaited One." She gaped at her Magic, finally understanding its urgency. "The one from the songs of old. The songs of Haven."

"Haven?" Haru used his firequill to scratch his head. "That's what the old kingdom was called. Like . . . a *really* long time ago, right?"

"Back when life was birthed into being, yes. When all was right in our world."

"What is the boy's name?" asked Haru, his quill hovering eagerly over the parchment. The scorched words inked there were already recorded in the *Legacy Hall of the Seers.*

"He is called Blue."

Haru scrunched his nose. "That's his full name? Just . . . Blue?"

Madera let out a long sigh, allowing these new revelations to settle deep into her bones. This was troubling indeed. The coming of the Awaited One meant also the coming of the end. And someone was definitely out there, trying to keep her from Seeing it.

"We'll have to be ready." She gave her Magic a knowing look and it huffed its agreement.

"So . . . is that the last of it, then, Madam Madera?" asked Haru, his voice sounding far away. The old woman nodded and Haru rolled up the scroll carefully. It rose into the air, blanketed by the blue glow of his Magic. Then the scroll disappeared with a *pop,* sending bits of magic dust everywhere and causing Haru to sneeze.

"That was amazing," Haru breathed, his teal Magic bouncing

up and down on his shoulder in celebration. "My first prophecy recording!"

Madera sighed, hobbling to the window, searching the night skies. Sometimes the stars mapped out a helpful message, winking their truths to those below who knew how to See. But tonight the stars lay hidden by clouds.

Keeping their secrets.

3.

IN WHICH THERE
IS A GREAT COMMOTION

TEN YEARS BEFORE THE FOURTH WAR

A great many years later, Blue the stable boy woke to the smell of Fear. It pushed down on him like a foal sitting on his rib cage. He scrambled up from his hay-pile bed, his clothes soaked through with sweat, trying to shake himself from his sleepy stupor. He stumbled through the stable gates to the training arena outside, strands of hay clinging to his trousers. Nothing looked out of the ordinary with the first bits of sunlight peeking over the tops of the massive stone walls of the castle. The quietness of the grounds rested gently against his thumping heart.

Where *was* it coming from?

To Blue, Fear always smelled of wood and oranges, though he was never sure *why*. For as long as he could remember, he'd been able to smell certain emotions the way someone might detect scents of different flowers. It took many years before he even realized what was happening, since none of the other castle servants shared his strange talent. For the longest time, no one even believed him, which only left him feeling confused and embarrassed.

Then one day, a very bored seven-year-old Blue had been exploring the eastern towers. He ran into—quite literally—Lady Zoya, the Royal Mage of Gerbera. Lady Zoya kindly explained his weird ability, assuring Blue it was an incredible gift.

Blue still wasn't sure about that. Most times his knack felt like a burden. Still, in time, he'd learned to pay attention to it—and so had everyone else.

Blue shivered in the dawn light, scanning his surroundings once more. Right now, the Fear clung to the air so fiercely, it could only mean someone close by was trapped in the worst sort of peril. But Blue couldn't place where it was coming from. The weight in his chest sank even deeper.

He'd smelled Fear this strongly only three times in his life. Once, when the stables had caught fire. Again, when Old Man Albert had fallen from the roof trying to repair a loose shingle. And lastly, when one of the kitchen servants had had a severe allergic reaction to strawberries. Each time, Blue had been right there to help. But now he couldn't see anyone. Silence hung in the air, except for the soft snores of the king's horses.

Then, like a weather vane shifting suddenly with a strong wind, the Fear dissipated, the scent of woody citrus nothing more than a memory. Blue frowned, running his hands through his hair as he scanned the castle walls once more for any clues. But the Fear was quite simply gone.

"And how'd I know you'd be up so early, Blueboy?"

Blue turned to see Suri Hakimi, one of the older stable servants, pushing her way through the gate. Her dark hair was pulled into a ponytail under a plum-colored beanie, and when she smiled, her deep brown eyes seemed to shine.

"What are you doing here?" asked Blue, though it was no stranger a thing for *him* to be standing outside barefoot at dawn.

11

"Finished my family chores last night, so my mom let me come early."

A small ache pierced Blue's chest. Whenever Suri or the other stable servants talked about their families, Blue couldn't help but feel a jealous longing.

"I checked the stable," Suri went on. "When you weren't in your bed, I figured you'd gotten an early start prepping Cedar." She rolled her eyes. "Don't think I didn't notice her shiny new horseshoes waiting by your bed. Trying to get that promotion, you are, you sneaky bugger."

Well, that was definitely true. Blue wanted nothing more than to get promoted to stable manager, and he'd been working overtime all year to prove himself to Albert, the stable master.

Suri's bronze cheeks flushed as understanding dawned in her eyes. "Oh. You had another . . . episode, didn't you?" she guessed, dropping her gaze to her shoes. It always made people uncomfortable to talk about Blue's ability. Even if they'd learned to trust it.

"It was some of the worst Fear I've ever smelled. I thought for sure the stable was on fire again. Then it just . . . disappeared." Blue's arms fell against his sides in defeat. "I just don't get it."

"Well, it might not be so hard to guess what it was," said Suri, nodding to the castle. Blue followed her gaze to the northernmost tower window.

"The king?" asked Blue.

Well, of *course.*

Today was Dragon Day.

At the nine o'clock gong, the king of Gerbera would set out beyond the kingdom, through the Peculiar Forest and up to Dragon Mountain—where he'd promptly be eaten. The king didn't *know* this, of course. He only believed he would set out to slay the dragon that had begun to terrorize the outer villages. The dragon showed up exactly every twenty-five years to goad the newest king into battle. And it always ended the same. Three days after the king departed, his horse would return with a note from the dragon, thanking Gerbera for another fine meal.

Everyone knew this except the king himself. The entire kingdom—and especially the castle staff—took great pains to keep it from him. From the moment a new king was crowned—always an orphaned infant from one of Gerbera's villages—he knew nothing of his fate. It was easier that way. There were no parents to miss him. And what kind of life would it be to *know* you would grow up to be eaten by a dragon? Better to let that be an unfortunate surprise. At least, that was how one of the kitchen servants had explained it to Blue when he'd asked so many years ago.

Blue frowned, eyeing Dragon Mountain rising far in the distance, its mighty peak hiding in the morning clouds. The end of the world. And soon enough, the end of the line for another valiant king of Gerbera.

He sighed, a small twinge of doubt throbbing against his temples. But Suri's theory made more sense than anything else. Of course the king would have fears about fighting the dragon, no matter how brave and noble he was raised to be. Still—why did the Fear disappear so suddenly?

"Come on. We might as well get an early start," said Suri, clapping Blue on the shoulder with a dubious look at the king's tower. "There's really nothing we can do for him, you know."

"I suppose you're right." Blue exhaled, a pang of sadness flitting through him. The poor king. Such a terrible fate. "Best we can do is give His Majesty a proper send-off."

"That's the spirit! Those horses will be shining pretty before breakfast."

With a defeated sigh, Blue followed Suri back to the stables. The large A-frame building stood welcoming, the morning sunbeams sliding across the timber roof like a slow golden yawn. Beyond the arched stone entrance, two rows of stables housed the horses of His Majesty's forty royal knights.

Blue had worked in the stables since the age of three—as soon as he was old enough for Albert to teach him how to use a grooming brush. Blue knew each horse better than the knights themselves did. He had the advantage, of course, since he lived in the stables, while the knights and other stable servants went home to their families each evening.

The stables *were* Blue's home.

By age twelve, he'd risen in the ranks, working hoof and horseshoe in hope of earning the promotion to stable manager. It would near double his responsibilities during the day, but it would allow him more free time in the evenings to ride Cedar, the colt he'd raised from birth. He'd only ever really wanted two things in life: to work with horses and to have a family of his own someday. If he did well prepping for the Dragon Day ceremony, that promotion was as good as his. He and Cedar could spend all their afternoons together.

Blue and Suri got to work washing, brushing, and saddling their teams. The smell of hay and manure set Blue into an easy rhythm. By the time Albert came to wake him, just as the other stable servants were arriving, Blue was already done with his morning duties.

"Up before the sun again, are you, Blue?" muttered Albert, giving Cedar's reddish-brown coat a once-over. He adjusted his messenger hat over his balding head. The old man was not one to give compliments easily, but Blue's horses were all immaculate. Especially Cedar. Grumpy old Albert had nothing to complain about today.

"And you think *this* horse be fit for a king?" asked Albert, crossing his beige arms against his chest.

Blue grinned confidently. "Yes, sir. Her coat's brighter than buttermilk. And her form is good. I even triple-braided her tail."

Cedar let out a snort, and Blue patted the bridge of her nose. He hated braiding because of how it aggravated Cedar, but the king preferred it. And Cedar had a real shot at being chosen for the Dragon Day ceremony. She was too young to be picked as the king's personal steed, but she stood in the running to be one of the processionals.

Albert's eyebrows scrunched together in what might've been the beginning contemplations of flattery, but Blue wouldn't get to find out. An earsplitting scream rose from outside.

Then another.

"That's coming from the castle," said Blue, his heart giving a knowing thump.

"Sounds like Pierre spotted another rat in the kitchen," grunted Albert, waving his hand in a dismissive manner.

Blue frowned. While the royal chef *was* prone to his fair number of shrieks at the sight of spiders, mice, or any other creature scampering about, this was something else. Blue smelled wood and citrus again. It came in spurts. Like not just one big Fear, but the Fear of many.

By this time, all the other stable hands had reported for work. They now followed Blue through the gates. Albert hobbled behind them reluctantly, muttering about Pierre's petty frights. Enzo, one of the gardener's sons, was sprinting across the castle lawn, his eyes wider than those of a feather-plucked chicken.

"Albert! Clear everyone out of the stables!" Enzo cried, his legs going wobbly beneath him.

"Eh? What you yelling about, Enzo?" croaked Albert, clearly annoyed at the interruption.

"M-my father sent me to tell you," Enzo sputtered between gasps, his curly dark hair a windblown mess. "The kn-knights need the s-stable for an emergency m-meeting. They're on their way n-now. You need to c-clear out."

"What's happened?" asked Blue. "What's this emergency meeting for?"

Enzo's light brown eyes blazed like wildfire, the smell of woody citrus saturating the air around him. "The king is dead."

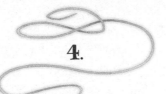

4.

IN WHICH A DRAGON TOOTH
MOST DEFINITELY DOES NOT
MAKE A MISTAKE

It took less than two clicks of a gallop for Albert to kick his twelve stable hands out on their rears. In the commotion, Blue scampered up to the enormous crossbeam that ran down the middle of the stable's A-frame ceiling. He'd discovered this hiding spot many knight-gatherings ago, mostly on a dare from Suri. From atop the wide rafter, he could squeeze comfortably between the beam and the ceiling, remaining hidden ten feet above the royal knights, now gathered below.

Blue was surprised that Lady Zoya had joined them. He hadn't seen the Royal Mage in years. Not since she'd explained his strange knack for smelling emotions. She looked just as mesmerizing as he remembered. Neither old nor young, but *fierce*. Her platinum hair was cropped short on the sides and underneath, and long on the top. Her dark blue eyes matched her glittering navy cloak, which hung to the floor, and her pale skin looked freshly painted with purple symbols on her palms and cheekbones.

It was rumored that Lady Zoya emerged from her tower only in times of dire emergency to offer guidance and counsel from a magical perspective. All Gerberans believed that magic was an evil born from dragons, so its use was permitted only during times of great peril.

And even then, with much reluctance.

Blue scooted carefully along the rafter, ignoring the puffs of dust threatening to bring on a sneeze attack, until he lay just above Lady Zoya. The room smelled of enough Fear to fuel the royal kitchen furnace as Lady Zoya's eyes scanned the room.

"For those who haven't heard, a tragedy of the worst sort has cast a shadow across our kingdom," said Lady Zoya. "Minutes ago, when one of the servants went to wake the king, he would not stir. Good knights of Gerbera, our king is dead."

The aroma of Sorrow—lilac and mint—mixed with the rising dust.

"Protocol is clear, written by the Gerbera knight Councils of Old," said Lady Zoya. The semicircles painted on her cheeks seemed to glow. She unfurled a long black scroll, blowing away a layer of dust before reading: "'In the dire case of a king's death before Dragon Day, a new king must be chosen from the Circle of the Brave.'"

"I will do the honors," said a short knight, stepping forward. Blue recognized Sir Huxley, his gray hair and mustache meticulously groomed, as usual. He'd always been kind to Blue, letting him ride a horse for the first time and slipping him extra sweets from the royal kitchen. "I'm the oldest, and it's only right."

"But you have a wife and children," another knight, Lady Camila, pointed out. She tightened her long dark ponytail for emphasis. "It would be cruel to leave them without a husband and father."

"Then I'll do it," said another. "I'm the youngest."

"*Too* young," argued yet another.

Lady Zoya held up her hands. "It is not up to any of you, noble ones. We must leave such a choice to the Fates."

There were several murmurs about the Fates being magical

mumbo jumbo, but no one seemed brave enough to challenge the Mage outright.

Lady Zoya raised her right palm, spreading her pale thin fingers slowly. From his vantage point, Blue saw the large white crescent before the others did. It stretched from one side of Lady Zoya's hand to the other.

A chorus of gasps filled the room.

"A dragon tooth?" someone breathed.

"Indeed," said Lady Zoya, with a hint of finality in her tone. "This tooth holds the only remaining magic in Gerbera, and it never fails. It will choose our next king."

Several knights shifted uncomfortably. Blue couldn't blame them: magic was nothing but bad luck. Everyone knew that. An icy chill worked its way through Blue's chest. At the same time, something glittered in the corner of his eye. He looked up to see a thick golden thread hovering about a horseshoe's length from his forehead. He craned his neck to get a better view. The golden string stretched to the far wall like a sparkling web woven by a mysterious spider.

And it *sang*.

A chorus of high fluttering notes poured from the thread. Blue peeked down, but if any of the knights heard the music above them, they paid no notice. They were too focused on the dragon tooth now spinning wildly in Lady Zoya's palm.

Blue shook his head. Webs weren't gold, and they didn't make music. As if to prove him wrong, the singing grew louder and louder, until Blue had to press his palms against his ears. Great torture of firebreathers, how could no one else hear that noise?

Maybe if he could just—Blue reached up and pulled the thread toward him. Instead of snapping from its grip on the wall, the thread only grew longer, as if it were being pulled *through* the wall. And before Blue could make sense of any of it, the thread disappeared.

"Cripes!" someone called out.

Blue jerked his head from the rafter to watch. The spinning dragon tooth now glowed emerald, a beam of light pouring out of it. The green glow swirled around the room in a wide spiral above the knights. Then the rafters started to tremble.

"What . . . Is that an earthquake?" cried Lady Camila.

"Stand firm!" Lady Zoya commanded as the ground beneath their feet continued to rumble.

A resounding *crack* ripped through the air, louder than a thunderbolt, its force knocking Blue from his hiding place. He tumbled off the beam onto a very startled group of knights—several of whom uttered a word or two *quite* undignified as they landed in a heap.

"It's that fool, Blueboy," someone muttered.

"Nearly broke my neck," said someone else.

Blue groaned. He'd landed mostly on bony shoulders, and thankfully, it was the burly Sir Kunma who'd broken his fall.

At least they'd all left their lances elsewhere.

"What you playin' at, hidin' up there, boy?" growled Sir Kunma, shoving Blue off him.

"I'm sorry," said Blue, pushing to his feet. His cheeks burned, and he couldn't meet anyone's eye.

"Are you all right, child?" asked Lady Zoya, her eyes scanning his face. Blue nodded and her eyes widened, staring at something on his right cheek. As soon as she looked at it, Blue's face itched something fierce.

"What's happening to his skin?" asked Sir Huxley, taking a step back.

"Got injured in the fall, most like," someone said.

"No," Lady Zoya breathed. She cupped Blue's face in her hands. "Look at this! These crescent markings on his cheekbones." She traced a finger along Blue's right cheek. "The dragon tooth . . . has chosen him."

Blue let out a sigh of relief at Lady Zoya's touch, the unbearable itching finally ceasing. But as his brain caught up to Lady Zoya's words, his stomach clamped tighter than stretched leather.

"Wh-what?" Blue asked.

"Chosen *him*?" scoffed Sir Kunma, hand on his sword hilt.

"Can't be," said another.

Sir Kunma shrugged. "Then again, he's got no family. So it's not really much of a loss, is it?"

Before Blue could blink, Lady Camila crossed the room and shoved Sir Kunma so hard he fell over on his rear. "You should be ashamed!" she thundered.

"That's right," Sir Huxley growled at Sir Kunma. "He's only a boy, for mercy's sake!"

"A *stable* boy," Sir Kunma grumbled. He pushed himself to his feet with a loud grunt of disapproval.

Lady Camila put a hand on Blue's shoulder. "It must be a mistake."

"Magic doesn't make mistakes," Lady Zoya said solemnly. She put a finger under Blue's chin. The smell of wood and citrus rose around her, and a deep shiver slithered through Blue's core.

"I don't . . . understand," said Blue, his voice barely a whisper.

"You must be very brave now," said Lady Zoya, trying to give him a reassuring smile. "You, stable boy, have been chosen as our new king."

5.

IN WHICH WREN BARROW SAYS THE HARDEST GOODBYE

SIX YEARS BEFORE THE FOURTH WAR

Some time later, and half a world away, seven-year-old Wren Barrow sat on the beach, holding her little brother, Cephas, tightly in her lap. Together they watched Mama's funeral canoe drift out onto the ocean under the light of a full moon.

Cephas pulled on Wren's tight curls absentmindedly as the incense bearers wafted their plumes of cedarwood smoke over the gathered Meraki people. Behind them, the Council Elders sang the Songs of Mourning with their Magics swirling around them. Each Elder wore a sleeveless white tunic to show off their Shoya, the slight glimmer and glow against their various skin tones. Shoya, noticeable only in the moonlight, represented a Meraki's mastery Bond with their Magics, and no one's Shoya shone brighter than the Elders'.

From her spot on the sand, Wren could no longer see the words etched onto the boat's wooden hull, but she knew they were there all the same. She'd carved one of the many goodbye messages to Rose Barrow herself.

I will try always to be brave, Mama. Just like you taught me.
And I promise to be your little dolphin forever.
All my love, Wren

The second part of the message was cloaked in a secret between just Mama and Wren. Mama was a scientist who studied ocean animals. She'd always said Wren reminded her of a dolphin because dolphins were both clever and curious. Unfortunately, the Meraki community didn't much approve of Wren's *persistently overactive imagination*—that was what the Elders called it, anyway. But Mama assured Wren her curiosity was a blessing, since brains were just as good for thinking clever thoughts as they were for asking questions.

And no one asked more questions than Wren.

"There will be many who don't understand your curious mind, love," Mama had told Wren on what had been her last day. "Especially the Elders, set in their old ways. They fear what they don't know, while you embrace it. In time, they will come to see how much they need a dolphin like you." Mama had given Wren her best smile, even though she'd been in great pain those final hours. "*You are enough, my sweet Wren. Just as you are. You don't need to change for anyone. Promise me you'll remember that.*"

Wren had promised.

And the weight of that promise now settled on her as a fresh waft of cedarwood filled her lungs.

Wren spotted Xayndra, the oldest of the island dragons, standing off to the side of the humans, her yellow scales glittering. Her large golden eyes glistened with tears as she caught Wren's gaze. The dragon let out a deep whine, bowing her head slightly. Wren nodded in response, an ache rising in her throat. Mama had always said that just because dragons couldn't talk didn't mean they couldn't communicate.

Wren hugged Cephas tighter against her chest as he pointed to the ocean's horizon, where Mama's ivory-colored canoe glided gently on the waves, suddenly glowing under the moonlight.

"That's the stardust activating," Wren told Cephas, though he was much too young to understand. "The natural magic transforms Mama's body into pure light, then sends her up to the stars, where she can watch over us."

Wren's people believed that the soul of a lost Meraki found peace among the stars, where companion Magics had originated. Wren wanted desperately to believe it. She needed to know Mama was at peace.

Even if Wren wasn't.

In the distance, the canoe glowed brighter, until bursts of pure white light shot up from the boat into the night sky. The lights danced among the stars, turning different colors. Cephas let out a delighted giggle, his eyes wide with wonder. It should've been beautiful. Instead, it was just wrong.

Everything was wrong without Mama.

Wren slowly lifted Cephas from her lap and kissed his pudgy brown cheek. He blinked his honey-colored eyes at her and then immediately toddled off to pluck seashells from the beach, leaving a trail of sunken footprints in his wake. Wren closed her eyes, picturing Mama's face. It had been six days since her mother's passing, and she was afraid of forgetting Mama's laugh. Her voice. Her warm brown skin and bright copper eyes—just like Wren's.

After a long while, Wren felt a hand on her shoulder. She looked up to find Granmama smiling over her, her violet eyes worn from a thousand tears. Granmama had lost her only daughter. And though Wren couldn't be sure, she wondered if that kind of loss hurt just as deeply as losing a mother.

The Elders and other Meraki started to get up and head home, companion Magic wisps following the adults like little multicolored clouds. People passed by Wren and Granmama, giving them nods and hugs. The adults glittered and glowed in a myriad of hues wherever the moonlight hit their skin.

Wren spotted Haru the Scribe, walking with his wife and young child. "So sorry for your loss," Haru whispered, his gaze flicking from Granmama to Wren as his teal Magic hovered next to him. "Rose Barrow was an extraordinary woman. The best of us, really."

Granmama gave Haru's hand a squeeze. "That she was, dear."

Several more people shuffled through with condolences, until Wren felt ready to burst with sadness. Her father was somewhere in the crowd, but he hadn't spoken to her all day.

"You ready to go, love?" asked Granmama, her purple cloud of Magic letting out a sniffling whimper.

Wren nodded. She called to Cephas, who stood with his arms full of colorful seashells. He stuck out a pouty lip and waddled reluctantly toward them. At the same moment, an old man in sleeveless white robes came up behind them, his rich brown arms and face glowing faintly with Shoya. Judge Santino Finlar wore his usual scowl beneath his narrowed eyes, which matched the color of his silver Magic. His salt-and-pepper hair was parted at the side and curved up slightly at the tips, always reminding Wren of an orderly ocean wave.

Wren tried to hide her grimace. She didn't like the judge, even though he was highly revered by the Meraki community. The old grump had caught Wren swiping flowers from the community garden and climbing the cherry trees during school hours more times than she could count. It was no secret that Santino Finlar considered Wren to be a *troubled youth.* He was one of the oldest Meraki— though not as old as Granmama. His was the deciding vote for any

Council matters at hand, as he was known for his swift justice. He was also the one who had first labeled Wren with a *persistently over-active imagination.* As if Wren's mind were dangerously contagious.

"It was a beautiful celebration, Madera," Judge Finlar said to Granmama with a small bow, his ocean-wave hair bobbing slightly. Granmama nodded briefly; then Judge Finlar's eyes flicked to Wren.

"You can take solace knowing your mother found her peace, Wren Barrow," Judge Finlar said a little louder, so others could hear. Then he waited patiently for her reply.

The judge's words were not random. They were a formality. A final blessing at Meraki funerals given by the judge. Wren knew her correct response should be "Yes, and may my mother remain at peace until we meet again."

It was the traditional reply expected from family members of lost ones. A way to promote the circle of healing for the Meraki commu-nity. Traditions were a really big deal to Wren's people—especially to the twelve Elders, who were all looking at her now.

Waiting.

But as Wren's sorrow burrowed deeper into her chest, she didn't feel like *promoting healing.* Not one bit. Instead, a simmering flame warmed her cheeks.

"There is no *solace* with Mama gone," Wren said coolly, her eyes starting to sting. A few people behind her gasped.

Judge Finlar stiffened, and his Magic let out a growl of disap-proval. Wren would definitely pay for her comment with a stern lecture from her father later. But for now, she couldn't care less. Shouldn't she be allowed to feel what she wanted instead of putting on a good face for the sake of some ancient custom?

"You would do well not to disrupt our traditions of honoring our lost ones, young lady," Judge Finlar scolded, his eyes narrowing. "Your mother never would have wanted it."

Wren's teeth clamped together, and her fists balled. This stuffy curmudgeon knew *nothing* about what Mama would've wanted! But since opening her mouth would only get her into more trouble, Wren instead threw the judge her best scowl and turned on her heel.

"I'm going to the Offering Tree," she told Granmama. "To pay my last respects." More than anything, she wanted to get as far from everyone as possible.

"This kind of disrespect is unbecoming of a Meraki," Judge Finlar warned loudly from behind Wren as she marched away. "The way she carries on, she may as well be a *Mainlander*."

Wren's breath caught at the insult. It was the lowest of all lows. Meraki considered the Mainlanders to be two things: *preposterous* for rejecting magic, and *dangerous* because of their ever-growing powerful army. To be called a Mainlander was to be called a reckless fool. Wren hated the shame that heated her cheeks. Hated that even on this wretched day, she was reminded how she didn't fit in.

"She's a seven-year-old girl who just lost her mother!" Granmama's fury seemed to crackle through the air. "Perhaps you would do well to summon some *grace*, Santino. And leave the girl be."

Wren wrapped Granmama's loyalty around herself like a shield as she walked on, wiping the tears from her cheeks. She wondered if her father was somewhere in the distance, watching. Or if he even remembered to think of Wren at all. After Mama got sick, he hardly ever looked at Wren and Cephas. And since Mama had passed, it was like Wren and her brother didn't exist anymore.

Wren tried to ignore the whispers and stares as she marched on toward the Offering Tree. She stormed past the Academy building and community gardens. Farther on, she passed the Council Chambers, where seven enormous gemstones—the Meraki crystals—twinkled in various colors to form the rooftops. The crystals glittered in the moonlight, ever a reminder of Meraki history, order, and tradition.

Ugh. Just what Wren needed right now.

She walked on, over the wildflower hills. By the time Wren crested the last hilltop, her breath came out in puffs as the enormous white tree came into view. It stood in the middle of a vast meadow, its massive branches stretching toward the stars.

Toward Mama, Wren realized with a new ache in her heart.

To one side of the Offering Tree sat Kado the dragon, his golden eyes twinkling. Even though he was the biggest dragon on the island, his plum-colored head didn't quite reach the top of the thirty-foot tree. Along with Xayndra and Kado, three other dragons were stationed on the island as a means to maintain peaceful order. As if anything disorderly *ever* happened on Meraki Island—hah! But the dragons also served as deterrents to keep the Mainlanders from getting any ideas of visiting.

Because no one got past a dragon.

Kado nodded a greeting as Wren approached the tree. The white bark seemed to almost glow in the moonlight, reminding Wren of powdery snow. She placed a palm on the smooth trunk, and it pulsed gently under her hand. All companion Magics were born at this beautiful tree—each one a bright wisp of smoke with different personalities, abilities, and colors. The Offering Tree was also where companion Magics came for their final rest.

"Thanks for looking after her," Wren whispered, though she knew Mama's Magic was now long gone. Had died three days before Mama, in fact. But it made Wren feel better all the same to speak her gratitude. "I know you did your best and . . . Mama loved you very much."

It was a rare thing for Magics to die before their human companions. Then again, it was a rare thing for a Meraki like Rose Barrow to die so young. Usually, Wren's people lived well near a thousand years, their long lives attributed to the natural magic in their blood as well as the help and restorative healing from their companion Magics.

Wren let her hand fall from the tree.

"She would've loved you wearing that dress."

Wren turned to find Granmama standing behind her, face glowing slightly Shoya purple in the moonlight as her Magic hovered at her side. Wren tugged at the sparkly pastel-blue fabric on her sleeve. She usually hated wearing dresses, but Mama had made this one herself.

"I can't stop thinking about how she died," Wren whispered, the words stabbing at her chest.

Mama had been out on her boat, studying a new species of large eel she'd named movlak. Somehow, despite her usual care and caution, she'd been stung multiple times by the creatures she was there to study. Normally, a venomous bite would be healed by one's Magic. But Mama's Magic was already dead when Wren's father reached the boat. Wren remembered her father's strong arms carrying Mama back to shore. The Healers did all they could, but after a few days, Mama was gone. Wren had spent the next few days studying Rose Barrow's science journals obsessively. There were plenty of sketches of movlak eels—huge yellow snakelike creatures with red eyes and tentacles tipped with deadly poison. Like monsters out of a nightmare. In fact, they'd haunted Wren's dreams for weeks.

"Nothing made my Rose happier than spending time in her boat, diving underwater and studying all those animals." Granmama shook her head. "In that way, she died doing what she loved."

Wren frowned. "Does that make it better—dying doing something you love?" Wren trembled at the thought of the terrible movlak eels. "Seems almost worse. Like the ocean betrayed her."

Granmama's mouth drew into a thin line. She got that faraway look in her eyes that meant she was lost in a lifetime's worth of memories.

And Madera Starling had a *lot* of lifetime behind her.

But whatever memories Granmama was reliving, she kept them to herself. She ran a hand over one of Wren's poufy pigtails. "Come on, love. I've convinced your father to let you have a late-night mug of cocoa."

Wren's eyes widened. "But he hates when we have sugar right before bedtime."

"Ah, but your grandmother can be very persuasive."

Wren smiled and took Granmama's hand as they made their way back to the house, where Cephas was already snoring in bed. Father, on the other hand, was nowhere to be seen.

After a cup of cinnamon cocoa, Wren's exhaustion finally caught up with her. She bade good night to Granmama, then slid into bed without changing into nightclothes. Through her bedroom window, the moon shone brightly. She thought she could still see wisps of Mama's dancing life lights, but she was probably just imagining it. Her eyelids drooped heavy, and she'd only just started to nod off when her father's voice carried through the walls.

He and Granmama were arguing in the kitchen again.

Wren sat up, straining her ears.

"She's only seven!" Her father's voice was getting more growly.

"We still have time," said Granmama calmly.

"How much time?"

"I . . . cannot be certain."

Her father scoffed. "Of course you can't." There was a pause; then her father said, "I won't lose her too."

Granmama blew out a long breath, and Wren imagined her grandmother rubbing her temples, like she always did when she was upset. "There is no stopping things. It's written clearly in the

Havensong! You know what I've Seen, Jarum. And the darkness that is coming—"

"Save your prophecies, Seer."

"It cannot be ignored. Wren *is* to be—"

"No!" There was a clattering of dishes. "I won't have it!"

"But the Fates—"

"Don't talk to me about the Fates, Madera! I want nothing to do with them."

There was a long silence.

"I don't like it any better than you do. But she needs us, Jarum. Now more than ever."

When her father didn't respond, Wren sank back onto her pillow. She steadied her breathing, knowing Granmama would be along soon to check on her. Sure enough, her door creaked open and Wren closed her eyes, pretending to be asleep. Granmama's cane clunked gently across the floor toward the bed. Wren felt a gentle kiss on her cheek.

"Rest well, my love. I am so proud of you."

Wren heard the door close, and she hugged her blankets tighter. The conversation she'd overheard swirled in her mind fast enough to make her dizzy. Songs and prophecies and darkness? She couldn't begin to guess what any of it meant.

But one thing seemed certain.

Something dangerous was coming. And according to Granmama, Wren would be part of it.

Not for the last time, Wren Barrow cried herself to sleep, with a Mama-sized ache in her chest.

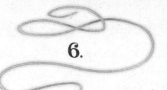

6.

IN WHICH SHENLI ZHAO
MEETS A STIRRUP

THREE YEARS BEFORE THE FOURTH WAR

Three years later, on the other side of the ocean, Shenli Zhao the Mainlander stood waiting in his new silk shirt, giving his jet-black hair a nervous ruffle. He was still shaking loose from the previous night's unsettling dream, instead trying to focus on looking presentable. Because Chancellor Cudek's soldiers would be here any minute.

Mama couldn't stop eyeing Shenli from the kitchen, trying to hide her sorrow with big smiles while feeding six-month-old Yiming her bottle. Shenli caught sight of the parchment scroll on the table, the broken crimson seal of the Mainland chancellor gleaming in the lantern light. The scroll explained that Shenli's older brother, Yuli, had fled his military post and hadn't returned. It had happened only three days prior, but that was enough time for all the neighbors to find out and to begin gossiping eagerly about the continued *curse of the Zhao family.* They shared the same single word on their lips for the eldest Zhao child:

Coward.

And they weren't wrong.

For a Mainlander, serving in the military was an honor. A sacred duty. Which meant Yuli's running away from his post not only was cowardly but also brought shame upon Shenli's entire family. Like a storm cloud darkening their doorstep. And quite frankly, the Zhao doorstep had been darkened enough already. Now Shenli had the chance to restore his family's honor.

"You look dashing, Shen," Mama told him. "You'll fit right in with the other castle servants."

Warmth flooded Shenli's chest, mixed with the slightest pang of guilt. His new clothes, including the outfits packed away in his travel bag, had cost Mama a month's income, since all the fancy fabrics were imported from the Mountain District. No one in Shenli's district wore silk, but Mama insisted that a personal steward to Chancellor Cudek needed to look the part.

Shenli's eyes flicked to the scroll again. The problem was, the Zhaos owed Chancellor Cudek a debt—even more than the average Mainlander family. By law, all Mainlanders had to pay their loyalty tax in one of two ways: donation or servitude. And while the rich Mainlanders in the Mountain and Middle Districts could afford to pay money or donate valuable goods like lumber or metal, Shenli and the rest of the Wedi people lived in the Coastal District, where everyone was a farmer, fisherperson, or soldier. And dirt poor. Which meant that Wedi Mainlanders were forced to pay the loyalty tax with servitude—each family had to send their eldest child to join the military for four years once they turned sixteen.

But the Zhao family's debt with the chancellor went even deeper.

Shenli hadn't known just how bad things were until a year ago, when his father disappeared in the middle of the night, leaving Shenli's mom with the kids, including baby Yiming, who was just starting to grow in Mama's belly. Soon after, the first scroll came, claiming that Jinbao Zhao had been found dead outside a tavern in the Middle District. No details were given.

But something about that didn't sit right with Shenli. He was certain there was more to the story. In fact, when Mama had sent a message to Cudek, asking that Jin's body be returned for a proper Wedi burial, the request was denied—without any reason given. Suspicious indeed. It was rumored that Jin's death was due to an enormous amount of unpaid—and publicly *undisclosed*—debt to the chancellor. But the usual punishment for a Mainlander family who failed to pay their loyalty tax was imprisonment, not death. So who had killed Shenli's father: the military, by order of the chancellor, or someone else entirely?

The Zhao family was left with zero answers. And they had little time to deal with their grief. Because along with the news of Jin Zhao's death, the chancellor had delivered a demand that Yuli, the oldest Zhao child, work off the debt in his father's stead by joining the military two years early, at the age of fourteen.

Shenli's family hadn't heard from Yuli since.

Then, three nights ago, the family had been celebrating baby Yiming's six-month birthday when the new scroll arrived, informing them that Yuli had deserted his military post, landing the Zhaos with four *more* years of family debt, bringing the total to seventeen years. But the chancellor had a solution for that. He'd invited Shenli, the next oldest, to come work for him at the castle as one of his personal stewards. And while Shenli knew it was a good opportunity for the family, he'd never left his village before, let alone traveled to a different district.

"You'll need a coat," said Mama, shaking Shenli from his thoughts. "It snows in the Middle District this time of year, especially at the castle." Mama handed the now-sleeping Yiming to Shenli and disappeared into one of the two tiny bedrooms, where his seven-year-old sister, Meili, still slept soundly.

Mama returned with a crimson tunic coat with golden embroidery on the cuffs and black buttons running up the front. Shenli's heart stuttered. It was his father's coat. Passed from one Zhao generation to the next. Traditionally, it was passed on to the oldest child, but with Yuli gone, Mama's message was clear.

Shenli was the oldest child now.

"Your father would want you to have it," Mama assured him as Shenli handed Yiming back to her and slipped into the coat. His fingertips barely poked out of the bottom of the sleeves.

Shenli thumbed the golden cuffs in wonder. "It's . . . fancy." He'd never seen the jacket close up before. Gold thread was a luxury non-existent in his village—in the entire Coastal District, for that matter.

"It's rather ancient. Gold thread used to be considered good luck because dragons have golden eyes. This was back in the old days, when Mainlanders felt differently about dragons."

"Like . . . they didn't used to hate them?"

Mama nodded. "There was a time, before the wars, when some Mainlanders and dragons were even friendly with one another."

Shenli winced. "Ugh. How could anyone be *friendly* with a fire-breather?" Dragons were all scales and smoke and danger. There were seven of them stationed across the Mainland. After the wars, part of the peace treaty called for the dragons on the Mainland to help the chancellor maintain peace and order. But the more widely circulated belief was that the dragons and their Riders were stationed on the Mainland to act as spies against Cudek.

"Times were much different back then," his mother continued. "But that was all a long, *long* time ago." She smiled. "Since then, this coat has been worn by many Zhaos. And now it's meant for you."

35

Shenli frowned. "Yuli was supposed to wear it, not me."

Mama blew out a long breath. "I really don't know what's gotten into your brother."

"I know what," Shenli huffed. "He's being selfish. As usual."

Mama's shoulders fell. "It's . . . complicated, Shen. Yuli was dealt a difficult hand in life. And I understand his anger. But I never thought he'd—" Mama blinked hard; then her light blue eyes locked on Shenli's. "Anyway, now we are all counting on *you*."

Shenli's heart pounded against his ribs. "I—I know."

This was the family's final chance to work off their debt. If he messed this up, it would mean prison. Maybe just for him. Or maybe his whole family. It would depend entirely on the chancellor's mood.

His father's coat suddenly felt much heavier.

An old memory stirred: It was the night before Yuli left to join the military, and everyone else was already asleep. Shenli had snuck out of bed to find his brother sitting by the hearth with a bottle of olive oil, shining an old pair of boots. Yuli had just cut his own hair, and the dark curly tufts still littered the floor by the fireplace. He'd always taken pride in his long silky hair, and though the military didn't require short hair, he'd chopped it all off in some kind of act of rebellion. Like becoming a soldier meant he was no longer Yuli, but . . . someone else.

For a long while, Shenli had watched Yuli scrubbing angrily at the shoes before his brother spotted him.

"Must be nice for you, eh?" Yuli had grunted. His eyebrows had been drawn together so fiercely he'd looked much older than fourteen in that moment. "Be glad you're too much of a runt to be punished for all of Dad's messes."

Runt.

Shenli *hated* that nickname, and Yuli knew it. But it was the only thing Yuli had ever called him. For Shenli's entire life, Yuli had made it clear he considered Shenli old enough to be a bother but too young to do anything right. This landed Shenli somewhere in the middle of being *annoying* and *useless*—at least to Yuli.

Shenli shook his brother from his thoughts and looked down at the coat hanging to his thighs. It was *way* too big for his ten-year-old body. But the proud look in Mama's eyes was enough for him not to make a fuss. He tried to smile but caught sight of the chancellor's scroll again, and his insides went all squirmy.

The chancellor wasn't known as a kind man. Cudek had spent many decades obsessively building up a massive army to stave off possible attacks from the Meraki and purge any remaining magic that lingered on the Mainland following the wars. While the magic folk hadn't bothered the Mainlanders in nearly a century, the Meraki had proved dangerous with their Magics in the past. They were a formidable enemy, and the Mainlanders' only hope against them was their military might.

Along with growing his army, Cudek had kept busy by keeping all five districts under a stern thumb. Grateful for Cudek's protection, the Mainlander people had cultivated a mix of feelings—both frightened and appreciative—about the chancellor over the years. So while Shenli did want to help work off his family's debt, he wasn't at *all* eager to be in such close proximity to the chancellor himself.

"Why do you think Cudek's giving me this job?" Shenli asked.

"Well, you're too young to be a soldier. But . . . it's more than that, I expect." His mother sighed. "Your father had a history with the chancellor. A rather long history, in fact. They grew up in the same village, long before Cudek ever rose to power."

"Were they friends?" The thought of his father and the chancellor running around as boyhood pals was weirder than the fact that Mama thought Yiming's baby toots were *cute.*

It was beyond ridiculous.

Mama's mouth drew into a thin line. "I'm not sure your father would've described them as friends."

"Why didn't you ever tell me?"

Mama let out another long sigh. "Their relationship has always been complicated, Shen. There are things in your father's past that are best left forgotten. And he didn't want his children mixed up in any of it."

Shenli bit his lip, considering. Maybe spending time at the castle would provide answers to the flurry of questions buzzing in his mind, like, what had really led to his father's death? And who had killed him? Surely Cudek knew. Angry as Shenli was at his father's foolishness, he still missed his dad terribly. And he longed for answers.

The recent disappearance of Yuli, however, was far less mysterious. Yuli had always talked about making a life for himself in the rich Mountain District someday. But their father's death, and the consequent arrival of Cudek's scroll, had dashed Yuli's dreams. Shenli wasn't the least bit surprised at Yuli's selfish choice to cut and run—leaving all the servitude debt for Shenli to shoulder.

The weight of leaving home sat on Shenli's chest heavier than a full-grown firebreather. And something else too. Something had been pressing on him from the moment he'd woken. And since he had only a few moments more with Mama, he figured she'd want to know.

"I had the dream again," he whispered.

"Of the same girl?"

Shenli nodded. He'd had the dream several times now. Of the girl with the sparkly copper eyes.

He could still see the memory of her, standing on the beach. A long golden thread looped over her in the night sky as ocean waves crashed against her feet. The girl wanted something desperately, and she needed Shenli's help to get it. The strange thread hovered, shimmering in the moonlight.

Waiting.

For Shenli.

Shenli had woken still feeling the pull in his chest.

"Your dad used to say having the same dream meant it held significance."

Shenli made a face. He didn't *want* the dream to be significant. Because he was certain the golden thread was magic. And there was nothing the Mainlanders hated more than magic and firebreathers.

"And you don't know what Dream Girl needs help with?"

Shenli shrugged. "I always wake up before I figure it out."

Mama was quiet for a long time before putting a hand on Shenli's shoulder. "Well, don't let it trouble you, son. You have enough to worry about with your new job."

"I thought it might be some kind of bad omen. Because of the magical thread." Bad luck was something that seemed to cling to his family, after all. Before his mom could respond, there was a loud knock at the door.

"That'll be the soldiers," Mama whispered, wrapping Shenli in a hug with Yiming gently squished between them.

Shenli's insides flip-flopped faster than hummingbird wings, but he did his best to keep a brave face. He was the oldest now. With a final kiss on the cheek for Mama and Yiming, he took his travel bag and slung the strap over his shoulder. Mama opened the front door.

Two gruff-looking soldiers stood on the doorstep. The man was tall, with fair skin and hair redder than Mama's tomato soup. His scowl was so deep it tied Shenli's insides in knots. The woman had light brown skin and amber eyes. Her dark hair was parted to the right and completely shaved on the left side. Her eyes flicked to Mama.

"Kayra Zhao?" she asked, and Mama nodded. "I'm Officer Anja Alizah, and this is Officer Graham. We are to escort Shenli to the chancellor."

"I'm ready," said Shenli, wishing his voice didn't sound so small.

The soldiers parted swiftly from the doorway and mounted two of the three horses standing outside. The third horse, a smaller white and gray, waited patiently. Shenli was sure he heard the male soldier utter something to his partner that sounded like *we came all this way for some kid!* before turning to Shenli.

Officer Graham nodded his chin toward the third horse. "Can you ride?"

Shenli shook his head.

The man grunted. "Well then. Today you learn."

Shenli bit his lip, approaching the horse slowly. He'd seen soldiers ride horses through his village, but he'd never been this close to one.

"You have to put your foot in the stirrup," Officer Alizah told him.

Shenli screwed up his face, wondering what part of the horse was a *stirrup*.

Officer Graham rolled his eyes. "You'll figure it out."

"Once you're up, it's all about squeezing your legs against the horse's sides to steer," Officer Alizah added.

"Er . . . thanks." Shenli reached a tentative foot upward, trying to place it in the dangling foot-strap thingy. But he couldn't quite reach.

Officer Graham scoffed. "While you sort *that* out, we've got a schedule to keep, kid." He flicked his reins, and his horse started off down the road. "You'd do well to keep up," he called over his shoulder.

Shenli sighed. Well, this day was getting off to a spectacular start.

Officer Alizah gave him a pitying glance. "You'll manage, Zhao. Just keep at it."

Shenli gulped. At this rate, he wouldn't make it to the castle before sundown. "Right. Thanks." At last, Shenli finally worked out how to put one shoe in the foot-loop thingy and pull himself up by the saddle. After a few tries, he was able to swing his other leg over and sit upright.

"Atta boy, Zhao. You'll make a fine soldier someday."

Shenli grinned and caught Mama beaming at him through the front window. He gave her a thumbs-up, then took hold of the reins.

"I'm going on ahead, but I'll keep an eye on you," Officer Alizah told him. Then she spun her horse to face the road and took off into a trot.

Remembering what she'd told him, Shenli squeezed his calves firmly against the horse's flanks, and the horse started walking forward. Shenli laughed, turning back for one more glance at Mama through the window. She grinned widely and held up Yiming's little hand to wave to him. Shenli fought off the lump in his throat and urged his horse toward the soldiers up the road.

Okay. He could do this. As long as the horse carried on steady. He would probably arrive at the castle just before sundown. How long before he met the chancellor? Would Shenli have the courage to ask Cudek what had happened to his father? Definitely not right away. But maybe eventually. Shenli was terrified at the thought of being in the same room as the chancellor, let alone asking him uninvited questions. But maybe if he worked hard, he could earn Cudek's respect over time—and then he could get some answers.

Maybe.

His heart fluttered in hopeful anticipation.

Just then, something flashed in the corner of Shenli's eye. Up to the right, floating in the air, an enormous loopy golden thread blinked into view.

Shenli nearly fell off his horse in shock.

Even having seen it countless times in his dreams, he never

41

could've imagined it showing up in real life. A deep flutter of foreboding rolled down Shenli's spine. He pulled the reins sharply, giving the terrible thread a wide berth, assuming that it must be some kind of magic curse.

The thread glittered innocently, hovering just out of reach.

Terrified as he was, Shenli had a tremendous urge to pull it. He gritted his teeth angrily. Had the cursed magic come to snare him in some kind of trap—to keep him from serving his new duty to the chancellor? Well, it wouldn't work. Because unlike his brother and father, Shenli would not be deterred.

"Leave me alone!" Shenli growled. "I want nothing to do with you!"

He flicked the reins again, urging his horse swiftly onward. As if in response to Shenli's rejection, the golden thread glittered out of sight. Shenli grunted his approval.

But somehow, deep inside, he knew it wasn't the last he'd see of it.

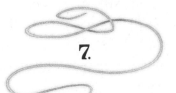

7.

IN WHICH THE GERBERANS MEET THEIR NEW KING

TEN YEARS BEFORE THE FOURTH WAR

Gerbera's newest king sat atop his horse, Cedar, surrounded by forty knights and their steeds, waiting for the castle gates to open for Dragon Day. The ceremony was always a complete and utter sham—in a very *respectable* way. Every quarter century, bright banners bearing the royal lion crest lined the streets. The villagers waved balloons as children stuffed themselves with too many sweets, cheering their king's bravery as he rode off to Dragon Mountain.

Normally, the facade at least made sense, as the king didn't actually *know* his own sealed fate, the way everyone else did. So they'd praise his valor from the streets, reciting their prayers for his hasty return.

All lies, wrapped in kindness.

But not today.

Word spread quickly of the king's death, and the streets were packed tightly, too crowded even for ample balloon-waving. Everyone gathered to see the new king. Many of the knightly wives clutched their children close, praying it wasn't their husband who'd been chosen. Their wait was agony. But how could they possibly know that in many ways, the truth was even worse than their deepest fears?

For when the castle gates finally opened, just past noon, and the new king's processional marched forth, the villagers looked past the forty knights riding in their perfect rows. Some people cheered—it was hard to break custom, after all. But when the new king's horse came into view through the gated archway, clearly recognizable with its emerald-studded saddle, a collective gasp of horror shuddered through the crowd.

"He's only a *child*!" someone cried.

Blue gave quiet thanks to the Fates that he'd skipped breakfast. If he hadn't, it might well have turned up all over the cobblestone street.

Thousands of people lined up for miles on end, all of them gaping at him with shock and dismay. He gripped the reins steadily, all too aware of the adult-sized royal-purple tunic hanging past his knees, clearly too large for his twelve-year-old body. His blond hair was parted to one side, as per royal custom; the glittering crown kept slipping down past his ears. It was all Blue could do to concentrate on Cedar's gentle steps underneath him. Her familiar scent was almost comforting enough to drown out the overwhelming scent of wood and citrus blanketing the air with Fear.

Almost.

"We can't send a *child* to the fire beast!" someone called out, and a chorus of agreement rose through the crowd.

Blue's lips trembled as he tightened his grip on the reins. It was rotten luck, really. This was the first time Blue had been chosen for anything. He'd never been *anyone's* first choice—not even his own parents.

Until now.

Thanks to that blasted dragon tooth.

But he would not let fear overcome him. Blue was Gerbera's chosen king. And sure, his coronation had been rather hurried and awkward, and his kingly reign might last only a few days—ending with him in the bowels of a fire beast.

None of it made sense. None of it was fair to Blue. Not in the least.

But why *shouldn't* it be him? The unwanted child abandoned on the castle steps at birth and raised as a ward of the king? Didn't Blue now have a chance to be significant? He could be brave for his kingdom, couldn't he? Or at least look the part? Inhaling deeply, he forced a smile, giving his best wave to the crowd.

Several people burst into tears.

"He *knows*!" someone called.

"It isn't right!" called someone else.

But the shouts of protest dwindled to a deep silence as the procession continued through the middle of the village, lilac and mint saturating the air with their Sorrow. The only sound was the clip-clopping of hooves against the cobblestone road, punctuated by the occasional sob from the crowd. After all, what else could be done? A king had been chosen. And the dragons waited for no man.

A deal was a deal.

On and on it went, through every village of Gerbera, for hours on end, until the royal procession at last reached the edge of the Peculiar Forest. As far as the eye could see, birch trees swept across the landscape, a blanket of silver-green lying in Dragon Mountain's shadow.

"We must leave you here, Your Majesty," said Sir Huxley with a small bow. He'd been kind enough to ride nearest to Blue, as he'd known the young king best. Blue nodded as if he understood. But how could he truly be *here*, about to enter the forest of a thousand deaths, and with the royal crown on his head, no less?

None of it seemed real.

"This will get you through the forest," said Huxley, handing Blue a small compass attached to a silver chain necklace. "A gift from the dragons, so they say. Handed down to each king. Usually it accompanies the king's horse when it . . . er, returns to the castle."

Returns to the castle *without the king* was Huxley's meaning, of course. Blue peered down at the brass compass, the weight of it heavy in his quivering palm. Two arrows pointed in different directions, one smaller than the other. At the top of the compass, a black triangle was etched in the space for *North*. Three dots were painted on the bottom, where *South* should've been.

The compass felt strange and wrong. Like everything else about the day.

"Follow the triangle to get to Dragon Mountain and the three dots will get you back to the castle." Huxley cleared his throat, the absurdity of his statement settling between them.

Because of *course* Blue would never need the three dots for anything.

Huxley leaned in closer and clapped the young king on the shoulder. "Be brave, Blue. May the honor of Gerbera serve you faithfully on your quest."

"Thank you, Huxley," Blue managed to choke out as he slipped the compass around his neck.

"It should've been one of us," Huxley told him, and several knights murmured their agreement. "You're a good lad, Blue—er, *sir*. Clearly as brave as they come. But it isn't right. And I'm just—" Huxley looked away suddenly, inhaling a shaky breath. "I'm just sorry, is all. We'll make sure your name is remembered. You have my word."

Blue's eyes stung. His name *remembered*. A name that wasn't really a name. He found this tragic and funny all at once. King *Blue*? It didn't exactly have a heroic ring to it. Still, he appreciated Huxley's heart. And suddenly the weight of what Blue was about to do squeezed him tighter than his new leather riding boots. He tried to respond, but all he could do was wipe his eyes with his royal sleeve and try not to notice all the knights before him doing the same.

Huxley gave Blue's shoulder a quick pat, then beat his right fist against his chest armor. Thirty-nine knights behind him did the same.

"Long live the king!" shouted Huxley.

"Long live the king!" the knights echoed.

Blue regarded the knights with a swell of gratitude in his chest. He was a phony king and they knew it. But they treated him as a *proper* king just the same. It was the kindest gift they could've given him.

"Thank you, all," Blue said in the strongest voice he could muster. He shot one last glance toward the villages and the castle in the distance. Somewhere past the stone walls sat the royal stables, which had served as his home these past twelve years.

Blue wondered briefly if his parents might've been out in the crowds today, and if they'd recognized him. He'd always wanted to meet them, but now he never would. In fact, now he would never get to have a family at all.

A familiar memory flashed in his mind. Two eyes, blue as the sea, gazing down on him. He shook the thought away and turned Cedar toward the Peculiar Forest. Dragon Mountain loomed in the distance, beyond the trees.

Funny how his first trip beyond the castle walls would take him to the end of the world.

"Come on, Cedar," said Blue, tugging the reins gently and turning the compass toward the black mountain. Without another look back, the king of Gerbera disappeared into the trees with the Sorrow stench of forty knights in his wake.

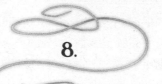

8.

IN WHICH THE PECULIAR FOREST IS, IN FACT, QUITE PECULIAR

Once Cedar stepped through the tree line, the Peculiar Forest swallowed Blue whole. Trees stretched in every direction, denser than morning fog. He shifted in his saddle and patted Cedar's head encouragingly.

"It's all right, girl," he soothed, though everything was most definitely *not* all right, and his horse could sense it.

As they padded onward, every legend Blue had ever heard about the forest came to life before him, the absurdities only increasing the farther they traveled. Birds that growled like bears. Golden bubbles that sang poetry. Trees growing upside down. But the worst of it came after they crossed a small stream into complete silence. As if someone had stuffed Blue's ears shut.

Blue had never known silence such as *this*.

It wasn't like nighttime at the stables, with the horses deep in sleep. Or the moment at dawn right before the royal rooster gave a holler. It wasn't even the quiet of being alone in an empty room. In fact, he was surrounded by critters. At least ten sets of eyes looked down on him from the treetops in every direction. He wasn't alone. And yet.

Nothing moved.

Unblinking eyes ogled him. Not a leaf fluttered. Even a row of red ants sat halted around a tree trunk. The smell of Fear soaked the air around him. But it wasn't only *his* Fear. Cedar slowed beneath him, her woody citrus scent swirling in with the rest.

Were the animals afraid of him? Were they so unaccustomed to seeing humans? No, that couldn't be it. If they were afraid, they would run away, wouldn't they? A large stag stared at Blue from behind a violet tree trunk, his beautiful antlers stretching toward the sky. Blue urged Cedar onward, the compass thumping against his chest as she broke into a nervous trot.

"You're a long way from home, two-legger."

The voice shattered the silence, sending Cedar rearing on her hind legs. Blue's heart nearly beat out of his chest. He patted Cedar's neck, calming her jitters enough to hold her still as he searched the trees.

No one was there.

"Oh, won't you *kindly* make haste?" said the voice. At that, Blue spotted a silver-and-orange fox sitting on a gnarled tree stump. The fox tilted its head and let out an aggravated huff. "I can't get on with my hunting until you've moved past," the fox grumbled.

Blue blinked. A talking fox?

"It's because of your compass," said the fox, nodding toward the frozen stag. "They know you're marked for the firebreathers. They don't dare disturb you."

"I . . . er—"

"And even though there is a burrow of plump, juicy rabbits only ten yards off, it isn't right for me to hunt them while you're here. Not in their state, you see. It isn't proper." The fox sighed. "No matter how *hungry* I might be."

"Why aren't you frozen like the other animals?" asked Blue.

"It's the dragon magic of the compass that compels them, but I am not bound by such spells."

"Why not?"

The fox scoffed, hopping off the tree stump. "Well, that's a rather forward question, isn't it? What kind of manners do they teach in Gerbera nowadays, anyway? Come to think of it, you don't seem the right size for a king. The two-legger king always comes at twenty-five years of age. Everyone knows it. So who are *you*, exactly?"

"I'm Blue."

The fox cocked his head again. "You're . . . what, now?"

Blue lifted his chin. "Blue is what everyone calls me. And when the king of Gerbera died, the magic of the dragon tooth chose me as the replacement." Blue wondered if it all sounded as absurd to the fox as it did him.

"The king *died*?"

"Just this morning," said Blue, wondering why the fox would care.

The fox raised a paw to his chin. "But that's *never* happened. And you, a mere *cub*, chosen to take his place? Humans. Sending their children straight to the mouths of the firebreathers."

Blue shivered, grateful that Dragon Mountain remained hidden behind the dense tree canopy. The fox started forward, and Cedar walked alongside him without being prodded.

"That's some bad luck you have there, Blue."

"How can you talk?" asked Blue, eager to change the subject.

"I made a deal with a dragon many moons ago." The fox grinned. "The firebreathers aren't all bad, you know. Though that won't do *you* much good, I'm afraid. No offense."

Blue wasn't sure what to say to that, so he fiddled absent-mindedly with his compass.

"A group of dragons used to dwell here, in fact," the fox continued. "In this wildwood, many centuries ago. Before they moved to the mountain. These woods are laced with dragon magic, even today."

"Is that why everything here is so strange?" Blue asked with a shudder.

"That's right. If you're very still, you can feel it."

Blue scrunched his nose. He had no desire to feel *anything* to do with dragons. Or magic.

"For example, those flowers there"—the fox nodded to some wilted white flowers with huge black leaves—"allow you to listen in on a conversation hundreds of miles away. And if you head that way"—he nodded to his left—"you'll get caught in the No Hunger Lands. You won't feel hungry, even when you actually *are,* and eventually it will kill you."

"And what about the shadow bears?" asked Blue, because everyone knew about the shadowy forest bears with razor claws.

"Well, they're not really the creatures you need to worry about, are they?"

Blue narrowed his eyes. "I feel loads better now, thanks."

The fox laughed. "I like you, human cub. The other kings were all so *somber.* Dreary. Death, after all, is an expected part of life."

"You've met former kings? Just how old are you?"

"Older than any human."

It wasn't entirely an answer.

"You're . . . *more* than the other animals, aren't you?" asked Blue. He wasn't sure how to better form the question. But there was clearly something about the fox—something *other*ly.

"I find humans just as repulsive as any animal does, if that's what you mean."

"And yet you're still walking with me," Blue pointed out. "Surely you could've hunted your rabbits by now."

The fox's furry grin seemed to falter as he turned his gaze toward Dragon Mountain, now peeking through the treetops.

"I am the Last Goodbye, young one. The guide of many kings."

Blue arched an eyebrow. "Our meeting wasn't an accident, then?"

"I've been waiting twenty-five years to meet you, Blue."

"Why?"

"I'd like to think it makes it easier for you. A bit of companionship before your journey ends."

The way the fox said it made it sound like a favor. And Blue *did* feel better. His heart rate had slowed, Cedar now trotted calmly, and Blue hadn't smelled any Fear since the frozen stag.

"But why?" Blue asked again.

"Curious—you're the first king to ask why. The minds of cubs are sharper than those of grown-ups, I've always said. It's because we're *grateful,* child. Have you never wondered why the forest animals leave your villages alone? Why your sheep and hens are never attacked by wolves of the forest? Why the deer do not graze on Gerbera's crops? The deal the humans made with the firebreathers protects us all. Humans are not the only creatures the dragons leave well enough alone."

Blue considered this. As far as he knew, his kingdom had always flourished. At harvesttime, farmers welcomed crops in abundance. Livestock roamed the hills freely. There were bedtime stories of the shadow bears with razor teeth who ate children in one gulp, but those tales were meant to keep children from running off to the forest. Blue had never heard of anyone actually being eaten by a bear.

"So this is your way of thanking us?" Blue asked.

"It is. My specific knack of magic deals with time," said the fox. "I can stretch it or bend it, just a bit. Dodge it, even." He laughed at some inward joke. "And for you, Blueboy, I can help pass the time in this dark lonely wood. In fact, it's been near seven hours that we've been talking."

Blue looked up. The violets and dark blues of the night sky seeped through the cracks in the treetops. He gasped.

"But—" Blue looked behind him. The stag was nowhere to be seen. In fact, his surroundings had changed entirely. Tall evergreens with glowing rainbow-colored pine needles loomed over him. He scratched his head in wonder. How had he not noticed he was in a completely different place? He held up the compass, one arrow still pointed toward the black triangle, while the other pointed home.

"Don't worry, I've kept us on the trail," the fox assured him. "I know the way."

"But how—" Blue looked up again, and now stars peeked down at him through the tall trees. Had they really just made a full day's journey in mere minutes? And why was the fox so certain this was a *good* thing? Wasn't he really only bringing about Blue's death faster?

"I'm not sure I'm so eager to reach the mountain, thanks," said Blue crossly.

"Would you rather have spent a full day in agony?"

"But these are my last minutes! Maybe I am frightened, but they're *my* minutes to live and breathe. And you've taken them from me."

"One need not fear death."

Blue scoffed. "That coming from a fox who apparently lives *forever.*"

The fox laughed. "Fair enough. But there's no use drawing it out. Better to end your misery swiftly. It is a kindness."

Blue remembered one of the king's horses that had been severely injured years ago, with no hope of healing. Old Man Albert had to kill it, he explained, to end its suffering. Blue might've been horrified, but the smell of Fear and Sorrow clung so strongly to the horse, Blue had understood Albert's action as a kindness at the time.

Was that how the fox saw Blue now? As a wounded animal, better off dead?

The fox was silent for a long time. Blue kept thinking he needed to stop and make camp for the night. But the starry sky was already giving way to the dawn. Blue gripped the reins tighter. At this rate, he'd be in the dragon's belly in the next five minutes!

"There's something different about you," the fox said, almost too quietly for Blue to hear. "You're not like the others."

"Well, I don't have a beard," Blue pointed out. "So there's that."

"No, no. It isn't your age. It's something else."

Blue scrunched his eyebrows together. "That'll be my knack for smelling emotions. Something I was born with."

"No. Nothing to do with knacks."

The fox jumped—much higher than a fox should be able to jump, Blue thought—onto Cedar's neck. His snout hovered so close to Blue's nose, Blue could smell rotten meat on the animal's breath.

"What is it, boy? It's almost as if . . ." The fox's silver eyes narrowed.

"Almost as if . . . *what*?" Blue urged.

"The . . . song . . ."

Blue blinked, completely bewildered. "Song? What song?"

The fox shook his head and laughed. "Nothing, nothing. I may be very old and very wise, but that doesn't mean I know everything. It's probably just because I'm hungry." The fox grinned. "Anyhow, we're here."

Blue peeked around the fox's silvery-orange head.

Here looked like the trees parting to reveal a wall of the great mountain.

"Down there," said the fox, nodding to the ground in front of them. Blue followed his gaze, his mouth dropping open. An enormous hole spread a good ten feet in every direction. Blue swung down from Cedar, his legs a little stiff—but not as stiff as they *should've* been on a full day-and-a-half's ride. Keeping hold of Cedar's reins, Blue inched closer to the massive void, his oversized royal tunic scraping the ground.

"What's this?" asked Blue.

"It's where you're headed."

Blue's eyes grew as big as two moons. "In *there*?"

"It's the entrance to Dragon Mountain," said the fox, jumping down next to Blue's feet.

Blue chanced another glance at the monstrous hole. It was too dark to see anything. He groaned. "Come on. Really? I have to go down the bottomless creepy hole of death and *then* get eaten by a dragon?"

"Your horse won't be able to join you either. It's too steep."

Blue's heart sank, and he clutched the reins tighter. He hadn't expected to leave Cedar so suddenly. Of course, he hadn't expected *any* of this. He pushed his forehead gently against Cedar's muzzle. She whinnied softly, jerking her head up, motioning for him to get back in the saddle.

"Sorry, girl. You can't come with me." Blue's voice hitched as he stroked her neck. It hadn't been that long ago that he'd helped nurse Cedar back to health when her mother died in labor. He'd moved his hay bed into Cedar's stall. Had sung to her when she was scared and snuck her carrots from the garden.

She was the closest thing Blue had to a friend.

"She'll get back home okay," said the fox. "I'll see to it. I always do." He grinned. "I even leave a note."

An enormous dread carved into Blue's stomach, hollowing him out. Cedar's Fear and Sorrow hung in the air, but there was nothing to do to make her feel better.

"You're a good girl," Blue whispered. "Some knight will be real lucky to have you."

Blue dropped the reins, and Cedar snorted her protest. He held one foot over the bottomless tunnel and his chest tightened. There was nowhere to stand. The hole dropped into complete darkness.

"It's funny," said the fox. "I have the strangest feeling we'll meet again someday."

Blue frowned. "I hardly see how that's likely."

"Stranger things have happened in these parts."

"If you say so."

With one last look at Cedar, Blue closed his eyes and held an image of her face in his mind. Ignoring the orange woodsy smell clinging all around him, the king of Gerbera stepped into the dark hole and fell into the nothingness.

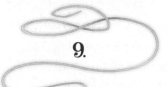

IN WHICH RIVER ROWAN
IS *NOT* IMPRESSED

TEN YEARS BEFORE THE FOURTH WAR

Not so far away from Blue, atop Dragon Mountain, River Rowan plucked a plump silver berry from the bush in front of her. She held it up in the early dawn light to examine it. The color was good. She sniffed: a perfect blend of lily and sweet cypress.

With a nod of approval, River dropped the final moonberry into her leather pouch and made her way to the ash trees. As she walked, she buried her toes in the soil, then let loose an enormous sigh of relief.

After years of hard work, everything was finally ready.

Like her grandmother before her, River had been born with a knack for growing magical ingredients. She was so talented, in fact, that she was set to officially be named Lead Harvester of the village. Her celebration was scheduled for that very evening, after today's Hibernation Day ceremony. Then, at the age of twelve, River Rowan would become the youngest Lead Harvester ever.

It was all she'd ever wanted.

"You taught me everything I know," River whispered. "Lead

Harvester, just like you were. Can you believe it?" She closed her eyes, soaking in the familiar deep ache. Her grandmother had been gone two years, but sometimes to River it felt like a lifetime. And today of all days, she longed for Nana's company.

It was moments like this when River was so certain of who she was meant to be that she thought she might burst from the sheer joy of it. The truth was, River knew her way around moonberries and firefruit the way most people know their way around their own skin. It wasn't that she *tried* to know. Not the way the other Dragon Growers fussed about, taking hourly samples of dragon manure or constantly monitoring the temperatures of the ash trees.

River simply *knew.*

She knew that when the starlight shone too dimly, the crushed dragon scales wouldn't activate. That moonberries harvested too early leaked out all their magic. And that phoenix honey with flecks of blue—no matter how much it glowed—would be instant death for a growing dragon. River Rowan came from nine centuries of Harvesters, and she was the best there ever was. And her people loved her for it.

Unlike the other children her age, who weren't yet sorted into their village job assignments, River had understood her destiny as a Harvester from her very first memories. She'd been drawn to the soil like an ember moth to the flame. Even as a toddler, she'd spent her time coaxing magical ingredients out of the ground while the other children played with one another. And all her passion and hard work had led to this very morning.

Today Gerbera's new king was coming.

So when she selected the absolute *best* firefruit at the first light of dawn, and her mother put a hand on River's shoulder and asked, "Are you certain, River, love?" River nodded.

She *was* certain.

58

River now plucked a square fruit from the ash tree, breathing in the charred-earth smell, and nodded. "This one is perfect," she said confidently.

The Elder Dragon Growers gave a shared sigh of relief. The Chief Elder, Cyrus, took the glowing crimson fruit in his bony golden-brown hands, raising it slowly above his head to a round of enthusiastic applause from the villagers. Then he held it over the preparation cauldron and started to peel it.

Slowly.

Off came the red layer of fruit skin.

Then the orange layer.

River held her breath anxiously. The ancient Elder worked so slowly she feared he might doze off before the ceremony could be completed. Father gave her shoulder a gentle squeeze, reminding her to be patient.

Patience was not River's strength.

At last, Elder Cyrus dropped the peeled golden fruit into the cauldron and set the contents ablaze. He nodded to River. She blew out a slow breath and held up her pouch, then dropped the moon-berries into the cauldron one by one until the pouch was empty. Another round of polite claps ensued.

"And just think: you don't have to do this for another twenty-five years, when the next king arrives," River's father whispered behind her. "That's a pretty cushy job you have, Rivs."

"Except if I do my job *wrong*, I'll murder a dragon, disgrace our family name, and put the entire village to shame," River pointed out.

"Right, there is *that*," her father agreed. "Not to mention it would be really embarrassing."

River held back her smirk. Normally, she would've given her father the playful shove he rightfully deserved, but Elder Cyrus was looking her way. His bushy eyebrows scrunched together in warning as the other Elders took turns adding the remaining ingredient—pinches of carefully measured stardust. Elder Cyrus then held the enormous wooden mixing spoon out to River. It was longer than she was tall, and she had to grasp it with both hands.

"You may do the honors, River Rowan," he said. "You've earned it."

River sucked in a deep breath, dipping the spoon into the thick golden liquid, taking care to only stir clockwise, for good luck. The Elders hummed their Growing Songs, and River didn't dare allow herself to lose focus until Cyrus raised his hands in triumph.

"It is finished!" Elder Cyrus announced, his pale green eyes shining.

The entire village let out a cheer that echoed off the surrounding mountains as they stomped their bare feet in the dirt, raising a celebratory dust cloud. River looked at them with pride. They smiled back at her, cheeks full of glittering freckles standing against their varying shades of light and dark skin.

Whenever a new baby was born, the village Elders performed a special ceremony that ended with spreading magical soil on the baby's cheeks. This always left behind a set of sparkly freckles—the mark of a Dragon Grower.

Her own freckled cheeks stretched into a grin. Another successful elixir after a quarter century of effort from them all. River peeked into the cauldron with immense delight. The golden mixture looked like a thick, bubbly smoothie. Just as it ought to. She exhaled a breath of relief and bowed to another round of applause.

River had always been a confident girl, but even *she* had nightmares about the elixir going wrong on Hibernation Day. And now she was one step closer to her new title as Lead Harvester. She bounced on her bare toes in anticipation.

Elder Cyrus raised his hands to silence the crowd. "And now we wait. Places, everyone. The king will be here soon." He nodded to one of the dragon keeper boys. "Felix, go fetch Ikor, won't you? It's time for our dragon to meet the new king."

Not ten minutes later, River tried to keep her foot from tapping impatiently as she stood along with the other four hundred Dragon Growers of the village. They all faced the gateway—the cave opening from which the king would emerge. Gathered on the southern hillside, they had just started to feel the heat of the morning sun warming the backs of their necks.

Ikor the dragon sat in the middle of them all, emitting puffs of ebony smoke from his nostrils. He flicked his tail impatiently. He was *most* eager to get on with the events of the day.

Almost as eager as River.

"Does it always take this long?" River asked her mother.

"Usually the king comes just after sunrise, love. You must be patient."

River bit her bottom lip and stared so hard at the gateway her eyes started to cross.

Patient, patient, patient.

Her foot started tapping again, and a muffled chuckle that sounded an awful lot like her father's came from behind her. Her foot tapped faster. She'd only waited her entire life for this day! All the planning and measuring of ingredients and sleepless nights hovering over the ash trees. She eyed the gateway with new fervor. The king could at least have the courtesy to show up on time, couldn't he?

A cough echoed from the dark tunnel.

"Finally," River muttered, earning another chuckle from her father.

A cloud of dust emitted from the tunnel opening, swirling upward. River squinted through the dirt fog as a purple tunic emerged and a wave of excited whispers erupted from the Dragon Growers.

Ikor snorted expectantly.

Then through the fog stepped a boy with a shock of hay-colored hair and eyes bluer than sapphires. Holding a golden crown in one hand, he used his other palm to block the sunlight sneaking up over the surrounding mountain peaks.

Ikor growled.

The boy coughed, peering up at the dragon warily.

"Er—hello," said the boy, his voice more of a squeak than a greeting. His gaze flitted to each of them, finally settling on Ikor.

No one said anything. The villagers eyed one another in confusion. Ikor stomped his enormous feet, past the point of patience.

"I wasn't expecting *people*," said the boy, at which point River stepped forward first to address the mysterious visitor.

"And just who are *you*?" she demanded, arms crossed.

"I'm Blue," said the boy.

"Why are you here, child?" Elder Cyrus asked him.

The boy's shoulders drooped, his eyes darting to Ikor. "They . . . sent me."

"Who sent you?" Elder Cyrus demanded. "And where is the king?"

The boy's face fell. He dropped the golden crown at his feet— much to the dismay of the Elders—and held up a round object in his hands. A silver chain weaved through an object hanging from his neck. River frowned. The boy's necklace sure looked an awful lot like—

"The king's compass," River's mother breathed.

"The king is dead," said the boy.

A collective gasp rose from the villagers, echoing off the surrounding mountains and sending a shiver down River's spine. The Dragon Growers glanced at one another in shock. River uncrossed her arms and stepped closer to the boy. The fear in his cerulean eyes flashed hot, like the blue bits of a campfire.

"Dead?" River repeated, her voice softer this time. "But what about the dragon ceremony?"

"I-I've come to fight the d-dragon," said the boy, reaching for his sword. But when he pulled it free, the blade instantly sank into the dirt, clearly too heavy for him. Ikor snorted loudly, finding the whole thing amusing.

"Let me understand this," said Elder Cyrus, taking a step forward with his cane. "The king of Gerbera has died, and in his place, the royal knights of His Majesty sent . . . you?"

"Yes, sir," said the boy. "Though they actually *did* make me king first. Technically, you know. Before they sent me." The boy sounded about as excited as a fly caught in a spiderweb. Then his eyes found River's, wide-open and terrified.

"Well, this won't do," said Elder Cyrus, thumping his cane against the soft grass.

"It's all wrong," agreed another Elder.

The murmurs of disagreement between the Elders rose louder still, until the boy cleared his throat.

"If it's all the same to you," said Blue, wringing his hands, "the dragon tooth chose me. It's the will of the Fates, and it can't be undone. My people are counting on me, and I swore to protect them." He paused, raising his chin to Ikor. "I'm ready to be eaten now."

River's mouth dropped open a little. Could the boy truly mean it? Was he really going to fulfill the duty of a king—the duty of a grown man? She stared at Blue in wonder. The boy's sunburned pale cheeks reminded River of her nana, who had worked long hours in the sun. Somehow this made her slightly less irritated with him.

But only slightly.

The Elders looked at one another, nodding in silent agreement. Elder Cyrus placed a hand on Blue's shoulder. "My boy, you are very brave. That kind of courage is exactly what's needed, you see. But

I must admit, you have come here under false pretenses, as all the kings have done before you." Cyrus paused, allowing the boy to process this.

"Wh-what does that mean?" asked Blue.

"It means, dear boy, you've not come here today to be eaten by a dragon," said Cyrus with a small grin. "In fact, today you will *become* a dragon."

10.

IN WHICH A VERY
BIG DECISION IS MADE

lue's heart thumped in his ears. The gray-haired man with the cane, smelling of sweat and spices, looked down at him expectantly. The man's freckles glittered strangely against his bronze cheeks as his bewildering declaration bounced around in Blue's head like a rubber ball, unable to settle.

Become a dragon.

He chewed on the words some more.

Become a dragon?

Nope. Still didn't make sense.

Finally, Blue couldn't ignore the entire crowd of people staring at him.

"I don't understand," he admitted, growing more and more uncomfortable. Anyway, who *were* all these people? They looked similar to Gerberans, with their varying body heights and skin tones. Their hair types varied too, anywhere from straight and blond, like Blue's, to curly and black, like Lady Camila's. But they all had glittery freckles pasted across their cheeks like flecks of shimmery soil. And why weren't any of them wearing shoes?

How could they sit so peacefully next to the dragon? And come to think of it, why did the dragon sit so calmly next to *them*? Why wasn't it attacking anyone?

"Come," said the old man. "All will be explained, I assure you. But you must be exhausted from your journey. We have prepared a feast in your honor, and we will tell you our Stories of Old around the gathering fire, as is custom."

Feast.

Stories.

Customs.

Blue's frown deepened. What in the Fates' trickery was going *on* here?

"So . . . that dragon there"—Blue pointed at the enormous black beast unfurling its scaly wings—"is *not* going to eat me?"

"He is most certainly not," agreed the old man assuredly. "Though he is rather eager to depart. As one new dragon—or *king*—arrives, another dragon leaves. Ikor has completed his hibernation, and he and his Rider will depart just after the feast. Such has always been the way."

Blue shook his head. Was he dreaming? Maybe he was still in the forest with the strange talking fox. Or maybe the dragon *had* eaten him already and he was stuck in some kind of alternate afterlife. He didn't know what to believe, and he suddenly felt as if the world around him was all going to topple in on him. The bossy girl stepped forward, her smile now friendly.

"It's all right," said the girl, her auburn hair fluttering in the breeze against her freckled beige cheeks. Her smile calmed his nerves a little. She took his hand gently and led him up a large hill, where the sun now cast a cheery aura of golden light.

From the hilltop, an entire village spread out before them. A lush valley lay nestled in the center of a perimeter of vast mountain peaks. From where he stood, Blue could see houses and farms and a small stream cutting through the green. Scattered throughout the village were bushes and trees and bright bursts of flowers growing wildly. It was a hidden paradise.

"What *is* this place?" asked Blue, dizzy with wonder.

"My people are Meraki Dragon Growers," said the girl, her hair emitting bits of sunlight like a reddish-brown halo. "We've lived in these mountains for nearly a millennium. We raise dragons for our family across the Wastelands."

"The Wastelands?"

The girl pointed north. "The desert on the north side of the mountains. The island Meraki live beyond the desert, in the Northern Sea."

Blue frowned. "But there *isn't* anything beyond Dragon Mountain."

"There most certainly *is.*"

"No, this is where the world ends," said Blue. "Everyone knows that."

The girl shook her head. "That's only what the Gerberans are taught to believe."

Blue couldn't tell if she was teasing him or not, so he thought it best to change the subject. "The old man said I'd *become* a dragon—what'd he mean?"

"That's Elder Cyrus. He's going to explain it all right now around the gathering fire. I'm River Rowan, by the way. The Lead Harvester. Well, *almost.* By tonight I will be." She grinned, and Blue thought she looked rather proud of herself.

"Harvester of what?" asked Blue.

"The magic crops," River said, her hazel eyes lighting up. The glittery freckles on her cheeks seemed to almost light up too. "I've spent my life growing them. They are truly the most beautiful and wonderful things."

"What are . . . magic crops?" Blue asked.

"The ingredients to grow dragons."

"To *what*?" asked Blue, completely exasperated. Magic ingredients and community campfires and *growing dragons*, for mercy's sake! The absurdity of this mountain village kept growing bigger and stranger, and Blue could hardly keep up.

"It's not your fault that you don't know anything," River told him.

Blue threw up his hands in frustration. "Is that supposed to be reassuring?"

"You just weren't taught the proper histories."

"And how do you know that you *were*?"

River shrugged. "My people moved to these mountains about a thousand years ago. We brought the histories of the Mainland with us. Your people, by the way, also came from the Mainland. But they chose to forget."

Blue's cheeks burned, a bit of heat starting to rise up the back of his neck. He'd had, quite possibly, one of the *worst* days a person could have. Now everything he'd ever known was slipping through his fingers like water. Could River be right? Did he really not know the true history of his people?

"Why did they choose to forget?" he whispered.

"We think Gerberans wanted a new life for themselves. You see, thousands of years ago, all humans lived north of here, on the other side of the Wastelands. In those days, magic humans and nonmagic humans lived together, and the land was called Haven."

"You said it was called the Mainland."

"It is *now*, but before that it was called Haven."

Blue arched an eyebrow. "So what happened?"

"People didn't get along very well—mainly because they fought about magic. That's what caused all the wars."

"Wars?" Blue had heard the word before, but only in reference to warring against the dragons if they attacked the Gerbera villages. He'd never thought about humans battling humans.

"Your ancestors and mine have seen three Great Wars," River told him. "When Magics came to Haven, most humans were accepting, but not all. Some chose to bond with Magics, while others thought they were evil. This caused a lot of tensions and fighting. The First War was fought over whether Magics should become a part of human society. Two wars came after, in the centuries that followed."

"All that fighting—over magic?"

River nodded. "Eventually, a large group of nonmagic humans— the Nordi tribe—had enough. Many Nordi headed to the Lands Across the Sea to get as far away from magic as they could. And a second group relocated to the Southern Realm, where your people live now."

"So . . . they became the kingdom of Gerbera?" Blue said, trying to fit together all the pieces of new information.

River nodded. "Over time, your people dropped the title of Nordi and stopped talking about the Northern Realm of the magic humans altogether. They started teaching their children that the world ended at Dragon Mountain. And after a while, they all believed it."

Blue frowned. It was definitely believable that his Gerberan ancestors would try to keep their children away from the magic of the Northern Realm. But it still didn't sit well in his gut that he'd been raised to believe a lie.

"Come on," said River, tugging his hand gently. "Everyone's waiting."

Blue gave a reluctant nod as he and River followed the crowd of Dragon Growers down the hill. On the far side of the village, rows of seating were cut away from the mountainside like an amphitheater. The stone seats faced toward a small stagelike area that held eleven flat-topped boulders forming a semicircle. It reminded Blue of the place where jousting tournaments were held at the castle. It seemed everyone in the village had showed up.

"You sit there," River told Blue, nodding to one of the boulders. "Along with the ten Elders, Ikor, and his new Dragon Rider. I need to go find my parents."

"Couldn't you sit with me?" asked Blue, who didn't much like the idea of being left alone with a dragon breathing down his neck.

"You . . . want me to stay?"

"If that's all right."

River looked to one of the Elder women, who was now taking a seat on the boulder next to Blue.

"He'd like me to sit with him," River told the Elder. "I think he's a bit nervous," she added in a not-so-subtle whisper.

Blue's cheeks grew warm and the Elder woman smiled. "Of course that's fine if the king wills it," she said.

It took a moment for Blue to remember *he* was the king she was talking about as he and River climbed onto his boulder. River waved to a man and woman in the crowd who Blue assumed were her parents. Then Elder Cyrus stood in the center of the semicircle of boulders and tapped his cane.

"We have gathered together to hear *The Story of History and Heroes* as was told by our ancestors before us!" he called, his voice echoing rather impressively off the mountainside.

There was a snort behind Blue, and warm breath trickled down the back of his neck. Blue's mouth fell open and River stifled a snicker. Blue didn't have to turn around to know that Ikor had taken his seat behind him as Elder Cyrus continued.

"In the earliest days, long ago, companion Magics lived amidst the stars. These Magic souls were *alive*. They were lonely and curious, so they came down to our world to explore and meet the hu-

70

mans of Haven. These were the First Magics. Some Magics touched the soil, and fire sprang forth, creating the very first dragons. Other Magics planted stardust into the ground, growing all sorts of plants and animals. Everywhere First Magics touched, natural magic was born in the soil. While not alive, natural magic was—and still is—a powerful force. It can be found woven throughout all of nature if one knows where to look."

Blue stared at the Elder, wide-eyed. He'd never heard anything like this before. Living Magics and natural magic? According to his people, magic was bad luck and came from dragons—Blue hadn't known there were different kinds.

"While dragons were born with natural magic in their blood, humans were not. They were given a choice. For those humans who wanted it, First Magics performed a special ceremony to bind natural magic into the human's blood. These magic humans were gifted with long life and eventually given a companion Magic of their own. Other humans refused the gift, too frightened of magic's power. Many humans still feel that way." Elder Cyrus gave Blue a meaningful glance.

"Wait—what are companion Magics, exactly?" Blue whispered to River.

"They're like little wispy clouds, I think. They sound really cute, but I've never seen them."

"Why don't your people have them? Aren't you magic too?" Blue asked, confused.

"Yes, the Dragon Growers are Meraki. We're born with natural magic in our blood, but we don't have companion Magics, since we don't have our own Offering Tree."

Blue knitted his brow, utterly perplexed. But before he could ask anything else, River shushed him and nodded toward Elder Cyrus. "Listen—this part's important."

"And so it was during the Age of Peace the three species—

dragons, humans, and Magics—coexisted in harmony." Elder Cyrus tapped his cane. "For a time."

Blue shared a look with River. "Then the wars?" he guessed.

River nodded solemnly.

"Three Great Wars were fought between those with the gift of magic—eventually known as the Meraki—and the nonmagic humans. The consequences of human warfare were dire even for the dragons. For some unknown reason, by the end of the wars, female dragons stopped bearing young. This is still known today as the Dragon's Curse. Eventually, the dragons came to the brink of extinction. It was decided that a select group of Meraki would devote their lives to helping new dragons grow with the use of natural magic."

A round of claps rang from the villagers.

"After seeking help from the Fates, the Dragon Growers learned to grow new dragons using magic ingredients and a nonmagic human host. Which meant we needed a Gerberan. We sent our Elders to Gerbera to propose a truce. From then on, the kingdom delivered one Gerberan every quarter century. In exchange, our dragons left Gerbera in peace." Elder Cyrus gestured a hand toward the seated villagers. "We need new dragons, you see, to protect our Meraki siblings in the Northern Realm," Elder Cyrus explained. "There is an evil chancellor who would see the island Meraki come to harm. The dragons proctor peace and help keep the two human groups in line."

A deep shiver fluttered through Blue. "And now you want to make *me* into a dragon."

"It is your duty, in fact," said Cyrus cheerfully with a thump of his cane. "One brave soul to protect the lives of thousands."

Blue didn't feel brave. Not one bit. But *protecting the lives of thousands* did seem awfully important.

And it sounded better than becoming Ikor's breakfast.

"How does it work?" asked Blue.

"You drink the hibernation elixir and go to sleep," River told him. "Part of my job is creating the elixir from magic crops. Over time, your body will transform. Then you'll wake up in twenty-five years as a dragon."

Blue turned back to look at Ikor. The giant creature gazed down at him thoughtfully.

"So . . . this dragon used to be a king of Gerbera?"

"Yes, he was. Though Ikor doesn't seem to remember it," said River.

"He can't remember being king?" asked Blue.

"He can't remember being *human*," explained Elder Cyrus.

Blue's mouth fell open. A swirl of shock tightened around his ribs. What must it be like to not remember being human? He inhaled sharply, letting this news settle as he eyed the black dragon sadly. "Can he talk?" asked Blue.

River shook her head. "Dragons can't talk. But they seem to understand us for the most part."

Blue gazed up at the dragon's big golden eyes. "Y-you don't remember being human?" he asked, his voice shaking a bit.

The beast regarded him with a curious expression. He lowered his face to Blue's level and shook his head.

Blue turned back to face the Elder and the rest of the villagers. "Becoming a dragon means losing my humanness?"

"Once the transformation is finished, you will be fully and completely dragon," Elder Cyrus agreed. "There will not be any human part of you remaining."

Blue stared down at his hands, a fierce pang of sadness swelling through him. He wouldn't remember Cedar or his life in the stables. He wouldn't remember the smell of hay or the taste of chocolate. His dreams of becoming stable manager and having a family of his own someday would be forgotten. And his oldest memory—of two eyes, blue as the sea, gazing down at him—would be lost forever.

Everything that made Blue himself.

All of it would be gone.

Then again, maybe it would be worse to be a dragon with a head full of human memories? Too painful to remember a life he would no longer be part of.

"Does it hurt?" Blue whispered.

"You'll be asleep the whole time," River assured him, patting his arm gently. "You won't feel a thing."

"But I won't be . . . me. Not at all?"

Elder Cyrus offered a kind smile. "Your soul will remain. Gerbera's kings are always incredibly brave."

"But I'm terrified," Blue admitted.

"So why did you come?" asked River.

Blue inhaled deeply, fidgeting with the end of his too-large royal tunic. The sharp edges of ache in his chest came spilling out in words.

"My whole life, I've never been wanted for anything. I've been liked well enough by the other castle servants, I suppose. But I've never . . ." He paused, squeezing his eyes shut. "Never been *loved*. I'm just a stable boy with a strange ability. My name isn't even really a name. Only what people called me because of my eyes. I guess I just feel like I've never mattered to anyone. Not really."

Blue hopped off his boulder and stood as tall as he could, facing the Elders. "Maybe I was no one's first choice to be king, but I *was* chosen nevertheless. So the way I figure it, at least now I have the chance to do something important."

A hushed stillness fell over the villagers. Then Elder Cyrus cleared his throat.

"You are of good heart, young king—perhaps the best and bravest we've ever known." He put a hand on Blue's shoulder. "You will make a fine dragon, Blue. And your life will *matter* more than you can imagine."

Blue inhaled, the weight of his kingdom settling heavier on his chest, and gave a decisive nod. "Just tell me what to do."

11.

IN WHICH RIVER SAYS GOOD NIGHT TO A KING

River was itching to get to her Lead Harvester celebration, but first she needed to help Blue get settled. The dragon caves lay just beyond the apple orchards, and after the feast and the send-off of Ikor and his newly chosen Dragon Rider, River and her parents took Blue to his hibernation cave. River's father, one of the village Architects, had spent the last several years readying the cave with steam vents and hibernation crystals. The center of the rocky floor had been smoothed as a bed.

"It's . . . really warm," Blue noted, stepping first into the cave.

"Dragons like the heat," River told him.

"It's pouring through the lava rocks on the perimeter," River's father explained. "And those crystals"—he pointed to the rainbow-colored gemstones jutting out of the rock—"give off a high-frequency melody, meant to keep your dreams peaceful."

"It smells like peppermint," said Blue, trying to smile. But River could tell he was nervous, as he kept rubbing the back of his neck.

"It really is as easy as going to sleep," said River. "You'll fall into a deep hibernation. Like . . . one long dream for twenty-five years."

Blue winced. "That's some dream."

"The elixir does all the work," said River's mother. "We'll make sure you get a steady dose each day as you sleep. Then you'll wake up in twenty-five years like no time has passed at all."

"And you will all be older," said Blue, looking at each of them.

"Older, yes," said River's father. "But still here to help you with your transition."

"And I'll get a Rider? Just like Ikor?"

"You'll choose a Rider once you've woken," River's mother explained. "Many young people are trained in preparation, but only one will be chosen."

"How will I know who to choose?" asked Blue, the crease in his forehead deepening.

"It seems to be a kind of instinct," said River's mother. "Don't worry, dear. A dragon always knows."

"I'll be here when you wake up," River promised. "Okay?"

A small smile pulled at Blue's lips, and he stepped gently onto the smoothed stone. "So how does this work?"

River walked over to the wall near the cave opening. There was a small cauldron, and a goblet on a table. She dipped the goblet into the cauldron, filling it halfway with the hibernation elixir, then handed it to Blue. "Drink this."

Blue peered down at the golden liquid. "Here goes nothing." He took a sip and his eyes widened in surprise. "Tastes like chocolate!"

"It's my nana's recipe," River told him. "I mixed it fresh this morning. It will help calm your nerves as you go to sleep."

"Will I meet many other dragons beyond Dragon Mountain?"

"Many like Ikor, yes," said River's father. "They'll be your new family."

Blue's breath caught. "My *family*?"

River studied him curiously. There was something about the way he said *family.* With a longing in his eyes. But before she could ask, Blue took another sip from the goblet.

"How will I know the way?" he asked.

"Your Rider will help you," said River's mother.

"Will they?" asked Blue, his eyelids starting to droop. He sat down on the floor.

River smiled. Her elixir was working perfectly. In a few minutes, Blue would be deep in peaceful sleep. Before he closed his eyes completely, he looked up at River.

"Will you be my Dragon Rider?" he asked. His pleading eyes twinkled in the dim cave light. "I know we've only just met. But . . . I like you."

River laughed, surprised by the request. "Sorry, but I haven't had any training." She gave him a sympathetic smile. "Besides, I'm about to become Lead Harvester, remember? Just like my nana before me. I'd be miserable up in the air so far from my beautiful gardens. Not to mention, I'm terrified of heights."

The boy's face fell a little. "I'm scared," he whispered.

River knelt down on the ground next to him. "That's understandable. Besides, I suppose it's doubly all right for a *kid* king to be scared."

"And for . . . a dragon?"

"I don't imagine dragons have any reason to be scared."

Blue smiled, then reached for the compass around his neck.

"Could you . . . take care of this for me?" he asked. "It's important to my people, but I"—he yawned—"I forgot to send it back with Cedar."

"Sure." River slipped the compass around her neck. She'd make sure it got back to Blue's castle somehow. She wanted to ask who Cedar was, but Blue's eyelids drooped heavily.

"I think . . . I think I'll go to sleep now," he said, lying down on the stone bed.

"Good night, Blue," River whispered. She studied his sunburned cheeks, trying to memorize his human face. She reached out and stroked his hay-colored hair, the way her mama had always done for her when she was little. Blue didn't have a mama, after all. So no one had *ever* sent him off to sleep properly, and here he was—in his last moments as a boy. Because *no one* soothes a dragon to sleep, of course.

"When we see each other again, I suppose we'll both look very different," River whispered, wondering what Blue would look like as a dragon. River would be grown by then. Someday, she could tell her own child of the time she sent a dragon off to his first sleep.

Blue began snoring softly and River wiped her cheeks. Had she been crying? What a silly thing to do on such a grand occasion as this. She stood with a sigh of deep satisfaction.

"You've done well today, Rivs," said her father.

"We are so proud of you," said her mother, wrapping River in a big hug. "Nana would be too."

River smiled, wishing with all her heart that her grandmother could somehow see her right now. She'd completed her first successful Hibernation Day, all thanks to years of Nana's loving patience and guidance in the gardens.

"And now"—River's father tapped his chin—"I hear there's some sort of party or celebration or something?" He pretended to look confused and glanced at River's mom. "Did you hear something about that, dear?"

River's mom laughed at the same time River rolled her eyes.

"Yeah. *Or something,*" River echoed, her heart thumping eagerly. Her Lead Harvester celebration was only moments away. River took her mother's hand. With one last look at Blue sleeping soundly, the three turned to leave the cave.

Then a surge of fire shot through River's right forearm. She yelped in alarm.

"River?" Her mother called her name, but it sounded far away.

"M-my arm—" Another shooting pain tore up her left forearm. She cried out, bright spots forming on the back of her eyelids as her eyes fluttered shut. Someone pulled up her sleeves hastily, inspecting her arms.

Her mother gasped. "But—that's impossible!"

"Just hang on, Rivs." Her father's voice swam around her. "It'll be okay."

River tried to form a question, but her mind couldn't put the words in the right order. She cried out again, this time swaying on her feet. Her father scooped her up in his arms and started to run. He was shouting now, but River could no longer understand him. The last thing River heard was her mother sobbing.

Then she heard nothing at all.

PART 11

SLEEPING
DRAGONS

12.

They say whenever a star dies, magic is born.

The trail of stardust floats down to our world, full of bits of flickering power. Much of it is lost, blown into the wind. But some of it settles into the soil.

How do I know?

I met a mouse once, who'd eaten bits of the stardust, thinking they were seeds. His fur was the most beautiful shade of purple and silver I'd ever seen—like the moonlight. Why am I telling you all this? Well, haven't you wondered why I've lived so long?

Perhaps you can guess what happened to the mouse? Yes, I'm getting to that part.

I ate him.

Yes, yes. I know. A tragedy. And I am paying penance enough, thank you very much. Turns out he'd been very good friends with a dragon who was furious to learn the fate of her small, whiskery friend. As retribution, she gave me the curse of Time.

Immortality is a lonely road to walk.

What is more, she tasked me with a sacred duty. It is my job to usher each human king to their path to Dragon Mountain. I believe she meant it as a punishment, but in all honesty, I quite enjoy the task.

Because I knew the day would come when I would meet the Awaited One. The One the Fates sang of.

Yes, kit. I believe I have met him. Led him to the dragons not that long ago, in fact. And so, young one, we must be patient. We hold on to the hope in our bellies that tells us all can be right again someday.

We only have to wait.

13.

IN WHICH A SEER REMEMBERS
A VERY OLD SONG

THE YEAR OF THE FOURTH WAR

Sometime later, half a world away, a swirl of purple Magic hiccuped.

From her rocking chair, Madam Seer Madera Starling cracked open an eyelid. Sticks, she'd fallen asleep reading again. An enormous and ancient book, *A History of Haven*, rested in her lap, inches from falling to the floor. She glanced at the purple cloud hovering above the nightstand.

Possibly, she'd only imagined—

The Magic hiccuped again and started swirling like a tiny tornado.

Wren Barrow looked up from the book she was reading, *My Magic and Me*, in the corner of the room. Her coiled curls bounced as she tilted her head in concern. "Granmama, was that a hiccup?"

Madera nodded and pushed herself up out of the chair. She'd promised her granddaughter some extra spell recitation practice this afternoon. Tomorrow was an immensely important day for Wren, along with all the other thirteen-year-old Meraki children. But the lessons would have to wait.

Madera eyed the purple swirl of Magic, now dancing in circles impatiently. "Well, let's get on with it, then." The violet swirl rose into the air and settled on Madera's head, helping her See.

"Is it a *prophecy*?" whispered Wren, eyebrows raised. "What do you See?"

"Not what—*who*."

"Okay, then. Who?"

"Your curiosity will need to be patient, love. I cannot speed up the Seeing process any more than I can hurry the sunrise." Madam Madera pressed her palms to her forehead. "Oh, it's the baby boy, Blue. I've Seen him before, long ago." The old memory stirred. "Strange, I've never received the same prophecy twice."

"It must mean something important." Wren hugged her book to her chest.

"The first came as a warning," Madera explained. She let out a weighty sigh, and her Magic did the same as it settled onto her shoulder. "This time is the announcement of his arrival. He is coming—and soon."

"Here—to the island?"

"Yes, child. And he won't be alone. It is like the old song says."

Wren rolled her eyes. "There are, you know, *lots* of old songs. Could you be more specific?"

Madera chuckled. "True enough. But this song is special, Wren. It is the Havensong." Speaking the name aloud sent a thrill of goose bumps across the old woman's flesh. Madera closed her eyes, remembering the ancient words her mother had taught her. "Most people only remember the ending: *For there is One who can make amends—with the aid of three Unlikely Friends.*"

"'One who can make amends'?" Wren tapped a finger against her lip. "So the Awaited One . . . is a little baby?"

"The prophecy is of the past, so I'm sure Blue has grown by now—though I can't tell you what he looks like." Madera started pacing the room, following the familiar path in the worn wooden planks in the floor. "His prophecy is especially concerning because of . . . the blurry parts. There are things I cannot See clearly. This happened last time too."

"That's unusual, isn't it?"

Indeed, it was. Ever since she was a little girl, Madera had received visions—brief bursts of a scene that felt ripped right out of someone's memories and dropped into her head—with clarity and precision, down to the most minute detail. And prophecies—full-length memories—though much more rare, had also come to her with remarkable clarity, both in physical detail and with any emotion attached to the memory. Almost as if Madera were living the scene herself.

But this particular prophecy about the boy had gaps and fuzzy images. Like someone had dumped water on a chalk painting. Madera sighed. "There's someone who doesn't want me to know of Blue's arrival."

Wren gasped. "Is that even possible—for someone to tamper with a prophecy?"

"It *shouldn't* be," Madera grunted.

"Who could be powerful enough to do such a thing?" Wren asked.

Madera stopped her pacing. There was one other who had matched her Seeing ability once. But that was ages ago. And he was now long gone.

"Why is Blue so important?" asked Wren.

Madera's heart fluttered. For weeks, her dreams had been filled with terrible shadow creatures and cursed flower gardens and grand tapestries of golden thread unraveling. They weren't visions, exactly. More like a premonition. But they left her insides feeling hollowed with fear that clung to her bones. "All I know is a terrible darkness is coming, love. And soon. And if I'm right, then the boy is destined to fight it."

"Along with his Unlikely Friends?" Wren guessed.

Madera had known the question was coming, but she still wasn't ready for it. A bead of sweat fell from her temple. She wondered, at times like this, if Wren was too curious for her own good. Still, she didn't have to tell her granddaughter everything.

Not yet, anyway.

"Yes, darling, I do believe the boy . . . and his friends . . . are going to attempt to save us all."

"Save us from what?" Wren whispered.

Madera eyed the sage flowers outside the window.

All is well. All is well.

The old woman shook her head sadly. "I'm afraid we're going to find out much sooner than we'd like."

14.

IN WHICH A YOUNG STEWARD BECOMES A SOLDIER

THE YEAR OF THE FOURTH WAR

The next morning, on the other side of the ocean, thirteen-year-old Shenli Zhao carefully fastened the last few buttons on his military jacket, examining himself in the small hand mirror propped up on the dresser. Through the fingerprinted smudges—suspiciously the size of Yiming's tiny fingertips—a young soldier stood before him.

This was truly happening, then.

A real military mission.

For the last three years, Shenli had proudly served as the youngest personal steward to Chancellor Cudek. He'd spent most of his time living and working at Cudek's castle, though he did get to come home a few days a month to see his mom and sisters if Cudek was pleased enough with his work.

Until now, Shenli had worked hard running errands, doing research in the library, bringing the chancellor his meals, and scrubbing his laundry. But recently, Shenli had been asked to do more important tasks, like delivering classified messages on horseback to

Cudek's military commanders all across the five districts, proving the chancellor's increasing trust in Shenli.

Still, Shenli hadn't yet been brave enough to ask about the mysterious death of his father. He'd learned early on that Cudek was notorious for his temper and didn't welcome unsolicited questions. There were more servants in prison for upsetting Cudek's mood than Shenli could count. He didn't want to do anything to land on the chancellor's bad side. Not with fourteen years of family debt remaining. And so Shenli was left with a desperate ache in his chest to learn answers to questions he didn't have the courage to ask. But he hoped that would all change after tonight's mission.

Yesterday, Cudek had told Shenli he wanted to give him more responsibility—as a soldier. At age thirteen, Shenli was three years younger than the typical cadet newbie, so he knew Cudek was giving him a major chance to prove himself.

"That cannot be my little Shenli."

Shenli caught sight of his mother's face in the smudgy mirror. Kayra Zhao tucked her long nutmeg hair behind her ears before wrapping her arms around him. She didn't have to stoop to hug him anymore.

"You sure it was your thirteenth birthday you celebrated yesterday, and not your thirtieth, my little duckling?" his mother teased. Then her breath caught as she spun him around. "Your hair . . ."

Shenli bit his lip, hoping she'd approve. He'd given himself a haircut for the first time and styled his hair the way his father used to wear his—cut short on the sides and long on top, parted mostly to the left. "Did I . . . do it okay?" If it weren't for the hand-drawn sketches of his father hanging in the kitchen, Shenli sometimes feared he'd forget what his dad looked like. It had been four years since the night he'd disappeared.

"You look just like him," Kayra whispered, her eyes glistening. "I couldn't be prouder, son. You've worked hard for this."

A swell of pride stole through Shenli's belly. He wondered if Mama was also remembering the night Yuli wore his first uniform. A familiar wisp of fury flared in Shenli's chest. Ever since he'd arrived to work at the castle, he'd been known as *Yuli's little brother.* It wasn't often that soldiers deserted—desertion was incredibly shameful for a Mainlander—and castle gossip spread even faster than village gossip, as it turned out. Shenli hadn't been able to live it down. It was like they were all expecting Shenli to do something just as terrible. He had received enough dirty looks around the castle to last a lifetime.

To make things worse, Shenli's family still hadn't heard from Yuli. Everyone assumed he was in hiding. Or maybe he was living a fancy new life in the Mountain District, like he'd always wanted. Either way, Shenli's anger toward his brother had only increased over time. His father's getting killed over unpaid debts was senseless, and bad enough for the family reputation, but Yuli's running away like a coward was pure selfishness.

Shenli squared his shoulders and gathered all the painful unspoken things leaking from his heart and stuffed them back down into the places inside him that he never visited.

He couldn't think about Yuli tonight.

"I'm coming back," Shenli said firmly, in case his mother needed to hear it. "I would never leave you and the girls—not ever."

His mother touched his hair gently. "I know that, son."

"I swear I'm going to make things right, Mama. Everything Yuli messed up."

A look of pain flitted across Mama's face as she rested her hands on his shoulders. "Tonight is your night. Cudek's right-hand man."

"Shen!" A shout from the other room was followed by the

thundering of tiny footsteps. A small face popped into the doorway. Three-year-old Yiming hopped into the room, her dark pigtails bouncing along with her. Ever since she'd seen a wild rabbit in the field behind their house, she'd decided hopping was the best way to get around.

"You look like a fluffy bunny!" Yiming said, beaming, hopping toward him and hugging his leg.

Shenli scooped his sister into his arms. "Well, coming from you, I'd say that's a compliment."

Yiming ruffled his hair, her brown eyes wide in amusement. "See? *Fluffy!*"

Shenli grinned. "Hey now. I think my new hairdo looks awesome." He tickled Yiming on the belly. She giggled delightedly, then wiggled out of his arms and slid back to the floor, where she promptly resumed her bunny bouncing.

"Sorry. I tried to keep her out of the way." Meili stepped into the room, hands raised in exasperation. Meili was nearing eleven, but she looked a lot older to Shenli these days. She had their father's dark hair and their mother's big blue eyes. "She just *had* to come see *Bunny Shen Shen*," said Meili, rolling her eyes.

"I'm all done getting ready." The truth was, Shenli was happy to soak up all the family time he could get.

Meili let out a low whistle. "Well, look at you, bro. All grown up."

"Not *too* grown up," Kayra argued playfully.

Shenli flexed his muscles. "I think my bulging biceps would have to disagree."

Meili took a sock from the dresser and threw it at Shenli's face. It landed smack on his nose.

"Gross!" Shenli plucked the sock away. "It's smelly."

"That uniform is going to your head, Mr. Macho," Meili told him.

Shenli waggled his eyebrows. "You're just jealous because I look awesome."

Meili rolled her eyes again. "Nothing *awesome* about becoming another military goon," she muttered. Then she clapped a hand over her mouth. "Er, I didn't mean—"

But it was too late. Kayra's eyes were already slitted narrower than sewing needles. Like the fury of firebreathers swelling in the air. Shenli took a step back for good measure.

"*Meili* Zhao!" Kayra shouted. "You *dare* speak disrespect for the military!"

Yiming halted mid–bunny hop to stare.

Meili held up her palms in surrender. "Ma, I'm *sorry*. I was just jok—"

"All it takes is one *joke*! One little wisecrack against Cudek to land you behind bars!"

Meili's shoulders fell. "I know. You're right, Mama. It won't happen again."

And before Kayra could protest—because they all knew it absolutely *would* happen again eventually, since Meili could never manage to hold her tongue—Meili sprang forward and wrapped her mother in a hug. Shenli and Meili had both learned long ago that the best way to defuse Mama Volcano was with big hugs.

Kayra pinched the bridge of her nose with one hand and hugged Meili with the other. "Your smart mouth will be the death of me, child."

Meili grinned. "Not before Shen's *bulging biceps.*"

Kayra laughed and Meili gave Shenli a playful punch on the arm. Shenli couldn't help but admire his sister. Her mouth *did* get her into a lot of trouble, but no one made Mama laugh like Meili did.

Fates. He wished he didn't have to leave again so soon. Everyone was in such good spirits. Last night, Mama had cooked his favorite dinner—honey-glazed salmon and fried rice. Then his sisters had gifted him a beaded bracelet in honor of his new assignment. He couldn't wear it for today's mission, since it wasn't uniform dress code. But it sat proudly on his desk, teal beads gleaming, awaiting his return tomorrow morning.

Shenli looked at each member of his family, a small secret hesitating on his lips. The truth was, Cudek had not only recruited him for a special mission—he'd also promised something. Shenli took a deep breath, praying he wasn't making the wrong decision by getting Mama's hopes up.

"Cudek said if I complete the mission tonight, he'll cut my service debt in half."

Kayra put a hand over her mouth.

Meili punched him on the arm again. "Get *out!*"

"In *half?*" Kayra gasped. "Shenli . . . you'd only have seven more years."

"*If* I do a good job tonight."

His mother pinched his cheek gently. "You *always* do a good job for Cudek. That's why he prefers you."

Shenli grinned and flexed his muscles playfully, earning another punch on the arm from Meili. It was true, Cudek had begun to favor Shenli above the other stewards. But it wasn't luck. Shenli had worked harder, paid attention, and used what his mom liked to call Shenli Charm.

"I guess that means you'd be home more often to boss me around," said Meili with an exaggerated sigh. Then she winked. "That would be fine by me."

"I'd like that too." Shenli grinned.

"It would be nice to have all my ducklings under one roof again," said Mama, pulling them into a hug. "Well, almost all of them . . ."

Mama's eyes fell away sadly, and Shenli and Meili shared a knowing look.

Shenli cleared his throat. "I'd . . . better get going. I need to meet the rest of the squadron before breakfast."

Mama nodded, biting her lip. The fear in her eyes was loud, but all she said to Shenli was "Be safe. I love you."

"Love you too. All of you."

They all wrapped him in another big hug before shooing him outside, where his horse waited patiently. He turned to give his family one final wave as he mounted his horse swiftly. Yiming blew him three kisses and he did the same back to her.

Fates, he loved that kid more than anything.

He flicked the reins and led the horse away from the house, riding through the sleepy village just as the morning sun crept over the hillside. As he picked up speed, a new hope pulsed through him with the pounding of every hoof. Tonight, Shenli would prove himself to Cudek, and finally end the Zhao family bad luck streak once and for all.

15.

IN WHICH A NEW MAGIC IS BORN

THE YEAR OF THE FOURTH WAR

As Shenli stole away to meet his new squadron, Wren Barrow stared at the ivory cherry trees, their blossoms sparkling with morning dew. She longed to climb their branches. After all, trees standing in a neat row along the side of the walking path *wanted* to be climbed. And the ocean view in the distance? The morning sun glittering off the deep blue depths? The beauty was too much.

"Your bowl is kind of ugly, you know."

Wren sighed, wanting nothing more than to hide away in the treetops with a good book.

Oh, wait. Had Cephas been talking to her again?

"Er—what?" she asked, looking down at her brother—not as far down as she *used* to, though. He'd hit a growth spurt since his eighth birthday. His honey-gold eyes rolled up in annoyance.

"Your bowl—it's junky-looking," he told her.

Wren scrunched her nose, peering at the handmade ceramic bowl she was carrying. She'd had to create it for Acquisition Day. Sure, the sculpting jutted unevenly. And the paint lines were crooked. But she'd loved the feel of clay at the potter's wheel. The way it smooshed between her fingers. A beautiful mess with endless potential, though she didn't have a steady hand like her other classmates.

"I did my best," Wren muttered, gazing longingly at the cherry blossoms again. She jumped up to pluck one, nearly losing her grip on her bowl.

"We're going to be late," Cephas scolded, furrowing his brow.

Wren frowned. Her brother looked so much like Father. Their light brown faces were all smooth angles, and they both wore their curly dark hair styled in the same faded haircut. Not to mention, their brows furrowed the same way in annoyance—it was uncanny.

"I'm never late unless I want to be," Wren told him.

"Well, *that's* reassuring," Cephas scoffed.

Wren twirled the tiny pink flower in her fingers. When had her brother started acting like such a little grown-up, anyway? She sighed. So much had changed since—Wren shook her head. No, not today. She couldn't dwell on Mama for Acquisition Day. It was bad luck and could upset her new Magic.

"So, what color do you think your Magic will be?" asked Cephas, picking up the pace, forcing Wren to walk faster.

"Oh, I hope *blue*. Like the ocean. Or purple, like Granmama's." She twirled the flower, lost in thought. "Pink might be nice too."

"Your eyes would look cool pink," said Cephas approvingly.

"Well, the eye-color change doesn't happen for a long time."

Wren bit her lip, trying to imagine her own reflection. Her eyes right now were brownish red with gold flecks—a mix of her parents' eyes and Magics. Her dad's eyes and Magic were honey golden, and her mom's had both been a bright shade of copper. But Wren's eyes would eventually change to match the color of her new Magic. It was the final phase of Shoya, signaling that the Bond with one's Magic was complete. After the glittery shimmer covered a Meraki's entire body—showing up only in moonlight—their eye color started to transform. This process could take hundreds of years, though. Only once a Meraki's eyes had totally changed color was Shoya complete.

It would definitely be strange. But exciting too.

The sound of a blown conch shell rose over the ocean, and the hairs on Wren's neck stood upright. The sound was faint, but loud enough to shatter the morning calm on her people's island. The call to military training drills was a Mainland ritual, sounding twice each day. Even all this time after the wars, Mainlanders loved to remind Meraki they weren't forgotten.

Or forgiven.

Even though her people had acted only in self-defense, many lives had been lost on both sides. Truthfully, Wren tried not to think about the wars of the old days. Instead, she marveled at how the two groups had once lived together in peace, back when the land was called Haven.

What might it be like to explore the vast stretch of Mainland and see what nonmagic people were like? Were they all serious and orderly like the Meraki? After the terrible wars, when all Meraki moved to the island, the Council had decided that people with Magics bore a great responsibility. For the sake of protecting their Magics and their way of life, the Meraki had long ago shaped a society of rigid protocols that shaped the Meraki creed: order, preservation, and tradition.

Wren also wondered how it felt for Mainlanders to live short lives—never beyond a century. What was it like to have multiple siblings? Meraki women usually bore only one child—Cephas being a miraculous exception. In fact, he was only the fourth Meraki sibling ever to be born—something not even Granmama could explain except to say Rose Barrow was clearly exemplary. The strangeness of it had always nagged at Wren, the fact that her family had this exceptional gift and no one knew why.

More than anything, Wren wondered this: Were Mainlanders allowed to be curious?

A whiff of apple pie tickled Wren's nose, sending a small ache to her chest. She gritted her teeth, giving a pointed look to the Memory Trees up the road.

Not today. Just leave me alone for once.

Cephas scooped up a star-shaped leaf fluttering by his foot. He sniffed the leaf and stuffed it in his pocket. "I always smell Granmama's cupcakes. Is it still apple pie for you?"

"Almost always," Wren admitted, the ache in her chest doubling. Apple pie had been Mama's favorite.

Wren took a shaky breath, pushing the simmering sadness away. She had to be brave for Cephas. He needed her to be strong. Ever since Mama had passed, she'd kept her sorrow to herself. Cephas didn't really miss Mama much, since he was too little to remember her. And there was no reason for Wren to let her grief leak out onto her brother. She wanted him to live a happy, *normal* life. Not like she did, walking around feeling like half of her was missing.

Like a misfit who didn't belong anywhere.

You are enough. Just as you are.

Mama's words settled into Wren's chest as she flashed Cephas her best smile. They walked in silence until the Memory Trees receded far behind them. As they crested the hill, the glittering sidewalk spilled out into the Gathering Place, a large valley blanketed in wildflowers.

On one side of the valley, wooden chairs sat in neat rows, awaiting the hundreds of Meraki who would gather for today's special occasion. The chairs formed a wide arc facing the Offering Tree, which stood in the center of the meadow. The enormous white tree glittered in the sun, its translucent heart-shaped leaves fluttering slightly, catching a hint of rainbow glimmer in the sunlight. Wren still visited the ancient tree often. It was the only place she felt free to speak her questions aloud, since there was no one around to scold her for it.

Next to the tree sat Xayndra, her gold scales shimmering beautifully, as always. Since the night of Mama's funeral, Xayndra had become Wren's favorite dragon. She was the oldest dragon on the island and the only female, and she was usually stationed at Wren's academy. Wren never had much luck making school friends, so she often spent her free time reading books in the shade of Xayndra's massive shadow.

Xayndra caught Wren's gaze and winked. Wren winked back just as Cephas gave her his best *good luck* grin before weaving through the crowds to find their father in the sea of immaculate chairs.

The sun crested the crown of the Offering Tree, signaling the eighth morning hour. Wren was right on time. But since everyone else had showed up ridiculously early, she was still the last to arrive. Even from this distance, her empty chair in the student bleachers stood out—a sad, gleaming hole amid the throngs of excited thirteen-year-old Academy students. Wren now had to walk in front of *every*one to get to her spot.

Ugh. Great.

She made her way through the student horde and took her seat. From there, she could see the Council Chambers in the distance and the seven large Meraki crystals twinkling from the roof, proclaiming the greatness of Meraki tradition.

Headmaster Leon Mikos stood from the faculty seats in the front row, pulling Wren's eyes away from the crystals. He dressed in a double-breasted pastel-blue suit, his brown hair slicked back for the occasion. The headmaster wiped his beige forehead with a handkerchief and then adjusted his glasses slightly as he walked toward the Offering Tree, where an enormous hollowed-out boulder sat steaming beneath. His pink Magic floated nearby, singing softly. Wren recognized the melody. It was the Song of Acquirement, and the headmaster's Magic had a knack for making beautiful music.

A lump Wren couldn't quite swallow formed in her throat as she watched the steam toss in the wind.

"Honored families and guests," Headmaster Mikos began, scanning the crowd of beaming parents with his pale pink eyes. "Today is a most sacred occasion. Your Academy students have been hard at work learning the responsibilities of Magics. They've prepared for this moment their entire young lives. Today, at last, they will become the newest Meraki to acquire their Magic companions!"

A round of dignified applause burst from the audience. Wren scanned the crowd for her father and finally spotted him and Cephas in the back row. Father wore his usual uninterested scowl.

At least he'd showed up.

"So without further ado, dear students—arise!" called Headmaster Mikos, clapping enthusiastically. "Come and claim your Magic!"

The students rose, one row at a time, and made their way to the cauldron. Wren gripped her bowl so hard she feared it might crack.

I can do this. Everyone else is doing it. I can do it too.

To keep calm, Wren turned her head south, toward the sea. From where she stood, she could barely make out the dark blur of the Mainland. She wondered if any Mainlanders might be on their beaches looking toward her at this moment. She knew it was silly, but she couldn't help imagining a Mainlander child waving to her.

"Wren Barrow."

Wren snapped her head forward. Headmaster Mikos stood with the twelve Meraki Elders and Judge Finlar around the cauldron. Her eyes drifted to Granmama, the Chief Elder, who gave her a wink. Headmaster Mikos beckoned Wren toward the cauldron. She kept her chin up, taking care not to trip, as she was so prone to doing. She stepped up to the enormous pot and peered inside. Dark liquid bubbled and spat, not unlike boiling, glittery mud.

The headmaster cleared his throat. "Wren Barrow, you may now submerge your bowl and acquire your Magic."

Wren gulped, slowly leaning into the steam. She chanced a look at Granmama, who nodded encouragingly.

"Go *on*, then," Headmaster Mikos muttered from the side of his mouth. His Magic hissed softly.

Wren dipped her bowl, allowing in just enough dark liquid to fill it halfway, like they'd practiced at school. Poppy Drenric, one of the younger Elders, with fair skin and long ginger hair, carefully plucked a large translucent leaf from the Offering Tree and held it up. It glimmered in the sunlight, flashes of rainbow colors skimming its surface. Elder Drenric smiled at Wren and dropped the leaf into her bowl, then held out the ceremonial dragon-bone dagger. Wren swallowed hard, staring at the ebony handle and the curved ebony blade. Elder Drenric's pine-colored Magic cooed encouragingly.

Don't be such a child, Wren scolded herself. It wasn't much larger than the knife she used to peel fruit with Granmama.

The dagger gleamed in the sun, beckoning her forward. And somewhere in the crowd, her father was watching. With gritted teeth, Wren reached out and ran her pointer finger along the blade. The cut burned as she held her hand over her bowl. Drops of red fell into the liquid with a satisfying sizzle. The dark liquid bubbled and churned, transforming into smoke. And then a small puff of periwinkle cloud, about the size of a cantaloupe, rose from the bowl.

"And now the Magic will bind itself to the child," Headmaster Mikos announced, waving his hands in dramatic fashion.

Wren beamed, the pain of her cut finger already forgotten. Her Magic! It swirled both blue *and* purple. Like Granmama's Magic and

Mama's ocean. It was a perfect periwinkle hue, and Wren's heart swelled with gratitude. She watched in awe as the beautiful little cloud rose higher into the air.

Uh-oh.

Too high.

"Claim it!" Headmaster Mikos spat. "Hurry, girl!"

Wren cringed. Right. She'd practiced the binding spell with Granmama last night. "I bind you to myself," Wren called to the hovering puff of smoke. "And bind myself to thee—"

Wren froze.

She couldn't remember the last part of the spell. Terror-stricken, she glanced at her grandmother, who tried to mouth the words, but Wren couldn't make them out.

Mercy.

She couldn't finish the spell. And the periwinkle Magic was starting to drift toward the audience, who watched in horror.

"C-come back!" Wren's voice was small and quivering, drowned out by the shocked cries from the crowd.

"Those aren't the proper words!" Headmaster Mikos gasped out, his pink eyes wide. "You've *ruined* the spell! You cannot undo it."

Wren's heart pounded against her ribs as she turned her pleading eyes toward the drifting Magic. Would it even listen to her if they weren't properly spell-bound as companions?

"Come back!" Wren tried, a little louder.

The periwinkle smoke paused, hovering. As if considering.

Headmaster Mikos shook his head. "Fates help us—what have you *done,* Wren?"

"Please. Please come back." Wren bit her lip, even though it was terribly bad etiquette, and held out her hands, beckoning.

Everyone held their breath as the headmaster muttered on about half a millennium of tradition going down the drain.

"Please."

After another beat, the Magic floated downward and wrapped around Wren's outstretched wrist, binding itself in a circle like a wispy bracelet. The crowd produced a smattering of polite applause, but the horror in their eyes was impossible to miss. Wren spotted Cephas in the crowd, his hand on his heart in relief. Next to him, her father had drawn his mouth into a deep frown.

He wasn't applauding.

Wren tried to swallow the growing lump in her throat as she made her way back to her seat. While her classmates showed off their new Magics to each other excitedly, Wren sat in silence. The most important day of her life, and she'd messed it up. Why'd she have to be so careless? No one else had trouble remembering spells.

Her eyes fell away once more to the Mainland. She wondered—and not for the first time—if the thirteen-year-olds across the sea had quite so much to deal with. They didn't have to tame Magics, for one thing. Or follow so many rules. Meraki children were expected to keep their head in their studies, mind their manners, and contribute to society. Meraki were a people of *order*. Of predictability. Being ordinary wasn't merely preferable; it was *required*. And Wren was tired of feeling so . . . *other*.

Wren sighed, peering at the periwinkle mist locked around her right wrist. It felt cold and tickly against her skin. The Magic let out a little growl.

Was it angry at her?

"I'm sorry," she whispered, her eyes stinging.

It was probably just embarrassed to be stuck with her as a companion.

And she couldn't even blame it.

16.

IN WHICH SHENLI IS GIVEN A TERRIBLE ASSIGNMENT

An icy wind tore up from the west as Shenli huddled on a deserted hilltop in the moonlight with a meager squadron of six other soldiers. According to Commander Anja Alizah, the squadron leader, their mission was classified. So they'd trudged on for hours under the cover of darkness with little idea of what to expect when they arrived. Now they awaited Chancellor Cudek, who was due to meet them any moment.

Shenli couldn't keep from shivering with anticipation. Or maybe it was just the cold. Whatever the mission turned out to be, Shenli and the others knew it was dangerous. Because in the valley below, next to two small pitched tents, an enormous cave loomed in the darkness.

A dragon lair.

Another deep chill shook Shenli, but he steeled his jaw. What could Cudek possibly want involving a firebreather? Cudek's army numbered into the tens of thousands, filling up the land like field mice. But even with those numbers, Cudek was no match for the dragons. Not with a thousand soldiers, let alone the mere six next to Shenli.

He shot a look at Commander Alizah, who adjusted her sword hilt. "You're doing great, kid," she assured him. "Just keep your wits about you."

"Sound advice," called a gravelly voice from behind them. "Especially since dragons can smell fear."

Shenli and the others stood to attention at the sight of Chancellor Cudek peering down at them. Even silhouetted in the moonlight, the man radiated a kind of strength and power that demanded people's attention. His pale face was all angles with a tidy goatee, his golden hair parted neatly at the side. He looked to be in his early forties, though strangely enough, no one seemed to know the chancellor's exact age. In fact, Cudek held many secrets. No one knew what his last name was, either. And no one dared ask.

"Chancellor, sir." Alizah saluted. "Awaiting your orders."

"I need you to deliver this package into the dragon lair," said Cudek, handing a small metal box to Shenli. Shenli kept his eyes from widening—but only barely. The chancellor was giving the box to *him*? The rookie? He was so surprised, in fact, that he almost missed the last part of Cudek's orders.

"*Inside* the lair, sir?" Shenli repeated, both eyebrows shooting upward.

There was a reason army bases were stationed at least a good thousand yards from each of the seven dragons posted around the Mainland. No one neared the perimeter boundaries of a dragon lair, let alone dared to *enter* one.

"Speak when you're spoken to, Zhao," Alizah scolded, and Shenli's face grew hot. He nodded, pressing his lips together.

"What are your instructions once we are inside the lair?" Alizah asked. Shenli had to give her credit. She didn't even look scared.

"Commander, I want you to personally accompany the package inside while the others secure the dragon companions," said Cudek.

Shenli could almost feel the relief pour from the other soldiers. *They* didn't have to go inside the lair, at least.

"I want the Riders taken into custody," Cudek continued. "Alive, if possible, though . . . it's not necessary. And these"—he held up two cube-shaped containers that looked like metal lunch boxes, each with a small door and a handle on top—"are specially constructed cages to contain their Magics. With their human companions' lives in peril, you will find Magics to be . . . surprisingly obliging."

Several soldiers shared uncertain looks. None of them felt comfortable getting so close to Magics. They almost preferred facing the firebreather.

Almost.

"Yes, sir." Commander Alizah nodded, handing off the Magic cages to two unlucky soldiers standing behind her.

"Any questions?" asked Cudek.

Alizah cleared her throat. "Sir, when you say you want me to *accompany* the package—"

"I am charging Shenli with the package. You are to be his lookout, Commander."

All the air left Shenli's lungs.

Cudek continued casually, as if he hadn't just given Shenli *the most dangerous mission in all the five districts.* "Once inside, open the package, Shenli. You'll find further instructions—which I expect to be carried out *completely.*" His cold gaze held Shenli's. "Then get the blazes out of there. If you do your job right, you'll be in and out before the dragon has a chance to stir."

After a few moments passed, Cudek cleared his throat. It seemed

Commander Alizah had gone into shock. And *that* was saying something.

"Is that going to be a problem, Commander?" asked Cudek.

"I . . . No, sir." Alizah's voice sounded far away. "That is . . . the boy's never had formal training—"

"Are you questioning my orders?"

Alizah stood straighter. "*No*, sir. Never, sir."

Cudek snapped his fingers. "Get it done." His ice-blue eyes shifted to Shenli. "You've always served me well—which is more than I can say for the other men in the Zhao family." Shenli's cheeks burned, but he held Cudek's unblinking gaze. "I acknowledge the danger this puts you in. But it is necessary. Now you understand why the mission cuts your years of servitude in half."

Shenli nodded obediently, digging his fingernails into his palms to steel his nerves before all the churning terror inside his chest burst out in the chancellor's presence.

"We won't let you down, sir," said Alizah, shaking Cudek's hand firmly. Shenli wondered if the commander really believed her own words. With a final curt nod, Cudek spun on his heel. He disappeared into the darkness, leaving Shenli with the mysterious box in his hands and a mountain-sized fear in his heart.

Because it was hopeless.

No one faced a dragon and lived. Even worse, there was no way to back out now. If Shenli refused the mission, he'd be a deserter. A failed soldier. Just like his brother.

Commander Alizah turned around to face the rest of the squadron. "Fan out and secure the perimeter. And ready those cages. We don't want those two Dragon Riders waking up and cursing us with their Magics."

As the other five soldiers stole away silently in all directions, Shenli eyed the two small tents on the perimeter and shuddered.

Dragon Riders were the only magic folk allowed on the Mainland—not to mention the only thing known to give Chancellor Cudek the jitters, other than the firebreathers themselves.

Alizah gripped Shenli's shoulder, causing him to jump.

"I don't know what Cudek's up to," she admitted. "But the way I see it, he's giving you a real opportunity. Chances like this come once in a lifetime, kid."

Shenli tried to speak, but his throat suddenly dried up worse than the Wasteland desert. Instead, he nodded. He thought of his mother and how he'd promised her he'd come home. Fates, he couldn't let her and his sisters down.

He was going to make things right for his family.

No matter what.

Alizah gave the signal, and with the package tucked under one arm, Shenli followed her down toward the dragon lair. With a dreadful pang in his chest, Shenli wondered if he'd ever see his family again.

17.

IN WHICH A SLEEPING
DRAGON STIRS

THE YEAR OF THE FOURTH WAR

A baby was crying.

Two bright silver-blue eyes stared down at Blue and blinked.

"He's beautiful," said a voice, but it was muffled and *wrong*. Somehow Blue knew it was his mother.

Two tears fell, wetting Blue's cheeks, the smell of Sorrow seeping into his every pore.

The eyes vanished.

Blue sat atop a golden horse, riding down a village road. No. Not a horse. A lion. The lion held a steady pace as the people waved their Gerberan flags and chanted Blue's name. The lion's giant paws shook the earth, the ground trembling in all directions.

Then Blue was standing in a never-ending meadow. Up on a hilltop in the distance, a boy stood facing him. The boy waved.

It was another Blue.

The sun sank low, just behind Hilltop Blue, casting a long shadow. The shadow jutted and shuddered, twisting into the shape of a massive dragon. Hilltop Blue vanished. As the sun sank lower, the dragon shadow grew, stretching across the entire meadow. The grass withered wherever the dark shadow touched it.

"He's so beautiful," said his mother's voice. "So brave."

The words took physical form and swirled around Blue like flower petals lifted by a gentle breeze. *Beautiful. Brave.* The words buzzed and sang, settling on Blue's head in the shape of a crown.

Suddenly Blue was flying, watching the dragon shadow bury entire villages. The sky around him caught fire. Blue tried to call out, but no sound came. He tried to catch his breath, but there was only rising smoke, saturated with woody citrus.

Then something shimmered in the sky just above Blue's eye.

A golden thread, stretching out into the distance.

It glittered and *sang*. Rich high notes throbbed behind his temple.

Blue reached up to the thread, plumes of dark smoke swirling around him, and he pulled. He kept pulling and the thread kept coming.

More, more, more.

"It's time to wake up now," said a new voice.

Something pushed Blue downward. He tried to right himself, but he twisted and fell from the sky, plunging into the darkness below. Somewhere in the distance, the song of the golden thread echoed across the sky.

FOR THERE IS ONE WHO CAN MAKE AMENDS—
WITH THE AID OF THREE UNLIKELY FRIENDS

18.

IN WHICH WREN'S MAGIC
PROVES TO BE QUITE STUBBORN

Wren sat with an untouched bowl of spiced porridge on her desk. She gazed out the window, following a little silverbird's journey back to its nest. Wren watched as the bird fed her chicks to the sounds of ocean waves lapping in the distance.

For the hundredth time, Wren let out a long sigh and wiped her tearstained cheeks.

Her father had disappeared after the Acquisition Day ceremony, so Wren had gone home and locked herself in her room, sulking. Thankfully, as the Meraki Dragon Master, he would be working late with the dragons again, so she wouldn't have to rehash her embarrassing fumblings of the day until tomorrow. Maybe he'd cool off by then.

She scoffed.

Right.

And maybe the dragons would all put on leggings and dance across the valley of the Gathering Place.

Wren sighed again, pressing her forehead against the windowpane. The sound of a cane thunked at her doorway.

"I'm fine, Granmama," said Wren without turning around.

"Child, you've hidden yourself away the entire day. Come celebrate."

Wren grunted, and her Magic did the same. She peeked down at her wrist, where her Magic was still bound like a periwinkle bracelet. She'd been too terrified to let it roam free yet.

"I made chocolate cupcakes," said Granmama.

Wren's stomach grumbled eagerly in response, but she didn't get up from her chair. "I just want to do something—just *once*—that doesn't embarrass him."

There was a creaking of floorboards as Granmama leaned on her cane.

"Your father is . . . complicated. And since your mother's passing . . ." Granmama sighed, a familiar sorrow filling the air. "I'm sorry to say, my son-in-law's lost sight of some things."

"Messing up that spell—in front of the entire Elder Council and everyone?" Wren held up her Magic-bound wrist. "I don't blame him for being ashamed of me."

"Your path has never been ordinary, child."

"Well, I wouldn't mind feeling *ordinary* for once."

The Magic let out a little growl, and Wren sighed, pressing her face back to the window.

Granmama didn't understand. Of course *she* adored Wren. That was what grandmothers were for. But could she really not see the way that everyone *else* looked at Wren? Like an apple on a pear tree—something that didn't quite belong, no matter how hard it tried?

While her peers focused on their classes and studies, Wren questioned and she *dreamed*. Of *other*ness and ridiculous things. She wondered at life on the Mainland and even in the faraway Lands Across the Sea. Wren lived with a thousand questions skipping against her skull like waves crashing against the rocks. And she kept them all inside, their silent protest relentless. Because the Meraki weren't supposed to ask questions or dream of things beyond the sea.

"What I've learned is that Magics are quite often stubborn for a *reason*," said Granmama. She winked at the purple cloud hovering at the window, and it chuckled in response. "Especially when they sense things beyond what ordinary Magics can feel."

Wren grunted, stroking the purply-blue cloud around her wrist.

"And another thing," said Granmama, tugging gently at Wren's tight curls. "True greatness doesn't come from *ordinary*. Do you understand what I'm saying, child?"

"You're trying to say there's beauty in my weirdness," said Wren flatly, resisting an eye roll. She knew Granmama was only trying to make her feel better.

"No," whispered Granmama, her eyebrows pulling together. She lifted Wren's chin with her finger. "Do you trust me, Wren Barrow?"

"Of course," said Wren, with a pang of hurt. Granmama shouldn't even have to ask such a question.

"Then believe me when I tell you you're going to become an incredibly powerful Meraki. Not just of your generation, Wren, but of all time."

Wren blinked back her shock. Granmama said a lot of things to try to cheer Wren up. Whispering of the work of the Fates and telling beautiful tales of enchanted forests and foxes. Of prophets and heroes and magical creatures of the days of old. But she'd never told Wren anything like *this*.

Or had she?

Wren frowned, trying to resurrect a long-lost memory. "Does this have anything to do with the Havensong?"

Granmama's eyes widened. Wren couldn't tell if it was shock or fear she saw.

Or both.

"What made you say that?"

Wren shrugged. "I never told you, but I heard you and Father arguing about me once. Something about a song. Then yesterday you had the prophecy about Blue, and now you're saying . . ." She made a face. "You know. What you just said about me."

"I probably oughtn't have told you that," Granmama admitted, sinking down onto Wren's bed with a deep sigh. "But I need you to believe it—for all our sakes."

Just then, a low rumble tore through the room, shaking the ground beneath their feet. Wren's mouth fell open. It was a deep earthy rumble—like the ground itself was angry. Her Magic trembled, pulsing in dark hues.

"What was *that*?" Wren breathed.

"That, my love, was the restlessness of the realm."

Right. Because *that* explained it.

"So . . . it was bad, then?" Wren tried to clarify.

Granmama thumped her cane. "More like a warning. But . . . bad, yes."

Wren waited, but her grandmother didn't reveal anything else.

"Well, I'm officially declaring it cupcake time," said Granmama after a long beat. She pushed to her feet slowly. "I'll save you one before Cephas eats them all."

"Do you think it's safe to let my Magic roam free?" Wren asked. Her Magic quivered adamantly around her wrist. "Even though we aren't properly spell-bound to one another?"

"You can't coop it up forever like a prisoner," Granmama pointed out as she held up Wren's wrist to get a better look. "The color is quite beautiful, isn't it? Still—it has a fierce temper." She laughed. "It'll definitely keep you on your toes, child."

Wren groaned.

"And as it often is with the extraordinary, your Magic will be greatly misunderstood." She smiled. "Much like you, my dear."

Wren touched her Magic lightly. It hummed softly, calming her scattered nerves. "It *is* beautiful," she agreed.

Granmama peered out the window. She nodded toward the sea that encompassed the Forbidden Pass—the water that separated the island from the Mainland. "I have a feeling your Magic possesses the same sense of adventure you do."

Wren raised a suspicious eyebrow. "Did you *have a feeling,* or did you *See* something?"

Granmama shrugged innocently. "Let's just call it intuition."

Wren let loose some major eye roll as the steady clunk of Granmama's cane traveled down the hall. Her Magic whimpered.

"I want to trust you," she told it. "But you're kind of an anomaly, you know."

An *anomaly.*

That was what Judge Finlar had called her after the ceremony. He'd leaned in close and told her: "It's an abomination for a Meraki not to be spell-bound to her Magic. It isn't proper. You're . . . an anomaly. Both of you are."

Wren's Magic, to its credit, had growled loudly at the judge in response.

Wren opened the window and pulled her chair in front of it. Then she rested her bare feet on the sill.

"I think rotten old Finlar might be right," she muttered. "We're both . . . anomalies." Before long, a steady rain started, sprinkling her toes, and the familiar scent of sage flowers filled the air. Mama had once told her that the smell of sage flowers meant all was well. It was a silly old superstition, but Wren still liked to believe it.

Maybe Granmama was right. Maybe Wren's strangeness wasn't *all* bad. Or at least she'd grow into it eventually.

Maybe then Father would even start smiling again.

Wren sighed and stood from her chair. She closed the window tightly, giving one last glance at the dark silhouette of the Mainland.

"Okay, you can go free—just for a bit."

She pushed two fingers down on her right wrist, her Magic cool to the touch. "Be free," she said. Instantly, the periwinkle swirl shot toward the ceiling and ricocheted back toward the bed like a bouncy ball.

"Okay, okay. Settle down," said Wren, hands on her hips.

Her Magic slowed, gliding coolly toward her through the air.

"You'll tire yourself out," Wren said. She crossed the room to her desk and flipped through the pages of one of her books, *My Magic and Me.* "See, here it says, 'A new Magic has limited energy. Ample rest is required, lest the Magic wear itself out.'"

The Magic let out an annoyed huff, then floated to the window. It bumped against the glass gently. Then it let out a high-pitched hum, sounding like the wind chimes hanging in the garden.

"Sorry, but you're not ready to go outside by yourself. You're practically an infant, you know."

Her Magic bobbed up and down eagerly in a purplish blur.

"Absolutely *not.* Especially after what happened at the ceremony today."

The Magic huffed and darkened in color, blue swirls mixing with violet.

"Ugh. You *are* going to be trouble, aren't you?" groaned Wren, rubbing her temples, then plopping down onto her bed. Her eyes felt heavy. "Maybe I'll . . . just . . . rest for a bit. . . ."

Her eyelids drooped.

She didn't mean to fall asleep.

She'd only just started to dream—of Mama and dolphins and the sunrise—when she sat up suddenly. Her eyes darted around the room, the moon outside pouring a dim glow across her floorboards. Then she spotted the window, cracked open. The smell of sage flower wafted toward her.

All is well, all is well.

With a start, Wren searched the foot of her bed, where her quilt sat empty.

The Magic was gone.

19.

IN WHICH SHENLI
FACES A FIREBREATHER

Shenli ducked under the patches of green moss growing on the back side of the dragon cave. Commander Alizah squatted next to him, her longsword at the ready. Shenli wasn't trained enough to have his own weapon. Not that a steel blade was any match for dragon scales. He rotated the small silver box in his hands, waiting for the signal from the other soldiers that they had secured the Dragon Rider tents.

"Smells kinda like fish guts," Shenli said, wrinkling his nose at the box.

Alizah laughed softly, shaking her head. "Couldn't care less what it smells like. I just want to get this done and then clear out."

"What do you think is in here?" whispered Shenli, shaking the box gently.

"I don't know," Alizah admitted, flicking a spider from her knee. "But I'll bet it has to do with dreamshade." She gave Shenli a significant look. "I know of another squadron that's been collecting ingredients for months—this is all classified information, of course."

"Come on, *dreamshade*?" Shenli arched an eyebrow. She must be pulling his leg to lighten the mood. "That stuff's just a myth." He'd done enough research for Cudek to know about some of the ancient magic legends.

Alizah shrugged. "You know Cudek. Always dabbling in magical exploration."

Shenli *did* know. Half of his assignments from the chancellor these days involved searching the castle libraries for books about ancient spells and the histories of magic. Everyone knew about Cudek's obsessive mission to locate and destroy any natural magic remaining on the Mainland, left over from before the wars. In the old days, magic folk had lived on the Mainland, and traces of their magic still lay hidden in certain plants and gems, and even in the soil. *A lingering nuisance*, Cudek called it.

"You can't destroy what you don't understand," Cudek had told him, before Shenli was tasked with sifting through a particularly massive pile of dusty old scrolls.

It made sense, of course. Cudek's obsession with wiping all traces of magic from the Mainland. Still, Shenli hated studying it. Even with the chancellor's permission, and even if it was for the greater good, learning about magic felt dangerous.

"Destroying magic is one thing," said Shenli. "But messing with a firebreather?" He shook his head. "I just don't get it."

"We don't have to understand the chancellor or his methods. I rose to the rank of commander by learning to obey orders without asking questions." Alizah paused, regarding Shenli carefully. "After all, we all have our debts to Cudek."

Shenli nodded, the mysterious box settling deeper onto his belly. A small green light glowed in the distance, beyond the tents. The signal from the squadron.

"You ready?" asked Alizah.

It was an absurd question. No one could be *ready* to face a dragon. But he nodded anyway. The urge to run away crept up Shenli's spine, and for the first time, he wondered if Yuli had been tasked with something just as dangerous. Was that why he'd fled?

Well, Shenli was not like his brother. He wasn't going to abandon his mission—not when his family was counting on him.

He followed Alizah; they slid their backs along the cave wall and slipped around the corner and into the entrance. The ground trembled beneath them, the deep snores of the dragon tickling Shenli's feet. He tried to ignore it as they crept into the dim light, but the enormous outline of the beast sent his heart to his stomach.

The dragon's backside loomed taller than two horses stacked on top of one another, its great lizard face tucked under its front arm. Crimson scales glistened in the moonlight trickling in from the cave opening. All Shenli could see was the color of blood wrapped around the beast's entire body. A few scraggly teeth—longer than Shenli's hand—poked out between the dragon's lips. Shenli knew that just one of those teeth was enough to slice him clean in two.

Shenli clutched the box tighter as he and Commander Alizah crept on. She kept her sword aimed at the beast's ginormous head as Shenli slid the top of the mysterious box open. Inside, two orbs stared back at him: one white and the other blue, with a small button on each. There was also a message carved into the underside of the lid. Shenli held the words up to a beam of moonlight.

Press the button and throw the orbs at the dragon.
  Then all will be revealed.
  It is time for the son of Zhao to learn the truth—because I know your secret.

Shenli tensed. His secret? This had to be about his father!
The most pressing question now was what the orbs would do

once he threw them. Alizah flicked her head toward the box, clearly wanting Shenli to speed things along. He didn't dare speak to ask for help.

Okay.

The box said to throw the orbs.

But which orb should he throw first? Or was he supposed to throw both at the same time? Did it matter? What if he did it wrong? Would Cudek still keep his side of the bargain? Shenli took another look at the inscribed message as precious seconds ticked by. The longer he hesitated, the more he and the rest of the squadron stayed at risk.

Time to choose.

He took a steadying breath and nodded for Alizah to make her way back toward the exit. No need for both of them to be this close to the beast when the orbs activated. When his commander reached the entrance, Shenli pulled the white orb from the box and held it up, beads of sweat trickling from his temples.

He pressed the button, a small *click* piercing the silence.

The dragon's yellow eyes shot open, making all the hairs on Shenli's neck stand on end. He thew the orb across the cave, where it rolled next to the beast's belly, emitting a steady stream of green smoke.

"Is that supposed to happen?" Alizah called from outside the cave.

Shenli's heart rate tripled. "I don't know!"

The dragon snorted, clambering to its feet. Shenli grabbed the blue orb and pushed the button hastily. Another click. Shenli threw the orb and started to run.

"Go—go!" he yelled.

Alizah took off as the dragon let out a fierce roar, one of its arms knocking the blue orb back in Shenli's direction, toward the cave entrance. There were shouts from outside. A fireball exploded, the force of the blast throwing Shenli into the wall. A sickening crack tore through his arm as he dropped to the ground and rolled to his side.

He could see the dragon lumbering overhead. Shenli gritted his teeth, pushing himself up with his good arm, the pain in his left side sending him staggering. The cave filled with black and emerald smoke, burning Shenli's eyes.

The dragon snorted, eyes pulled into slits. It opened its mouth, and just as Shenli grew certain his life was about to end by dragonfire, the beast swayed on its feet. Its eyelids drooped. Then the dragon crashed to the ground, the earth trembling beneath Shenli's feet. Shenli bolted toward the exit through the smoke as a second explosion rippled through the air. Shouts rang out from the Rider tents, and Shenli ducked back around the lair's wall. The smoke was too thick to see anything, but the shouts of the squadron were getting farther and farther away. He couldn't make out what they were yelling except for three words.

Magics have attacked.

Shenli couldn't risk being seen by the Dragon Riders, so he followed the cave wall around to the back side, blue flames licking his heels.

Wait. Blue flames?

That wasn't dragonfire.

Blue flames were the aftermath of military explosives.

It didn't make sense. Explosives were never wasted on dragons— dragons were fireproof. Shenli pushed his palm against his forehead, willing his brain to work faster. He had to piece together what had happened in the cave. The white orb—the one that emitted the smoke . . . That must've been some kind of poison gas for the dragon. But the blue orb—had it been a bomb?

Before he could sort it out, another explosion shook the ground, knocking him off his feet again. A loud *crack* rang through the air, and Shenli barely had time to look behind him before the back wall of the cave cracked and tumbled down on top of him, burying him in darkness.

20.

IN WHICH WREN RUNS
INTO SOME TROUBLE

"It's *gone!*" Wren sobbed, bursting into her grandmother's room. She readied herself to wake the old woman from sleep, but instead, Granmama was sitting up in her bed already, staring out the window.

Like she was waiting.

"I knew that Magic of yours was extraordinary. I just didn't realize how *persistent* it would prove to be."

Wren paused, catching her breath. "Wh-what?"

"I've just Seen it happen, child. Your Magic's gone to the Mainland."

Wren's face went ashen.

No, no, no.

She couldn't have lost her Magic on her *first* night! It was unheard of! Reckless! And to the *Mainland*—she'd never see it again. She pressed her palms to her temples and started pacing the room, trying to keep her breathing steady.

A Meraki without her Magic was no Meraki at all.

So what did that make her?

"I . . . I have to go after it," she realized. Saying the words aloud sent a shock of fear through her whole body, enough to make her knees wobble. But what else could be done?

"Wren. I can't See what will happen if you go," said Granmama as her Magic settled onto her shoulder with a whimper. "We've tried to See, child. But it . . . I couldn't—"

"It's okay," whispered Wren, placing a hand on her grandmother's arm. She knew that when a Seer received a vision or prophecy, it was alarming and strange but relatively harmless. But for a Seer to *try* actively to See the future was incredibly painful, and often didn't work.

Even now, she noted the sweat on her grandmother's brow and her labored breathing. The extra tremble in her Magic.

"Thank you for trying." Wren squeezed Granmama's hand and touched the purple cloud gently. A sinking stone formed in Wren's gut. But she knew what she had to do. "I have to go to the Mainland."

Granmama's Magic whined.

"Child, do you understand what the Council would do to you?"

"The Council hates me anyway," Wren muttered, quivering in her nightgown. It wasn't exactly true, but it fired enough courage in her belly to shut out all the other thoughts—the ones warning her that *this would be an act of treason.* In her mind's eye she imagined her father's face once he found out she'd lost her Magic.

But she couldn't think about that now.

She pulled one of Granmama's cloaks from the wall and wrapped it around herself. "I have to fix this."

Granmama thumped her cane. "Then I will not stop you."

Wren stopped fastening the buttons on the cloak. "You won't?"

"No." Granmama held Wren's gaze. "Even before you were born, I Saw the darkness that is coming. And how you and Blue and the others must face it. I didn't know it would happen so soon, but I've always known. So have your parents."

"I'm scared." The words sounded so small, barely a whisper, but the truth of them pushed heavily on Wren's chest, gripping every part of her.

Granmama stroked Wren's cheek. "Ever since you were a little girl, I've told you that you were born extraordinary. You thought I was feeding you compliments. Dear one, I was feeding you *truths*." Granmama unhooked her necklace and fit it onto Wren's neck. Hanging from a silver chain was a small black stone.

"Your messenger pendant?" asked Wren. The stone was incredibly rare, enchanted by natural magic. It allowed the wearer to communicate over long distances. As far as Wren knew, only two pendants had ever been created.

"I imagine you'll find it useful. Also, take my canoe. It will keep you hidden on your way to the Mainland." Wren nodded, and Granmama wrapped the cloak tighter around her. "Now, listen, child. That first prophecy about Blue was a long, *long* time ago. Not long after, I received a second prophecy, linked to Blue's." She paused for several moments, her eyes locked with Wren's. "I never recorded the second prophecy in the Legacy Hall of the Seers. In fact, I've never told anyone about it."

Wren couldn't keep from shivering. It was a crime for a Seer to keep a prophecy hidden from the Council.

"There's a Mainlander soldier boy named Shenli," Granmama told Wren, squeezing her hand. "He doesn't deserve your trust, child, but you must give it. He is part of the Story."

"Why doesn't he deserve my trust?"

"The boy has a tremendously complicated path ahead of him, and much of it is shrouded in uncertainty. I tried to See more, but—"

Granmama let out a long sigh. "All I can tell you is that he is important."

Wren's arm hairs prickled. This boy sounded dangerous. "Why haven't you told anyone about him?"

A single tear ran down Granmama's cheek, and Wren sucked in a breath. She hadn't seen Granmama cry since Mama's funeral. "That, my dear, is a story for another day."

Wren hugged her arms tight to her chest. "How will I find him?"

"I'm not even sure you can. But you must try." Granmama reached down, cupping Wren's cheeks, trying to will courage into her granddaughter's bones. The purple cloud purred gently. "Also—Blue. He is coming soon. And, Wren, he is *everything*. But he can't do it alone. He will need your help."

Wren nodded without understanding anything.

The old woman's violet eyes blinked back tears. "Your Magic did not run out on you, Wren—it senses something. And it is trying to help." Granmama kissed her on the forehead. "Time to be brave, little dolphin."

Wren wrapped her arms around her grandmother's frail frame and breathed her in. Then, before her brain could catch up to what her body was doing, she ran back to her room and grabbed her school rucksack. She raided the kitchen for a few bits of food and water, then hauled the bag over her shoulder and stole away through the back patio door and into the gardens. She followed a familiar footpath through the lavender shrubs, all the way to the beach, holding her hands out until they bumped into unseen oakwood in the marshes. Wren gripped the side of the magic canoe, her hands turning invisible, and pushed it out into the water. She lowered herself over the side of the boat and took a seat, as she'd done so many times as a little girl playing Mainlander spy.

Only this time, it wasn't a game.

From inside the boat, she could see the world, but the world could no longer see her. A small navigational orb rose to hover over the middle of the canoe. Wren spun it forward, and the boat sped off in the same direction. The sudden breeze whipped her hair back as she started across the midnight sea toward the Forbidden Pass. She didn't dare look back to her island for fear her shaking limbs would betray her and turn the boat around.

Could Granmama still see Wren, even in an enchanted boat? Wren clutched the dark gemstone gently, wondering at the centuries it had lived around Granmama's neck. How many messages had been written from it? In urgency? In secret? Who did the other pendant belong to? Granmama had never told her.

A cool tingle tore across the underside of her left wrist in the moonlight. She let out a squeak, flipping her hand over. In violet letters, a small message had scribbled itself across her wrist.

> *I'm only linked to the magic of the pendant for a few*
> *moments more.*

Wren gasped. A message from Granmama! Wren touched the message, and it faded, replaced by a new one:

> *But I wanted to tell you that I am so very proud of you.*
> *And your mother would be too.*

Tears pricked at Wren's eyes, lost in the wind.

She rubbed her pendant, thinking of a reply. She had a million questions, but she was too terrified to think straight. Instead, a single request bubbled to the surface: *Hug Cephas for me.* Wren imagined her brother's face when Granmama told him what had happened. His little eyebrows scrunching up in disapproval. At the edges of her thoughts, another face came to mind, but she pushed it away.

She couldn't think of Father now.

Wren kept a steady pace all night as the canoe raced through the Forbidden Pass. She hugged her knees, grateful for Granmama's cloak to help stave off the icy wind tearing over the bow. The salty smell was usually a comfort, reminding Wren of her mother's love of the sea. But tonight all she could think of was what lurked below.

And how Rose Barrow had died.

Wren blinked away tears and wrapped Granmama's cloak tighter around herself. She kept seeing dark shapes rush past her in the water. She peered over the boat's side, her heart fluttering. She'd never been this far out in the deep water.

Something bumped the boat.

Wren scrambled to the centermost part of the canoe, where the navigation orb hovered. Was there a way to go faster? She touched the orb, gently prodding it forward, and the boat picked up speed. Just then, an enormous shadow rose behind her.

Something was coming up from the water!

Panicked, Wren felt her fingers slip backward on the orb, bringing the boat to a sudden halt. The momentum threw Wren from her seat and up over the front of the canoe. She barely sucked in a terrified breath before hitting the water.

The last thing she saw before sinking was a dark shadow slithering overhead.

It was coming right toward her.

PART III

WAKING
DRAGONS

21.

You feel it, don't you?

The way everything's gone wrong? We hear it in the way the wind carries sadly through the wildwood. We see the extra droop in the flowers and the shriveled leaves on the trees. Even the musty earth breathes her scent of sadness. We feel the echo of sorrow all around us as the ground trembles in trepidation.

But it wasn't supposed to be this way.

They were all meant to live in peace, you see—Magics, humans, and dragons. They were supposed to rule the land honorably and care for us creatures and all living things. They've made quite a mess of things, haven't they? The earth shakes and churns in great fury. And there is a darkness coming, threatening to swallow us whole.

It's all gone very wrong.

But there is also hope.

The paths of the four friends are soon to cross, and once they do, nothing will ever be the same again.

What's that, kit?

Yes, I entirely agree. Things would've been far less complicated if foxes had been put in charge.

Quite right.

22.

IN WHICH WREN
IS SUNK

THE YEAR OF THE FOURTH WAR

The watery darkness pressed up against Wren like an uncomfortably tight hug. Her chest ached, her lungs desperate for air, as she sank farther into the ocean. She knew how to swim, but her body was frozen with fear. Dark yellow shapes slithered through the water. Pairs of glowing red eyes stared at her from every direction.

Movlak eels!

They were even bigger than in her nightmares, and when the nearest one opened its mouth, Wren spotted two rows of razor-sharp teeth. Something slimy brushed her ankle. That was enough to cut through Wren's frozen panic and motivate her body to *move*. She swam upward as fast as she could. She was only a few feet from the surface when the Slimy Thing wrapped around her left wrist and yanked her back down. The shock of it let all the remaining air out of Wren's lungs. She watched helplessly as the last of her oxygen slipped away in a stream of bubbles as she was pulled deeper, with the snake-like yellow bodies surrounding her. Wren kicked furiously, but the harder she tried to swim upward, the weaker she became as the slimy tentacle held fast to her arm. Just as the edges of Wren's vision started to go black, something grabbed her leg and pulled swiftly.

With great force, Wren was yanked upward and ripped out of the water upside down. She breached the surface, sucking in gasps of air. It was a few moments before she recognized the giant golden creature flying overhead.

Not another eel.

Xayndra, hovering in midair.

The dragon held Wren's leg with her front claw as her great jaws clamped around the eel's long tentacle, which stubbornly held fast to Wren's arm. There was a loud squeal; then the eel released its grip and plunked back into the water. Xayndra laid Wren gently in the boat, where she coughed and gasped until she had finally sucked in enough air for her body to be satisfied.

Only once she'd caught her breath did she realize she was crying. Fates. She'd nearly just *drowned.* She waited for the eels to jump up and pull her under once more, but the water stayed calm except for the ripple effect from Xayndra's powerful wings beating a steady rhythm.

Trembling in her wet clothes, Wren met Xayndra's gaze. "You saved me."

The great beast nodded, the expression in her golden eyes filling Wren's belly with affectionate warmth. Then Wren remembered. "Hang on—how did you even find me? The canoe is invisible."

Xayndra brought her head low so her snout was level with Wren's face. The dragon's gaze rested on Wren's neck for a moment; then Wren felt a tickle on her left wrist. She tugged her wet sleeve out of the way, and beneath the red tentacle welts was a new incoming message.

I know the scent of Madera's Magic. This boat is drenched with it, and I can see past it.

Wren knitted her brow in confusion for several beats before understanding settled. Her eyes flicked back to the dragon in shock. "*You* sent me this message, Xayndra?"

"I did. Though it's much easier to speak openly, if you don't mind."

Wren's mouth fell open as she realized that the voice, rich and earthy, was coming from the dragon herself. She stood in alarm. "You can . . . *talk*?"

"I can communicate with you because you wear the amulet."

"But . . . Granmama always wears the amulet! Does that mean you talk with her too?"

A toothy grin spread across Xayndra's face. "Your grandmother is full of secrets, dear."

Wren blinked. She was *talking with a dragon*! A thousand questions flooded her brain at once, and it was almost enough excitement to make her forget how freezing she was, standing in her wet clothes.

"Tell me, Wren Barrow, what are you doing all the way out here on the Forbidden Pass?"

Wren shuddered, thumbing her grandmother's pendant, her arm still throbbing where the eel had taken hold. She could lie. Maybe she could say the Council was sending her on a secret mission or something. Wren rolled her eyes. Right. Because *that* would ever happen. She decided the truth was her best option.

"My Magic's run off to the Mainland." Wren looked out to the horizon, wondering how far she still had to travel. She was maybe halfway? With another half day's journey ahead? "I told Granmama I needed to go after it," Wren continued. "I also need to find a Mainlander soldier boy, and someone named Blue."

"That is quite the to-do list, Miss Barrow."

Wren let out a shaky breath, her finger tracing the strange red welts on her wrist. They were starting to sting. "I'm . . . pretty terrified, actually."

Xayndra let out a long sigh, her eyes drifting back toward Meraki Island far in the distance. "This puts me in a difficult situation, child. I am supposed to protect you. Letting you travel to the Mainland—especially unaccompanied—goes against every ounce of my judgment."

Wren's shoulders fell as she met Xayndra's eyes. The dragon let out a huff of smoke from her nostrils. "And yet . . . I know you speak the truth. So if Madera did not stop you, then I will not either."

"You won't?" Wren wasn't sure whether to be relieved or disappointed.

"I will accompany you through the Forbidden Pass, but I can go no farther."

Wren nodded. After the postwar peace treaties, a magic enchantment had been constructed that now physically prevented the five island dragons from entering the Mainland and the seven Mainland dragons from leaving. Wren had always wondered how the dragons felt about the agreement. It meant they could never visit each other, and nor could the Dragon Riders, who were essentially stuck on the Mainland as well, since they were duty-bound to their dragons.

"Also, you'll want to mind that injury," said Xayndra. "The eel did not have hold of you for very long, but the poison has already left its mark. Perhaps you can find some enderberries as a remedy. They used to be common enough on the Mainland—though that was many years ago."

Enderberries? Wren had never heard of them.

Wren hugged herself tighter as her head filled with thoughts of Mama. By the time they'd found her boat, there had been movlak welts all over her body. It had been too late for any remedy.

How close Wren had been to suffering the same terrible fate, all because of her clumsiness driving the boat! She couldn't make that kind of mistake if she was going to survive on the Mainland.

"I owe you my life, Xayndra."

"Child, it is an honor to watch over you. I only wish . . ." The dragon's watery eyes closed. "I only wish I'd been able to do the same for her."

Warm tears left trails down Wren's cheeks. "I know," she whispered. The two shared a significant gaze before Xayndra shifted her position in the air.

"Now sit tight." Xayndra hovered directly over Wren, then grabbed both sides of the canoe. With an extra beat of her wings, Xayndra lifted Wren and the boat out of the water more easily than one might pluck a wildflower. Together, the girl and dragon soared toward the Mainland so fast Wren's cheeks flapped in the wind. She let out a delighted giggle, momentarily forgetting about her throbbing arm and the dreadful journey ahead.

They flew onward and Wren thought of her father again. As Dragon Master, he'd be amazed to see her now—talking to a dragon! She wondered why dragons had never used Granmama's pendant to reach out to humans before—or had they? But she had too much on her mind to focus on that now.

At last, as the morning sun peeked over the ocean's horizon behind them, they reached the Mainland shore. Xayndra let out a grunt, and Wren figured the dragon must've reached the enchanted barrier that kept her out.

A smattering of lush trees and greenery greeted them as Xayndra lowered Wren and the boat back down to the water and pushed hard. The canoe glided several yards before landing gently on the shore.

"I've come as far as I'm allowed," Xayndra told her. "I have tried mind-speaking to Hezu, the dragon who patrols the Coastal District. I wish for him to keep an eye on you. But I cannot seem to reach him."

Wren bit her lip as she hopped over the side of the boat and pulled it all the way onto the sand, between two bushes. "Mind-speak? Dragons can communicate with each other using their minds?"

"Usually, if they are within a certain distance. Hezu's the closest dragon to the Mainland border. I've never been unable to reach him. Something feels . . . amiss." The dragon narrowed her eyes, scanning the landscape carefully. "Perhaps he's merely gone out of range. I will keep trying."

Wren didn't miss the worry in Xayndra's face, but before she could ask about it, the great dragon bowed her head. "I wish you much success on your quest, Wren Barrow. Be well."

Wren bowed in return. "Thank you, Xayndra. For everything."

Xayndra gave one final nod, then turned and headed back home.

Wren spun to face the Mainland, slinging her soggy rucksack over her shoulder, where it landed with a wet *plop*. Off in the distance, a rooster crowed as Wren took in her new surroundings. The Mainland! She was standing on enemy soil! A mix of excitement and dread rose in her belly. Somewhere on this mysterious land of non-magic people, she would find her Magic.

And Blue.

And the dangerous soldier boy, Shenli.

As she blinked away the morning sun, she could see the big slithery eels behind closed eyes. She trembled so hard her teeth chattered. If Wren was going to find her Magic, she couldn't make any more foolish mistakes. After a final glance at Xayndra's shrinking form in the distance, Wren stole silently down the beach, her figure casting a long shadow as she ran into the unknown.

23.

IN WHICH RIVER AWAKENS AND EVERYTHING IS WRONG

THE YEAR OF THE FOURTH WAR

That same morning, half a world away, River Rowan stirred. She could hear voices as she melted into and out of consciousness, until finally her eyes fluttered open.

Her parents knelt over her, smiling. They cupped her cheeks and kissed her forehead. Right away, something felt . . . off. While their freckled faces looked mostly the same, even in her sleepy stupor River could see the *wrongness.*

Father's chestnut hair was too long, past his ears. And—a goatee? He'd never let any hair grow on his face because River didn't like the pokiness when he kissed her. Also, Mother's beloved dark hair was cropped short. Why was it dyed with streaks of purple—a traditional symbol of loss?

Wrong, wrong, wrong.

"What's happened?" River tried to say, but the words wouldn't form. Her tongue stuck to the roof of her mouth.

"River, love," her mother whispered, two big tears spilling down her freckled bronze cheeks. "We have missed you, dear."

River blinked. Missed her? What did *that* mean? Her mother handed River a cup of water as Father helped her sit up to drink it. The liquid cooled her throat, and River drank eagerly until it was gone.

"What's happened?" River managed to say at last. They were still in the cave where she . . . well, what *had* happened, exactly? Had she passed out? She remembered her arms feeling on fire, then everything bubbling to blackness.

"The dragon has started to wake," said her father.

"What?" River gasped. "But he's only just gone to sleep."

Her parents shared a look. A *dreadful* look.

"Darling, it's been ten years since Hibernation Day," said her father.

River blinked. Her father's words circled her, refusing to land properly. Ten years? No. She'd only just said good night to Blue moments before! Besides, ten years wasn't even half the time it took to grow a proper dragon. The Dragon Growers had learned long ago that the best dragons were ripe at exactly a quarter century.

River winced as the fuzzy memories took shape: Her father carrying her out of the cave. Her mother sobbing.

"What's wrong?" she asked.

"Rivs . . . ," Father started, rubbing his awful goatee. "You've been . . . hibernating too."

River blinked. "Sorry . . . what?" She glanced around the cave, squinting in the dim light. It seemed colder. And something else too. Something *big* was missing. She groaned. Why couldn't her brain wake up *faster*!

Mother cleared her throat. "Honey, when you were saying your goodbyes to the boy, something . . . happened."

Blue. Yes, she'd stroked his hair as he went to sleep. He'd been so frightened. And then the pain—oh, the pain in her arms!

"Usually Dragon Riders aren't selected until the dragon wakes . . . ," said Father, his voice trailing off. He hung his head, like he couldn't finish the thought. River frowned. Of course she knew that. Everyone knew that. Why was her father talking to her like she was a little child? Unless—

Her heart rose to her throat as realization washed over her.

The pain.

The pain she'd felt in her arms.

She raised her arms slowly. Patches of cerulean dragon scales were stuck to her skin, wrapping around her forearms like shackles.

The markings of a Dragon Rider.

"He chose you somehow as he was going to sleep," said her mother. "And then you two were bound together."

"No," River whispered, hugging her scaled arms to her chest.

No, no, NO.

Riders were *never* selected until after dragons woke from hibernation. There was an entire ceremony with at least a dozen potential Riders who'd been trained for the opportunity. Then the dragon would consider each one before officially choosing his Rider. How could Blue possibly have chosen River before he was even a dragon? She eyed her new dragon scales again, and her whole body swayed. She tried to stand, but apparently, her legs had gone all wobbly in her hibernated state. Her parents each wrapped an arm around her waist to help her up. Leaning on them, she limped outside, where she was immediately blinded by daylight.

"Ashes!" River cried out, shielding her eyes. Even the *sun*—normally a welcome companion to grow her crops—seemed to be against her. She paced back and forth, getting the feeling back in her legs, grunting and kicking the dirt for several minutes as her eyes adjusted. "I hate this," she sniffed.

"It's completely wretched," her father agreed, crossing his arms for good measure.

Aster Rowan put her hands on her hips. "Calder, don't make her feel worse than she already does."

"Not possible," River muttered, and her mother hugged her tight. There was something about the hug that felt different, but River couldn't sort out what it was.

"We came to visit you every day, and you always looked peaceful, but still—" Aster pulled out of the hug and kissed River's forehead. "We've talked to the Elders loads of times over the years to try and get you out of it, but there's nothing to be done." She touched River's strange blue scales gently. "There's no undoing *this*."

Her father's jaw quivered, his freckles glowing slightly against his pink cheeks. "I desperately wish I could make this all go away, Rivs. But you and that dragon are bound together." His soft green eyes blinked, and River watched a tear fall down his stubbled cheek. "I'm so sorry."

River thumbed her scales. They were solid but soft. Like sturdy flower petals. Mostly, they were just *wrong*. "I can't believe ten years have passed," said River.

"Not too much has changed," said Calder, wiping his cheek. "We added another room to the school building. We lost Elder Flores to sickness after the terrible storm two years back. Also, four babies were born—" He shared a look with Aster that River couldn't quite interpret. "But for us, it's been an eternity of waiting for you to wake up."

"And yet, still not enough time," said Aster. "At least we got to see you every day, but now—" Her voice broke.

"It . . . hasn't been easy, Rivs," said Calder, clearing his throat. "Your mother and I . . . haven't exactly been ourselves."

Aster's gaze fell. "There were days when I thought . . . that I wasn't sure I could—" She closed her eyes, and tears fell freely down her cheeks.

Calder took her hand, and River really studied her parents for the first time: The dark circles under their eyes. Her father's unkempt hair and scruffy face. The dyed purple streaks in her mother's dark hair—something villagers often did when someone died. And River realized. Her fate as a Dragon Rider felt like a death sentence to her parents. Dragon Riders didn't come back for visits. They were bound to their dragons, protecting the island Meraki across the vast desert from the evil chancellor's armies. It was a lifetime arrangement. Once she left with Blue, they'd never see her again.

And the grief of her parents, on top of her own, sent a shock wave through River. It swirled like a simmering fire and awakened a new fury in her chest. This wasn't fair! Dragon Riders trained for this— their parents *prepared* for their departure. But River's parents had been blindsided by grief and then left to pick up the pieces.

"There's more bad news, I'm afraid," said her dad with a grimace. "The Weavers are waiting to see you. They need to fit you for your new Rider clothes."

The dread in River's chest sank even further. She hadn't thought it was possible to feel any worse. New clothes? She'd been happy to wear the same green and brown cotton Harvesting clothes her whole life. She stared down at her bare feet.

"Ugh. They're going to make me wear *shoes,* aren't they?"

"Dragon Riders wear boots, I'm afraid," her mother said softly.

River burrowed her toes into the dirt in a sort of anti-shoe defiance. "Everything is terrible."

"It most definitely is." Her father looked like he wanted to say more, but squeezed his eyes shut for several moments. He blew out a steadying breath before meeting River's gaze. "Still, I . . . I believe in you, Rivs. I know you're going to do great things, wherever you go."

New hot tears ran down River's cheeks. "I was meant to be Lead Harvester! I want to spend my days in the garden—just like Nana." Then another terrible thought took root and her breath caught. "Hang on . . . if it's been ten years, then someone else was chosen as Lead."

Her parents shared a mournful look, and her mother squeezed her hand. "Since you were . . . unavailable, the Elders eventually decided on someone else."

River could hear her heart pound in her ears. "Who? Who is it?"

Her father rubbed the back of his neck. "Mind you, the Elders took their time choosing. Especially since we protested pretty fiercely those first few years. That is, I don't want you to think they rushed their decision—they were very sorry to lose you as an option."

"Who?" River repeated, balling her fists.

"Sage Jackson," said her mother.

River's mouth fell open. "Sage Jackson! He's still in diapers!"

"Well, he was ten years ago," her mother agreed gently. "But Sage just turned thirteen, and since you've remained twelve—"

River groaned. "Ugh. So he's *older* than me now?" Somehow that made things feel even worse.

"Sage is quite gifted, Rivs. I think you would approve—"

"I *really* don't want to hear about it," River growled. She had helped change Sage's stinky diapers a few times, for Fates' sake! The thought of someone stealing *her* job as Lead Harvester was enough to make her want to explode. How could she possibly leave her beautiful ash trees and moonberry bushes to someone else?

They walked in silence to the Weavers' hut near the center of the village. She normally felt too old to hold her parents' hands, but this time she gripped them like her life depended on it. Villagers greeted her excitedly as they passed by, but River could barely muster the strength to smile at them. It was too strange seeing her classmates all grown up. Or how different the trees and gardens looked. She hated how life had changed while she'd slept away, completely unaware.

All too soon, they reached the hut of the Weavers.

"I have to do this now?" River muttered. "I don't *want* new clothes."

"With the dragon showing signs of waking soon, you'll need to be ready." Her father gave her an apologetic look. "For what it's worth, I think you'll make a great Rider, Rivs. You're wicked smart, and more determined than anyone I know. Just like—"

"Nana," River finished for him.

"You're so much like her," he agreed.

"I only wish she could see you now," her mother added, wiping River's cheeks. "I think she would tell you that it is an honor to be chosen as Rider, I really do."

River's eyes stung with new tears. "It's like . . . I'm betraying her."

Her mother hugged her close. "She would be so proud of you."

River wiped her tears, and both parents kissed her temples before she ducked through the rickety door. She took a deep, steadying breath as two women greeted her: Freya, the Head Weaver, and another young woman River didn't recognize at first. And then it came to her. The girl's tanned face and deep brown eyes were familiar, but older. Ten years older.

"Luna?" said River incredulously. Luna was the daughter of Calla—one of the other Harvesters—who used to help River water the ash trees. "But you were nine years old the last I saw you!"

"It is rather strange," Luna admitted. "To see you still so young."

"Come, child," said Freya, leading River to a full-length mirror propped against the wall. River glanced at her reflection, catching sight of the blue dragon scales on her forearms. She cringed, her eyes darting to the trappings of the little hut. Animal furs and dyed fabric hung on the walls. A giant weaver's loom and set of spindles stood in the corner.

"You'll have to forgive the mess," said Freya, pulling her thick wavy hair back into a ponytail. "We weren't expecting you for another fifteen years, of course. But what an honor it is—the youngest Rider ever!"

River scowled with about as much enthusiasm as a goat getting milked. *An honor.* River repeated the words in her head, but they fell flat. She felt empty and awful.

An *honor* that would take her away from home and everything she loved.

"Now hold still, dear, while Luna gets your measurements," said Freya. "This is her first Rider fitting."

River stood in silence as the Weavers took her measurements. Luna scribbled furiously in a notebook as she worked, pulling her measuring rope in every direction against River's skin to the point where River was ready to throw the blasted thing out the window. It took nearly all afternoon for the Weavers to make a vest out of iron flakes to keep her chest protected from dragon scales when she rode in the saddle, as well as leggings and boots—ugh, *boots!*—from oiled leather, sturdy enough for all weather but light enough to run long distances.

When at last they were finished, Freya wiped her brow and helped River change into her new clothes. The iron vest fitted over a long-sleeved green tunic and brown leggings made from enhanced cotton to stave off harsh winds. The clothes were strange to River. They hugged her tighter than she was used to, but she was surprised by how lightweight and comfortable everything felt.

Except the blasted boots.

Lastly, she slipped Blue's compass over her neck. She wasn't sure what else to do with it. "The vest is made of askalt iron, which can only be found in the caves at the top of Dragon Mountain," Freya told her. "The flakes are as thin as grass but sturdier than a sword blade. It takes our blacksmiths well over a decade to make them." The Weaver smiled proudly.

"It is impressive," River admitted, tapping the vest. The metal flakes felt soft, like her scales.

"Have you thought about what you'll call him?" asked Luna.

"Er—what?"

"The dragon. Riders get to name the new dragon, remember?"

"Oh. Right." River frowned. "It's hard to think of him as anything but Blue, honestly."

"But he won't remember that name from before," Freya pointed out.

"He won't remember anything about his human life," Luna echoed, as if River didn't already know that.

"And besides, Blue isn't much of a name, is it?" said Freya. "Especially for a dragon."

River pressed her lips together and wished they'd stop talking about it already. She didn't *want* to give Blue a new name, and she didn't want to be his Rider. She didn't want any of this.

Just then, Elder Cyrus poked his head into the tent. His ancient eyes were wide with alarm. "River, you must come at once!"

River's heart crumbled into a million pieces. Because she knew exactly what the Elder would say next.

"The dragon has woken!"

24.

IN WHICH THERE
IS A GREAT YAWN

THE YEAR OF THE FOURTH WAR

Blue let out an enormous yawn, blinking his eyes open. His lids drooped heavily with a deep weariness, tempting him to settle back to sleep. He might've done so, except he spotted a girl standing in the cavern doorway with her arms crossed. She had fair skin, auburn hair, and big hazel eyes—which were currently narrowed significantly—and wore . . . a metal vest? Blue shook his head. But when he blinked again, the girl still stood there, wearing her strange armor. Like a knight.

Wait. He knew her. Only, her once-kind eyes were practically shooting daggers at him.

"River?" he whispered, his voice coming out garbled and dry. He tried to stand to greet her, but his arms and legs weren't right.

The girl's mouth fell open. "You . . . can *talk*? Wait—you *remember* me?"

"Of course I do," said Blue, finally managing to stand. "You were the last person I saw before I . . ." He couldn't finish. Already, his head felt fuzzy, and when he exhaled, it sounded funny. Come to think of it, why was he looking *down* on River? Was he floating? Had she gotten shorter?

And then it hit him—a single word shook him like thunder.

Dragon.

He remembered all at once.

I'm a dragon.

Blue let out a yelp, shrinking back in terror.

"Blue, it's all right," said River, her eyes softening slightly. "I can't believe you can actually talk. That's never—" Then she gasped. "Are those *feathers*?"

Blue looked down—what a long neck!—where the outside sun barely trickled into the cave. The light was dim, but it was enough for him to see blue feathers on his dragony arms and legs. And then he spotted a whole belly of shimmering silver scales.

"S-scales," said Blue, blinking rapidly, his mind spinning.

"The scales and feathers on the rest of you are deep sky-blue, just like your eyes." River frowned. "Well, your old eyes, anyway. Actually, hang on. Can you bend your head down a bit?"

Blue knelt so his head was level with River's. He found this height far more comfortable.

"Well, what do you know? Your eyes are still blue as the sea," she said with a half smile. Then her face became hard. "Dragons usually have golden eyes. Whatever. Not that it matters." She crossed her arms again.

Blue might've asked about River's obvious coldness toward him, but at the moment he was too stunned about everything else. "But . . . I can *remember.* You said I wouldn't be able to, but I can remember everything! The castle, the dragon tooth, Cedar."

A sharp pang rose in his chest, and his new eyes prickled with tears.

Wait, dragons could *cry*? The shock of this shook him from his sadness. Then he realized something else.

"Why aren't you older?" Blue asked.

River turned away from him then as the sharp smell of Sorrow rose swiftly in the air around her.

He could still smell emotions!

"River?" a voice called from outside the cave.

"We'll be out in a minute," she grunted, then turned back to Blue, fists balled.

"River, what's happened?"

She rounded on him. "You've *ruined* everything, that's what!"

Blue shrank back as her voice echoed off the cavern walls.

"I don't—"

"You've woken up fifteen years early, for starters."

Fifteen years early? That meant he'd slept ten years. But that couldn't be right either. Because River looked exactly the same.

"And that's not even the worst of it!"

It was that moment that Blue noticed the bits of color wrapped around River's wrists.

"River?" The voice called again from outside. "Is everything all right?"

"Coming!" she called back.

"Is that your dad?" Blue guessed.

"The whole village is out there waiting for you," River told him, ignoring his question. "They've all aged. Except me. I've been hibernating."

"But . . . why?"

"Don't *you* know?" The fury in River's eyes was enough to make Blue's head sink several feet.

Hibernating.

Blue markings around her wrists.

Blue gasped as understanding hit him. Because he remembered one single thought swirling through him as he'd drifted into hibernation. A wish. About River. "You're . . . my Rider."

Her silent fury was enough of an answer.

"But *how*? I don't understand what happened. Your mom said there would be some kind of choosing ceremony once I woke up. I didn't say any magic spell words or anything—did I?" And then he added, because he felt he ought to say it, "I'm really sorry."

She'd told him how much she loved her gardens. This really *did* ruin everything for her.

"Whatever. Let's just get this over with." With that, River stormed outside.

Blue went to follow her on clumsy legs to the gathered crowd outside. He ducked his head—how *tall* he was!—through the cavern entrance and into the dusk light. At full height, he stood a head taller than any of the horses in the royal stables. River stood off to his left, still sulking, while her parents stood behind her. They'd been so kind to Blue before, but now they couldn't seem to meet his eye.

The Dragon Growers, meanwhile, gaped and gasped, whispering to one another. Instead of applauding, the villagers all stared at him wide-eyed, like they'd never seen a dragon before. Their shocked expressions didn't exactly sit well in Blue's gut. He expected his cheeks to heat up with awkwardness, but in fact, as he thought about it, his entire body felt warm. And then he wondered: *Can dragons get embarrassed?*

When no one spoke, all Blue could think to do was clear his throat. Which sounded more like a growl.

"Why's he got *feathers*?" said a little boy. The boy's mother reached down to shush him, her cheeks crimson.

Blue craned his neck—he could turn his head completely around

152

now!—to see the rest of himself for the first time. He nearly fainted at the swarm of cerulean feathers covering every inch of him. A long curled tail—a *tail!*—twitched slightly when he set his mind to flick it. But most of all, he was in awe of his wings. Two enormous feathery silver-blue wings expanded when he told them to. He turned his gaze back to the gaping Dragon Growers.

"This is definitely strange," Blue announced, at which point another great round of gasps rose through the crowd.

"He talks!" said one.

"Impossible!" said another.

"We all heard it, clear as day," said a third, settling the matter with certainty.

Blue's massive new heart pounded like a drum in his chest. Part of him couldn't believe any of this was real. But the crowd continued to stare at him, so because he could think of nothing else to say, he decided to try using some manners.

"Er, it's nice to see you all."

At once, the crowd turned to each other. Their shock shifted to admiration. They grinned up at Blue, their hearts settling back again in their chests.

"So polite," said one.

"He's small, but quite *beautiful,* really," said another.

"I like his feathers," said a third, and everyone nodded their avid agreement.

At last, an old man stepped forward with an exaggerated bow, one hand on his knobby cane. "I am Cyrus, Chief Elder of the Dragon Growers."

"I remember you," said Blue, which sent another round of shrieks from the humans.

"*Do* you?" asked the old Elder, his mouth falling open a bit. "How . . . unconventional. Right, well. You must forgive us, great dragon. We mean no disrespect. But we've never seen a dragon . . . quite like you."

Blue nodded. "And as this is my first time *being* a dragon, I suppose it is a lot for all of us to get used to."

"You are most gracious," said Elder Cyrus with another bow. Blue really wished the man would stop, but he didn't quite know how to politely say so.

"Have you, eh, decided upon a name?" asked the Elder, looking from Blue to River.

"A name?" Blue repeated. "Haven't I already got one of those?"

Elder Cyrus laughed nervously. "It is customary for a new dragon to be named by his Rider. Although this is a most . . . uh, delicate situation, as usually the dragon cannot *remember* his human name."

River wouldn't look at Blue. "Let the dragon pick his own name."

Blue frowned—a new frown for a new face!—and considered. He knew nothing about dragon names. And while it was tempting to choose something impressive like *The Mighty One* or *Great Protector*, he didn't feel like either of those things. Even in this strong, shiny new body, he didn't feel much like a dragon.

He was just Blue.

"I'd like to keep my name," he said at last. "I know Blue isn't much of a name. But it's mine."

Elder Cyrus winced, then nodded. "Right, *ahem*. I suppose there's no way to persuade—" The old man stopped. He waved a dismissive hand through the air. "That is . . . if I may introduce you properly, then. It is my honor to present the newest dragon of the Southern Realm, Blue."

Blue couldn't help but chuckle. The name *was* rather small for someone his size. But it seemed fitting.

"And now—a feast has been prepared," Cyrus told him. "Quite

hastily, you can imagine, as we weren't expecting you to wake yet. Such a wonderful surprise!"

Blue wasn't sure about *wonderful*. In fact, everything about this day felt terrible. Still, he reluctantly followed the crowd to the circular arena with the twelve flat-topped boulders. How small the rocks looked to him now. Baskets of fruits and breads and meats lined the stones as the villagers gathered.

"And now—we feast!" announced Elder Cyrus, his hands raised. There was a great cheer as everyone swarmed the food baskets. Blue looked back at River and her parents. River's mother whispered something in her ear, though to Blue, it was spoken with perfect clarity.

"You should go talk to him," Aster Rowan urged her daughter.

"I don't *want* to talk to him."

"You're going to have to make nice sooner or later, Rivs," said Calder Rowan.

"Then I definitely choose *later.*"

Blue turned back to the food baskets and watched the Dragon Growers fill their plates, eyeing him curiously as they passed. At last River and her parents joined the line. At the prodding from her parents, she put one fruit on her plate and stomped her way over to Blue. She stood by him in silence.

"I don't feel all that hungry," Blue said after a while, only because it felt like the safest thing to say.

"Dragons don't need to eat," River muttered, taking a big bite of what looked like a magenta banana.

"Won't I starve?"

River shook her head. "The magic in your blood keeps you nutritionally sustained."

"Really?" asked Blue, amazed. And maybe a bit grossed out at the thought of *magic blood.* Then he frowned. "I think I'll miss eating, though."

"Well, you *can* eat if you like. But you don't have to."

The two stood in silence as the last people in the food line, the Elders, prepared their plates. Several of them patted Blue's arms gently as they passed.

"It feels weird to be petted like an animal," he told River.

River flicked her eyes up at him. It was the first time she'd made eye contact with him since the cave. He got a whiff of something. Something like . . . leather and mud. Then the scent shifted to lilac and mint.

River's Sorrow.

Blue held her gaze, and she looked like she was about to say something when a boy about her height walked up to them, holding a plate piled high with meats and fruit.

"Hey, River." The boy's dark hair was pulled into a short ponytail, and his sand-colored tunic was stained with dirt nearly the same color as his tan skin.

"Um, sorry, who are you?" River asked.

"I'm Sage," said the boy with a friendly grin as he popped a small berry into his mouth. "Sage Jackson. I suppose I look a lot different than the last time you saw me."

River's Sorrow from moments earlier turned to fury faster than a cricket chirp. She shot the boy a scathing look. "Last I saw you, you smelled like a poopy diaper."

Sage stood stunned for a moment, then laughed—much to River's obvious annoyance.

Before Blue could ask any questions, a low bell sounded, echoing loudly off the surrounding mountains.

Clang. Clang. Clang.

The ten Elders stood from their seats, peering somewhere in the distance. Blue turned, and some two hundred yards off—how could he see so far?—a small boy ran from the bell tower at the edge of the village, a tiny piece of paper clutched in one hand.

"What's happened?" Blue asked River. All her fury had fizzled. Now she stood rigid, her eyes scanning the horizon.

"Those are the bells of proclamation," explained Sage, his green eyes following River's gaze. "They ring once when a new baby is born and twice when someone dies."

"What's three rings for?" asked Blue.

River hugged her arms against her chest. "A message from our Meraki relatives."

The small running boy finally passed through the crowd and handed the paper to Elder Cyrus. The old man adjusted his glasses to read properly. Blue could smell the man's Fear. Elder Cyrus looked over the top of his spectacles, shaking his head sadly.

"There is trouble brewing for our Meraki siblings," Cyrus announced. "Dark times indeed. Dragon Master Jarum has lost contact with several of the Mainland dragons."

A hush fell over the villagers.

"The island dragons cannot travel to the Mainland to investigate because of the enchantment that compels them to stay away. That's why you two"—he looked from Blue to River—"are needed at Meraki Island immediately. Madam Madera has Seen that you've awakened, Blue. And you are the only dragon who can help the Dragon Master search for the cause of this troubling state of affairs."

Blue's heart pounded against his ribs. "You mean I have to . . . *fly*?"

"Most hastily, yes," Cyrus told him. Then the Elder turned back to the gathered crowd. "Prepare the saddle! The dragon and his Rider are to leave at once!"

25.

IN WHICH SHENLI IS NOT, IN FACT, DEAD

The next morning, Shenli Zhao woke to the smell of charred earth. His eyes fluttered open to darkness. At first he thought it was still nighttime, but then he remembered that he lay buried under a mountain of cave rubble. Somehow he'd managed to remain uncrushed as the heavy boulders landed in a tripod formation over him.

It was a miracle.

Beams of light trickled at odd angles through the cracks between boulders. But it was enough for Shenli to see a small opening in the rubble. He pushed himself to his belly and slithered forward. The boulders above him shifted, threatening to collapse. Just as he started toward the exit, he heard someone hiccup.

His head snapped up. Was someone else trapped too?

"Hello?" he called.

There was no answer.

He hurried his pace, elbow-crawling to the opening. The sudden sunlight blinded him as he passed through and the rubble behind him collapsed into a heap.

Fates, that had been close!

Shenli pushed himself to his feet, his entire body feeling like one big *ache*. He rubbed his eyes and gave himself a once-over. He certainly *looked* like he'd been in an explosion. His new uniform hung tattered and charred. He heard another hiccup and spun around, raising a hand to shield his eyes from the sun. A tiny purple-blue blur raced by at the edge of his vision, but when he turned, no one was there.

Except . . . that wasn't entirely true.

On the far side of the cave rubble was the firebreather. Red scales glittering fiercely in the sun, the great beast lay on its belly, arms sprawled, snoring in a deep sleep. That didn't stop Shenli's heart from jumping in his chest. He stepped back slowly, scanning his surroundings. The two Dragon Rider tents lay flattened on the ground, with no sign of the humans anywhere.

Shenli frowned. Dragons didn't sleep during the day. And Riders never abandoned their dragons. Cudek must've captured them and their Magics. And everyone must've left without Shenli, thinking he was dead.

Shenli stiffened.

Mama!

He had promised her he'd come home in the morning, and now she'd be worried sick. Would she think he'd run away, like Yuli? Or that he was dead, like his father? Shenli had to let her know he was okay!

He took off in a stumbling run, ignoring the ache in his limbs as he weaved through a maze of dense trees until he found a river his squadron had passed the night before. He remembered a boat. He ran a shaky hand through his hair, scanning the marshes until he spotted it: a small fishing boat docked on the shore. It would carry him downstream to where his family lived.

He'd just started to push it into the water when he noticed that his right palm was bright blue. Like he'd dipped it in paint. He sniffed his hand tentatively, but all he could smell was smoke. He reached down into the water to wash away the strange coloring, but the weird blueness remained like a stain. Ugh. Great. Like he needed more problems to deal with.

He started to push the boat again, when a sudden cool breeze whisked by, flapping his hair every which way. He turned just in time to see a little purple-blue cloud zoom overhead and disappear down the river.

He was pretty sure he'd heard the cloud hiccup.

He blinked.

A *periwinkle* cloud? That hiccuped?

Well, that couldn't be right. His injuries must've affected his brain. "Hello?"

Shenli whipped his head around. A girl burst out of the marshes downriver. Her jaw dropped as she spotted him. The smallest bit of recognition tickled Shenli's mind: This strange girl coming up from the river . . . had he seen her before?

The girl's chin-length dark curls bounced freely. Her clothes looked expensive and fancy. Beneath her traveler's cloak, her shimmery violet nightgown and gray leggings seemed better suited to the eclectic fashions of the Middle District or, better yet, the rich Mountain District. She looked lost yet . . . *determined.* She hesitated, her glittery copper eyes locked on his. There was something unnaturally *bright* about them.

The girl raised her chin and then moved toward him with purpose.

Shenli's breath caught as she spoke.

"Are you . . . Shenli?"

26.

IN WHICH WREN MEETS
HER FIRST MAINLANDER

Wren watched the boy's eyes grow wide. She'd spent the past twenty-four hours chasing whispers in the wind. She'd thought she'd sensed her Magic and had followed it upstream only to find this boy with his tattered military uniform and small fisherman's boat. She hadn't meant to be so blunt, but one look into his deep hickory-colored eyes and the question had popped out. Granmama hadn't warned her the boy would be handsome, with dark hair and rich tawny skin. But Wren knew the moment she saw him.

It was *him*.

At least . . . she was pretty sure.

The boy blinked. "Wh-what did you say?"

Wren gulped, silently scolding herself for not keeping her mouth shut—how would she explain how she knew his name? But it was too late now, wasn't it? She wished her thumping heart would settle down so she could think straight.

"You're Shenli, aren't you?" she asked again, trying to muster some of Cephas's confidence. If her brother were the one in this mess, he would already have a plan. A cover story, even. Cephas was the master of keeping his cool under pressure.

"Yeah. Do I . . . know you?" the boy asked.

"*Don't* you?" asked Wren, ignoring the heat in her cheeks. Answer a question with a question, Cephas had taught her, especially when trying to weasel out of trouble.

The boy's eyebrows scrunched together in confusion. "Do you work at the castle? Are you one of the other servants or something?"

Wren tried to keep her face composed. She was a terrible liar. But she couldn't very well tell him the truth. A Meraki on the Mainland was treasonous. "Or . . . something," she repeated.

Shenli took a step toward her. "Okaaaay. So what are you doing out here?"

Wren bit her lip. She wasn't even sure where she was. Probably still somewhere in the Coastal District. But how could she explain wandering around by herself? "I'm . . . lost," she said at last. It was the truth, after all. Even if it left out a *lot* of details.

"Your accent is funny."

Wren tried to smile innocently. "*Is* it?"

"Where are you from?"

"Er—north . . . ish," she tried.

"North? Like in the Char District?" Shenli's eyebrows furrowed into a hard line. "No one lives there because of the volcano. It's uninhabitable."

Wren's cheeks flushed hot. "I meant, like, more north . . . m-middle."

"North . . . middle," Shenli repeated as his frown deepened.

This was going terribly. Wren felt like the boy could see right into her mind to the big flashing *I'M LYING* sign. The best she could do now was to be sort-of truthful. "I really don't want to talk about home, to be honest," she said quickly. "I've only just run away."

"You've *only just*," Shenli repeated, shaking his head. "You sure do talk funny. You're dressed strangely too." He tapped his chin, as if considering. Then he snapped his fingers. "You're from one of the *settlements*, aren't you?"

Wren made a face. She hadn't been taught much about Mainland geography in school, only that there were five districts ruled by a chancellor with a massive army. She knew there were villages and towns, but she hadn't heard of any settlements. Best to answer with another question.

"From the settlements?"

"Yeah, those religious settlements are in the northern part of the Middle District. *North . . . middle.*" He imitated Wren's accent as he said the last part, and laughed. "I've had to deliver a few messages to military commanders out there. Everyone speaks old-timey, and the disciples—I think that's what they call themselves—only leave home to sell things at the castle market." He snapped his fingers. "That must be where I met you, isn't it?"

Well, it was as good a story as any, Wren supposed. She smiled. "You're clever, aren't you?"

"*Clever?*" Shenli repeated, again imitating her accent. A smile spread across his face, and butterflies swarmed Wren's stomach without her consent. She took a small step back. "Okay, I get it. You've run away from your settlement to make a new life for yourself. You're not the first kid to do it." Shenli sighed, swiping his bangs out of his eyes. One of his palms looked like it had been painted with blueberries.

"What's wrong with your hand?" Wren asked.

Shenli shrugged. "I . . . had a really weird night. Besides, I could ask you the same thing." He nodded to the Wren's left forearm, with its dark circular welts. "That looks infected."

"I was attacked by a movlak eel," Wren said with a wince, an image of the awful creatures flashing in her mind. The welts were stinging terribly now, and fear wedged farther into her chest. Xayndra hadn't seemed concerned about poison, but maybe the damage was worse than the dragon had realized. "I was told enderberries could heal it— do you know where I can find some?"

Shenli crossed his arms. "Yeah, I can get you some enderberries. They're usually grown in the rich Eadi gardens in the eastern Mountain District, but my mom has a stash."

Wren's eyes widened. "She does?"

Shenli shrugged. "She likes collecting rare herbs and stuff."

Wren bit her lip. This all seemed too easy. But maybe that was why she was supposed to find Shenli—so he could help heal her.

Unless he was lying.

"But I've never heard of *movlak* eels. The Wedi are farmers and fishers, you know. My people know every creature in the sea."

"Well. Perhaps . . . my people . . . have a different name for things."

Shenli eyed Wren skeptically. "Sure, whatever. Anyway, we have to leave now." He pushed the boat farther out into the water and looked back at her. "I'm in a hurry."

Wren eyed the boat. Uncertainty knotted tighter in her belly.

All her life, Wren had been taught that the Mainlanders were dangerous and selfish. Was Shenli really going to help her—just like that?

"You're truly going to let me come with you?"

"It's only a few hours south of here." He flicked his head downriver. "I live in Sankala village."

"But you don't even know me."

Shenli glared at her. "It's not like I *want* you to come, exactly. But you clearly need help. That injury looks bad."

As if in response, a renewed stinging struck Wren's wrist. Granmama's words echoed through her.

He doesn't deserve your trust, child, but you must give it.

The boy before her couldn't have been much older than she was, and yet he might as well have lived an entire lifetime. His ragged uniform flapped gently in the breeze, holding its secrets. What could cause clothing to singe like that? His eyes held her gaze, a wildness to them that surprised her.

He was scared.

But of what? *Her?* Or something else? He kept glancing around like he was expecting someone to jump out at them.

The word *danger* sent a deep shiver through Wren. Life on the island was many things—boring, monotonous—but never dangerous. She was supposed to go with him, wasn't she? She needed to find out why Granmama believed this boy was so important. Whether he was dangerous or not, she wasn't going to let Shenli slip away. She would follow him through all five districts and back, if that was what it took.

"All right, I'm coming with you," she said firmly, hands on her hips.

Shenli grunted. "Geez, you don't need to be all *serious* about it. Hurry up, will you?" Wren jumped into the boat, and Shenli climbed in after. "By the way, what's your name?" he asked.

Wren hesitated only a moment before the name hit her lips.

"My name is Rose."

27.

IN WHICH SHENLI
REMEMBERS

Shenli was having second thoughts about inviting the strange Rose girl to come along with him. The more he thought about her story, the less it made sense. The settlements were located about a day's walk north of the castle. If Rose was really running away, why would she come all the way to the Coastal District? There was nothing out here but farmland and the smell of fish. Not much to start a new life. It would've been better to hide somewhere in the Middle District. There were loads of overcrowded towns and villages where it was easy to disappear and find work. Even the Mountain District would've made sense. The rich Eadi people were always looking for more servants to hire.

There was so much about Rose that didn't make sense. Her night-gown looked like something royalty would wear—not exactly settlement garb. The religious disciples wore strange clothes, all right, but mostly boring white robes. Not silky pastel-purple pajamas. With glitter.

Maybe she'd stolen it.

"So you said you met me at the royal markets?" Shenli pressed.

Rose pulled her eyes away from the apple orchards and met his gaze.

"Actually, *you* said that," she pointed out.

"Okay. But you knew my name."

"I'd only heard it spoken once before. But I'm so glad I ran into you." She winced, hugging her wounded arm to her chest. "I . . . I think it's getting worse."

Shenli's eyes flicked down to her wrist. The dark welts *did* look bigger. But he couldn't help feeling that she was also using her injury to change the subject.

Rose smiled at him. He hated the fluttering in his chest.

"Your eyes are really, *really* bright," Shenli told her. "Like shiny copper metal."

Rose squirmed on her bench. "Uh . . . thank you?"

"It wasn't a compliment—they look unnatural. I'm just pointing out something that's strange about you. There's a lot that doesn't add up."

Rose sighed. "Even back home, people think I'm strange."

Shenli gripped the oars tighter. "Again with the vagueness and the secrets."

"Well, I'm not exactly inclined to trust strange soldier boys in the woods." Rose arched an eyebrow. "Even if I do know your name."

Shenli considered this. "Fair enough."

"Though you *have* been really kind so far," Rose admitted with a sigh. "Thank you for letting me come with you."

Shenli shrugged. "My mom would want me to help. Also Yiming. She's always helping the wounded animals in the field behind our house. Guess her helpfulness rubbed off on me a bit."

"Yiming is your sister?" Rose guessed.

Shenli nodded. "She's rescued a rabbit with a broken foot, starving kittens without a mom, and a whole bunch of baby birds who fell out of their nest." He smiled, imagining his little sister carrying her furry bundles back to the house. "We even looked after a grasshopper once. Really, it's my mom who restores them to health."

"So your mom's a Healer, then?"

"A Healer?" It was a strange word to use. "Do you mean a doctor?"

"Oh. Right. Sorry, they're, uh, called Healers where I'm from."

Shenli pursed his lips. The girl's strangeness continued. "Not a doctor, no," he told her. "Just good with herbs and stuff."

"Herbs? You mean magic?"

Shenli nearly dropped the oars. "What—*no!*" He hastily scanned the shoreline on either side of them, half expecting Cudek's soldiers to pop out of the bushes and haul them off to prison. He lowered his voice. "You can't talk about *magic* out in the open like that! You want us to get in trouble?"

Rose's eyes widened. "No! I definitely don't want trouble."

Shenli scoffed, catching sight of his tattered uniform sleeves as he rowed. "Then you picked the wrong person to travel with."

Rose didn't seem to know what to say to that. Her gaze fell back to the orchards as the two sat quietly for a while. They passed long stretches of farmland, where cotton and silkworms grew in abundance. Off in the distance, vast rice fields cut into soggy hillsides. The familiarity of it all settled warmly in Shenli's chest. Though he spent most of his days at the castle, the peaceful Coastal District would always be home.

"Do you live much farther?" Rose asked, breaking the silence. She was hugging her injured arm to her chest.

"It's getting worse?"

Rose nodded, showing him her arm. The welts now wrapped all the way to her elbow, like ugly snakes.

"My house is a few hours south of here, on the southern edge of the Coastal District."

Another silence settled between them as Shenli fell into a calming rhythm of rowing. He used to go fishing with his father in this river. He remembered catching his first carp and bringing it home to Mama, his pride near bursting out of his little four-year-old chest.

"My, my, what a strong and clever fisherman you are." Mama had beamed, preparing the hearth for a fish dinner.

His father had laughed, ruffling Shenli's hair. "Course he is. He's Papa's little helper."

Another old memory stirred, uninvited.

A memory he'd pushed so far down deep, it frayed and blurred rising to the surface. But now it came at him full force. Shenli had been nine when his father had snuck out of the house one evening. Shenli had followed, in the dead of night, as his father crept through the sleeping village and down to the beach. From his hiding spot, Shenli had seen two soldiers meet his father in the moonlight. There was shouting. His father pushed one of the men, and the other bound his father's hands with rope. The soldiers took his father to a nearby horse-drawn carriage and shoved him inside. The carriage took off into the night, the soft sound of hoofbeats in the sand pulsing in Shenli's ears.

He'd never seen his father again. And Cudek's scroll had showed up days later.

For years, he'd been furious at his dad. Only a fool didn't pay his debts to Cudek, after all. And his father's foolishness had left his family's lives in ruins. Shenli only wished he knew the whole story. His dad had always been a loving father, and his mom had endless stories of Jin's courage and goodness. There was still a part of Shenli that believed his father was a good man who'd gotten mixed up in some unlucky trouble. Over time, Shenli's anger had simmered into a deep sadness.

Shenli also couldn't help but wonder if his father's disappearance had any connection to Yuli's running away. Unlike his dulled anger at his father, Shenli's fury at his brother had only grown over time. He'd always believed Yuli was being a selfish coward by leaving. And yet, after everything that had happened the night before at the dragon lair, Shenli wondered if there was more to the story. What had Yuli's assignment been—what exactly had he run away from? Had Yuli also been tasked with facing a firebreather?

Not that it mattered. In the end, it all added up to Yuli's cowardice. Yuli was meant to take care of the family. But instead, he'd abandoned them all—by choice. Not like their dad, who'd been taken by force.

Shenli let out a slow breath, trying to ease the dull family-sized ache lodged under his ribs as he shook his brother from his thoughts. Rose was looking at him thoughtfully. He tried not to notice the golden flecks in her coppery eyes, glinting in the sunlight. There was something about this girl that still bubbled in vague recognition. Like he knew her. He *must've* seen her in the markets, as he'd first guessed.

"Why do you need to get to your family so badly?" she asked.

Shenli frowned. He couldn't explain a classified military mission to a complete stranger. Or his family's private business. "I need them to know I'm okay," he said simply.

Before Rose could respond, the boat trembled beneath them, water sloshing up over the sides. Shenli stopped rowing. Pebbles bounced slightly along the riverbed. The bushes and trees shook violently, their quivering leaves causing a terrible wind to whip up around the boat.

Then the rumbling halted, as quickly as it had begun.

Shenli sat frozen. "What. Was. THAT?"

Rose sighed. "Guess it's here too."

"What is?"

"The restlessness of the realm."

Shenli made a face. "Uhh . . . I have no idea what that means."

Rose stiffened a moment before her features relaxed. "My grandmother is very superstitious, that's all." Her eyes flicked to a large singed hole in Shenli's right sleeve as he resumed rowing. "You seem young to be a soldier," Rose told him.

"It's only my second day," Shenli admitted. Again he thought of his dad, and clenched his grip tighter on the oars. He'd been so close to finally learning more from Cudek! Now he had completely ruined his chances.

"And how's military life going so far?"

"Definitely . . . interesting."

"You look like you got blasted out of a volcano."

"That's not too far from the truth, actually."

"Really?" Rose leaned forward with curiosity. "What happened?"

"Er—I'm kinda not supposed to talk about it. You know. Classified."

"Oh." Rose rubbed a small black gemstone hanging around her neck. "Here," she said, shrugging off her traveler's cloak and holding it out to him. "You need this more than I do."

"No way. I can't take your cloak."

"Please, I insist. You look worse than a fire-roasted boar sausage."

A flicker of a grin tugged at Shenli's lips as he held Rose's steady gaze. "It's not that I don't see your point. But you need it more than I do. Once we're in my village, you're going to stand out like a sunflower in a snow patch."

"You mean because of my clothes?" she guessed.

"Because of your . . . everything."

"Oh." Rose frowned and slipped her cloak back on. She was staring at him intently again. There was something about the sunlight hitting her eyes that made them seem . . . otherworldly.

Then it hit him.

He realized where he recognized her from. The shock knocked into him so hard he stopped rowing. His dreams! Rose was the girl who'd visited his dreams all those years ago! His mouth dropped open a bit.

"Are you all right?" she asked.

"I'm . . . It's just that . . ." Shenli cleared his throat. No way was he telling her about the dreams. It was too weird. "It's nothing. I'm just eager to get home."

With a grunt, Shenli resumed his rowing with new fervor. The sooner he could get Rose out of his life, the better.

28.

IN WHICH WREN
BECOMES A SPY

After a few more hours of traveling downriver, Shenli pulled the boat ashore and Wren followed him down a narrow path stretching along the beach. Wren breathed in the familiar salty air. Somewhere across the vast blue of the Forbidden Pass, her classmates were at school, learning how to train their new Magics. Did they all know she was gone? What would Father say? She steeled her jaw. No need to think about *him*. Didn't she have enough to worry about?

Because the mysterious Shenli made her uneasy.

What kind of secrets was he hiding, anyway? Not that he was the only one. Wren still wasn't sure what had made her give him her mother's name. Maybe it was because where she was from, names held weight and meaning. They could be used for spells, for one thing. And living on an island where news traveled fast meant everyone knew your name—and your personal business. So it felt safer to give herself a new name.

Plus, maybe by being Rose, Wren could be as brave as her mom, the bravest person she had ever known.

"There it is," said Shenli, pointing up ahead. "Sankala village."

Wren followed his gaze to a smattering of buildings clinging to the lush green hillside. "It's beautiful!"

"I was born here. Along with Meili and Yiming, my two little sisters."

"Two sisters!" Wren gasped. Then she remembered—Mainlander women could bear many children. How strange and wonderful to have such a large family. "So you're the oldest, then? Me too."

Shenli grunted, kicking a pebble through the sand. "I have an older brother, but I haven't seen him in three years. He ran out on us only a year after my dad died."

"Oh. That sounds . . . complicated." She could relate to *complicated*, at least.

"That's just life." Shenli's voice was gruff, but Wren didn't miss the sad look in his eyes.

"I'm sorry," she said, knowing it wasn't enough.

Shenli nodded, and they continued in silence for a while, the ocean waves lapping in the distance as they made the steady climb up the hill. They passed through a small market spread out on a grassy lawn. All around, people gathered under rows of pop-up tents, buying and selling goods. Wren's mouth watered at the heaps of colorful carrots, pears, and dragonfruit. Her stomach growled at the smell of fresh fish, shrimp, and oysters. Some of the fish were still alive, swimming in large glass containers. One of the vendors held up a live crab, trying to tempt the people passing by.

"It's the Sankala wet market," Shenli explained. "You won't find fresher fish for sale anywhere on the Mainland."

"How exciting!" Wren breathed, taking in the vendor stalls with renewed wonder. Everything was so crowded and loud—nothing like the orderly markets on Meraki Island. And just like back home, people's skin colors ranged anywhere from sun-pink to darker than Wren's own. Their eyes were noticeably different, though. Here, everyone's eyes were nonmagical shades of blues, browns, or greens. She knew her own copper eyes stood out brightly—and *strangely,* as Shenli had rudely pointed out—among the mix.

She had so many questions—why was it called a wet market? How did people transport the live fish home once they bought it? And most of all, why was everyone wearing the same brown and gray clothes? In fact, once she noticed it, it was impossible to ignore. Back home, Wren's people dressed in a variety of beautiful pastel-colored clothing. But here, every man, woman, and child in the market wore simple cotton trousers and a tunic, in bland shades of brown or gray. The only pop of bright color came from the produce and seafood.

Before she could ask Shenli about it, one of the fruit stand owners caught sight of them and the man's mouth fell open. The man ruffled the small tuft of charcoal hair atop his balding head, then gave a sweeping look in both directions before beckoning them over.

"That's Naveed Farhad. He's one of my neighbors," Shenli told Wren, leading her to the small wooden stall stocked with tiny squid and spotted blue pears.

"Morning, Naveed." Shenli waved. "Sorry to be rude, but I really need to go—"

"Keep your voice down!" Naveed hissed, adjusting his rectangular glasses against his tan face. Very quickly, he slipped out of his charcoal traveler's robe and held it out to Shenli. "Take it—you look like you got into a fight with a bear."

Naveed noticed Wren for the first time, and his brown eyes widened behind his glasses, causing them to appear extra-large as he gave her a once-over. "And you're bringing home strangers, I see." He shook the cloak at Shenli, who finally took it and slipped it on. "Keep that hood up!" Naveed warned; then his eyes flicked to Wren. "You too."

Shenli obeyed and Wren followed suit, both pulling their hoods up.

"What's wrong?" asked Shenli.

"Fates, boy. I heard you were dead!"

Shenli flitted a nervous glance at Wren. "I nearly was," he admitted. "But what's up with the hood protocol?"

"I don't want anyone else to recognize you—though it's surely too late for that." Naveed lowered his voice. "Shenli, I saw soldiers enter your house this morning."

Shenli's face fell.

"They were still there when I left for work at sunrise. I don't know what's happened, but there's definitely trouble."

"I need to get to Mama." Shenli started to leave, but Naveed grabbed his shoulder. Wren could tell the grip was firm. Like a warning.

"Shenli, I've known your family a long time." The old man's eyes glistened. "Your father and I were dear friends. I'm telling you . . . it's not safe for you to go home right now. You know soldiers only show up on Cudek's orders."

Shenli shook his head. "I have to make sure they're okay!"

Wren looked down at her welted hand. It was starting to burn like fire. Could they still get the enderberries? Of course she wanted Shenli's family to be safe too. But Naveed was making her jumpy. What had she gotten herself into here?

"You're not in trouble with the chancellor, are you?" Naveed shot a questioning look at Shenli's tattered military uniform under the cloak.

Shenli stiffened. Suddenly he didn't look so sure. "I . . . I don't think so."

Wren shifted uncomfortably, her heart thumping wildly against her ribs. The danger surrounding this boy kept swirling higher.

"Your house is obviously being watched—there's no point in handing yourself over."

"I can't just abandon them!"

"No, but you need to lie low for a few days until things blow over.

Whatever this is, Kayra would want you safe." Shenli started to protest, but Naveed cut him off. "Your mama is stronger than you think. This isn't her first run-in with Cudek's soldiers."

A look of understanding settled between them, and Wren could feel the weight of sadness in the air.

"What if this is somehow all my fault?" Shenli whispered, his eyes glistening with tears.

Wren thought about her failed bonding spell. She remembered standing frozen and helpless as her Magic drifted away, out of reach. She knew what it was like to feel that everything was your fault.

"Maybe I can help," said Wren, putting a gentle hand on Shenli's shoulder. "What if I go check on the house for you?" She turned to Naveed. "Would that help keep Shenli safe?"

Naveed eyed the violet nightdress beneath her cloak. "Well, you're clearly not from around here. I suppose they wouldn't suspect you were connected to the Zhao family." He looked at Shenli. "It's not a bad idea."

Shenli turned to face her. "You'd do that for me?"

"Of course I would."

Shenli's deep brown eyes regarded her for a long moment. Then his face hardened. "Oh. Because you want those berries, right?"

Wren's cheeks flushed. "Well, *sure*. But I also want to help."

Shenli looked away.

"Both of you need to be quick about it," Naveed warned.

"Thanks, Naveed." Shenli nodded his goodbye, then motioned for Wren to follow as he led her away from the market and down side roads through a maze of small mud-brick houses with shake roofs. Up one street, down another. It felt like they were going in circles.

Or trying to make sure they weren't being followed.

Finally they settled behind a cluster of peach trees in someone's yard. Shenli gestured to a row of houses up the dirt road. "The one with the orchids." He pointed to a cluster of pink and purple flowers growing from clay pots next to the front door.

"I see it."

"The berries will be in my mom's room. In the dresser. Do you know what they look like?"

Wren shook her head.

"I'm pretty sure they're pink."

"Okay."

"If anything goes wrong, head back toward the market. I'll find you."

Wren nodded, clenching her shaking fists tightly. She started toward the hillside just as Shenli gripped her arm.

"I still don't understand why you're doing this, Rose."

She turned to face him. "It's only a *little* about the berries, Shenli. I want to help."

He narrowed his eyes as she stepped onto the road, heading toward his house. He didn't believe her. But she was too nervous to really care.

Wren blew out a slow steadying breath.

She could do this.

She could wander through the streets of a dangerous Mainlander village.

And visit a house of a strange soldier boy.

Who was clearly in some kind of trouble with the scary Mainlander chancellor.

The knots tripled in Wren's belly as she headed up the winding pathway. A few people greeted her on the road. She couldn't miss the suspicion in their eyes and the swell of silence halting their conversation as she passed. Once more she noted their earth-toned clothes as she hurried by, hugging her cloak around her. She exhaled her relief as she finally reached Shenli's house. An orange cat lounged between the flowerpots next to the door.

"Well, hello," said Wren, crouching down to give the cat a scratch on the head. Its steady purr calmed her jitters. Mama had always loved cats. Wren's family used to have three of them, and they had adored Rose Barrow more than anyone else, though they'd sometimes slept at the foot of Wren's bed on the nights Mama worked late. But after Mama was gone, the cats ran away, and they hadn't come back. Wren always wondered if they'd gone to look for Mama.

Wren stood, and the cat meowed its protest.

"Sorry, little one. I have a job to do." Wren knocked on the door. It creaked open a few inches and she peeked inside, into the sliver of darkness. She swallowed the lump of fear lodged in her throat. "Hello?" she called.

She couldn't hear anything inside. No voices. No footsteps. She knocked again, the door creaking inward a few more inches. She hesitated. They'd come all this way. She had to be certain.

She opened the door slowly. It was a small house, not even half the size of her own. A table was pushed against the corner to her right. In the kitchen, pots lay haphazardly along the countertop next to some freshly rolled dough. The fire in the hearth had gone out, leaving a cauldron of cold porridge that looked like it hadn't been stirred since that morning. Like the inhabitants had left in a hurry.

"Anyone home?" she called a little louder. Across the kitchen, two doors stood ajar. Three beds lay empty in the first room, the biggest one right beneath a window overlooking the fields in the backyard. Clothes and a few toys were scattered across the floor. Wren picked up a small cloth doll with black yarn hair, two black buttons for eyes, and a red dress. The doll smiled up at Wren. The smile seemed out of place in the quiet empty house.

A small tickle crawled up her neck, and she looked around. She felt she was being watched. Wren quickly crossed the room to a small oak wardrobe against the back wall. This must be where Shenli's mother kept her herbs. She pulled open the top drawer. A black spider scurried out, disappearing up and over the top of the ward-robe. Wren bit her lip to keep from squealing as she glanced back at the open drawer. Little girls' clothes sat folded neatly. She pulled open the second drawer: Shenli's mother's clothes. An eerie sadness clung to the air around her. Wren looked down at her own night-gown, with its glittery white flowers decorating the sleeves. It had belonged to her mother. One of Mama's favorites. But it had drawn plenty of attention in the village, and the last thing they needed was eyes looking their direction. With a decisive nod, Wren took a pair of simple black trousers and a gray tunic from the drawer. It felt forbid-den, holding a stranger's clothing. She hoped Shenli's mother would understand. She hoped Shenli would understand.

Wren quickly changed out of her dress and slipped into the new clothes, tying the waist belt firmly and slipping back into her cloak. They fit a little loose, but they'd do. Folding her mother's dress care-fully, she tucked it in her rucksack along with the little doll. Maybe it would cheer up Shenli.

She opened the bottom two drawers, which were stuffed full of bottles and bags of all kinds of liquids, powders, and herbs. One small jar in the corner was filled with magenta berries. She lifted it carefully and added it to her rucksack, then slipped out the door.

She meant to leave, but then she caught sight of the second bed-room. It stood empty except for two mattresses, a chair, and a small desk with a compact mirror sitting on top. Two sets of boys' trousers lay folded on the smaller mattress. Shenli's room. Something glit-tered from the desk chair. She crept across the room and pulled the chair out. A teal beaded bracelet lay on the seat. Something about the bracelet sent Wren's heart thumping wildly. Something *significant*. But that was silly, wasn't it? How could she possibly know the signifi-cance of a bracelet? She reached for it and held it up to the window light, the beads casting a deep blue-green glimmer on her chest.

A floorboard creaked behind her. Wren turned just as two hands grabbed her, spinning her around. A uniformed soldier with dark hair peered down at her, his pointer finger pushing into her shoulder.

"You're on confiscated property!" the soldier growled, giving Wren another poke for good measure. "You are not permitted to be here." Then he unsheathed his sword and hauled her out to the kitchen, where a second soldier was standing. Wren's eyes flicked to the sword blade and she nearly fainted. She'd never seen a real weapon up close.

"I—I was looking for s-someone," Wren stammered, slipping the bracelet into her pocket. "But they've all g-gone."

The second soldier stepped toward her. "You're joking, right?" she scoffed, her yellow ponytail swaying when she talked. "Everyone knows it's forbidden to trespass on seized property."

"I'm—sorry. I'm not from around here," said Wren, her heart thundering louder than a dragon's roar.

The woman gave Wren a once-over. "You're a thief, aren't you? Looking for scraps."

"No! I wasn't trying to make trouble," said Wren, her palms sweating. Were thieves a common thing in the Mainland? "I was . . . only looking for Yiming." Wren hoped she'd gotten Shenli's sister's name right.

"Who's Yiming?" grunted the man.

"One of the sisters, I think," said the woman. "Look, kid, the family is gone. They were moved out of here this morning."

"Moved . . . out?"

The soldiers shared an incredulous look.

"You know . . . *moved out*. Transferred." When Wren only blinked, the male soldier narrowed his eyes at Wren, pointing his sword tip at her. "I think we need to take her in. Something's fishy about her."

Just as he grabbed Wren's wrist, a loud buzzing echoed through the house. The sound was coming from behind the soldiers. Like a swarm of bees—but more bubbly and high-pitched.

The male soldier scowled. "What the—"

The buzzing intensified, and the soldier released Wren and swung his sword around to face the sound. "There's nothing there!" he growled, and both soldiers searched the kitchen and living room. "I don't see anything."

There was a clang outside. A cat howled.

"It's coming from out back." The woman grunted, unsheathing her sword.

"Rotten neighbor kids," the man muttered.

"We better clear them out before Commander Perez makes the rounds. He's in one of his *moods* today."

With a grunt of agreement, the man followed his partner out the door. Before they could remember she was still there, Wren ducked out the door and sprinted down the hill as the soldiers headed to the back side of the house. She didn't stop until she had passed through the market, where vendors tried to tempt her with chicken and nets full of fish. Catching her breath, she circled back around a cluster of buildings nearest to the sea, and spotted some old crates behind a carpenter's shop. She felt safer here than in the crowd of people at the wet market.

Heart pounding in her ears, she sat down on a crate and hugged her knees to her chest. She forced herself to take slow breaths as she scanned the alleyway for Shenli. He would find her.

Wouldn't he?

She wasn't so sure. Everything had gone wrong. For all she knew, Shenli had abandoned her, and she was completely alone. Left to fend for herself on the dangerous Mainland.

29.

IN WHICH RIVER CAN'T
TAKE IT ANYMORE

All too soon, River sat atop Blue's back, the wind whipping around her as they soared over the great mountain range. There had been no time for the Makers to create a new saddle, given the urgency of Madam Madera's summons. So an old harness was found in the back of the blacksmith's shed and hastily fitted to Blue's too-small frame. Thankfully, Blue had mostly worked out the flying thing and hadn't thrown River off his back.

At least, not yet.

She now clung shakily to harness straps, terrified of the dizzying drop beneath her. As the mountain peaks passed by below, River held fast to her last memory of her parents. Before she'd left, they'd told her they were expecting a baby. It was a miracle. Although the Dragon Growers enjoyed very long lives like their island Meraki brethren, the women in River's village only had one child in their lifetime. To have a second child was considered incredible good luck, and as far as River knew, it had happened only a handful of times in all of Meraki history—and never in the Dragon Growers' village.

River was overjoyed for her parents. Grateful, even, that they would gain a child to fill the hole she was leaving behind. And yet it broke her heart to know she had a little brother or sister she would never meet. She wouldn't even know their name.

All this new grief hung on River, the ache in her chest swelling until she could hardly breathe. But she didn't have time to grieve. Instead, she had to keep her balance thousands of feet up in the air while holding on to the very worn old map the Elders had given her to navigate her way to Meraki Island.

It didn't help that she was terrified of heights.

Of course, a *proper* Dragon Rider would've received years of navigational training before their first flight. As it was, River could hardly sort out the best path through the mountains. She grunted for the umpteenth time, trying to keep the map flat without losing hold of it—not an easy task, considering Blue was still shaky on his wings.

Blue, for the most part, remained silent, following River's uncertain directions with little nods and grunts. River didn't know if he was sad or frustrated, but she couldn't quite muster up compassion for either. Truthfully, *he* was the reason she was sitting up there in the frigid air, missing her family. Whether he'd meant to or not, he'd chosen her for this. And in doing so, he'd completely ruined everything—for her and her parents.

"That must be the desert up ahead," said Blue, his voice rumbling beneath her.

"The Wastelands?" River narrowed her eyes, peering into the distance. All she could see were endless trees and mountaintops.

"It's still another hundred miles away," said Blue, with a slight cock of his head. "I . . . I'm not sure how I know that."

"Dragons have an impeccable sense of direction and distance," River told him. She had no idea where their location was on the map, but she wasn't about to admit it.

"And yet you're the one stuck navigating."

River scoffed. "Oh, I'm definitely stuck. Here. With you."

Blue turned his head slightly to look back at her. River could feel her anger bubbling just under her rib cage. It felt like water heating over a fire. She'd managed to keep her mouth shut for most of the trip so far—everything was too painful to talk about. But now that simmering water was starting to boil.

Blue dipped a little lower, through a cloud.

"Watch it!" River scolded, beads of water clinging to her face. On the one hand, River knew she was being a bit of an irritable monster. They'd been in the air nearly the whole day, and she'd done nothing but grunt and fume the entire time. On the other hand, she wasn't done being mad at Blue, and thought he maybe deserved a bit of her anger.

She couldn't stop picturing her parents the last time she'd seen them. The pain in their eyes when they said goodbye.

"Sorry," Blue muttered. "I didn't know clouds were so wet. I just thought it might be fun."

"Yeah? And how'd that work out for you?" River growled, clenching the map tighter. That was when she realized how wet it was. Half of it was soaked through, the ink completely smeared. "Oh, great! Now the map is drenched. Your little cloud maneuver ruined it."

Blue let out a low growl. "Well, maybe your people could've trained me a bit before sending me off *as a dragon*! How was I supposed to know clouds are filled with water?"

The anger in his voice only riled River's fury. "Maybe if *you* had chosen a *proper* Rider, you'd be prepared!"

"I didn't *mean* to choose you, River!" Blue turned his head around abruptly to fully face her. This caused his flying body to tilt, and River had to grip the harness to steady herself. "I don't even know how it happened!"

"Doesn't matter what you *meant*," River yelled. "You still did it!"

Blue narrowed his eyes. "Well. I'm kind of regretting it at the moment."

River clenched the harness tighter. "I told you! I was meant for Harvesting! I wasn't meant to be a Rider."

"Clearly!"

"You ruined my life, Blue!"

"Yeah, well, *you*—"

But Blue didn't get to finish. Because at that moment, something strange glittered into view, right in front of them. "Hey, look!" River called, momentarily forgetting her frustration. "There's something up ahead. What *is* that thing?"

Blue whipped his head back around, spotting the *thing* a moment later. River leaned forward to get a better look. The *something* was gold and glittery, floating just overhead. A long thin line, hovering in the sky like a lost kite string without a kite. And the string was gold.

"Is that . . . a thread?" asked River. "It's— Blue, can you see it?"

"Ugh. Yes. And I've seen it before."

"You *have*?"

The string let out a chorus of fluttering notes.

"Oh, there it goes again—singing," muttered Blue. "It showed up just before all the dragon tooth trouble began, so whatever you do, *don't* touch—"

Before Blue finished his sentence, River reached out and tugged the thread. It trembled for a moment before fading out of sight. Something lurched in the air, an invisible force. It rattled River's teeth, and Blue surged downward.

"You touched it!" Blue cried.

"I couldn't help it!" she yelled as Blue shot forward so fast she nearly lost her grip on the harness. "Watch where you're going!"

"I can't . . . control . . . my flying."

River could feel Blue straining his wings. But the strange invisible force pulled them farther down.

"Wrong way!" River called.

They plunged faster, the scenery whipping around them. They were headed straight toward a high mountaintop.

"Can't . . . slow . . . down!" Blue grunted, flapping his wings harder. But the more he struggled, the stronger the force pulled. To River it felt much like getting squeezed through a tight space. With a final push, Blue skittered downward, straight toward the oncoming mountain peak. It rose like a scraggly rock monster topped with snow.

And they were going to crash right into it.

IN WHICH BLUE AND HIS RIDER HAVE SOME WORDS

River screamed loud enough to rattle Blue's eardrums, and Blue realized two terrible things at once:

First, he couldn't slow down.

Second, they were most definitely going to crash into a mountain.

The only mercy was that the mountaintop was blanketed in snow. Blue tried to angle his body so as not to crash headfirst, but in doing so, he dipped too far forward, and the momentum threw River off his back. Both dragon and Rider slammed into a muddy snowbank at the same time.

The impact left Blue breathless. He ached all over. He'd never had a boulder dropped on his body, but he wondered if this was what it would feel like. After a few moments, he rolled onto his back with a loud grunt and wiped the snow off his face with the back of his clawed hand.

Okay, so he wasn't dead.

But something was . . . wrong.

"You okay, River?"

After a beat, River groaned in response.

Blue pushed himself up and shook the snow from his back and wings, sending loose a few of his feathers. He winced, realizing he probably looked like an overgrown dog shaking himself off. Ugh. He hated this new animal body! There was also a sharp pain searing through his left wing. He spotted River a few yards away, brushing snow off her clothes. Her eyes were like fire.

"You threw me off on purpose!" she yelled.

Blue recoiled at her fury—couldn't she lay off him for just five minutes? And though he most absolutely had *not* thrown her off on purpose, he was too irritated to say so. "Well, it got you to stop yelling at me, didn't it?"

"You deserved it."

"Stop acting like this is all my fault, River." His wing felt on fire now. "You're the one who pulled the thread when I told you not to."

"This *is* your fault. You ruined my life!"

"You—you already said that earlier!"

"Well, I meant it." River stamped her foot.

Blue couldn't help but notice her normal human footprint. He glanced down again at his own dragon-sized print in the snow. Then the pain in his wing flared so badly he started seeing stars. He suddenly felt like he was going to be sick.

River, on the other hand, was clearly only getting warmed up. She stomped through the snow, shaking her fist at him.

"I was supposed to become Lead Harvester, Blue. It was a really big deal."

"Clearly you think *you're* a big deal," Blue shot back, trying to extend his wing to examine it. But it wouldn't budge.

"Well, I kind of *am*, if you want to know the truth!" River's cheeks were flushed pink. "The ceremony was all set for after your hibernation. Then you had to go mess everything up!"

Blue grunted, little wisps of black smoke coming from his nostrils. "And what about me, River? *I am a dragon!*" Great big tears leaked down his cheeks, and he turned his face away. "Don't talk to me about your life being ruined. At least you still get to be human."

River sucked in a breath. The two stood in silence until River finally met Blue's gaze.

"*Nothing* about me is the same," Blue told her as his tears kept coming. "My walk is different, my senses are all on overload, and my head is so high off the ground it makes me dizzy. Not to mention flying is totally frustrating. I just . . . I miss my old body." He inhaled a shaky breath. "I really don't know how to do this. How to be a dragon."

River blinked at him, her own eyes glassy. The two stood still for a long moment, the only sound the wind howling between them. River looked like she was going to say something, then changed her mind. Instead, she kept her mouth drawn into a thin line and tapped her foot.

"Do you smell that?" Blue asked after a beat.

"Smell what?"

He inhaled deeply. "It smells like . . . earthy leather."

River stopped tapping her foot and sniffed. "I don't smell anything."

"I smelled it right before we crashed too. It was really strong. It was almost like—"

Suddenly, River's mouth fell open. "Blue! Your wing is bleeding!" At once, the anger drained from River's face and she raced toward him, swinging her shoulder bag around to the front. "Lie down so I can get a better look."

Blue obeyed, gritting his teeth as he lay down on his belly. "I can't move it."

River studied the wing, touching it gently in certain places.

"Ashes. I think it's broken." She turned her head back to their crash site. "You must've hit rock under that snowbank."

Blue winced as she gently tugged at feathers to survey the damage.

"This is really bad, Blue. I can clean the wound, but"—she gaped at him wide-eyed—"I don't think you'll be able to fly."

Terrible understanding settled into Blue's belly. And it felt even worse than the fire in his wing. "We're stranded," he whispered.

River's face went pale. Then she closed her eyes and took a few deep breaths. They came out in little fog puffs. "Do *not* freak out," she whispered—whether to Blue or herself, he wasn't sure. "You can take control of the situation, River. You. Can. Do. This."

Okay. Definitely talking to herself, then.

"Uhh . . . what are you doing?"

River peeked an eye open. "I'm claiming my confidence."

"Er—what?"

"Look. We can either freak out or make a plan. I, for one, am a big fan of plan-making."

"Yeah, but—"

River wagged a scolding finger. "*No buts!* We make a plan. List the steps. Follow each one. We will sort this out."

Blue wanted to point out that his wing hurt so badly he probably couldn't even walk, let alone fly anytime soon. But the determination on River's face gave him some hope. "Okay," he agreed weakly. "Then what's the plan?"

River nodded her satisfaction. "I'll clean this wound best I can. I have a few things in my bag that should help numb the pain, at least temporarily."

"Well, I definitely like that plan."

"Now hold still."

Blue laid his head down as River went to work. She used melting snow to wash his wing—Blue had to look away from all the red-stained water running off his body—and then she took a variety of bottles from her bag. After a while, the fiery pain cooled to a simmer. His wing still hurt. A lot. But the pain was no longer paralyzing. Blue could breathe easier.

"Earlier," said River, "you said you smelled something."

"Oh. Right."

"You said it was like earthy leather. Do you think you smelled your wound? Dragons are supposed to have an incredibly strong sense of smell, but I wasn't sure about you—since you're so . . . young."

Blue took a whiff. The smell of leather and soil was still there, but fainter. "It's not the wound."

"Oh? Then what is it?"

Blue sampled the air again until he was sure. "I think . . . I smell Anger."

River raised a skeptical eyebrow. "You can smell emotions?"

"It's this weird thing I can do. Ever since I was little."

River looked up at him, pausing her application of green paste to his wing. "That *is* pretty weird."

"But I've only ever smelled Sorrow and Fear. This . . . is something new."

"Well, I'd say your nose is accurate, anyway." River stood up and wiped her hands in the snow. Her teeth chattered as she hugged herself tighter. "I m-mean, with the two of us s-s-screaming at each other, there was probably enough Anger scent in the air to knock you sideways. No wonder you c-c-crashed. Anyway, I'm all done."

"You're freezing, River," Blue realized aloud.

"Uh . . . yeah. Snow will do that to you."

"But I'm *not* cold!" Blue gasped.

"How n-nice for you," said River, rubbing her hands against her arms. "I bet all that f-fire in your belly keeps you warm."

"I have fire in my belly?" He pushed himself slowly to his feet.

"Well, dragons breathe f-fire. Grown-up dragons do, anyway. Guess I don't really know where the f-fire comes f-from."

"We need to get you out of here," said Blue. He stretched his neck over the cliffside. "Let's head down, where it's warmer."

"F-fine. But for the record, I'm still f-furious with you."

Blue snorted. "Oh, I know. I can smell it."

The corner of River's mouth turned upward ever so slightly. "Good."

"If we check the map, we can still head in the right direction," said Blue, making his way down the mountain as River trailed behind. "The desert was directly north of here."

There was a long pause, until Blue turned his head around to look at River. "So, which way?"

"I . . . lost the map," River told him.

Blue's mouth fell open. "You lost it? How? Wasn't it . . . you know, *huge*?"

"It was a *regular*-sized map!" River shot back, crossing her arms.

"But . . . definitely large enough to hold on to," Blue pointed out, kicking angrily at a nearby rock. River shot him a scathing look. Her cheeks flushed a peculiar shade of red as a new waft of dirt and leather filled Blue's lungs.

"Maybe if you weren't flying all *wild*, I could've kept hold of it!" River yelled.

"The only *wild* one was the one who grabbed the weird magic thread!" Blue growled back. "Anyway, without the map—"

"I told you—I will figure it out! One step at a time."

"Right," Blue scoffed. "Well, it would be great to know *which direction* to step, wouldn't it? And you know what would be helpful for that?" He narrowed his eyes. "A map."

River snapped her mouth shut, and suddenly there was enough earthy leather smell in the air to choke a giant.

"Ugh. Fine. I'll just start walking," Blue muttered, snapping his head forward and ignoring River's fury. "I think we should go right."

"No, *left*," River grunted.

Blue craned his long neck to look both ways. To the right was a sprawling meadow leading toward rolling hills in the distance. To the left, the mountain sloped down into more forests.

"The map was clearly meant to lead us through mountains to get to the Wastelands," River argued. "The hills and meadows are in a completely different direction."

Blue frowned. While it made sense to keep to the mountains, something deep in Blue's gut trembled. Like a warning. "I really don't think we should go that way."

"I'm the navigator. And I say we go left."

"You said dragons have an impeccable sense of direction," Blue challenged, his eyes narrowing.

River gritted her teeth. "While that might normally be the case, you aren't exactly full-grown." She put her hands on her hips. "So you can't be fully *reliable* either."

Blue paused a long moment, the unsettled feeling in his belly bubbling higher. "I have a bad feeling about the mountains, River."

"Well, you're wrong," she snapped. "The mountains are the most logical choice." River marched toward the forest. Blue followed reluctantly, the terrible warning in his gut growing with every step.

31.

IN WHICH SHENLI
UNCOVERS A SECRET

S henli sank back farther into his hiding spot behind a row of huckleberry bushes, clutching a bundled cloth and trying to catch his breath.

He'd watched Rose enter his house minutes ago, which he'd taken as a good sign—until two soldiers followed her inside. Shenli had snuck in through his mom's bedroom window and scrambled under her bed to hide, all set to cause a distraction so Rose could flee, when the roaring buzz of a bee swarm had filled the room.

And that was when two *really* weird things had happened at the same time.

First, as he'd peeked out to the kitchen, where Rose and the soldiers were, he didn't see any bees. He *heard* them, but all he could see was a strange little blue-purple cloud hovering in the kitchen.

This might've unnerved him, except at that same moment, his hand had bumped into something under his mom's bed. He'd shifted slightly to get a better look. There, wedged into a large crack in one of the wooden boards on the underside of the bed, was a small bundled cloth held up with tape.

What in the world?

Shenli grabbed the bundle from its hiding place and stole back through the window. He was just sorting out how to cause some kind of distraction to draw the soldiers outside when the strange purplish cloud—the same one he'd seen that morning near the dragon lair, he realized!—flew out the front door and ran into poor Whiskers before shooting out of sight.

Soon after, Rose had fled and headed down the hill while the soldiers checked the backyard. Shenli now waited for the soldiers to clear away. Once they were gone, he inched out of the bushes, still clutching the mysterious bundle. He knew he should go after Rose before he lost sight of her.

But . . . he also had to know what his mom had been hiding under her bed.

A light breeze rose from the field behind him as Shenli slowly removed the tape and stared at the strange gold cloth. *Gold!* Where had Mama acquired such expensive fabric? The cloth was dusty, like it hadn't been touched in years. He unwrapped the fabric, and there sat a small blue wooden dragon statue, no bigger than his thumb. He dropped the statue in alarm.

Hesitating slightly, he scooped it back up to study it closer. The dragon was sitting up, with his wings folded behind him. His head was tilted slightly, and he looked at Shenli with a toothy grin. Shenli traced his thumb along the intricately carved blue scales.

What could it mean?

Dragons were nothing but bad luck. So why would his mom hide one under her bed? A sliver of fear swept through him. His mom was keeping secrets from him. His dad had kept secrets too—and look where it had landed him.

Shenli stared at the smiling dragon. The fire beast looked like it held secrets of its own. Shenli gripped the little statue angrily before wrapping it back up and shoving it in his pocket. It seemed like everything around him was suspicious—Cudek and the lair, the strange purple cloud, Rose, and now this statue.

He stormed down the hill after Rose. He weaved through the back roads until he finally spotted her behind the old carpentry shop, where she sat on a wooden crate.

He stopped in his tracks.

She was wearing his mother's clothes. The soft gray tunic with the double stitching Mama favored in the winter. Fury boiled through him.

"I'm guessing this isn't the first time you've stolen clothes," he growled.

Rose's head whipped up. The relief in her eyes wilted once his sharp words sank in.

"You stole the purple dress too."

"No. I didn't."

Shenli scoffed. "Right. The disciples in the settlement don't wear pastel colors, Rose."

Rose's eyes fell to her lap. "I'm sorry. I should've asked. But my old clothes were vastly conspicuous."

"*Vastly conspicuous?*" Shenli repeated.

"It means . . . really noticeable."

"I *know* what it means!" Shenli crossed his arms. "But kids don't talk like that." Another bout of fury bubbled through him. She was a thief. And a liar. And he never should've let her tag along.

"Shenli, there's something I need to tell—"

"Fates, your arm!" Shenli winced. Her sleeve was pulled up, revealing the eel-sting welts well past her elbow, and they'd turned bright red. "It's *so* much worse."

Rose bit her lip. "I've been trying not to think about it."

Shenli eyed her wounds with new horror. "How could you *not*?"

197

"Because my mom—" Rose squeezed her eyes shut. "I'm super scared, Shenli."

"Did you get the berries?"

"Maybe?" She pulled a small jar from her bag.

"That's them. We'll need to boil them before we can apply them to your wound. Hang on, I'll be right back."

Shenli ducked around the corner to the back side of the carpentry shop. He knew the owner, Mrs. Miller, wouldn't mind if he borrowed supplies. But he also didn't want to be spotted or he'd be forced to answer a lot of questions. He snuck through the door and into the tiny kitchen. He found a few filled canteens on the counter and grabbed them, along with a small pot, then snuck back outside to Rose. She looked so miserable, hugging her arm, he nearly forgot his anger about the clothes.

"You were pretty brave back there," Shenli said quietly, setting the supplies on the crate. She'd been more than brave. She'd been selfless. Shenli wasn't used to kindness from strangers.

"Happy to help," said Rose, still wincing. She nodded to the pot. "What's that for?"

"Prepping the enderberries. We shouldn't do it here, though."

Rose blinked at him. "I really am sorry for taking your mom's clothes. It seemed like a good idea at the time."

Shenli frowned. Her old clothes *had* been drawing too much attention. It was a smart move. But he still didn't like it. He cleared his throat, ignoring her apology. "So what did the soldiers say?"

He already knew it must be bad news. But he needed to hear it.

"No one was home. They were"—she bowed her head, reaching into her bag—"transferred."

Shenli dug his fingernails into his palm. Transferred? That happened only by order of Cudek himself. It meant his mom and sisters had been hauled away to prison like dangerous criminals. He'd never heard of children getting locked away—what could the chancellor possibly want with them? His whole world started to spin; then he felt Rose press something into his hand.

He knew before he saw it: soft, worn, with button eyes . . .

Yiming's doll.

The one he'd given her right before he first left to work for Cudek, when she was only six months old.

"I can't believe this," he said, his voice catching.

"What does *transferred* mean, exactly?" asked Rose softly.

"It means they've been put in prison." The thought of his mom and sisters holed up in one of Cudek's prisons right now made his blood boil.

"Oh. Shenli, I'm so sorry."

"Yiming is only three years old." He gripped the doll tighter.

"I can't believe the chancellor would imprison children," whispered Rose.

"Yeah. Terrible luck is kind of a thing in my family." Shenli thought of the dragon statue, then slipped Yiming's doll into his pocket right next to it. "Naveed was right. We're not safe here. But I know someone who can tell us where my family's been taken. We can prep the enderberries along the way."

Shenli held out his blue palm to help Rose down from the crate; then the two started down the road together, out of the village, each keeping their hood pulled up. Rose, who was now dressed like any common Coastal District villager, kept a steady pace with him. Shenli found her presence both suspicious and comforting at once.

There was still so much he didn't understand. About the blue orb and the explosion. Now his family had been taken. The two things must be related, though he couldn't see how.

After his village was long out of sight, Shenli led Rose to a small tangle of trees. He started a fire from dried twigs, set Mrs. Miller's pot on top, and filled it with water. Then he dumped in half the enderberries and sat on the ground, waiting for the pot to boil.

"Once the berries have boiled, we'll mash them up."

Rose took a seat across from him. "Then what?"

"Then you'll need to eat it. Cripes, I should've swiped some sugar to sweeten it."

"Couldn't I just eat the berries?"

"Ugh. You could, but they're disgusting. At least when they're mashed, they go down easier."

Rose shuddered, eyeing the pot tentatively. "Okay, so then where are we headed? After I eat the nasty berry mash, that is."

"My friend Ranji. He has a lot of military connections and he'll know what's happened to my mom and sisters—and hopefully what in the five districts is going on. He's stationed at the southern watchtower, about a half day's walk from here. But . . . it might be dangerous."

Rose frowned, touching her pendant gently. "Shenli, I need to tell you something."

"I'd understand if you don't want to come with me."

"No, it's not that."

There was a sputtering sizzle coming from the pot, where the water was boiling over. Shenli shrugged off his cloak, wadded it up, and used it to take hold of the pot and dump out most of the water.

"You know, you probably shouldn't come with me," Shenli told her, grabbing a nearby rock and using it to mash the cooked berries. "Because if Cudek has my family, then I'm probably a wanted criminal."

Rose held his gaze. Her strange glittery eyes started to water. "And I'm a traitor to my people," she said quietly.

Shenli frowned, pausing his berry-mashing. There was a kind of significance hanging in the air, building up around them.

Rose looked at him for a long time, wiping her cheeks.

"What did you want to tell me, Rose?" he asked finally.

"My name . . . isn't Rose. And I'm not a disciple—" She took a shuddering breath. "I am Meraki."

32.

IN WHICH SHENLI LEARNS
THE TRUTH

Shenli dropped the stone he was mashing berries with.

"Meraki?" he repeated. The word felt sour and awful on his tongue. "You're . . . *Meraki*?"

Rose—or *not* Rose, apparently—nodded. "My name is Wren Barrow."

Shenli stood abruptly. "I mean, I knew you had secrets, but *this*?" He couldn't meet Rose—no, *Wren's* gaze. He paced back and forth, running the day's events through his mind: Dragon lair. Strange girl. His family taken. Purple cloud.

His dream.

All this time he'd been dreaming about a *Meraki* girl? Though he knew he couldn't control his dreams, it still felt . . . dangerous. And wrong.

"I . . . can't deal with this," he told her, backing away. "Just . . . eat the berry mash once it cools. Then you're on your own. I need to find my family." Shenli spun on his heel and marched down the road.

"Shenli, wait."

He didn't turn around. He marched onward until he reached a

forest of birch trees. The quickest way to Ranji's was to cut through. As he weaved through the tall pale trunks, he did his best to ignore Wren's leaf-crunching footsteps behind him.

He needed to focus. And make a plan. He *really* should report to Cudek, but he was desperate to know where his family had been taken. Cudek wouldn't tell him. It would be just another link in the long chain of Zhao family secrets the chancellor kept from Shenli, and he wasn't about to let the rest of his family disappear without a trace. No, best to get Ranji's help first and then report to Cudek.

"I need to talk to you, Shenli," Wren called out. "Please, it's important."

Shenli whirled to face her. "Stop following me!"

Wren held the pot of berries in her hands. "You need to know the truth."

"What? About you being Meraki?" Shenli threw her a hard glare. "It's actually not hard to believe. Your weird accent and freaky eyes." Her shoulders fell, and he immediately felt a little bad. Her eyes were actually really pretty. But *strange.* Probably magically cursed or something. "And now that fancy dress makes sense. The magic folk are rich snobs who love to dress up."

"It was only a nightgown," Wren muttered.

Shenli scoffed. "There's a reason why people in my village don't wear fancy colors. Colored dye is ridiculously expensive. I could sell that dress and feed my family for weeks."

She dropped her gaze. "I . . . didn't know that."

"Whatever. Why are you *here,* Wren? Are you some kind of spy?"

"No!"

"Mm-hmm. Sure. Did someone send you or something?"

Wren thumbed her necklace. "I guess my grandmother did. Kind of."

Shenli made a face. "Your . . . *grandma* sent you?"

"Well, it started because my Magic ran off, and I've come to find it." Wren threw up her noninjured hand in exasperation. "It was only born yesterday, Shenli! And it's stubborn, and unruly, and bound to get into mischief."

Shenli's mouth hung open a bit. He knew the Dragon Riders had Magics on the Mainland, and he'd read some about Magics because of Cudek's assignments, but he'd never thought about Magics as thinking creatures with wills of their own.

"Magics can run away?" he asked, too curious to care that he was asking dangerous questions. "Also, you need to eat those berries soon."

Wren sighed, looking down at the pot. She tilted it and let the contents drip into her mouth, then gagged. "Ugh. This is disgusting."

"Yeah. Pretty much." Shenli gave her a pitying glance. "Try not to think about the smell."

She took another mouthful of berry mash. "Anyway, Magics don't *usually* run away. But mine wasn't properly bound at the Offering Tree, so it's a bit of . . . an anomaly." She winced. "I really hate that word."

"What's an Offering Tree?"

"It's where Magics are born. Also where human and Magic companions are bound together with a spell."

"Okaaaay." Shenli took a step back. He'd crossed the line of curiosity. Now he was in Weird Magic-y Danger territory.

"My Magic's not even the half of it, though!" Wren went on, taking another helping of berry mash. "My granmama is a Seer. She told me your name and that you are part of my story."

Shenli tried to keep his face composed, but the truth was, his heart was thudding triple speed. His Meraki Girl dreams kept playing in his mind on a loop, no matter how much he tried to shove them away. Wren. On the beach. The golden thread.

Was he part of her story? What did that even *mean*?

A few beads of sweat trickled down his temples. He was already in enough trouble with the chancellor; the last thing he needed was to get mixed up in some weird magic conspiracy nonsense.

But even worse than that, he couldn't stand not knowing the truth. He'd spent too many years in the dark. His dad. His brother. His mom's dragon statue. Now his family had been taken. All of it meant something. Was it possible Wren could somehow help him get answers? He gritted his teeth as a battle warred inside him. He wanted answers. But he didn't exactly trust Wren—she could be lying. Again. It was what the Meraki were good at, after all.

"All done," Wren declared, setting the empty pot down on the ground and wiping her mouth with her sleeve.

His mom's sleeve.

Shenli's words came out like ice. "What do you mean I'm part of your story?"

"Well . . . Granmama couldn't See specifics, exactly."

He rolled his eyes. "Of course not."

"Seeing isn't always so straightforward. Also, someone is clouding her visions with darkness."

"Something to do with the *restlessness of the realm*, I'm sure."

Wren's eyes widened. "Yes, exactly!"

Shenli gave an even bigger eye roll. "I was *making fun* of you, Wren. You're talking about superstitious nonsense. I don't believe in any of that."

"Well, you should. Because you're part of it."

"I am not a part of *anything* to do with magic." His mind flashed back to the dragon lair and the golden thread, but he shook the thoughts away. He stomped off again, toward the watchtower, and Wren hurried after him.

"Look, I know this is a lot. And it probably sounds strange since your people aren't used to magic."

"Because it's evil."

Wren narrowed her eyes. "*Anyway.* Something bad is coming. Granmama believes I'm meant to help stop it. And you too. Oh, and also Blue."

"Who's Blue?"

Wren shrugged. "I don't know. Haven't met him yet. But I will."

"You know how weird that sounds, don't you?"

"It's not weird when your grandmother is the greatest Seer in the world."

"Right. So why did she want you to find me?"

Wren rubbed her stone pendant a few times before answering. "I think you are meant to help too. To stop the darkness that is coming."

Shenli dragged a palm down his face. "Ugh. I've got enough troubles of my own. I really can't deal with"—he gestured to her—"all *this* right now."

"Quite frankly, I don't think you'll have a choice."

"*Quite frankly.*" Shenli matched her accent. "And now I know what your accent really is. Snootery."

"Snootery?"

"Uh. Yeah. Meraki snooty talk."

"You think the Meraki are snobs." Wren didn't say it like a question. More like she was considering his words. She looked at him thoughtfully. "Well, you're not totally wrong. But we're not all like that."

Shenli ran an angry hand through his hair and turned again to walk away. "Just . . . leave me alone."

"I don't think I'm supposed to. I'm meant to help you."

"With *what*?"

"I guess we'll see."

"Fates," Shenli muttered, kicking a pebble. "You're more persistent than a hungry mosquito." He shot her a look. "And just as annoying."

It was Wren's turn to roll her eyes, and Shenli quickened his pace. He supposed he couldn't stop her from following him. So follow him she did. Like a little lost sheep. He found the best thing he could do was ignore her as he trudged through the forest.

The trek to the watchtower took nearly the rest of the day. They snacked on whatever fruit and berries they could find. At one point Wren started blabbing about the Meraki—even though Shenli hadn't asked her about them. She told him about a Council of strict Elders who made all the rules—and there were So. Many. Rules. Their government building sounded like Cudek's castle, except with magical gemstones for a roof—the Meraki crystals, Wren called them. There were magical gardens, trees that smelled like memories, and of course the companion Magics, born from a sacred tree. By the time she started on about invisible canoes, he'd had enough.

"Isn't there *anything* I can do to get you to leave me alone?" he groaned. "You talk more than Meili, and *that* is saying something."

"I suppose if you helped me find my Magic, then I'd leave."

"Hah. Hard pass." Shenli chanced a look at her. She had leaves and twigs in her hair, and she seemed exhausted. Probably because the Meraki were used to lounging around in their fancy houses, not hiking through the wilderness. He almost felt sorry for her, then thought better of it when he remembered she'd stolen his mom's clothes. "Just . . . stop talking, then."

Wren sighed. "Fine."

"Fine," Shenli agreed. Then the two hiked through the dark woods in silence, completely unaware that a little purply-blue cloud was watching them from a distance.

IN WHICH RIVER
LOSES HER WAY

It was a hopeless mess.

Without the map, River had no clue which way to go. Back home, she knew how to tell time and direction based on the position of the sun—any Harvester worth their salt knew that—but that was from her mountaintop. Surely the sun's position meant something different this far north.

They took a chance with Blue's compass but soon found it useless. There weren't proper north and south symbols, just a triangle on one side and three dots on the other. Blue told her the triangle was supposed to lead toward Dragon Mountain. But since the compass was meant to be used in Gerbera, they weren't sure it would work correctly on the other side of the mountain, which was now leagues behind them. They'd also tried to summon back the strange golden thread to lead them, but it had vanished. And neither River nor Blue had any idea what it was, where it came from, or even if they could trust it.

So River did the best she could, since it was the Rider's job to navigate. But every few minutes she mentally kicked herself for losing the blasted map. A few times, the beginnings of an apology hesitated on the tip of her tongue, but each time she stopped herself. She was still too angry about everything.

"Can we stop for a drink?" Blue asked. "There's a river up ahead."

River craned her head. "I don't see it."

"I can hear it."

River grunted. She'd filled her canteen with the cleanest snow she could find at their crash-landing spot, but that had been hours ago and it was already running low.

"Dragons don't have to drink," she told him.

"Well, I want to," Blue grumbled.

"But dragons don't need—"

"River. I *am* a dragon. And I'm telling you. I want a drink."

River clamped her mouth shut grumpily as she followed Blue—who followed his ears—until they found a small river cutting through the woods. The water trickled gently, and a few fish darted by. River's stomach growled. While she'd been taught to fish and hunt, she wasn't particularly good at it.

Blue bent down to take a drink, and River filled her canteen. For some reason, Sage Jackson's annoying grinning face came to mind. Sage was probably a great hunter. River muttered a few choice words under her breath. Then she picked up a rock and threw it into the water. Her blue dragon scales glittered in the sun, which only darkened her mood.

"River?"

"Ugh. What?"

"I was wondering how your people grow dragons. Your Elder said your ancestors visited the Fates to learn how—is that true?"

River nodded. This was one of her favorite stories, actually. She sat down on a smooth boulder and took a long swig of water. "There is an old woman, older than time, who is the Knower of All Things. Some say she's one of the Fates. Others believe she created the universe."

"She must be *really* old."

"Hush, and listen to the story," River scolded. "So remember, during the wars, the dragons were dying, with no way to repopulate because of the Dragon's Curse. And the Dragon Riders of the age were understandably devastated. To lose one's dragon is to lose one's self—or so the old saying goes." River winced at this as she took another drink of water. She would *never* feel that way about Blue.

"Some of the Dragon Riders made the trek north, across the ocean, to the Knower. It's a treacherous journey, and some lost their lives. But those who made it were given an audience with the Knower. She heard their stories of the female dragons unable to produce younglings. And the Knower wept and wept. Her tears became rain, falling back down to the earth. From the ground where her tears touched, firefruit grew on the world's very first ash tree—on top of Dragon Mountain."

"Did that really happen?" Blue asked. "Or is it like . . . you know, just a kind of nice bedtime story?"

"Our Elders say it's what really happened, but who knows?" River furrowed her brow thoughtfully. "What I do know is our mountain is teeming with natural magic. Supposedly, we have more magic crops than anywhere else in the Northern and Southern Realms." A sharp pang tightened in her chest. She missed her gardens fiercely. What she wouldn't have given to bury her hands in some nice cool magic soil at that moment. "Anyway, the Knower said to grow dragons using three magic ingredients: firefruit, moonberries, and stardust. Given to a nonmagic human host."

"Okay. And why do you need kings?"

"We don't. But Gerbera keeps sending them."

"Uh . . . what?" Blue sat down beside her. "I thought kings were essential to the whole growing-of-the-new-dragons bit."

"Nope. We don't need kings specifically. We only need a non-magic human. It's Gerberans who decided it would be their king and made it tradition. But it could be anyone."

"Huh." Blue pondered this. "I guess it's because Gerberans believe the king should be the bravest of us all. We're raised to be that way."

River scoffed. "Gerberan traditions are totally outdated. If you're going to insist on having a royal ruler, why not let a woman give it a go?"

"What . . . you mean like a queen?"

"Are you saying girls can't be brave?" River snapped.

"I—no! I didn't mean that!"

"It's *ridiculous*, Blue. Your people migrated from the Mainland to the Southern Realm over a thousand years ago, and they've always *only* had kings. As if men are the only ones good enough to rule."

Blue's head drooped a bit. "I've . . . never thought about it before."

"Of course you haven't. You're just as stuck in the past as all the other Gerberans."

Blue stayed quiet for a long while, lost in his pondering. "You're right, you know. There's nothing about being a boy that makes a better ruler. I mean, Suri is the most talented and cleverest of all the stable servants. It isn't fair to only have kings." He tilted his head, considering. "Do other kingdoms have queens?"

"Well, my nana was our Chief Elder for hundreds of years until she . . ." River fought the lump in her throat. "Anyway, that's when Cyrus took over. And the island Meraki Chief Elder is Madam Madera, the one who summoned us. Our ancestors have always seen all people equally. Even the Mainlanders have had non-male leaders, though not currently." She shrugged. "It's really not that hard to understand. Only Gerberans can't seem to get their act together."

"Did you know women weren't even allowed to become knights until, like, a decade ago? And that was only after a lot of protests." Blue frowned. "It's pretty unfair, but I don't see things changing anytime soon."

River let out a long sigh. "Yeah, well, my point is, if Gerbera sent us queens, we would happily use them. In fact, our first magic-grown dragon was female."

"Really?"

River nodded. "We messed up, though. We weren't supposed to use a magic human. The Knower was very clear. But this was early on, when the Dragon Growers had first relocated to Dragon Mountain. We hadn't found a way to use a Gerberan yet, so we wanted to try a host of our own. The Chief Elder at the time, Daya, volunteered."

"What happened?"

"She was . . . unstable. Once Daya transformed into a dragon, she still had her human magic in her blood. Plus the new dragon magic. It was . . . too much."

"What do you mean?"

"With so much magic inside her, she couldn't control her fire-breathing. She ended up burning down half of the orchards and some of the houses. When she accidentally burned a little boy, she left. We assume she went to live by herself where she couldn't hurt anyone else."

"That sounds really lonely. Is Daya still alive?"

"We don't know. She never came back. Some of my ancestors went to visit the Knower a second time, and she scolded them for using a magic host when she'd told them not to. And she said that

Daya would forever suffer because of it." River sighed. "We never made that mistake again."

The two sat quiet for a while, lulled by the gentle trickle of the river.

"I can't stop thinking about kings," Blue told her. "I'll admit, it's rotten that my people haven't allowed women to rule. But . . . it's also pretty rotten that your people have been lying to us. All this time, we thought our kings were being eaten."

River pondered this, rubbing sleep from her eyes. Fates, she was tired. "I suppose either way, the king's human life comes to an end. It is a sort of death, isn't it?" She paused, wondering how to phrase her next question. "Do you think it makes it worse for you? Remembering your human life?"

A low whine rumbled through Blue's chest. The saddest sound River had ever heard.

"It's like . . . there's a Something Missing–shaped hole inside me."

"Something missing? Like you've forgotten something?"

"Forgotten my whole *self*. All the human parts are just . . . gone. But I can still feel the hole . . . where they should be. Where *I* should be."

"Oh." Something in Blue's sorrow broke River's heart in two. Stuffing all her frustrations with him deep in her chest, she reached down and laid a hand on his feathery tail.

All this time she'd focused on how terrible it felt to be chosen as a Rider. But like Blue had said, at least she was still human.

"River?"

"Yes?"

"I'm sorry you are sad too."

"I didn't say I was sad."

"You didn't have to. I can smell it."

River wasn't sure what to say to that. Her mind wandered back to her parents. To her mother's swollen belly.

"You must miss your parents."

River arched an eyebrow. "How'd you know I was just now thinking about them?"

"Your Sorrow smells very strong."

"Meraki women usually don't have more than one child. My mom's pregnancy is a miracle," River told him. She picked at the iron flakes on her vest absentmindedly, trying to push her sibling from her thoughts before she completely broke down. "What about you? Who do you miss the most?"

"Cedar. And Suri too."

"Your friends?" she guessed.

"Cedar was my horse." Blue chuckled. "What would she think if she could see me now? And Suri was the closest thing I ever had to a friend, other than Cedar."

"I don't really have friends either," River told him.

"Not a single one?"

River pondered this. There were a bunch of kids she'd grown up with. They went to school together and saw each other often for village gatherings. But truthfully, River was always happiest alone in her gardens. Or at home with her family, poring over whatever books she could get her hands on.

"Is it terrible that I'll miss my plants more than people? Except my parents, of course."

"Well, I'll mostly miss my horse, so I guess we're even."

River laughed for the first time in days, and the homesickness ache in her chest throbbed painfully, only this time making a sliver of room for Blue's sadness too. She was still a little mad at him, but whether she liked it or not, their fates were now wrapped up together. They were meant to be a team.

Just then, a low growl rang out across the water. Blue pricked up his ears and jumped to his feet. He sniffed the air, then crouched to his belly. "River . . . get on my back slowly."

"But the harness is all wonky. I haven't had a chance to readjust—"

"River. *Now.*"

Blue's icy tone shot through River as she obediently climbed onto his back. Since he'd been sitting, the oversized harness had slid uselessly to one side, so she sat on Blue's bare back, gripping handfuls of feathers.

Blue stood up and started to run. He leaped across the water just as a pack of wolves burst from the bushes. River hugged Blue's neck as five wolves spread out into a V formation behind them. Blue may have been a powerful dragon, but he was still shaky on his feet. And these wolves were fast. They all seemed to have their yellow eyes fixed on her. And they looked hungry. One of them managed to jump onto Blue's tail, but Blue flicked it off, slamming it into a tree trunk. The other four raced ahead, undeterred.

As Blue pounded onward, River was too focused on the wolves to take note of where they were going. The forest around them started to change. The tree trunks were thicker here, and stretched so high River couldn't see the tops through the dense canopy that plunged them into darkness. The smell was different too. Old and musty, like they were in a damp cave.

Suddenly, as Blue raced past the next tree, an enormous boulder sat in their path. Blue slid to a halt, and the force of his sudden stop threw River forward. She flew through the air and landed on some prickly shrubs. In a flash, the wolves surrounded her, baring their dagger-sized teeth.

Then the biggest one, the leader, crouched, ready to pounce.

34.

IN WHICH WREN ONLY
MAKES THINGS WORSE

Wren trekked on after Shenli, through forests and over hills, with the sun sinking behind them. Wren had tried to be friendly, sharing stories from home, but Shenli was colder than an icy wind. She was beyond exhausted and not at all enjoying Shenli's rude company, but Granmama had told her this boy was important, so she felt she needed to stick around and find out why. Besides, it wasn't like she had anywhere else to go until she found her Magic.

If she found her Magic.

"Why'd your Magic leave, anyway?" asked Shenli, breaking several hours of silence.

Wren's head snapped up. "I was just thinking about it—how'd you know?"

"Maybe I'm a magical Seer too." Shenli waggled his eyebrows, then frowned. "Ugh. Nope. Can't even joke about that. Makes my stomach queasy."

Wren rolled her eyes. "You're the one who brought it up, you baby."

"Hey." Shenli put his hands on his hips. "I was just trying to make conversation. Turns out I can handle only so much silence."

Wren adjusted her rucksack on her shoulder. In the past few hours, her eel welts had nearly disappeared, thanks to the enderberry mash. She'd tried to thank Shenli for this countless times, but he'd just grunted at her. At least now he was talking to her. That was an improvement.

"I'm not sure why the Magic ran off," Wren admitted.

"Now you're calling it *the* Magic? Instead of *your* Magic?"

Wren frowned. She hadn't meant to call it that. But truthfully, it hardly felt like *her* Magic. Not with all the trouble it had caused. And besides, they weren't even properly bonded. So *was* it hers? "Granmama thinks it's trying to help somehow."

"You don't sound like you believe that."

Wren shrugged. "I really don't know what to believe. Magics are supposed to be helpful to their human companions. But all it's been to me is a pain." Even as she said it, regret blossomed in her chest. It was a terrible way to talk about a newborn Magic. But the truth was, her feelings were hurt. What if the Magic had only left because it didn't want to be Wren's companion?

What if it had never liked Wren, even from the start?

"Huh. Well, maybe it didn't want to stay with your people because it knows how rotten you all are."

A new kind of fury bubbled through Wren, and she shot Shenli a simmering look. She was tired of trying to be friendly. *"Enough* already."

"What? I'm only speaking truth here."

"Are all Mainlanders so insulting?"

Shenli scoffed. "Are you honestly trying to tell me the Meraki don't deserve it?"

Wren rounded on him. "Are you kidding me right now? Everything that's happened between our people was, like, a *century* ago. Nothing but old war stories!" She stamped her foot. "Let. It. Go. Not that I'm surprised. The Mainlanders know how to hold a grudge. Like your dumb military drill rituals—we can hear the stupid conch shell blaring all the way on our island, you know."

"That's the idea."

"Why can't you let the past be the past? The wars are ancient history."

"The *wars* were only the beginning," Shenli spat. "And they were bad enough, but that's not the *main* reason my people hate yours so much."

Wren stopped walking. "What do you mean?"

Shenli halted beside her. "It's because of the hurricane. Obviously."

Wren's eyebrows scrunched together. "The hurricane?"

"Yeah, *the hurricane.* Sixty years ago, a terrible hurricane hit the west shores of the Mainland. It flooded nearly half of the villages in the Coastal District, including mine."

"You're talking about Declaration Day. A group of Mainlanders broke the peace treaty, crossed the Forbidden Pass, and came to our island by rowboat."

Shenli tightened his jaw. "We only broke the treaty because we were desperate for help."

"Help?" Wren leaned closer. "Uh, your people came to our island and *blamed* us for the hurricane—not to ask for favors. They claimed the storm was caused by magic, but that wasn't true. They then *declared* that they'd build an army and seek revenge. Like I said. Declaration Day."

Shenli gritted his teeth so hard it made a terrible squeaking sound. "That. Is not. What happened. My grandfather was one of the men who was on the boat, Wren. He lost his home and two children in the hurricane. He said they traveled to your island and met with a Meraki man who promised he'd go to the Council and get them to send a rescue party. He *swore* they'd send aid. Only the help never came. The Meraki man *lied*."

Wren clamped her mouth shut. There was no point arguing about the past, anyway. She knew the truth. Most of the Meraki population was old enough to have been there when it happened. Well, it explained why the Mainlanders hated them so much. Even if it was all based on a lie.

Shenli grunted again. "What I don't understand is why the Meraki hate *us* so much."

"Mainlanders are dangerous. I mean, you've built up a massive army for revenge against us." Wren's eyes passed over Shenli's tattered uniform to prove her point.

"The army was because of Cudek. Once he rose to power, he claimed the Meraki would attack us again. We needed an army to protect ourselves. But it had nothing to do with the hurricane or *declaring* anything."

"Either way," Wren said, "your army is a threat. I learned in school that one-tenth of the Mainlander population is in the army—is that true?"

Shenli shrugged. "Well, we don't have Magics to fight with."

"Is *that* what you think Magics are for?" Wren shook her head. "We use Magics to help, not harm."

"Hah. Sure you do."

Wren gave an irritated sigh and shoved her hands in her pockets. Her fingers brushed against a row of round beads. Suddenly, she got an idea. "Hey, I can show you." She pulled out Shenli's bracelet and slipped it onto her wrist. "Magic isn't evil."

Shenli's eyes widened in recognition. "That's mine."

219

"Sorry, I forgot I had it."

"You stole it."

"I didn't really mean to. I was holding it when the soldiers grabbed me and I panicked and shoved it into my pocket."

Shenli balled his fists. "You had no right to take it."

Wren bristled at his tone. He'd been annoyed with her all day, but this was something different. A simmering anger. She took a step back. "I'm really sorry. I'll give it back. I only want to show you something first. Please."

If she could just show him how clever and useful magic was, maybe he wouldn't be so afraid of it. Before he could respond, she rubbed Granmama's amulet and thought up a message to send him. She grinned. "Look at your wrist."

"Umm. Is this a joke?"

"Just look. At your left wrist."

He flipped his hand over and frowned.

"'Hello, soldier'?" he read. Then his eyes shot to hers. "What have you *done*?"

His look of horror dropped a boulder in her gut. "This is a messenger pendant," she said quickly. "I can send you messages because I have something that belongs to you."

"You used *magic* on me?"

"You can send a message back if you want," she tried hopefully. "Touch the message and think what you want to say. It's . . . kinda fun."

"Fun?" The anger in his eyes was hot enough to burn down the forest.

She took another step back. "I—I thought you could see—"

"Wren! That bracelet was a gift from my sisters. Now you've defiled it with *magic!*"

Wren's shoulders crumpled. "Shenli . . . I'm really sorry." She took off the bracelet and held it out to him.

"I can't take it back now—it's cursed!"

"It's not—" Wren sighed through her nose. It was no use.

Shenli turned and took off without her. Wren was tempted not to follow. More than anything, she longed to go back to Granmama's canoe and head home. She'd rather be a weird outcast at home than hated here on the Mainland.

The Magic probably would never even miss her.

Wren wiped her cheeks.

And then her grandmother's voice floated through her, like thick, persistent fog—the kind where you can't see where you're going.

Trust will not be easily won—for either of you.
All I can tell you is that he is important.

Wren's whole body folded into a new level of exhaustion. She missed home. She didn't want to be here. She was furious at the Magic for getting her into this mess. Still, she knew she had to keep going. Returning home empty-handed—and without following Granmama's guidance—would be the worst mistake of all.

So she put one foot in front of the other and followed Shenli like a reluctant shadow. He responded with only a grunt. The two pressed on as the trees parted into a vast golden meadow bathed in dusk light. In its center, an old stone watchtower stood ominously against the rising moon.

35.

IN WHICH AN OLD
WATCHTOWER HOLDS
MANY SECRETS

The watchtower stood taller than three dragons stacked on top of one another, and Wren couldn't remember ever being so high up in her life. By the time she and Shenli had scaled the cold metal ladder to the tower platform above, she felt she was soaring with the falcons. For a moment, all the drama with Shenli faded away as she whirled around in wonder. The stars! She could nearly touch them. The moon! It dipped down to her ear, ready to whisper its secrets.

She could see *everything*. Forests hugged the earth, right up to the land's edge. Fires winked at her from villages far away. She even imagined Cephas waving at her from across the ocean. She waved back with a big grin.

Shenli eyed her strangely. "You really are something, you know that?"

Something.

Yes.

She felt a whole lot of *something,* up on the tower that reached to the heavens. The Mainland—the *Mainland*!—stretched out before her like a vivid map. Her people, in all their elegance and wisdom, had never seen *this*. Not this beauty. This land. Maybe the Mainland was dangerous. But it was breathtaking too. With golden meadows and wet markets and flowers she'd never seen before. And so much life happening. All of it was new to her. And Granmama was right— the Mainland called to Wren like a song.

"Let me do the talking, okay?" said Shenli.

"Sure, sure," said Wren, reluctantly pulling herself from the singing hills below and turning to the small metal door set in the stone wall.

Shenli knocked three times, waited, then knocked twice more. The uncertainty in his eyes was hard to miss. The door creaked open and a dark figure peeked through the gap.

"State your business," said a gruff voice. Wren took a step back in alarm, glancing at Shenli. He'd better be right about this.

"The water's looking fine this evening," said Shenli. "And I thought I'd go for a swim."

Wren scrunched her eyebrows. What in the world was he talking about?

The door opened wider, and two russet-brown arms flung outward so fast Wren felt certain Shenli was about to be attacked. Instead, the arms wrapped around Shenli in a hug.

"You death-defying rascal!" A face emerged. It was a young man with wavy black hair, several years older than Shenli.

"I'm surprised you remembered the password after all this time," Shenli told him.

"How could I forget?" The young man laughed. "Come inside. I'm on solo duty for another two hours."

Wren followed Shenli, the door clicking shut behind them. They stood in a circular room with a large desk and floor-to-ceiling windows on one side that overlooked the surrounding forests. The other side of the wall was completely covered in maps and an assortment of posters about military protocols and procedures.

Wren eyed the largest map with interest. It showed the five districts of the Mainland: The Coastal District, where Shenli lived, was to the west, and the enormous Mountain District to the east—Shenli had said that was home to all the rich people, who wore expensive colorful clothes. The Middle District sat right between the two. The sketch showed a large stone castle surrounded by towns filled with trade markets. Wren could even see little vendor stalls sprinkled about. To the north was the Char District, its ominous volcano surrounded by scorched earth, completely devoid of people. The Parch District, to the far south, was equally abandoned. The vast Wasteland desert filled up most of the district, with a smattering of village ruins dotting the borders. Seven dragon symbols were showed scattered through the various districts.

Those markings must be where the Mainland dragons were stationed.

Wren stared in wonder. She'd never seen a modern map of the Mainland. Other than her father and the Council, she might be the only Meraki who had. Most of the maps in the history books were from centuries ago, when the Meraki used to live on the Mainland—long ago when it was called Haven.

She turned her attention back to the boys. A single lantern lit the room, casting long shadows across the hardwood floor. A wave of goose bumps rose on Wren's arms and neck. She took a seat next to the windows, peering below. She wondered how far they'd walked from Shenli's village. Ten miles? More? She sighed.

The Magic was out there somewhere. She hoped it was safe. And keeping out of trouble.

Wren scoffed. *That* was unlikely.

"Ranji, this is Wren."

Ranji's dark brown eyes narrowed slightly. "New friend of yours?"

Shenli didn't answer. Instead, he turned to Wren. "Ranji used to live next door before he got drafted into the military. He's a scoundrel, but a good-hearted one."

"Nice to meet you," said Wren, though her manners felt stiff in this strange cold place. She couldn't help noticing that Ranji's eyes kept flicking to the door.

But then his face broke into a wide grin as he ruffled Shenli's hair. "I used to run around with Shen's older brother, Yuli, before . . ." Ranji cleared his throat, his gaze dropping to his boots for a moment before he looked back at Wren. "Anyway, Shenli here's always been a good kid." He gave Shenli a playful punch on the shoulder. "And now he's growing up and going off on special missions for the chancellor, from what I hear."

"The mission didn't exactly go well," Shenli admitted.

Wren leaned forward, eager to hear details about Shenli's mysterious story.

"And my family's been transferred."

Ranji nodded sadly. "I heard. Terrible shame."

"Do you know where they've been taken? I know you keep in contact with Alizah."

"Alizah?" Wren asked before remembering that Shenli was supposed to do the talking.

"Commander Anja Alizah is my aunt," Ranji explained, puffing out his chest a bit. Clearly this information was supposed to be impressive.

Wren tried to follow along. "Commander . . . in the military?"

Ranji shot her a questioning look, as if she should have already known that.

"Why were they taken?" Shenli cut in.

Ranji let out a slow breath. "Alizah sent me word this morning.

Your family still owes Cudek a big loyalty tax, so . . ." He shrugged. "I mean, *you* can't pay off debts if you're dead."

All the blood drained from Shenli's face. "But it hasn't even been twenty-four hours since my mission! Doesn't Cudek have better things to do than deal with the family debts of a random servant boy?"

"Clearly, it's important, because Cudek had your family transferred to level-one prison in the Middle District."

"Level *one*?"

Wren could almost feel the fear rising hot off Shenli's body.

"But my sisters . . . They're just kids."

Ranji shook his head. "It's terrible, it really is. Cudek's real amped up these days. He's lashing out at everyone. And as for your family? Well, the Zhaos have burned too many bridges. They're all out of chances."

Shenli shifted his stance, eyeing the Mainland map on the wall. "Ranji . . ." Shenli started slowly, as if uncertain. "What word do you have of the dragon lair in the Coastal District?"

Ranji's eyes grew dark. He gave Wren a long look before answering. "They say the dragon's been put to sleep—permanently."

Wren gasped. "Permanently?"

"Not dead, mind you," said Ranji. "Just in a deep sleep. The same thing's happened with the Parch District and Mountain District fire-breathers. All of them asleep."

"So Cudek's taking out the dragons, one by one," said Shenli, crossing his arms.

Something terrible churned in Wren's stomach.

Taking out the dragons?

"It's some kind of sleeping gas," said Shenli. "I saw it myself."

"That have something to do with your blue hand?" Ranji asked.

Shenli shrugged. "Not sure how that happened, actually."

Wren hugged herself. Even the Meraki knew of the chancellor's cruelty and hunger for power. Her father heard all kinds of stories when the Mainland Dragon Riders checked in with him. "Without the dragons protecting the people, Cudek is free to do whatever he wants, right?"

Ranji scoffed. "The dragons don't *protect* us. They're the enemy." He shot a look at Shenli. "Where'd you find this girl, anyway?"

Shenli hesitated a moment, then waved a dismissive hand. "It's okay. She's cool."

Wren shivered. Shenli considered her to be many things, she knew, but *cool* wasn't one of them. Was he trying to protect her? She frowned. *That* was unlikely.

"There's something else too," said Ranji, his voice dropping to a whisper. He gave a sidelong glance at the window wall. "You've been spotted. Earlier today, leaving your village. Cudek thought you were dead this morning. But he's surely been informed by now. You're most likely being tracked."

Shenli let out a long breath, running his blue hand through his dark hair. "I don't know what to do, Ranji."

Ranji frowned. "You're in a tight spot, Shen. I don't envy you. Honestly? You might want to lie low for a while, while Cudek cools off. Maybe then his punishments will be less . . . severe." He walked over to the wall and tapped a finger on the map. "I have some cousins in Mackinaw village, Phillip and Skye. They're right on the border of the Parch District. You could hide with them for a few days while you sort things out."

"I don't want to put anyone else in danger."

"Nah, they owe me a favor—lots of favors, actually." Ranji reached down to the desk and scribbled something on a piece of paper.

"Mackinaw village is only a few hours on foot. Just let them see this note from me and you'll be good to go." He folded the paper and handed it to Shenli.

Shenli nodded and tucked the paper into his pocket. "I owe you one."

Ranji shook his head. "I'll never understand why the Zhaos get all the rotten luck. Keep your head up, Shen, you hear?"

Shenli's lips stretched into a grim line. "Course I will."

"I wish you success, friend," said Ranji, gripping Shenli's shoulder. "You have my thanks."

Ranji grinned. "Just *try* to stay out of trouble, eh?"

Shenli laughed. "No promises." He turned to Wren. "Time to go."

Wren's gaze flicked to Ranji. His easy smile fell away as Wren tailed after Shenli out the door and shut it behind her. A slow chill worked up her spine. Something seemed . . . off. Wren took one last look at the beautiful landscape spread out below before following Shenli down the ladder. When they were a few yards away from the tower, she fell into step with him.

"So . . . did that seem weird to you?" she asked.

"What?"

"Ranji. He seemed . . . nervous."

"What are you talking about? He was totally normal."

"He kept looking at the door."

"He did not." Shenli shook his head. "You probably just don't like him because he hates dragons."

"What? No! I mean, you hate dragons too," she pointed out.

"Yeah, and you don't like *me*," he shot back.

Wren frowned. "Why'd you tell him I was cool? Why'd you cover for me?"

Shenli grunted. "Would you have preferred I tell him who you are? He would've had you hauled away to Cudek himself."

"So you were . . . helping me?"

Shenli gave a one-shouldered shrug. "I don't know, okay? It was a split-second decision. And while I find you *annoying*, I don't think you deserve a lifetime locked away in prison—which is what Cudek would do to you, by the way."

"Well, thank you." She paused a beat. "But about Ranji. I really think—"

Shenli threw up his hands. "Ugh. Enough with the Ranji conspiracy already!"

"Shenli, I'm trying to help. And I think something's off about him."

"You don't know what you're talking about. Ranji is basically family. You met him for, what, twenty minutes? And you think you know him?"

"I'm just telling you what I saw."

"Not everything has to be a dramatic story, Wren. It's all darkness and dread with you, isn't it?"

Wren frowned. She'd been called many things back home: clumsy, a dreamer, *an anomaly*—ugh. But never a pessimist. She looked at Shenli, trying to *really* see him. The way Granmama would want her to. With compassion and understanding. But the more time they spent together, the more the edges around Shenli seemed to harden. He went from grumpy to annoyed to truly angry. And she kept doing the wrong things and saying the wrong things.

She didn't understand her purpose here.

Maybe she was only supposed to help him sneak into his house. And he was meant to help heal her wounds. And that was it. Was it possible she was trying to force some kind of invisible thread between them?

"What?" Shenli asked, meeting her gaze. "What is it?"

"I . . . I just . . ." A single tear slipped down her cheek, and she swiped it away. Shenli was the last person she wanted to cry in front of. Then again, she felt so tired and emptied out. . . . What did it really matter, anyway? "I thought once I came to the Mainland I'd know what to do next. I mean, I found *you*. But I still don't know who Blue is or if I'll ever see the—my—*my* Magic again." She squeezed her eyes shut to keep them from leaking. "Nothing makes sense."

Shenli stopped walking. He put his hands on his head and let out a heavy sigh, peering up at the sky. A few stars winked down on them. Wren thought of her mother and her heart clenched with an impossible ache.

"My dad used to take me stargazing," Shenli said after a long while. "He said the stars connect all people because we all see the same sky." His arms fell to his sides and his gaze snagged on Wren's. "There's something I haven't told you."

"What's that?"

"I . . . Geez, this is embarrassing." He ran a hand through his hair. "I've had dreams about you."

Wren's mouth fell open a bit.

"Nothing *weird*," he said quickly. "Just you standing on a beach. With this magical golden thread thingy."

Wren's heart quickened. "When was this?"

"I've had the same dream a handful of times over the past few years." He shrugged. "Last time was right before I went to work for Cudek. I remember because I actually saw the thread on the way to the castle."

"You . . . saw a golden thread?" Wren bit her lip, trying to remember some of Granmama's old stories about foxes and Fates and golden thread on a loom.

Shenli made a face. "I mean, I *think* I saw it. But I was also super nervous that morning, so I probably just imagined it. Anyway, I'd forgotten about the dreams. Even when I first met you, it didn't click. I didn't realize it was *you* until later."

Wren sucked in a deep breath. Everything about this boy was peculiar and unexpected. "Thank you for telling me."

"I guess what I'm saying is . . . today has been really weird. Like, *epic* strangeness."

"Agreed." Wren smiled.

"And I've been angry about a lot of other stuff with my family, and then you showed up with your sparkly eyes and your magic talk."

"You think my eyes are *sparkly*?" Wren teased, raising an eyebrow. Even in the moonlight, she caught the red in Shenli's cheeks.

"I . . . *No*, that's not the point. The point is I've been in a hard place, and you came along and, quite frankly, made things harder." He threw up his hands again. "Basically, you're just . . . impossible. And I don't know what to do with you."

"If it helps, I don't know what I'm supposed to do either."

"Mmm. Nope. Doesn't help."

Wren laughed. Shenli smiled at her then, and it sent Wren's insides spinning into unforgivable flutters.

"So maybe we can call a truce," said Shenli. "I'll try not to be such a jerk, and you stop talking about all the Magic Story Destiny stuff. Because it's freaking me out. I mean, not that I *believe* any of it."

"Uh-huh. Of course you don't. And you have a deal."

The two of them shook hands.

It was only when they started walking again, in the moon shadow of the tower, that Wren remembered what Ranji had said. That they were being watched. As they hiked on, Wren's shoes sinking into the wet grass, she couldn't shake the feeling that someone was going to jump out and grab them at any moment.

36.

IN WHICH A SPOOKY FLOWER
IS RATHER SUSPICIOUS

The snarling wolf leaped at River before she could blink. Its sharp teeth sank into her left shin as she kicked its head hard with her other foot. It let go of her leg, momentarily stunned. River looked around frantically for somewhere to hide, but she was wedged between the prickly shrubs in front and a massive tree trunk at her back.

She was trapped.

Just as the wolf was about to lunge at her again, Blue barreled forward with a swift swipe of his claw. The wolf was tossed into the shrubs with a yelp. The small dragon threw his body between River and the remaining wolf pack as he let out a low growl.

The wolves snarled angrily in response.

A low rumble sputtered from Blue's throat. He coughed a few times, then let out an earsplitting roar like nothing River had ever heard. Like wild thunder cracking open the sky, shaking River's entire body.

The wolves each slunk down with their ears flattened against their heads. Blue bared his teeth and pawed the ground with one foot, like he was readying to charge. One by one, the wolves tucked their tails between their legs and scampered off, whimpering all the way, kicking up a trail of blue feathers in their wake. Once they were out of sight, River jumped off the shrubs, little prickly burrs sticking to her everywhere.

"I'm molting," Blue said, wincing at the blue feathers now tossing in the wind, his silvery chest still heaving.

River gaped at the dragon wide-eyed. "You . . . saved me."

Blue turned to face her. "I . . . didn't know I could roar like that."

"That was really brave." River exhaled her relief. "I thought I was a goner."

Blue sat down next to her. The feathers on his head were ruffled like he had a bad case of bed head. "Sorry about your leg."

She looked down at the deep bite marks in her left leg, which throbbed something fierce. Her boot had taken most of the damage—turned out boots were useful after all!—but there was a deep red stain forming on her shin. She swung her bag around and pulled out a small bottle. She uncapped it and poured the silvery liquid onto her puncture wounds.

"Smells like . . . musky honey?" Blue guessed.

"It's poplar-tree venom."

"Trees have *venom*?"

"Ghost poplar trees do." River held still until the liquid hardened. "That'll stop the bleeding for a little while."

Blue stared at the silver patch curiously; then his gaze flitted to hers. She wondered if she'd ever get used to his bright blue dragon eyes. She cleared her throat a few times. "You are doing the dragon thing just fine, by the way," she told him. "That was an excellent roar."

"Er—thanks." Blue sat up a little straighter.

River's eyes fell to her boots. "I shouldn't have blamed you for my losing the map. It was my job to take care of it."

Blue lowered his head to match her eye level. "I shouldn't have given you such a hard time. We're both new at this."

"You said you had a bad feeling about the mountains." She sighed. "I know dragons have great instincts and I still didn't trust you. Now we're stuck here."

"We'll find a way out. Just one step at a time, right?"

"Right," River agreed. That had always been Nana's mantra. There was no problem that couldn't be solved by attacking it one step at a time. "First, let's try to get our bearings."

River spun around, taking in their surroundings as she plucked the burrs from her clothes. They stood in a large, dark clearing surrounded by enormous ancient oak trees. "These trees . . . Don't they look—"

"Like they're grouped in a perfect circle all around us?" Blue finished for her. "Yup. It's freaking me out."

It was true. The trees formed a circle around the clearing. The boulder River and Blue had nearly crashed into was one of five, each at a different point around the circumference, equidistant from the others.

"You were right to have a bad feeling about going this way," whispered River. "We should've gone through the meadow. This place gives me the chills."

"Hey, what's that?" Blue nodded to the center of the clearing.

While the sun stole through a few patches, the center of the clearing was completely dark. Still, even in the dense shadows, River could see something small taking shape. She held her breath as they stepped nearer.

"It's . . . a flower," Blue whispered.

Sure enough, a single glowing flower stood several feet tall in the gloom. Two large black leaves spread out, like a bat in flight. In the center of the flower were three wilted white blooms with long thin red tendrils twisting out of them all the way to the ground.

"I've never met a flower I didn't like," whispered River. "But *that* is creepy."

Blue snorted, then took a step back into one of the small beams of sunlight peeking through the treetops. "Do you . . . smell that?"

River threw one last look at the flower, then made her way to join him. She sniffed. "Hmm. I think so. I'm getting hints of chamomile. And burned lavender, maybe? And . . ." She gagged. "Ugh. And something rotten."

Blue's head drooped. "Mmm-hmm."

River glanced around the clearing. Her arm hairs started to prickle. "Blue, we need to keep going."

Blue stumbled a bit, nearly knocking into her. "I think you're right, but I'm just . . . so tired. All of a sudden."

"Blue, we aren't safe here." River's eyes darted to the shadows around them. A wolf howl echoed in the distance. She gave Blue's leg a shove, but she might as well have been trying to move an elephant.

A feathery blue elephant.

"Blue, *please*." But the dragon wouldn't budge. Instead, he plopped down on his rear and stretched his front legs. He looked like an overgrown cat. When he fell to his knees and slumped over on his side, River threw her hands up in the air in defeat.

"Ugh! Now is *not* the time to be difficult, Dragonboy!"

Blue laid his head down, totally oblivious to River's pleading. He looked at her, droopy-eyed, with his tongue hanging out. "S-sorry. Just s-sooo s-sleepy."

"Worst time ever for a nap! Because we need to— Whoa," River swayed suddenly on her feet. All at once she felt like someone had wrapped her in a weighted blanket that was trying to pull her to the ground. Her eyes felt ridiculously heavy.

She fell to her knees. Blue was already snoring beside her. She knew she shouldn't sleep. Not here. They weren't safe. And yet all she wanted to *do* was sleep. The ground called to her, warm and inviting. Her eyelids drooped and she fell over, her body resting on Blue's fluffy side. Before she closed her eyes completely, she could see the creepy flower, glowing through the darkness.

And the last thing she heard before drifting off was a voice, slithering in the air around them. A gravelly whisper that said:

"At last. We've found them."

37.

IN WHICH THERE IS A MOST UNFORTUNATE DEVELOPMENT

By the time Shenli and Wren neared Mackinaw village, the moon hung high overhead and crickets were singing their midnight songs all through the meadow. Looking past the tall grass, Shenli eyed the small twinkling lights up ahead, where the village slept soundly.

Shenli rubbed the back of his neck. "Hope Ranji's cousins don't mind us coming in the middle of the night."

"Shenli, why is Cudek after you?"

Shenli blew out a long breath. He wasn't sure how much to tell her. He felt a connection to Wren somehow. Maybe because of his dreams? It was confusing and unsettling. But he didn't trust her. He could never fully trust a Meraki. Because even though she'd been kind to him, Wren was a thief who was willing to betray her people's laws and loyalty—what did that say about her?

Besides, Shenli still wasn't sure what Wren really wanted.

"I don't know why he's after me," Shenli answered carefully. "But I do know he's planning something big with the dragons." He opted not to talk about the exploding orbs. "And for some reason, he's roped me and my family into his plans."

"Because your family owes him a debt, like Ranji said?"

"My family's done a lot to upset Cudek. Our debt was supposed to be reduced to seven years after last night's mission." Shenli gritted his teeth, again furious at himself for blowing it. "But I guess it will all depend on Cudek's mood."

"He seems like a horrible person."

"He's not horrible, he's *powerful*," Shenli told her. "He's got a terrible temper, maybe, which makes it scary to work for him sometimes. But he protects us. He built an army from nothing, and he's kept our people safe."

Wren frowned. "The Meraki think Cudek finds magic on the Mainland and steals it for himself. Our Mainland Dragon Riders have shared reports of—"

"*That* is just absurd," Shenli cut in, shaking his head. "He hates magic. He hunts it down and destroys it. That's half of what the military does these days."

"But what if he *is* hoarding magic? Couldn't that explain what makes him so powerful?"

Shenli scoffed. "I'm telling you, there's no way Cudek wants anything to do with magic except to destroy it." Shenli let out a shaky sigh, his eyes falling to Wren's amulet swaying in the moonlight. He was more than ready for a change of topic. "Can you tell me about your family, Wren?"

He wondered. Were they all so . . . strange? So brave? So impossible?

Wren smiled. "I live with my grandmother, my father, and my little brother. Granmama is wonderful and whimsical—always hinting at prophecies and old songs and such. She's my best friend. My brother is clever and responsible and my whole world. And growing up *way* too fast for my liking, by the way."

"My sisters do the same, completely without my permission," Shenli agreed. "What's your dad like?"

Wren frowned. "My father . . . is complicated. He used to be kind and attentive. But after Mama passed—" She closed her eyes. "Well, he'd rather hang out with the dragons than me."

Shenli made a face. "He *hangs out* with dragons?"

Wren smiled. "Hanging out with dragons isn't scary where I'm from, especially for my dad. He's the Dragon Master. He trains dragons and Riders to work together. He's also in charge of giving them their assignments—where they patrol. That kind of thing. He sometimes helps with medical stuff too. Dragon injuries and such."

Shenli's stomach tightened as he thought of the red dragon he'd nearly blown up the night before. Wren eyed him curiously.

"Your mother . . . ," Shenli said softly, knowing he was treading on painful ground. "I thought your people were basically immortal."

"No," said Wren, inhaling in a sharp breath. "Our Magics help us live a long time. And the island is a very safe place. But accidents"—she winced—"can happen."

Shenli shoved his hands in his pockets, tapping the little doll and the dragon statue with his thumb. He gazed up at the sky. Out here in the meadow, without any lanterns, the stars seemed to stretch on forever.

"Your mom's name was Rose, wasn't it?" he guessed.

Wren nodded, and Shenli could nearly feel her sorrow sweep over him.

"My dad was killed when I was little." He closed his eyes. "He got into some big trouble with Cudek, and, well, my mother's never been quite whole since then." Shenli sighed, pushing away the swelling of grief in his chest. "And neither have I."

"I understand."

239

There was a stillness in the night air as they finally reached the edge of Mackinaw village. Through a smattering of trees, small dilapidated houses lined the main road. A light breeze whipped through the village, lifting a swirl of dead leaves. Shenli's neck hairs stood up abruptly. Something didn't feel right. He took a step in front of Wren just as a shout rang through the silence. Then a squadron of soldiers poured into the street up ahead, swords raised.

"Fates, it's an ambush!" Shenli turned to Wren, who gaped at the soldiers creeping closer to them.

Then her terrified eyes flicked to Shenli.

"You . . . you set me up?"

Shenli staggered a step backward. "What? No! This wasn't me."

"You wanted them to capture me?" She took a step back.

"Wren, no! Ranji must've sent us into a trap."

Fates, she'd been right about Ranji all along! She held Shenli's gaze. Her copper eyes shone even brighter in the moonlight, wide with terror.

"Wren, I didn't do this. *Please* believe me."

Sucking in a breath, Wren took off running back through the meadow. Shenli watched her go with a stab of sorrow in his chest. He took a step to go after her, but the sound of cold metal sliding from a sheath stopped him.

"Shenli Zhao!"

Shenli turned to face the squadron of soldiers as one of them stepped forward. Commander Alizah. She held her sword pointed right at him. "Don't take another step, Zhao," she warned.

Shenli shot one last look at the meadow. He could barely see Wren's outline fading into the night as a handful of soldiers ran after her. Mercy, he hoped she'd get away. Behind him, the wind whipped over the tall grass like a sad song.

"You are under arrest, by order of Chancellor Cudek," Alizah told him.

Shenli stiffened. "But I haven't done anything wrong!"

Alizah narrowed her eyes. "We'll let the chancellor be the judge of that." She nodded to the horse next to her. "Get on. You're to report to him immediately."

Shenli swallowed hard. With much reluctance, he mounted the horse and turned to follow Alizah north, toward the castle. Apparently Bad Luck wasn't through with the Zhao family after all.

PART IV

SENDING
DRAGONS

38.

*T*here *is a song whispered through every creature across the realms. The Fates warned us, but no one pays any mind to the Fates anymore.*

Even though they should.

And because we wouldn't listen, the Fates had to write it across our hearts.

Can you hear it, kit?

No. I suppose not. You are so very young, after all.

Well, I can sing part of it for you:

A DRAGON WAKES WHEN THE FULL MOON PEAKS
HE AND HIS RIDER MUST FIND THEIR TRUST
WHEN THE MAGIC FLEES
THE COMPANION SNEAKS
THE SOLDIER BOY WILL DO AS HE MUST

39.

IN WHICH WREN IS VERY MUCH ALONE

Wren raced through the moonlit meadow. A small group of soldiers took off after her, swords drawn. Legend had it that the ancient Meraki, in the throes of war, could run like the mighty lions of the mountains, and she believed it now as she fled across the meadow as if death reached for her heels. She could hear the soldiers breathing as their feet pounded after her through the tall grass.

There was an explosion behind her, and a flash of purple light. Were they throwing bombs at her? A gust of wind swirled around her; then she heard only silence. She raced onward until she couldn't anymore, clear past the watchtower and into the coastal forest where she'd tried to teach Shenli to send magic messages.

She collapsed into some leaves, her chest burning as she gasped for air. She shivered, drenched with sweat, her stomach knotted with fear. She couldn't shake the image of all those soldiers with swords and bombs. How long before they found her again?

And what would happen to Shenli?

She gritted her teeth. No, she wouldn't worry about *him*. He'd set her up! She was sure of it now. That was why he'd allowed her to accompany him to talk to Ranji. Somehow, Shenli had secretly passed along the message that Wren was Meraki, and the trap had been set. Catching a Meraki would surely be enough to put Shenli back into the good graces of the chancellor. He'd get to see his mom and sisters again.

If they captured Wren.

Slowly, Wren pushed herself to her feet, her legs throbbing in protest as she limped onward. She tried to convince herself that the pain in her chest was only because of her long sprint. But she knew it was more than that. She felt betrayed. First the Magic. Now Shenli.

And her whole body ached with it.

It was ridiculous, really. That a boy she'd just met could hurt her this deeply—and a Mainlander boy at that! They weren't even friends! But during the last few hours, it had felt like they were starting to connect. Shenli had apologized and opened up about his father.

Now she knew it was all a ruse.

Wren hugged her arms tighter against her chest. What was she supposed to do now? Finding Shenli had almost been too easy. As if she'd been drawn to him by an invisible thread. Now there was no thread.

Then, like the flicker of a lantern coming to life, terrible images filled her head. Of glowing eyes and huge snakelike bodies. The darkness around her suddenly felt like deep water pushing in on her. And though she knew it was impossible for eels to reach her in the forest, she started imagining them slithering through the trees, coming for her. She let out a sob, trying to blink the terrible nightmares away.

A deep groan crackled through trees, and the ground trembled beneath her. The eel echoes vanished, and Wren gritted her teeth, shooting an angry glance at the grass under her vibrating shoes.

"I know that everything's gone wrong! But I can't see what there is to be done about it!"

The ground rumbled in response.

"You can just take your restlessness somewhere else, thank you very much!" Wren shouted, and crossed her arms for good measure.

Ugh. Right. Because yelling at the ground was going to help. But she was too angry and exhausted to think straight. When was the last time she'd slept, anyway? The trembling beneath her finally ceased, and she cast her gaze to the twinkling stars.

"You would know what to do," Wren whispered, wiping a stray tear from her cheek. It was in these moments when everything felt hopeless that she missed Mama the most. "I just feel so lost."

She'd been so sure she was meant to stick with Shenli, but that had clearly turned out to be a disaster. She'd thought she understood her mission. But there was no Blue and no Magic, and now Cudek's soldiers were after her. All she could do was push on and find somewhere safe to hide. So she stumbled through the night until the forests gave way to meadows and grassy hills.

Eventually, she came upon a farmhouse perched atop a hill. Sheep and goats lay snoring in their pens. Wren crept along until she reached a rickety barn full of sleeping cows. A few of them peeked at her with one eye as she scaled the ladder to the hayloft; then they went on snoozing. She dropped down in the middle of the hay piles, exhaustion settling over her like a blanket. She needed to rest. She could make a new plan in the morning. Through a small skylight in the barn roof, stars twinkled down on her.

"I'm sorry, Mama," whispered Wren. "I've made a mess of everything. Like I always do."

And then, somewhere between exhaustion and sleep, the feeling of *aloneness* crashed down on Wren, cracking her chest wide open.

Her tears turned to sobs.

For six years Wren had stuffed down her sadness about Mama's death. She'd tried so hard to be positive and *whole* for Cephas, but she wasn't either of those things on the inside. She'd kept all that from her brother, trying to shield him from sorrow. Because he needed Wren to be strong. The loss of Mama had left not just one hole in their lives, but two: their dad was also gone. He was like an unsmiling shell of himself, spending most days and nights with the dragons. It was like Wren didn't have any parents left. Granmama's kindness was the only thing keeping her going most days.

But Granmama wasn't here.

Mama wasn't here. Mama, who'd always been the one to help Wren find her bravery, was gone.

Really and truly gone.

Even though it had been six years, the pain felt fresh as Wren sobbed into the hay bales well into the night. She wanted so much to be a brave dolphin—to be fearless like Mama. To believe that *she was enough.* But ever since Wren had left home, she'd made one terrible mistake after another. With the eels, with the soldiers, with Shenli.

So she cried for her mistakes. She cried that her mom would never be there to help her navigate her endless tangle of blunders. And somewhere amid the gut-wrenching sadness and tears, something happened to the Mama-shaped hole in Wren's heart. Wren's grief filled it up. It was still painful, but she no longer felt an emptiness. More like a dull throb of *significance.* The hole became . . . a scar.

As Wren finally drifted off to sleep, her mind whirled with terrible nightmares. Of Mama disappearing into the stars. Of slithering eels trying to strangle Wren. Of dragons being poisoned and falling from the sky. Of uniformed soldiers chasing her with fire swords.

And of the brown-eyed Mainlander boy who had betrayed her.

40.

IN WHICH SHENLI HAS A
VERY IMPORTANT MEETING

Shenli had ridden through the night to the castle without a wink of sleep, haunted by the look in Wren's eyes just before she'd run away. It was eating at him that she clearly believed he'd betrayed her. Shenli certainly hadn't entirely trusted Wren, but he'd never meant her any actual harm.

Shenli now sat at a large oak desk next to an oversized fireplace in Cudek's private study. Vast bookshelves spread from floor to ceiling along the walls, filling the air with the scent of musty parchment. He'd been summoned here countless times over the years, whenever Cudek had a new research project for him or errands to run. But Shenli had never been invited for a formal meeting. Whatever Cudek was up to, Shenli would have to convince the chancellor this was all just a big misunderstanding. Then everything would get sorted out to how it was before, wouldn't it? With Shenli just two breaths away from getting his family debts cut in half and finally getting answers about his dad?

Shenli closed his eyes, his last memories of his father and the two soldiers on the beach painfully resurfacing. By now, Shenli had convinced himself that *the secret* mentioned in the orb box had something to do with his dad. Maybe even something to do with his mom and the little dragon statue. Whatever the secret was, it would lead Shenli one step closer to understanding the truth about his family. But he would have to be careful. Cudek was apparently furious with him, and there was nothing to stop the chancellor from making Shenli's mother and sisters disappear permanently.

To pass the time, Shenli scanned the various papers and books scattered all over Cudek's desk. There were rolled-up scrolls and sketches of various plants. Maps and charts and things written in a language Shenli didn't recognize. On the paper closest to him was a drawing of a strange flower. Two huge black leaves fanned out like bat wings behind some droopy white blooms. Red stringy things hung down from the center like long thin snakes. It was eerie and disturbing. He couldn't stop staring at it.

The study door creaked open. The quiet footfalls on the carpet made Shenli's neck hairs shoot up. Chancellor Cudek sat down on the other side of the desk, the firelight casting strange shadows on his face.

"I see you've discovered the chimera bloom." The chancellor nodded to the flower drawing.

"I've never seen anything like it."

"It's remarkable, isn't it?"

Shenli frowned. "It's . . . super creepy."

"Legend has it, the chimera bloom allows a person to spy on someone on the other side of the world. You can see them. Hear them. Even speak to them."

Shenli eyed the drawing again. "Do you think it's real?"

Cudek pushed his fingertips together. "That would really be something, wouldn't it?" He leaned forward across the desk. "But we aren't here to talk about mythological flowers."

Shenli inhaled a shaky breath. "Sir, my mom and sisters—"

"—are not your concern."

Shenli paled. "Can I see them?"

"Absolutely not. Do not ask again." Cudek shifted in his chair. "Now. Tell me why you abandoned your mission, Zhao."

Shenli gripped the armrests. Each of his words mattered now. "I didn't abandon it, sir. I completed the mission."

Cudek narrowed his eyes. "I assumed you were dead. Then I get reports of you showing up in your home village, when you *should* have reported back to me immediately. Given your family's history of treasonous betrayal, I thought you'd have more sense. Especially traveling around with that strange companion of yours."

Shenli looked at his hands, his blue palm shining in the firelight.

"I didn't think it through, sir. I apologize. I thought I was dead too, buried under a heap of rubble. The next morning, when I came to, everyone was gone except the firebreather. I got scared, and I went home to check on my family." *The family you stole,* Shenli wanted to add, but he held his tongue.

"Do you know what happened in the dragon lair, boy?"

Shenli frowned, thinking of the orbs and the explosions. "Not really," he admitted. "I know the dragon got knocked out by the green smoke, but that blue orb . . ."

Cudek nodded for him to continue, his eyes revealing nothing. "Go on. I want to hear what you think happened."

"Well, the blue orb was an explosive, sir. Which didn't make sense, because we both know explosives don't work against dragons."

Cudek narrowed his eyes. "The blue orb was for *you,* Shenli."

Shenli's throat went dry.

Mercy of the Fates. Had Cudek tried to *kill* him?

"The explosive was never meant to harm you. It was . . . enchanted."

All the air left Shenli's lungs.

He blinked.

Then he blinked again, replaying Cudek's last word in his mind on a loop.

Surely he'd misunderstood.

"En-enchanted?" he repeated. "Like . . . with *magic*?"

Cudek tapped his fingertips on the table in a steady rhythm. "There are many powers at work here, Zhao."

That didn't answer Shenli's question.

"So . . . you're saying you used *magic*?" Shenli clarified.

"I do what is necessary." The chancellor maintained his steely gaze. "It is not your place to question me."

Shenli was too stunned to register his usual fear of the chancellor's threats. "But . . . magic is evil."

"And we have a war to win."

Shenli slumped in his chair, his mind whirling. His whole life he'd been taught the horrors of magic. How it had been used to kill thousands of Mainlanders during the wars. And *no one* hated magic more than the chancellor. Cudek had spent his entire career snuffing it out, wherever it lingered on the Mainland.

"So all that research on magic you had me do . . . You weren't trying to destroy it. You were learning how to"—Shenli swallowed hard—"*use* it."

Fates. That was exactly what Wren had told him. It was what the Meraki had believed about Cudek all along.

First Ranji. Then Cudek. What else was Wren right about?

Shenli stared at the man before him. He'd always feared Cudek because of his power and respected him for his accomplishments, and he'd felt certain what Cudek stood for—and against.

But now he didn't know anymore.

And that made the chancellor all the more terrifying.

"What's the best way to win a war, boy?"

Shenli shook his head, still too stunned to answer.

"Use your enemy's strengths against them. Or, as the old saying goes: fight dragonfire with dragonfire." He tapped his fingertips against the desk. "In this case, magic is the secret weapon."

"So the blue orb was a weapon?"

"Ah. That was an experiment. My own little protective spell." Cudek sat up a little straighter, clearly proud of himself.

Shenli wanted to be sick. Then something besides nausea rose in him too. A sharp kind of fury, pulsing under his rib cage. The chancellor had risen to power on the promise of purging the Mainland of all magic—of keeping the Mainlanders safe *from magic.* He'd lied to everyone.

"Your little spell didn't work," Shenli scoffed, his fury fueling him with more courage than usual. "It didn't protect me at all. The explosion threw me into the wall and nearly broke my arm."

"And how is your arm now?"

"Actually . . . it's fine," Shenli admitted. Truthfully, he'd forgotten about his injury until now. It hadn't hurt since he'd woken up in the rubble. "But the cave collapsed on me," he pointed out.

"And yet here you are."

Shenli remembered the rubble, arched around him but not actually touching him—was that because of a *spell*? His eyes widened. But then he remembered something else: the strange purplish-blue cloud had been there too.

"The explosion was just a diversion, Shenli. So you could make it out of the dragon lair. Something to distract the others."

"Why?"

"I *had* to know."

"Had to know what?"

"Your secret."

Shenli's heart pounded eagerly. "The orb box said you already knew my secret. Does this have something to do with my father?"

Cudek regarded Shenli for a long moment, the man's mouth pressing into a thin line, all of Shenli's hopes hanging on his next words.

"I have . . . a theory. About you. And I know a great many secrets. Many of them you would be very keen to learn. But now isn't the time."

Shenli's heart plummeted. *"Please—"*

Cudek raised a hand to silence him. "You haven't earned that kind of trust yet. And you're walking a fine line as it is, wouldn't you say?"

Shenli sank back in his chair.

"Speaking of trust—show me your hands."

Shenli obeyed. His blue palm glinted in the firelight, and Cudek nodded, clearly pleased at the sight of it.

"I needed to know if I could trust you to do a job even when it was dangerous. There was a special powder coating the orbs. That's why your hand turned blue. It's proof that you were the one who handled them. Just like I told you to."

"So this whole time my hand's been covered in"—Shenli winced—"in *magic*?"

"Now I know you can be counted on to follow orders."

"Does this mean my debt's been cut in half?"

Cudek considered for a moment. "Sure. Sure it does. I'm a man of my word."

A wave of relief washed through Shenli. This hadn't all been for nothing, at least. "And now that I've returned, you'll let my mom and sisters go, right? I mean, you have no reason to hold them anymore."

Cudek's eyes flashed. "*You* don't get to decide what my reasons are."

Shenli's chest tightened. "Oh, n-no. Of course not, sir. I only meant—"

"Maybe you're not understanding the situation fully." Cudek leaned forward, and the motion caused the creepy flower drawing to flutter slightly. "Your little disappearing stunt was beyond reckless. It was *Yuli* all over again!"

Shenli's cheeks burned.

"And I am not inclined to release your family until you've made it up to me—are we clear?"

Fear squeezed Shenli's insides, but he forced himself to nod.

Cudek inhaled sharply, then sat back in his chair. "As it is, you're off to a decent start." He nodded to Shenli's blue palm. "So that's something."

"This whole thing with the orbs . . . was some kind of test?"

"A test, yes. In more ways than one." Cudek grinned, the hint of a secret on his lips. "We're going to war, Shenli. And I'm going to need soldiers I can depend on."

The word *war* hung in the air, snatching the breath from Shenli's lungs. There was always talk of a new war with the Meraki; it had been so for the past hundred years. But something new flared in Cudek's eyes. Something . . . *immediate.*

"Now, tell me about the girl you were traveling with. No one seems to recognize her."

Shenli hesitated. Wren's glittery copper eyes burned in his mind—that hurt look on her face. Cripes, he didn't want to get her into any trouble. But he also desperately needed to get on Cudek's good side. Another face bubbled into his thoughts: little Yiming, lying on a cold prison floor. Locked away behind bars. She must be terrified. Were they even feeding her?

Shenli squeezed his eyes shut.

"I'm waiting," said Cudek, drumming his fingers on the desk.

Tap, tap, tap.

The truth was, until now, Shenli had always considered the chancellor a man of justice. His rules were strict, and the consequences of breaking them swift, but there was an order and logic to them. A predictable consistency Shenli took comfort in. But keeping children in prison? This was something else. Something . . . darker. Awful as the idea was, Wren's secrets might be the key to his family's freedom.

"I only met her yesterday," said Shenli, trying to ignore the throbbing guilt in his chest. "She claimed . . . to be Meraki."

Cudek sat up straighter. "Meraki?"

"She knew a lot about the island."

"How did she get through the Forbidden Pass with the island dragons on patrol?"

"I—I don't know."

"Why were you two traveling together?"

Shenli gritted his teeth. This next part was going to sound totally wonky. But he didn't know what to say except the truth. He tried not to think about the soldiers tracking Wren this very moment.

"She seems to think we are meant to work together. Some sort of . . . prophecy? From her grandmother."

Cudek stood from his chair. "A prophecy—are you *sure*, boy?"

"That's what she told me."

Cudek paced the floor in front of the fire. He mumbled something about *the grandmother*, but Shenli couldn't catch it. "And what of the girl's Magic?"

"She said she lost it."

"*Lost* it?"

"She'd only just bonded with it at some ceremony thingy—or *mostly* bonded, I guess? Then the Magic ran away to the Mainland for some reason. She doesn't know why."

"It's looking for them," Cudek muttered to himself. Then he put two fists on the table and leaned forward. "Shenli Zhao, did she tell you where the Meraki get their Magics?"

Shenli wiped the sweat from his temple, trying to sort through all of Wren's stories. Cudek's eyes bored through him, hungry for information. They made it impossible to think straight. Then Shenli remembered—there was a special tree. Wren had told him that all new Magics were birthed at the tree when Meraki kids turned thirteen.

"This is *incredibly* important, boy."

Shenli nodded, the answer on the tip of his tongue.

Then he realized something terrible.

If he told Cudek about the tree, Cudek would do something horrible to it—Shenli was certain of it by the eager look in the chancellor's eyes. And what would that mean for Wren's people? But if he *didn't* tell Cudek about the tree, his family would stay locked in prison. He could feel Yiming's doll pressing against his leg from inside his pocket.

"Tell me what you know."

Cudek's threat prickled against Shenli's skin. *I am not inclined to release your family until you've made it up to me.*

Shenli clenched the armrest tighter, whispering a silent apology to Wren for what he was about to do. "It's a tree, sir. That's where the Magics are born."

"A tree?" Cudek ran a hand through his hair and started pacing the room again. "A tree? A *tree!*" The chancellor leaned back his head and laughed.

Shenli looked on, dumbstruck. He'd never heard the chancellor laugh—not once. A terrible pain sank in Shenli's gut.

What had he done?

Cudek snatched a scroll and unfurled it on the desk. Shenli recognized the crescent shape of Meraki Island as the chancellor tapped his finger somewhere near the middle of the map, where there was a large oaklike tree. "There were always rumors, of course, but it was believed to be impossible." He shook his head. "But they actually managed to do it."

"To do what, sir?"

"To grow a new Offering Tree."

"A *new* one?"

"Shenli, my boy, you have been tremendously helpful." Cudek rolled up the map. "To think—I almost got it wrong." His eyes flicked to Shenli. "I have a very special job for you. You've earned it."

Shenli waited, his insides swirling with hope and dread.

"As a steward, you've always served me well. When you ran off, I'll admit, I had my doubts." Cudek resumed tapping his finger against the desk.

Tap, tap, tap.

"After all, the Zhao family has done very little to earn my confidence. But you're a smart kid and you follow orders. I'd like to think I can trust you."

Tap, tap, tap.

Shenli shifted in his chair uncomfortably.

"*Can* I trust you, Shenli?"

With seven years of debt to still work off, the lie fell from Shenli's lips as slick as oil. "Yes, sir."

"Good. Because completing this special job will rid you of all your debt to me."

Shenli's jaw dropped.

"*All* my debt?"

"It wasn't really your debt to begin with, but that of your traitorous father and cowardly brother."

Shenli's cheeks burned, but he forced himself to push the insult aside. "What's the job, sir?"

Cudek took a seat. "That part's going to be a surprise."

Shenli inhaled deeply, summoning the courage to ask Cudek a question that was none of his business. "When is this . . . war?"

"Very soon. With all seven Mainland dragons nearly asleep, there will be nothing to stop me." He considered Shenli for a long moment. "I'm after the Meraki crystals."

Shenli remembered Wren talking about the gemstones that formed the roof of the Meraki Council Chambers. They were super old and held great significance to the Meraki, but he couldn't remember what else she'd said about them—he'd pretty much tuned her out by that point, since she'd been making him so squirmy with all her magic talk.

"The crystals have magic?" Shenli guessed.

Cudek leaned back in his chair. "Times are changing. Magic has become . . . a necessity. If we use it correctly, we will own the Meraki. They will learn to fear us."

"Er—yes, sir," said Shenli, somehow keeping his face from scrunching up in disgust.

"I have big plans—plans I'd like you to be a part of."

A cold fear churned in Shenli's belly. He was on dangerous ground now. But he could play along. To get out of debt, learn the truth about his dad, and keep his family safe. He only had to earn Cudek's trust.

Shenli put on his most convincing smile. "I'd like that opportunity, sir," he said, willing himself to believe it.

Cudek smiled. "Excellent. Because in two weeks' time, we're going to war with the Meraki—and you, young man, are going to help me steal a whole lot of magic."

41.

IN WHICH SHENLI
HAS A VISITOR.

Shenli woke with a start. He lay in a cold sweat, waiting for his racing heart to settle. It had been three days since his talk with Cudek, and he'd spent each of them locked away in a small servants' bedroom at the castle. Shenli knew he was being punished. He was in time-out, like a toddler. There was even a guard posted outside his room.

He stood, still shaky from his nightmare, and propped his elbows on the small open window that overlooked the castle gardens. He'd dreamed of Wren getting captured by Cudek and thrown into a volcano. He'd had similar dreams the past few nights—Wren getting crushed by gigantic crystals or strangled by the branches of an enormous magical tree.

He blew out a long breath into the chilly night air. At the meeting with Cudek, Shenli had thought he was doing the right thing for his family by giving up Wren—and her secrets. But now he wasn't so sure. He still hadn't been allowed to see his mom and sisters or even been told where they were being kept.

He had requested more meetings with Cudek, but each time, the guard outside his room had given him the same message: the chancellor wasn't to be bothered. So Shenli had betrayed Wren's trust, and his family was still stuck in some prison somewhere, no better off than before. The only sliver of hope Shenli had was this mysterious upcoming job Cudek had for him.

His last chance to make things right.

He was about to head back to bed when something glittered in his peripheral vision. At first he thought it was the stars twinkling, but then a long thin shimmering strand looped through the sky, coming straight toward him.

Fates. It was that freaky golden thread.

"No," Shenli told it. "Get out of here."

The thread paused, gleaming gold in the moonlight, hovering a few feet from the window. Shenli could feel that same irresistible pull he'd felt when he'd first seen it three years ago. But his answer was still the same.

"Whatever you want, I'm not interested," Shenli growled. "I want nothing to do with magic!"

The thread disappeared with a *pop*, much to Shenli's relief. Then another strange sound came from behind him. It almost sounded like . . . a hiccup. Shenli whirled around to find a small purply-blue cloud floating in the middle of his bedroom. It looked like glittery fog, about the size of a coconut. It moved and shifted, and its color darkened, almost like a mini-storm brewing.

Shenli stood transfixed.

And horrified.

Because seeing it up close, he finally understood what the cloud was.

"You're Wren's Magic."

The cloud bobbed up and down, and Shenli took a step back.

A Magic—a *Magic!*—was in his bedroom! Cripes, what if the guard came in to check on him?

"What are you *doing* here?" Shenli lowered his voice to a harsh whisper. "You've been following me, haven't you?"

The Magic sank a few inches lower, flattening like a collapsing sandpile. It let out a little whimper.

"Oh, uh-uh. Don't try to act cute," said Shenli, wagging his finger for a proper scolding. "I don't know what your deal is, but you've caused nothing but trouble for Wren. And I don't want anything to do with it."

The Magic let out a huff.

Shenli made a face. "Did you just . . . *scoff* at me?"

The Magic started bouncing in all directions, and Shenli mustered the sternest voice he could manage: "Get out of here. *Now*."

The Magic let out a low whine, and a pang of sadness shot through Shenli as the sound brought back a memory of Yiming running on the beach. She'd fallen and skinned her knee on a seashell. She'd managed the saddest little whimper, until Shenli had scooped her up in a hug and bandaged the injury.

Shenli ran a palm down his face.

Ugh. Okay. The Magic was here for a reason. And what if it had something to do with helping Wren? Didn't Shenli owe it to her to at least listen?

Shenli exhaled in resignation. "Fine. Tell me why you're here."

The little cloud hummed; it almost sounded like soft music. Then it rose and took the shape of a wispy cloud dragon.

"Hey, that's pretty good," said Shenli, impressed. "Can you do a duck?"

The cloud scoffed again, then shifted, taking the form of four humans. One of the human shapes started to shift back into a dragon.

Shenli shook his head. "Uh . . . I don't understand."

The Magic growled.

Shenli crossed his arms. "Hey, it's not my fault I don't speak Magic."

The Magic pulled together to form the shape of a human head. The cloud features sharpened, until Shenli recognized the scowling face.

His mouth hung open. "That's me! Hang on, do I really look that grumpy?"

The Magic snickered.

"Are you saying you came here, to the Mainland, to help *me*?"

Part of the Shenli cloud split off, forming a second face: a girl with short curly hair.

"Wren?"

The Wren cloud and the Shenli cloud hovered steadily.

"You're trying to help *both* of us?"

The Magic gave a chittering sound like a squirrel as it bobbed up and down.

"But . . . you ran away from Wren. I can't see how that was helpful."

The Magic shifted into a single human form—only, this human had a tail and wings, so Shenli wondered if the cloud was confused, or starting to tire. It brightened in color until it was a deep teal blue.

"Blue . . ." Shenli frowned at the cloudy human shape. "Oh, *Blue*. The mysterious Blue."

The Magic bounced up and down.

"You're looking for him too, huh? You've been pretty busy."

The Magic let out a mournful whimper and floated down to the floor.

"I'm guessing that means you haven't had any luck finding him."

The Magic sighed again, shifting back to its original periwinkle cloud shape.

"And by helping me and Blue, you're somehow also helping Wren, aren't you?"

It made sense. This Magic had clearly gone to a lot of trouble. It must have good reason—even if that meant leaving Wren. Like all the times Shenli had to leave his mom and sisters in order to help the family. A new fondness for the little cloud sank into Shenli's chest.

"You'll go back to her, though, won't you? When your other work is done? I think she really needs you."

The Magic let out a few singsongy notes and whirled in a slow spiral. Then, at its center, a red heart shape emerged. It pulsed gently.

"And you need her." Shenli had no idea why he was so certain of this strange little cloud's loyalty to Wren. But somehow he knew. Felt it in the deepest parts of him. "You're more bonded together than she realizes, even if that spell didn't work," he said with a sigh, praying for the thousandth time that Wren was okay, wherever she was.

He ruffled his hair, confusion and frustration swirling through him. He couldn't believe he was sitting here so calmly *talking with a Magic*! But if he could help Wren somehow, after what he'd done to her, he had to try. And besides, this little Magic didn't look evil. It was even cute. He shuddered, shaking the thought away.

No, it didn't matter how adorable it was. Magics were still the enemy.

"Look . . . ," said Shenli. "I know you're trying to tell me something important, but I don't know what you want from me. Is it something to help Wren?"

The Magic sat silently for a few beats; then it drifted to Shenli's left hand. A small wisp of cloud formed into a pen. It looked like it was writing something on his wrist, but there was nothing there. Shenli trembled at having a Magic so close to his skin. It was warm at first, but then it grew cold and tingly. It felt an awful lot like—

"Wren's magic messages?" Shenli took a step back.

The Magic flipped through the air excitedly. Then it took the form of cloud-Shenli and cloud-Wren, facing each other. The little human mouths were moving, as if in conversation.

"You want us to . . . communicate?"

The Magic made a musical sound and spiraled upward through the air.

"I forgot she said I could send messages back to her. Will it still work? She's so far away now."

The Magic cloud-humans bounced up and down.

Shenli gasped as realization hit him like lightning. "Fates," he breathed. "I can *warn* her—about the war! With a message."

The Magic shifted back to its original form and let out another round of happy chittering sounds as it continued to bounce up and down, making circles around Shenli's head.

"But . . ." Shenli stared at his wrist. "It would mean I would have to"—he gulped—"use magic."

Shenli stood rooted to the spot. It was dangerous enough to stand here talking to a Magic. Didn't that alone make him a traitor to his people—even if he was only trying to help Wren? But if he *used* magic, he could never un-use it. There would be no going back. He would become . . . something else. A magic user. Not a proper Mainlander anymore, that was for certain. Then again, the chancellor himself was using magic. Everything felt so backward.

"Can't *you* warn her?" Shenli asked hopefully.

The Magic sighed, forming a Shenli face.

"It has to be me?"

The Shenli face nodded.

"But why?"

The Magic formed three humans and a dragon again, then chittered excitedly.

Shenli shook his head. "I don't know what that means."

The Magic grunted, and the four cloud shapes glowed brighter.

"Sorry, I still don't get it."

The Magic sighed, pulling back to its original shape. It squeaked out a few sad whimpers.

"Hey, you did your best," said Shenli, and the little cloud sighed again.

Shenli ran a hand down his face. "Okay, look. Whatever your reasoning, I agree that Wren needs to know what Cudek is planning."

The Magic hovered, waiting.

"Honestly, I feel awful for telling Cudek that Wren is Meraki. And maybe if she can warn her people about his attack, they can give up the crystals peacefully. No one will have to get hurt."

For some reason, his mom's little blue dragon statue came to mind. Shenli had looped some twine through a little hole at the top of the dragon's head and tied it around his ankle. He hadn't meant to bring it with him back to the castle. And he was too worried to hide it anywhere in his room for the guards to find. So it was part of him now, wherever he went. And there was something about his mom's secret rebellious dragon that gave Shenli the strength he needed to make his choice.

"Okay, I'll do it." His heart thumped in his ears as he touched his wrist and thought of what to say. The Magic chittered its encouragement. Closing his eyes, Shenli pictured Wren's face and felt a small jolt run through his arm as he mentally scripted the message. His eyes flew open.

He'd done it.

He'd used magic.

It felt strange and disorienting. But . . . he didn't feel all that different.

"Huh. I thought I might sprout dragon claws or something."

The Magic snorted.

"I'm kidding . . . mostly." Shenli raised his hands to the moonlight just to make sure: no evil claws. "Er, so I guess there's no way to tell if it's worked unless she writes back?"

The Magic shot up into the air.

"Now you're off to find Blue, I suppose?"

The cloud hovered for a long moment. Then it slowly shifted shape. Minutes ticked by as the cloud transformed into an intricately detailed landscape. A river threaded between two hills. At the top of one hill was something Shenli recognized: a partially collapsed building with enormous pillars in its courtyard.

"Oh." Shenli's eyebrows hitched up in amazement. "That looks like the temple ruin in Croydon village. I've been there before."

The Magic immediately shifted back to its original form with a grunt.

"That one was challenging, huh?" said Shenli.

The cloud grunted again, collapsing into a flattened pile of wispy smoke.

"Super-impressive, though," said Shenli. "You even got the carved symbols on the pillars. But why'd you want to show me Croydon?"

The Magic shifted into a rectangle with bars—a jail cell, with three humans inside.

Shenli's eyes widened. But it couldn't be. "My family—are you saying that's where my mom and sisters are?"

The Magic gave a chittering sigh as it swirled upward and toward the window.

"I've delivered Cudek's messages to the commanders in Croydon—it's only an hour's ride from here!" Shenli ran a hand through his hair in excitement. "Cudek's bound to let me out of here sooner or later. Then I can borrow a horse to go visit them." Shenli bit his lip as warm tears fell down his cheeks. He looked at the periwinkle cloud with gratitude. "Thank you."

The Magic hovered for a moment more before taking off through the window and into the night. Shenli tried to watch, but it was already out of sight. He instead watched the stars, thinking of his mom and sisters and the little wooden dragon tied to his ankle.

There was so much that was still uncertain. So little that made sense.

But maybe, just maybe, he'd finally done something right.

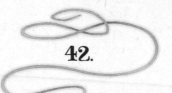

42.

IN WHICH
AN OLD FRIEND RETURNS

River's eyes fluttered open in the musty-smelling darkness. Two cerulean dragon eyes peered down at her.

"You've been out for hours," Blue told her.

"I . . . What?" River pushed herself to a sitting position. Her head pounded terribly.

Blue snort-laughed, and River shot him an irritated look. "What's so funny?"

"You've got feathers in your hair."

River pushed the hair off her face and redid her braid, plucking out leaves and blue feathers as she went. "Guess that's what happens when I use a fluffy dragon for a pillow," she muttered. "Ugh. I can't believe we fell asleep in the creepy forest."

"Yeah. And I think we've been sleeping for a while."

River closed her eyes, willing the throb in her temples to stop. "My brain is still so foggy."

"There was some kind of sleeping gas or something," said Blue.

"Sleeping *spell*, more like."

Blue scrunched his nose. "This place is the worst. There aren't any animals here—isn't that strange? And the air seems too thick. And tingly. It reminds me of—"

"Hang on—I remember hearing a voice!" River cut in, suddenly spotting the glowing flower in the distance. "Right before we dozed off."

"What voice?"

"I'm pretty sure it was coming from"—she lowered her voice to a whisper—"the flower."

Blue followed her gaze. "I feel like that thing's been staring at me this whole time while I waited for you to wake up."

"How long do you think we've been here, anyway?" River's stomach growled hungrily in response. Just then, an echoing whisper swirled around the clearing, like a voice caught in the wind. River stood. "The voice is back."

"It's about time." It was a male's voice, deep and gravelly, echoing all around them. *"You're sure that's them?"*

"You dare doubt me?" a second voice hissed, also male, but higher pitched. And very irritated.

"I'm inclined to doubt everything until it proves itself true. Wait—" The gravelly voice paused. *"Can they hear us?"*

Blue and River both took a step back.

"Don't just stand there!"

A new voice shot through the clearing. Both girl and dragon jumped in alarm. They whirled around to find a silvery-orange fox standing in a small beam of light peeking through the tree canopy. A long bloody scar stretched from his snout to his shoulder.

River's mouth fell open. "Did that fox just—"

"It's you!" said Blue.

"Fools!" The fox lowered his head. "The longer you stay, the more easily they can trace you!"

"Trace us?" River frowned. "Who are *they*? And hang on—who are *you*?"

"What's happened?" the gravelly voice demanded.

"They're getting fainter. . . ."

"We cannot lose them!"

"There's no time!" the fox growled, shooting a look behind him through the dense trees, where there was a faint thumping. And it was getting louder. "You must get out of here—*now*."

Before River could argue, Blue knelt down and nudged her with his snout. "He's a friend. We can trust him."

"But—"

"*DON'T LOSE THEM!*" the gravelly voice boomed.

At the same time, the faint thumping coming from behind them became more like a loud crashing . . . the pounding of feet. Big feet.

River grunted in frustration and jumped onto Blue's back. She hated not knowing what was going on, but if Blue trusted the fox, then she'd just have to go along with him. She owed Blue that much.

The fox took off running, and River could hardly follow the silver-orange streak as Blue pounded after him.

"We have to get to the light!" the fox called from somewhere up ahead.

Blue heaved heavily as he bounded on, keeping his wings tucked tight against his body. Even still, he clipped branches and shrubs as he struggled to keep pace through the winding trees.

Behind them, the crashing sound broke through the clearing. River turned back to see three hulking bears racing after them. Only, these bears didn't have fur; they looked to be mostly bone and shadow. One of them let out a wild scream, and River clung tighter to Blue's neck feathers.

"How much farther?" she called, but either the fox didn't hear or he didn't know the answer. The bears were gaining on them.

As Blue raced on, the scenery whipped around them. It was a

confusing sight. In a matter of moments, trees shifted from tall and skinny to short stout evergreens with rainbow nettles. At one point, the trees looked as clear as glass; then, seconds later, they seemed to be made of wafting smoke. River blinked in disbelief, whipping her head back around.

The shadow bears were now only yards away from Blue's tail. She could smell their rancid breath. Their eyes glowed yellow and orange, like fire. River's heart thundered in her chest with terrible realization.

Blue wasn't fast enough.

"Blue!" River screamed in horror as one of the bears slashed its front paw across Blue's tail. Blue let out a terrible howl but didn't slow. The bear reared back, ready to pounce. It leaped through the air, fast as a blink, just as Blue and River broke through the trees. All three bears slammed into some kind of invisible barrier where the tree line ended. River watched them paw angrily with shadowy fists as they snarled and snapped their jaws.

As Blue slowed, River blew out a breath of relief, her heart still pounding in her ears. Before them lay a small green meadow on top of a cliff. Beyond that, deep blue water stretched endlessly, disappearing into the horizon.

"Is that the ocean?" cried River. She'd learned about the sea but never could've imagined how massive it was. She turned to the fox. "Meraki Island must be somewhere off in the distance!" Then the memory of the last few minutes caught up with her. "I *did* hear you speak back in the forest, right? It wasn't a hallucination?"

Before the fox could answer, River felt a trembling beneath her. At first she thought it was an earthquake, but it was Blue. He took a shaky step, stumbling forward, then crashed to the ground. River tumbled off him headfirst into a patch of dandelions. She pushed herself to her feet. "Blue! What's wrong?"

But Blue didn't answer. He let out a low whine and his eyes rolled back into his head.

"He's been poisoned," said the silvery fox, sniffing Blue's tail, where long trails of black goo cut deeply into his feathers and scales. "The shadow bears," the fox explained. "One scratch from their claws is all it takes."

"All it takes to what?" River asked frantically.

The fox's silver eyes met hers. All at once, the creature looked ancient. "To kill," he whispered.

Then, somewhere off in the very far distance, a periwinkle cloud hiccuped.

43.

IN WHICH WREN
TAKES CHARGE

W ren Barrow gasped as she ducked behind a fallen log and
slowly pressed herself to the ground.

She'd heard her Magic hiccup!

It wasn't anywhere close by, but she was *sure* she'd heard it
somehow—impossible as it seemed. She'd never heard of a human
and Magic companion to be connected long-distance, but she was
too exhausted to question it. All that mattered was that her Magic
was in trouble.

Right now she had to focus on keeping still. The dead leaves tickled her face, but she didn't dare move. On the other side of the log,
not twenty yards away, a small squadron of soldiers marched through
the woods, most likely on their way to patrol a nearby village. Wren
held still until the squadron was out of sight before peeking her head
up over the log. The coast was clear. She bolted across the main path
and stole to the shadows of the trees on the other side.

It had been a very lonely and terrifying three days.

After the first night, in the hayloft, Wren had woken with a new
plan. She'd find one of the Mainland dragon lairs and ask the Riders

for help. She could only hope Cudek hadn't yet taken out all the dragons with his poison gas.

The problem was, she didn't know where the dragons were. Not specifically. She had a vague recollection of Ranji's map. She remembered that a dragon was posted somewhere on the border of the Coastal and Parch Districts, near the coast—which was about where Wren was now. Or at least, she thought so. It was hard to tell. In any case, it was the only plan she'd had—until now.

Because her Magic had hiccuped! And though it was still far away, she'd felt the hiccup in the very core of her being. Wherever it was, it needed her help. She wasn't sure how she knew, but Wren was certain. Her Magic—yes, it was *her* Magic!—was in trouble. She tore through the trees toward the coastline, following a tugging inside her chest.

She felt different now. Three days on the Mainland, along with the new Mama scar throbbing steadily in her chest, had summoned a bravery from Wren she hadn't known existed. Her arm had completely healed, thanks to the enderberries. She felt strong. And ready.

And as she broke through the trees and strode down the beach toward a little fishing village, she realized something for the first time. She hadn't felt the pull of her Magic when she first reached the Mainland because she hadn't fully claimed it as *her* Magic. But now it *needed* her. And that need had awakened a new mama-bear instinct in Wren.

"I'm coming!" she told it, pounding through the sand toward a small dock of fishing boats. She scanned the sea before her, squinting into the sun. To her right, she knew, were Shenli's village and the river. To her left, down the coastline, she could see the beginnings of the Wasteland desert off in the distance.

"Where *are* you?" she whispered, closing her eyes. The pull toward her Magic thumped so loudly in her chest her whole body trembled. "I want to help—show me where you are!"

Then her eyes popped open.

Something glittered in front of her. A little golden dot hovered in the sky, just out of reach. She took a step to the left, and the speck stretched into a thin golden line. It went on endlessly, as far as she could see, into the clouds beyond. And it *sang*. High twittering notes filled her ears.

Wren sucked in a breath. She'd never seen this kind of magic before.

"You're Shenli's thread, aren't you?" asked Wren in wonder as the thread looped closer to her. It felt familiar to her somehow. But what *was* it? Where had it come from?

A memory stirred in Wren's mind. She was a little girl, curled up in bed while Granmama told her wonderful stories. Stories of foxes befriending dragons. Or when Time played tag with the moon and set the days of the week all out of order. And there was another story of two children, a brother and sister. They sat at a magic loom, day and night, weaving lives together with golden thread. Wren scrunched her brow. The story was important. *So* important. But she couldn't remember who the children were. What was the thread for?

The golden thread above her looped through the air slowly, its joyful song burrowing deeper into Wren, like a promise. And then Wren knew what to do. She reached out and pulled. The thread disappeared, her hand tingling wildly where she'd touched it.

In its place, a small periwinkle light appeared.

"Oh! Hello."

It wasn't her Magic. More like . . . an echo of it. The light floated out toward the ocean, and Wren shot into action. She had to follow it! She scanned the line of rowboats and pulled the smallest one into the water. She hitched her rucksack onto her shoulder, then jumped aboard, took the oars, and dunked them into the water, rowing in a smooth, steady motion.

It took a great deal of effort to get past the oncoming surface waves, but once she cleared them, the water calmed. Keeping her eyes on the traveling light ahead, Wren rowed steadily south, toward the Wastelands. And toward the Southern Realm, she realized. As far as she knew, no island Meraki had ever traveled this far south. Only the Dragon Growers had.

She wasn't sure how long she'd been rowing when the landscape to her left changed. The beautiful lush scenery of the Coastal District fell away to hot cracked desert stretching as far as Wren could see. She stayed well clear of the land, thankful for the steady breeze on the sea. After a while, her arms started to tire. She longed for her grandmother's magic canoe. Still, she kept a steady pace, determined not to lose sight of the mysterious light.

Wren stopped to take a drink from her canteen and wipe the sweat from her brow. The periwinkle light didn't stop to wait for her, so she hurriedly took one more drink before once again grabbing the oars.

Something bumped the boat.

Wren's breath caught. Maybe she'd only imagined it? She leaned over as much as she dared to scan the water. Long dark shadows slithered underneath her.

No, no, no.

She gripped the oars tighter as one of the shadows broke the surface. A long yellow eel rose through the water, slimy tentacles outstretched, until it was eye level with Wren. Its razor teeth flashed wickedly in the sunlight. She scanned the boat for something— *anything*—to help fight it off. At the very bottom of the bow, a rusty knife sat next to a pile of dead fish in a barrel. Wren inched forward just as another eel popped out of the water. Then another.

Fates, how many were there?

Her Mama scar throbbed loudly in her chest.

Be brave, be brave.

You are enough.

Wren gritted her teeth and wrapped her hand around the hilt of a knife and brought it up over her head. Two more eels—now five of them altogether—surrounded the boat, all of them staring at her, teeth bared, and inching closer. She watched helplessly as the periwinkle light drifted onward, nearly out of sight.

The eels let out a low hiss, filling Wren's whole body with dread as their writhing tentacles wriggled closer and closer. She gripped the knife tighter as the first eel started to lunge.

Then something most peculiar happened.

From somewhere deep inside her, a single word burst forth from Wren's throat:

"Stop!"

The command crackled through the air for a moment, and then, quite absurdly, the eels *stopped*.

All five of them froze where they were, staring at her. The first one, now rooted mid-lunge, cocked its head like a confused puppy.

"We ssstop," it hissed.

Wren's mouth hung open. "You . . . can talk?"

"You ssspeak our tongue."

"Uhh . . . what?" Wren lowered the knife, flicking her eyes from one eel to the next. Then she realized. Her grandmother's necklace! If the pendant allowed her to talk to dragons, then why not bloodthirsty villainous eels?

She gulped.

"Right," she clarified. "So when I asked you to stop—"

"*We mussst obey.*"

"You must? Why?"

"*It isss our curssse.*"

"You mean . . . like a magic curse?"

"*Yesss.*"

"Hang on—you're cursed to obey me?"

"*We are cursssed to kill you.*"

Wren tightened her grip on her knife hilt. "You are cursed to kill humans—*and* obey them?" This was getting confusing.

"*Not to kill all humansss. We are only to kill the Barrowsss.*"

"The Barrows." All the air left Wren's lungs. "M-my family?"

"*You are Wren of the Barrowsss, yesss?*"

"And you are cursed to *kill* me?"

"*Not only you. Any of the Barrowsss will do.*"

Wren's Mama scar pulsed again.

Thump.

Thump.

Thump.

Time to be brave. Wren stood a little taller. "You said you must obey me!"

"*We mussst obey the One who can Ssspeak to usss.*"

"Who ordered you to kill my family?" Wren demanded, holding the knife out in front of her.

"*He isss one who can Sssee.*"

"He?" Wren shook her head. "My grandmother is the only Seer left."

But then she remembered Granmama getting the vision about Blue. She'd said someone was keeping things from her. Preventing her from Seeing properly.

"Who is he?"

"He hasss Ssseen for a very long time. And he'sss waited."

"What's his name?"

"We only know him as Massster."

"Is he Meraki?"

"We do not know. But he made usss."

"He made you . . . to kill my family." Wren gritted her teeth.

"To kill you, yesss. But alssso . . . we mussst obey."

Wren considered this. Obviously, this murderous monster wasn't factoring in Wren's ability to talk to the eels like he could. So couldn't she use that to her advantage? The beginnings of an idea took shape, and a small smile slipped onto Wren's face.

"So if I tell you to pull this boat, you'll do it?"

"We mussst obey."

"And you won't kill me."

"We mussst obey."

Wren arched an eyebrow. "That's not exactly reassuring."

Still, it couldn't hurt to try. "All right, then. I want all of you to pull this boat as fast as you can—and don't touch me." She pointed toward the little periwinkle light, which had all but faded in the distance. "Take me that way."

The first eel nodded. "We mussst obey."

Wren grinned. "Do it, then."

All five eels plunked back into the water. A moment later, five sets of tentacles popped up and secured themselves to the sides of the boat. Wren had barely sat down to get a grip on her wooden plank seat when the boat took off. It whipped through the water so fast tears streamed from Wren's eyes. Soon the ball of light came floating back into view.

Wren's heart soared as the small boat whipped over the water.

"Hang on!" she shouted to her Magic, which she knew was waiting somewhere in the distance. "I'm coming."

44.

IN WHICH IT'S ALL TOO LATE

Blue's eyes shot open and he screamed. Well, he tried to scream. It came out as a roar. River was at his side immediately.

"I'm so sorry, Blue. It's your tail," she told him. "You've been poisoned."

Blue gritted his teeth and tried to get up. He was lying on his side and couldn't see his tail properly.

River put a firm hand on his shoulder. "Er . . . you'd really better not," she warned. "It's pretty awful-looking."

Blue ignored her and shifted his weight. He immediately regretted it. Every part of his lower half felt on fire. Worse even than the pain of a broken wing, this was like every inch of him was boiling in lava. He settled back down, but not before he caught sight of the thick black goo clinging to his tail in crisscross patterns like a giant spiderweb.

"What kind of poison is *that*?" he grunted.

"That's wyvernarix."

Blue tilted his head to find the fox perched on a tree stump.

"It *is* you," said Blue. "How'd you end up all the way out here?"

"I'm known to . . . wander every now and again." The fox grinned. "Anyway, I barely smelled the shadow bears before they went after me. Then I spotted you two, smack-dab in the middle of the Haunted Hollow—like a pair of fools."

"Haunted?" repeated Blue.

"That flower—it's cursed," said the fox. "It . . . sees things. *Knows* things."

"I heard a voice," said River.

The fox narrowed his eyes. "It's likely someone lured you to the Hollow. They wanted you there."

"But why?" asked Blue.

"Who's to say?" said the fox, cocking his head. "Bet you thought I wouldn't recognize you, eh?"

"How *did* you recognize me?" Blue suddenly wondered.

"Hah. New body. Same ol' Blueboy smell."

Blue tried to smile, but the fire in his lower half flared again with a vengeance. He squeezed his eyes shut until the worst of it passed.

A small squeak rang through the air.

"What was that?" asked Blue.

"Ah, yes. That's been happening quite a bit," said the fox, flicking his head toward River. Blue followed the fox's gaze to where River sat, legs crisscrossed, at Blue's belly. Then a little purply-blue cloud appeared over her shoulder. There was another squeak.

"They're hiccups," said River.

Blue scrunched his dragon brow. "The cloud . . . has hiccups?"

"It's a Magic companion," River explained. "At least, I'm mostly certain it is. I've never seen one before."

The little cloud rose higher, coming closer to Blue.

"It showed up not long after you blacked out," said the fox.

"It must be exhausted," said River, petting the top of the cloud gently. The Magic let out a low purr. "It must've come all the way from Meraki Island."

"But why?" asked Blue.

River shook her head. "We don't know. It's been chittering adamantly, and hasn't left your side. But we have no idea why it's come."

"It seems to be friendly," said the fox. "And very concerned about you, Blue. But we still don't know what it wants."

"It's waiting for *me*," said a voice.

Blue craned his neck and the others turned. A strong breeze blew up over the cliffside just as a girl's head popped into view. She pulled herself over the edge, staggering a bit, her copper eyes shining in the sun. Then she smiled.

"That's my Magic," the girl said. "And it meant for me to find it here."

River and Blue shared an incredulous look as the fox hopped down off the tree stump.

"Who are you?" asked the fox.

"*More* talking animals?" said the girl, shaking her head. "This is getting ridiculous." She knelt down next to River, and the Magic cloud bounced into her hands. "I'm Wren," she told everyone. "And I think"—she hugged the Magic to her chest—"I'm here to help."

Before anyone could respond, Blue let out another roar. The poison fire had returned, only this time it was worse. "I can . . . feel it in my chest now," he grunted.

"What's happened?" asked Wren.

River gave a quick rundown and Wren turned to her Magic. "How can I help?"

The periwinkle cloud hummed softly. Then it shifted, breaking apart into a cluster of small orbs. Clumped together, the little orbs almost looked like—

"Berries!" Wren gasped, swinging her rucksack around to her front. "I still have the rest of the enderberries from Shenli!" She pulled out a small jar of magenta berries and held it up triumphantly. Blue tried to get a better look, but suddenly he felt impossibly sleepy.

"Enderberries?" breathed River. "I've only ever heard of those— they're supposed to be incredibly powerful. How do you just *happen* to have them on you?"

Blue closed his eyes.

"Long story." Wren unscrewed the lid. "We have to boil them into a paste," she said. "It'll counteract the poison."

"There's no time for boiling," said the fox, leaning his head down to sniff Blue's chest. He sucked in a sharp breath and his ears flattened. "Whiskers of mercy—we're too late. The poison's already reached his heart."

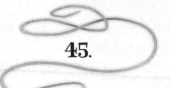

45.

IN WHICH THE MAGIC
HAS ITS MOMENT

River watched in horror as Blue's eyes rolled back and his body started convulsing. Wren's Magic shot up toward the jar of enderberries and knocked it from her hand. Then the little cloud moved so fast it was nothing but a blur, whipping up dust and grass. When it was finished, it collapsed onto the ground. And right beside it was a steaming hot pile of pink goo.

"You heated *and* mashed the berries?" Wren cried, her smile stretched wide with admiration. "You're *brilliant*, you are!" The cloud let out a small whimper. Then Wren scooped the pink goop off the ground in her palms and turned to River. "He needs to eat this. Help me get his mouth to open."

River followed Wren's lead and held Blue's mouth open—minding his incredibly sharp teeth—while Wren dropped the paste onto his tongue.

"You need to swallow it, Blue," River urged, praying the dragon could hear her as Wren went to scoop more berry goo from the ground.

Blue's body continued to jerk and tremble. Once all the remaining enderberry glop had been scraped off the grass and dripped onto the dragon's tongue, River closed his mouth and held it together. After a few moments, Blue's body went completely still.

River shot a desperate look at Wren.

"Now all we can do is wait," Wren told her.

The girls sat next to each other, anxiously stroking Blue's neck and belly, while the fox paced back and forth. Wren's Magic hummed a slow sad tune.

"You've done this before?" asked River.

"Well, not to a dragon," Wren admitted. "And . . . it was eel poison last time. But that was deadly too, so . . . this should work, right?"

River tried to sort everything she knew about magic curses and crops. But the truth was, she had little experience with poisons. And zero know-how with enderberries.

"I honestly don't know," River whispered, fear freezing her insides. What she *did* know was this was all her fault. She'd forced Blue to go left when he'd wanted to go right. She'd been too angry at him to trust his instincts. And after he'd saved her countless times back in the terrible forest—would they now be able to save *him*?

After a few more agonizing minutes, Blue finally took a shuddering breath.

River rushed to his head, relief washing through her as his big blue eyes fluttered open. "You're okay!" She kept a hand on his cheek as his breathing steadied. "How do you feel?"

His voice came out all croaky. "Like . . . death." Then a small smile tugged at his lips.

"You *talk*?" Wren gasped as she knelt down next to River. Her Magic did big loops through the air above them. "I mean, you can all hear him talk, not just me?" she asked, clutching her black stone pendant.

"Yup, he's one of a kind," said River, her heart swelling with something new toward her dragon companion—*pride.*

287

"And he's truly all right?" Wren asked.

"He's stable," said River, feeling a steady pulse on Blue's neck. Then she turned and threw her arms around Wren. After a few seconds of surprise, Wren returned the hug. "I don't know what we would've done without you," River said, her voice cracking. "You're a miracle, sent by the Fates."

Wren blushed. "You have my Magic to thank for that. And . . . some really creepy eels."

"Huh?" River pulled out of the hug and Wren laughed.

"*That's* a story for later."

The fox jumped to Blue's back, sniffing the length of the dragon's body.

"The poison's dissolving!" the fox cried. Even as he said it, the black gooey spiderweb started to shrink in size. "I've never seen anything counteract wyvernarix before." He looked from Wren to her Magic. "I think . . . you truly *were* sent by the Fates, weren't you?"

Wren's cheeks blushed scarlet and she shared a look with her Magic. "Perhaps . . . something like that." Her eyes flicked back to River. "The real question is how we're going to get you out of here."

"We were on our way to Meraki Island when we crashed," River explained. "But Blue broke his wing and then we lost our way."

"Because *someone* pulled that blasted golden thread," Blue croak-muttered.

Wren gasped. "Hang on—your name is Blue?" She looked at her Magic. "*This* is Blue?"

The purply cloud bobbed up and down.

"You know him?" asked River, puzzled.

"Blue is a *dragon*," said Wren, shaking her head in amazement. "No wonder Granmama had trouble sorting out her visions."

"Granmama?" said River.

Wren stood to her feet. "My grandmother is Madera Starling."

River's eyes widened. "The Seer! She's the one who summoned us! She said we're needed immediately."

Blue coughed and slowly pushed himself to a sitting position. River noticed he had ruffled bed-head feathers again.

"We're obviously a bit behind schedule," he said.

River frowned. "And we've lost our way to Meraki Island."

Wren turned and pointed a finger out toward the ocean. "It's just west of here. But . . ." She looked from Blue to River. "I have no idea how we're going to get you there if Blue can't fly."

The fox cleared his throat as he sat down on Blue's shoulder. "As for getting to places quickly . . ." He grinned. "I can help you there."

46.

IN WHICH SHENLI
IS RATHER SNEAKY

The air was heavy with the stench of sweat and musty earth as Shenli made his way down the long cobblestone street to where two soldiers stood guard at the entrance of Croydon's level-one dungeon.

The day after Wren's Magic had paid Shenli a visit, Cudek gave the order to let Shenli go back to work. The next night, Shenli was able to sneak away and, er, *borrow* one of the military horses from the castle stables. After a breezy midnight ride, he'd arrived at the small town of Croydon, where the Magic had claimed his family was being held.

Now was the moment of truth.

Shenli held his head high and walked with as much confidence as he could muster.

"Oi, state your business," said one of the guards, brandishing his sword.

"Shenli Zhao, personal steward to Chancellor Cudek." Shenli kept his face composed, though his heart was pounding against his ribs at triple speed. If he botched this, he'd most likely be earning a jail cell of his own tonight.

"I recognize 'im," said the second guard, putting a hand on her hip. "That's your mum and sisters in there, is it?"

Shenli nodded and the woman narrowed her eyes. "I'm surprised to see you here. I heard you were locked in your room on account of *suspicious activity.*"

Shenli steeled his gaze. "Nothing but a misunderstanding. The chancellor and I are squared away."

"We weren't expecting any royal emissaries this evening," said the first guard, his sword still raised.

Shenli lifted his chin. "I'm here for a personal visit."

The woman stepped forward. "And the chancellor's given clearance for this . . . personal visit?"

Shenli scoffed. "You think I'd *be* here if he hadn't?"

"Why you coming at this hour?" the male soldier challenged.

Shenli rolled his eyes. "I only *just* finished all my other chores for Cudek, like, an hour ago, so this is my free time. If you don't believe me, you can go wake him up and ask him yourself."

The two guards shared a look.

No one would dare wake the chancellor for anything less than fire in the castle. And even then, maybe not. The man really took his sleep seriously.

Shenli held his ground while the guards weighed their options. Then the woman sighed.

"Fine," she grunted. "You've got ten minutes."

Shenli nodded, keeping a straight face in order to mask his immense relief. Then he followed the male guard underground via a spiral staircase. They stopped at the bottom, and the guard pointed down a long dark corridor flanked by iron bars.

"There," the guard grunted. "The last cell on the right."

As Shenli passed, some of the other prisoners looked up at him with momentary interest, but most were either asleep or staring off into space. In the farthest cell in the corner, his sisters slept pressed up against his mother, leaning against the back wall. A tiny wisp of moonlight shone through a small window, falling on his mama's face.

A ripple of anger trembled through him. At himself, for putting them in danger. And at Cudek for putting Shenli in an impossible position.

But they were here. They were safe.

"Mama," he whispered.

His mother's eyes fluttered open. When her tired gaze found Shenli, she brought a trembling hand to her lips. She gently laid Yiming and Meili down one by one and stood shakily to meet him. Hot tears settled into the corners of Shenli's eyes.

"I knew you couldn't really be dead," she whispered, cupping his cheek through the iron bars. "But when you didn't come home . . ."

"I know. I'm so sorry to worry you, Mama." Shenli pressed his face to the cold iron bars. "I completed my mission, but . . . things got complicated."

"I'm just glad you're okay."

Shenli frowned, reliving the past few days in his mind. He wasn't sure how much to tell her with the guard listening in.

"Cudek has another special mission for me," he whispered. "He says it will cancel all my debt."

"*All* of it?"

Shenli nodded. "No more debt hanging over our family."

"And what is this job?" Mama whispered, shooting a glance at the guard, who stood at the far end of the corridor but was staring right at them, clearly eavesdropping.

"Cudek hasn't told me yet," Shenli admitted, which was only half true.

War.

The word hung on Shenli's lips. He was desperate to tell her, but it felt too dangerous to speak aloud.

"I heard the guards talking, Shen. Something about the dragons. Are they in danger?"

Shenli frowned. Mama's mysterious little wooden statue pressed up against his ankle, and he was desperate to ask her so many things.

"I—I don't think they're in danger, exactly," he whispered. "Only sleeping."

Mama gave him a measured look for several moments before her eyes flicked to the guard. "I just want you to be safe."

"I know," said Shenli softly, the night in the dragon lair flashing through his mind. The smoke. The terrible explosion. What did Cudek have planned for him next? It was likely anything but safe. But he couldn't worry Mama any more than he already had.

Mama turned Shenli's wrist over and kissed his palm. As she did, she caught sight of the teal letters still inked on the underside of his wrist. *Hello, soldier.* It was the last message Wren had sent him. Mama's mouth dropped open.

In fear? No.

In *recognition.*

Shenli frowned. That couldn't be right. How could his mother possibly know about magic messages?

"You must be more careful, son." She looked at him knowingly. She unwrapped her red headscarf and tied it around his wrist, covering the message. "This is something to remember me by, as is tradition in my family."

Shenli hitched an eyebrow. There *was* no tradition in Mama's family for wrapping scarves around the wrist. That ruse was clearly for benefit of the guard, who was watching them like a firehawk. A hundred questions burned in Shenli's mind, but he could ask none of them.

A heavy silence settled between them. He was due to meet Cudek in the morning, and he couldn't stand leaving his mom and sisters in this terrible place. Even more, he feared what kind of job Cudek had planned for him.

And what would happen to his family if he failed.

"I'm scared, Mama." The tears burst forth then, dripping down to where his mother's hands cupped his face.

"Oh, my sweet duckling. It's okay to be scared. But you will also need to be *brave*. Like your *mama*." She winked at him, and a small smile broke free on Shenli's lips as she wiped his cheeks.

"Yes, ma'am."

There was a shout from above, down the hallway.

"Time's up, kid," said the guard.

Shenli frowned. He hadn't gotten the chance to speak to his sisters. He hoped they'd forgive him.

"I'll come back to visit when I can," he promised.

Shenli dropped his hands from the cell bars with tremendous reluctance, glancing at Yiming and Meili one last time before turning on his heel. As he followed the guard back down the hallway, a familiar ache of loneliness swept over him. And Shenli whispered a silent prayer—to the Fates or whoever was listening—that he was brave enough to do what it took to save his family.

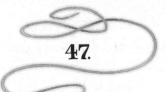

47.

IN WHICH WREN RETURNS

The trip back to Meraki Island was the strangest journey Wren had ever taken—and that included the one being pulled in a rowboat by a swarm of murder-eels.

How the fox did it, Wren couldn't be sure. But after Blue had gone down the cliff, onto the beach, and into the water, everyone had piled onto the small dragon's back. The fox had told Blue to swim. And then everything whipped by them faster than a sneeze. They'd moved so fast that the wind had iced Wren's cheeks and blown her curly hair into a frizz-puff. In a blink, the afternoon sky had darkened to night, morning, dark, and then morning once more. Had two full days truly just passed in a matter of moments?

Before Wren knew it, they'd slowed significantly, and Blue was paddling them all up onto the Meraki shore, at the southern part of the island, where the dragons slept and Wren's dad worked.

The girls—with their spectacularly windblown hair—stumbled off Blue in a wobbly stupor, and Wren turned to the fox. "How'd you do *that*?" she breathed.

The fox grinned. "That's just my knack. And now, if you don't mind, I'm off to home, with a head full of new stories for my kit." Then, in a blink, the magnificent fox was gone, racing back across the water toward the Southern Realm.

After a beat, Wren realized everyone was waiting for her to lead the way. "Er, right. So this is Meraki Island." She stepped forward and they followed, her Magic trailing behind her. It felt so good for the two of them to be traveling together like proper companions.

She led everyone across the beach and into a vast meadow. "We're on the smaller side of the island, where the dragons live. They're trained and tended by my father." Wren pointed to the right, where a long land bridge fed into a much bigger part of the island. "That's where the humans and Magics live. There are several housing regions, kind of like small villages. I live in the Council region, on the north side of the island. You can barely see the rooftops nestled among the white cherry trees, off in the distance."

"How many Meraki are there?" asked Blue as they plodded along through the meadow.

Wren was leading them toward the dragon caves on the other end of the island. "Nearly five thousand, at last count," she answered. "The Council is big on taking a yearly census."

"Five *thousand*," River repeated. "There aren't even five *hundred* Dragon Growers."

"Nothing like the nonmagic humans, though," said Wren. "Our Dragon Rider reports estimate nearly *a hundred* thousand Mainlanders!"

River tapped her chin thoughtfully. "Because even with their shorter life spans, they can have lots of kids, right?" she said. "Interesting."

"Does each Meraki have their own Magic companion?" asked Blue.

"Everyone who's thirteen or older, yes." Wren pointed again

toward the bigger part of the island. "Also over there is the Gathering Place and the Offering Tree, where the Magics are born." She stood on her tiptoes. "You can see the very tops of the Academy buildings from here too. I should be in class right now, if you can believe it." She imagined her classmates in their pastel-colored school uniforms, carrying on with mathematics exams and science labs without her. She shivered, realizing her life would never be what it was before. Would she even be allowed to go back to school? Or would the Council send her straight to prison?

"What's that big white domed building with all the shiny rainbow gemstones?" asked Blue, craning his long neck.

Wren gulped. "The Council Chambers. That's where"—she closed her eyes—"they'll put me on trial. For treason."

Treason. The word turned Wren's stomach sour.

"Oh." Blue lowered his head a bit. "Sorry I asked."

Wren tried to ignore the flutters beneath her ribs. "Anyway, I suppose we should get you settled in, Blue. My father will want to meet you."

As they crossed the field, Wren spotted someone coming toward them. It was Granmama with her cane, hobbling out to meet them, waving excitedly. Wren grinned from ear to ear and ran to her grandmother's arms. The warmth of *home* swelled around her.

"My extraordinary girl has returned!" said Granmama, wrapping Wren in a big hug. After several moments, she held out Wren's right wrist, where her Magic now slept soundly with loud snores. "Glad to see you two reunited." Granmama nodded to River and Blue. "And you've brought *friends!*"

"How'd you know we were coming?" asked Wren, breathing her grandmother in.

"We saw you, dear."

"You had another vision?" Wren guessed.

Granmama smiled. "No, I mean, we saw you swim up." She turned to Blue and River. "We've been expecting you for several days now."

River's shoulders slumped. "I . . . lost the map and we crashed." She looked at Blue. "We were lucky to make it out alive."

Granmama frowned. "I imagine you both have quite the tale to tell." She turned to River. "It's an honor to meet you, River Rowan."

River blinked. "You . . . know me?"

"*Know* you? Child, soon your name will be known across the realms!"

Wren grinned at River's baffled face. "Um, yeah," said Wren. "She talks that way sometimes."

"And *you*." Granmama stroked Blue's snout. "My beautiful brave Dragonboy Blue—look at you! So happy to finally meet you, my child."

"You might've warned me he was a dragon," Wren pointed out, putting her hands on her hips.

Granmama laughed. "I'm just as shocked as you, dear. While I *had* Seen the newest dragon waking early, I had no idea who he was until Elder Cyrus sent word."

Blue gave a shy toothy smile. "You must be Madam Madera."

"I am known by many names," said Granmama with a wink. "And it is *lovely* to hear your voice, dear. Cyrus says you've retained all your human memories?" Blue nodded and she shook her head slowly. "Such a blessing and a curse, I imagine. You both understand why I've called you so urgently, don't you?"

"Your message said something's gone wrong with the Mainland dragons," said River. "And you need me and Blue to scout out what's happened."

"That was the original mission. Since Blue's the only dragon who hasn't been officially initiated, the barrier enchantment doesn't work on him. But we've had to terminate the mission, I'm afraid," said Granmama. "Wren's father has lost contact with all dragons and their Riders."

Wren gasped. "*All* of them?"

"So we're too late to help?" said River, her face crumpling.

"Admittedly, we would've benefited from your presence a few days sooner." Granmama put a hand on River's shoulder. "We're just happy you've both made it safe, dear. But now it's too dangerous to travel to the Mainland until we know what's happened."

"I know what's happened!" said Wren. "Cudek's taken out the dragons with sleeping gas."

Granmama's mouth fell open a bit. "How do you know that?"

Wren's eyes dropped to her feet. She had so much to say, but the thought of talking about Shenli caused her chest to tighten.

Granmama gave her a knowing nod. "We can save your stories for a bit later, dear. As it is, we shouldn't linger here. Let's get you safely tucked away."

Wren hugged her arms against her chest, understanding Granmama's meaning. Tucked away *from the Council.* How much time did Wren have before Judge Finlar and the Elders came for her?

With a deep inhale of dread, Wren went with Granmama quickly across the grass field with River and Blue following. Some hundred yards away, a group of caves clustered along the seashore.

"Is Father here?" Wren whispered.

Granmama nodded, pointing. Up ahead, Wren spotted her father standing with his arms crossed in front the nearest cave opening. The churning in Wren's belly wrenched tighter.

"He must be furious with me."

"It is . . . complicated, child." Wren eyed her grandmother curiously, but the old woman's eyes hid away their secrets. "Did you meet the soldier boy?"

"I—I did."

Granmama nodded again, almost sadly. "My sweet Wren. I sense you have much to share of great urgency. Very soon, you will have the chance to speak your truths to the Council, and from that moment on, everything—*everything* will change."

Wren released the air in her lungs. The sleeping dragons. Cudek the Horrible. Shenli. Each thing pressed at her chest. Wren would be set before the Council soon enough, and then what would happen to her? Prison?

Everything will change.

"I am proud of you, child. So very proud of my extraordinary girl."

Wren tried her best to smile, ignoring the pear-sized lump in her throat, as the two walked on in silence toward the dragon caves—and her father—at the far end of the island.

"This is where all new dragons are brought," Granmama explained to Blue and River. "You can see the Rider tents pitched next to the caves. River dear, one of those tents will be yours. And this"— she nodded to Wren's father—"is our Dragon Master, Jarum Barrow. Jarum, this is River Rowan and Blue."

Jarum stepped toward Blue without a glance in Wren's direction, his yellow Magic fluttering along behind him, his honey-gold eyes wide with wonder. "Look at the radiance of the scales, and *feathers!*" He shook his head in awe and ran a swift hand over his tightly curled hair.

Blue's head drooped lower. "Er . . . Nice to meet you, sir."

Jarum jumped in alarm, as did his Magic. "You . . . *talk!*" He put a hand on his chest and gave Blue another once-over. "I have studied and trained dragons for nearly my whole life. I understand their anatomy, their temperaments, and how to cure what ails them. But never, not *once,* have I heard a dragon speak." He gave a very formal bow. "It truly is an honor to meet you, Blue."

Blue, clearly taken aback, gave a small bow in return. Then Jarum stepped toward River and shook her hand. "It is an honor to meet you as well, River Rowan. The youngest Dragon Rider in history— imagine that!" Jarum finally turned to Wren, his eyes unreadable. His steady gaze set her cheeks aflame. He started to say something, then seemed to think better of it.

Wren swallowed hard. "I'm sorry for leaving, Father."

Jarum crossed and uncrossed his arms. Then he shot an irritated look at Granmama, who stood tapping her foot.

"Don't *you* have something to say, Jarum?" urged Granmama, her tone stern.

Jarum bit his lip. "If it were up to me, Madera, none of this would have ever—"

"But it *has* happened!" Granmama cut in. "And Wren needs us now more than ever."

Jarum sighed heavily and shook his head. "I'm sorry, but what you did was reckless, Wren. And no matter your reasons for going to the Mainland, you committed treason. There's no way around that."

Wren stood rooted to the spot, feeling completely gutted. She blinked desperately to hold back her tears. Of course, she knew she shouldn't be surprised not to have her father's support.

But it still stung terribly.

Granmama looked angrier than a cat dunked in water. "*That's* all you have to say to your daughter?" she hissed.

Jarum clenched his fists. "Look, you made your choices, Wren. So now you must face the consequences." He let out a long breath, his eyes finding Wren. They almost looked sad. "I'm glad you're back safe. I really am. Honestly—"

Wren's father didn't get to finish. Because Wren had been nervously fidgeting with the bracelet—Shenli's bracelet—still on her wrist, and at that moment, she'd moved the beads aside, revealing a new message inked on her skin in teal letters.

Cudek's preparing for war! In two weeks! He's after the Meraki crystals.

Wren's mouth hung open. How long had that message been there? It must be from Shenli! But she couldn't imagine him using magic—not unless threatened with death or something.

And maybe not even then.

She stiffened, only vaguely aware that everyone was staring at her.

"What's wrong?" asked Granmama.

"It's a message." She frowned, showing it to Granmama. "From Shenli."

Her father stepped closer to read it too.

"The crystals?" said Granmama at the same time her father asked, "Who's Shenli?"

"Do you think he's telling the truth?" asked Granmama.

A wave of uncertainty shuddered through Wren. She started walking in a circle, running everything through her mind. Shenli had set a trap for Wren, so why would he be warning her now? Was it possible he felt guilty for what he'd done? And he was trying to make it up to her? Or was this just another lie? But . . . why? Why would he lie? What if it wasn't even Shenli who sent the message? What if the mysterious eel master had something to do with it? She made ready to tell everyone about what she'd learned from the eels, when her father stepped in front of her.

"*Who* is Shenli?" he repeated.

"Let her think a moment, Jarum," Granmama scolded.

Wren met her father's eyes. "I don't know if I trust him," she admitted. "But he works for the chancellor. So it's possible he's telling the truth."

Her father put his hands on his hips. "Are you telling me this message came from a *Mainlander boy*?"

"Are you more upset about the *Mainlander* part or the *boy* part?" Granmama teased.

Jarum shot her a look, running a palm down his face. "I'm honestly not sure," he muttered.

"Anyway, it all makes sense, doesn't it? Wren says Cudek's found a way to put the dragons to sleep. Now we know why. He needs them out of the way to get to the crystals."

Jarum gasped. "He's done *what*?"

Wren nodded. "It's true. He's taking out the dragons with some kind of sleeping gas."

Jarum uttered a few choice words under his breath. "That's why I haven't been able to make contact? Are you sure about this, Wren?"

Wren sucked in a breath. Her father hadn't held eye contact with her for this long in years. She wanted nothing more than to make him proud—for once. "I didn't see any dragons myself," she admitted. "But I heard loads of people talking about it." In fact, during her three days hiding out, it seemed the whole kingdom was abuzz with news of the sleeping dragons. "The dragons are most definitely asleep—some of them, anyway. I don't know what happened to their Riders."

Jarum pressed his fingertips to his temples. "And Cudek's after the Meraki crystals?"

"Well, that's what Shenli is saying." Wren shook her head. "But the magic drained out of the crystals a long time ago, didn't it? So that doesn't really make sense."

"They're purely decorative now," Granmama agreed. "Seven monuments to the past and not an ounce of magic in any of them. They're useless. But it's likely Cudek doesn't know that. Once upon a time, the Meraki crystals held the most powerful natural magic in the world. And Cudek's been greedy for magic for a long time."

River started pacing. "So if what Shenli is saying *is* true, then the

Mainlander chancellor is going to war . . . for crystals that don't even *work*?"

No one seemed in the mood to confirm such a horrible truth. Instead they all shared sorrowful glances.

"It's possible he does know the truth of the crystals," said Jarum. "And he has other plans for them." He turned to Wren. "How certain are you that this source is trustworthy?"

Wren hesitated. She didn't want to be wrong about this.

At that moment, her Magic hovered between the humans. There was a small crackling sound, and the cloud shifted into a new shape. A human face that Wren recognized instantly.

"It's Shenli."

Every Meraki mouth fell open, gaping at Wren's Magic. Magics had never made shapes like this before. They watched in awe as the little cloud shifted into three human shapes and one dragon. Two human clouds bunched together with the dragon. The third human—with the Shenli face—was off by itself at first; then it slowly joined the others in a big group hug.

"You're saying we need to trust Shenli," Wren said to her Magic, looking from Blue to River. "I mean, that's *us*." She nodded to the cloud shapes. "The four of us."

The little cloud whimpered, pulled back to its original shape, and drifted downward into Wren's arms. Everyone stood in shock for several moments.

Granmama thunked her cane on the ground. "Well, *that's* new," she said.

Wren held her Magic close to her chest. "You've been busy, haven't you?" Her Magic purred. "This settles it, then," she declared. "I may not be sure about Shenli, but if my Magic says to trust him, then we will."

Granmama gave a stiff nod of agreement. "Indeed." She shared a look with Jarum. "The Council needs to know."

Wren winced, the knot in her gut tightening.

"I'll . . . keep reaching out to the Riders," said Jarum. "The Council's going to want confirmation about all this."

Granmama took Wren's hand. "I'll go with you to see them. It's going to be okay, dear. Just tell them the truth."

Wren nodded, wondering if she could absorb some of Granmama's courage.

Wren's father started to take a step toward her, then hesitated. He cleared his throat. "Right. Um, good. I need to ready the dragons. We need to figure out a strategy to guard those crystals. And, Wren . . . your grandmother's right. Just tell the Council the truth."

Wren nodded, but she couldn't ignore the doubt in her father's eyes.

"That's right," said Granmama encouragingly. "You'll make them believe, one way or another, that your handsome soldier boy is going to help save us all."

"Hold up—" Jarum's eyebrows shot upward. "You never said anything about *handsome*—"

Jarum's Magic chuckled as Granmama pulled Wren along and shooed her father away. "Calm down, Jarum. Go focus on your dragons."

With one last look at Blue and River, Wren stumbled beside Granmama, her father's eyes following her as she walked.

I'm glad you're back safe.

She tried to hold on to his words from earlier. It was the kindest thing he'd said to Wren in years. But the small sliver of hope had already fizzled in the face of her trial. And somehow the divide between Wren and her father seemed wider than ever.

48.

IN WHICH BLUE MEETS
A VERY OLD DRAGON

A good many hours later, Blue woke from an exceptionally long nap in his new cave. It was warm and spacious, and to his delight, it even held a pile of enormous feather pillows. After Wren left, Blue had spent several hours with the Meraki Healers, who'd tended to his wing. They'd determined he had a double fracture, and after he'd downed a large quantity of elixirs, they'd assured him his wing would be good as new once he woke from his nap. So he'd happily drifted off to his first pleasant sleep since hibernating.

He now pushed himself up and stepped out of the cave with a yawn, stretching his front legs much like an overgrown cat, testing his wing. It felt so much better! He glanced up to find a large yellow dragon peering down at him.

"Hello, Blue." Her voice was like an old woman's, rich and welcoming. He straightened to stand at full height. He barely reached the dragon's middle. "My name is Xayndra."

"You can talk," Blue noted.

"All dragons can talk, dear."

"Oh?" Blue then caught a whiff of something in the air. "Strange,

I smell . . . hay and chocolate." Perhaps the last bits of a dream still clung to his senses?

"How interesting," said Xayndra. "For me, the smell of Joy has always been cinnamon and rainwater."

Blue's eyes widened. "I'm smelling Joy?"

But he'd never smelled *Joy* before! He let out a bubbly laugh, much to the old dragon's amusement. Then Blue realized something else.

"You can smell emotions too?"

"All dragons can, youngling. Though it takes much training to use it to our advantage."

"It was something I could do as a human boy. And even then, it wasn't all emotions. I only ever smelled Fear and Sorrow. Well, and now Anger too." He shot a look at River's tent, sitting a few yards from his cave. "But that one's new."

"Yes, Madera told me you've retained all your human memories. How fascinating."

Blue frowned. *Fascinating* wasn't the word he'd use.

"And it *is* a rather strange ability for a human," said Xayndra. "How very odd indeed."

"So emotions smell different for each dragon?"

Xayndra nodded. "Ten dragons would smell Joy in ten different ways. Each scent holds a special significance. For some reason, to you, Joy is represented by the smell of hay and chocolate."

"Sir Huxley used to sneak me chocolate treats after dinner." Blue smiled at the memory. He remembered going back to his hay bed and savoring the treat as slowly as possible until the moon came up. Everything was so peaceful and easy back in those days.

"You'll learn to detect even more emotions, and their complexities, as you get older," Xayndra told him. She lowered her beautiful reptilian face level with his. Two giant tears pooled at the corners of her golden eyes. "Forgive me," she whispered, the tears sliding down her cheeks. "But I haven't seen a youngling in many centuries. Dragons usually come here full-grown, you know. Look at all those beautiful *feathers*!" She laughed. "Well, I suppose we should get started. Jarum's asked me to train you today. We'll start with simple flying techniques to test that wing of yours." Xayndra pumped her wings a few times, hovering in the air. "If it goes well, I'll even teach you to fly upside down."

Blue stretched out his wings tentatively. He hadn't tried flying since he and River had crashed into the mountains. "Okay, here goes." He flapped his wings a few times and took off into the air, hovering next to Xayndra.

"How does it feel?" she asked.

"A little sore, but nothing too terrible," he said, amazed. "The Meraki Healers really know their stuff."

Xayndra grinned. "They do. But Jarum thinks it has more to do with the healing properties of the enderberry remedy. The Healers said it's been in your system for several days now—not only ridding your body of that terrible poison, but also healing you."

"Several days?" Blue shook his head. "But I only just met Wren and her Magic this morning." Then he thought of the fox and his knack for traveling quickly. "Then again, maybe it was days ago." That fox was really something.

He hadn't even thanked the fox—the creature had taken off back across the sea before Blue had had the chance. Come to think of it, he hadn't properly thanked Wren and her Magic either. Everything had happened so quickly, with the fox taking them to the island, then Wren being whisked away to see the Council.

But soon Blue's guilt was pushed to the side. Because he was flying again! As much as he missed his human body, he had to admit:

flying was pretty amazing. He loved to be so high off the ground, away from any troubles that lurked below. He felt so *free.*

"Ah, and now I'm smelling cinnamon and rainwater." Xayndra turned to smile at him.

"My Joy?" Blue realized.

"It's quite strong."

Blue grinned, and for the first time in a long time, a wave of pure happiness swirled through him, until his whole body tingled with it. "Can dragons truly fly upside down?"

Xayndra laughed, the sound beautiful and earthy. She circled the large meadow, then flipped onto her back, still flying seamlessly. Blue took off after her, his mouth hanging open.

"That. Was. Awesome."

Xayndra laughed again. "There are many *awesome* things about being a dragon, I assure you."

"Where are your Riders?" Blue asked, looking around the meadow.

"I don't have any. My Riders passed long ago, during the wars. Same with Kado. He's the other elder dragon—have you met him yet?"

Blue shook his head.

"Come, let's circle the island a few times, and I can take a look at your form."

Blue nodded and the two soared higher. It was still so strange for him to see things from this height. Everything looked so tiny. He caught sight of his dragon shadow on the grass below. Had it really only been a week since he'd woken from his hibernation? It felt like ages.

"Your form isn't bad," Xayndra told him. "But if you stretch your neck forward"—she elongated her neck so her whole body looked more snakelike—"then you'll be able to go even faster." After a bout of silence, Xayndra slowed. "I don't suppose you breathe fire yet?"

"Uh . . . not that I know of."

"Usually fire-breathing starts about the same time a dragon loses all their feathers." She smiled. "In your case, I imagine you have another year or two. It's a shame, though. It would be useful for you in battle."

Blue cringed. "I don't know much about battle," he admitted.

"I fear I know *too* much."

"You lived through the old human wars?" Blue guessed.

"All three of them," Xayndra confirmed, looking out over the ocean toward the Mainland. "Humans never seem to keep the peace for long."

Blue didn't know what to say. His people of Gerbera hadn't had any wars—though now he knew his ancestors had all come from the Mainland. And *they* had fought in wars.

Before long, the sun sank lower on the horizon, painting the sky with pinks and oranges. The two dragons touched back down by the caves and spotted River walking along the beach in the distance. She saw them and waved. Blue hated that he couldn't wave back. His reptilian arms didn't bend that way.

"So, Blue." Xayndra's eyes looked thoughtful. "You've had quite the journey. And with such . . . unique circumstances, you must have many questions."

Blue frowned. He was still uncomfortable in his new dragon body, but he didn't want to offend Xayndra by telling her this. When he didn't respond, Xayndra leaned forward.

"Most younglings want to know about their special abilities," she told him.

"Abilities?" Blue repeated. He remembered River saying something about dragons having natural magic in their blood. "Do dragons do spells?"

"No, we don't do spells like humans or have companion Magics.

But each dragon does manifest their own special ability, which is different from the standard abilities."

"Like fire-breathing?"

"Also, all dragons have strong hearing, exceptional eyesight, and a keen sense of direction. And we can speak telepathically to other dragons."

Blue considered this. And he realized Xayndra's mouth didn't move when she spoke. "We're speaking with our minds?" he asked, amazed.

"Well, I am. That's why humans can't understand us. But you are speaking aloud with words somehow."

"Is that my special ability, then?"

"It might be. Special abilities are different for each dragon. Some can see in the dark. Others can breathe underwater or call upon weather. Each dragon has one."

"What's yours?"

"I know when someone is lying."

"Humans also? Or just dragons?"

"Humans too."

Blue tilted his head, considering. All of this was still very strange. It was hard enough coming to terms with his new dragon body, but breathing underwater? Seeing in the dark? The Something Missing feeling suddenly swelled so big it hurt his insides.

"Are you all right, youngling?"

Blue tried to shrug, but he couldn't quite get his dragon shoulders to cooperate. Which only made him feel worse.

"I can smell your deep Sorrow, dear."

Blue met Xayndra's steady gaze. Her golden eyes were intense. Strange. But also kind.

"I don't think I'll ever stop missing my human self."

Xayndra nodded solemnly. "You have gained so much in retaining your human memories. But also, I imagine, there is much heartbreak and loss."

"Being a dragon isn't *all* bad," he admitted. "I love flying. And I like the idea that I can help protect people. Even if I'm scared to do it."

"We don't have to talk about dragon things, if you'd rather not."

"Actually, I was wondering about you." Blue paused, hoping it wasn't rude to ask. "I didn't know there were any female dragons left. River told me about Daya, and how she disappeared. But I thought all the other dragons were males, ever since the Dragon's Curse."

"I am naturally grown—that is, not at the hands of the Dragon Growers. I came long before the Dragon's Curse, born to two dragon parents."

"Did you know Daya?"

"It is kind of you to ask about her." Xayndra frowned. "Yes, I knew Daya, long ago."

"Was she ever able to have a baby?"

"Sadly, no. The Dragon's Curse was still in effect, even for her. Such a tragedy."

"What happened to her?"

"She had the hardest time being around humans. So after a while, she flew off to the Lands Across the Sea."

"River told me some of the nonmagic humans fled there during the wars."

Xayndra nodded. "Humans and dragons both left."

"Where are the Lands, exactly?"

"All I know is it's a very, *very* long journey. I've had to say more goodbyes to dragons traveling to the Lands than I care to recall." She sighed. "Since Daya left, I am the last female of the Northern Realm. And only because I am wise and *very* stubborn." Xayndra grinned.

"But I have long been past childbearing age, which is why it is such a treat to meet you, Blue. A proper youngling."

"How old *are* you?" asked Blue, curious about how long dragons could live.

"Hmm. I honestly lost count after the second thousandth year. Females tend to outlive male dragons, you know." Xayndra winked. "I happen to think it's because females are more clever."

Blue grinned just as River came into view, heading back from the beach with an armful of sticks and seashells. She nodded her hello, then came to sit on a tree stump by the fire pit, setting her collection at her feet. "I'd like to study these specimens for their magical properties," River explained.

"Speaking of cleverness," said Xayndra, one eyebrow raised, "I did not think the humans allowed Dragon Riders so young."

"It was sort of an accident," Blue admitted aloud.

"What was an accident?" River asked Blue, with a small wave to Xayndra. "Hello there."

"Hello, Rider," said Xayndra. "What is her name?"

Blue realized Xayndra was talking to him. "Oh, this is River Rowan."

"Who are you talking to?" asked River, clearly puzzled.

"Xayndra. She asked your name."

"She did?" asked River, looking to Xayndra in wonder. "Wait— she's a *she*?"

"Remember, youngling, the humans cannot understand dragon mind-speak," Xayndra told him.

Blue nodded. He'd have to interpret for River's sake. "River, this is Xayndra. She is the last remaining female dragon in the Northern Realm. She was born naturally."

"How extraordinary!" River whispered, holding her hands over her heart. "And mercy, Xayndra, you are absolutely *stunning*. Those scales! They look like pure gold."

"I *am* rather exceptional," Xayndra agreed with a big grin.

"She seems to like you," Blue told River, and she returned the smile.

"Where's Jarum?" asked River. "I thought he might be here too."

"Jarum was summoned to confer with the Council," said Xayndra. "Wren Barrow's trial is tomorrow morning."

Blue repeated the information to River.

"Poor Wren," said River, hugging her arms to her chest. "I hope they go easy on her."

"That child has been through enough as it is," Xayndra agreed.

"Xayndra's been giving me flying lessons all afternoon since my wing's feeling better," Blue explained. "And answering my dragon questions."

"Oh! I have a question, Xayndra," said River, perking up. "If you don't mind?" Xayndra nodded for River to proceed. "My people have been growing dragons for nearly a thousand years. Before that, dragons—like you—were born naturally. I've always wondered . . . how many dragons are there out in the world?"

Xayndra sighed, bits of smoke puffing from her snout. "There were once *hundreds*, child. We roamed all the realms freely, male and female, in every size and color you can imagine. The human children called us flying rainbows." Xayndra grinned at some faraway memory as Blue translated her words to River. "Back then, all humans were at peace—until they *weren't*."

"War," Blue muttered. The word now took on newly shaped fear in his chest.

"Yes, youngling. In those days, there were many humans who greatly feared Magics. So the people became divided between those who chose Magics and those who rejected them. The humans worked it out as they always do—with eras of peace crested by the devastation of war. The dragons were caught in the middle."

"Did the dragons fight in the wars too?" Blue asked.

Xayndra frowned. "Many dragons wanted nothing to do with the human wars, so they left, never to be heard from again."

"But you stayed and fought?" asked Blue, wondering what it must feel like to have lived so long and seen so much.

"My love for the humans was very strong, and I believed the dragons would be crucial in helping them make peace." Xayndra sighed, shaking her head. "I was so young and naive then."

Blue was quiet for a while before gathering his courage to ask, "Are you glad that you stayed?"

Xayndra lowered her head, her eyes bright with fresh tears. "I will admit, there were times I wished to leave. Someday you'll learn that serving the humans can start to feel like an enormous burden. It wears on the soul, dear."

"Then why have you stayed all this time?" asked Blue.

"Because I believe it is *right*. Dragons are creatures of justice, youngling. The desire to protect others surges strong in our blood. And, despite the humans' many shortcomings, I have never lost sight of that."

"What's she saying?" asked River.

Blue frowned, inhaling the ancient dragon's deep Sorrow. "That being a dragon can be very hard and very lonely."

"I fear it will be loneliest for you, young one, with your human memories intact." Xayndra smiled. "But I am so very thankful you are both here with us now."

"Xayndra, do you have any idea why Blue's hibernation ended early?" asked River.

"I imagine it's because you are both needed. You are each crucial to the war that approaches." She lowered her gaze, and her eyes seemed to bore into both River and Blue. "In fact, Madam Madera believes you both to be Heroes of Havensong."

"Havensong?" Blue repeated, then translated for River.

River's eyes widened. "Heroes?"

Xayndra nodded. "Back when the world was born, these lands were all known as Haven. Even then, the Fates could see a darkness coming. They wrote the great Havensong for humans to learn across the realms. Singing of the Heroes who would one day save us all."

Blue's mouth hung open in surprise. Once Blue translated, River had to take a seat on a tree stump, trying to absorb Xayndra's words. It all seemed like too much. Impossible. Blue and River definitely didn't feel like heroes. Not even a little bit. They'd barely managed to make the journey to the Meraki without yelling each other's heads off.

Or getting eaten by wolves.

Or mauled by poisonous shadow bears.

Xayndra closed her eyes and inhaled deeply. "There is a great restlessness in the realm—can you feel it, Blue?"

Blue shook his head.

"You will learn, in time, to sense it. I know this feeling all too well. It is the edgy stillness just before war." She sighed. "So far, Jarum and I haven't been able to make contact with any of the Mainland dragons or their Riders, which is gravely concerning. We can't confirm anything that's happening."

"You do believe Wren about the sleeping gas, though, don't you?" asked Blue.

"I know the girl speaks the truth—remember my special ability? But convincing the Council will be another matter entirely. Very soon, I fear we will all be facing battles on multiple fronts."

A shiver ran down Blue's spine.

Because as Xayndra was speaking, there was a trembling beneath his feet.

49.

IN WHICH WREN FACES
THE COUNCIL

The Meraki Council Chambers felt colder than a snowstorm. Or maybe it was Wren's fear, chilling her from the inside out. The enormous glass ceiling hung overhead in a large dome, making her feel incredibly small. From where she sat, the seven glittering Meraki crystals on the roof could be seen through the glass ceiling, casting a shimmery array of rainbow lights across Wren's lap.

The same gemstones Cudek was after—if Shenli was telling the truth. She looked down at his message on her wrist, wondering what he was doing right now. She'd sent him a quick thank-you response last night but hadn't heard back from him since.

Wren's Magic gave a little chittering sound, and Wren stroked it. It remained bound to her wrist, per order of the Council, and she could tell how it hated to be constrained. It quivered as she shifted uncomfortably in her chair.

The chair of *the accused.*

Across from Wren, the high-back chairs of twelve Elders of the Meraki Council formed a semicircle behind Judge Santino Finlar, who loomed over Wren behind his tall podium. The Council

Elders, in keeping with the Meraki fashion of wearing pastel hues, looked like their own kind of rainbow crystals. Each Elder donned a different-colored robe with a formal ivory sash across the chest, reserved for trial hearings.

The crisp, clean sashes only made the fear in Wren's gut burrow even deeper.

As she scanned each Elder's face, she suddenly thought of the people in the wet market in Shenli's village. The Wedi people might've worn bland clothing, but as a whole, they looked as diverse as the Elders sitting before her. Some were older, with gray hair and wrinkles. Some were tall and had dark skin; others short, with pale skin. Some looked grumpy, while others always held a hint of a smile in their eyes.

Did the Elders really think the Mainlanders were so different from them? Weren't they all just . . . people?

From the middle of the Elder row, Granmama gave Wren a reassuring smile. Maybe her grandmother could sense how the knots in Wren's stomach seemed to be mass-reproducing.

And it was no wonder. It seemed the entire island had turned up for Wren's trial. Not a single seat sat empty in the gallery behind her. At least children weren't allowed in the courtroom. She couldn't have stomached Cephas watching this.

Her father was nowhere to be seen. Wren had expected him to escort her to the chambers that morning, but he'd never showed. She tried not to let it get to her. After all, he'd missed a lot of things these past few years. But her trial was a big deal—how could he just *not* show up! She exhaled through her nose, and her Magic whimpered its sympathies.

Judge Finlar cleared his throat, and the courtroom fell silent. His silver eyes seemed darker somehow, his rich brown face full of more anger wrinkles than usual. His white-and-black ocean-wave hair, however, was as perfectly side-swooped as ever.

"We are gathered here today for the trial of Wren Barrow, age thirteen." Judge Finlar's eyes flicked to Wren as his silver Magic settled onto the podium. "The felonious charges are as follows: magical negligence, breaking curfew, and traveling illegally to the Mainland. Wren, we will hear your testimony; then the Council will render their verdict. Do you understand?"

Wren nodded, her gut full of boulders.

"Very well. Go ahead and tell us what happened on the night of your disappearance."

Wren tried to inhale a steadying breath, her eyes bouncing from Judge Finlar to the Council members. Granmama gave an encouraging nod.

"I woke up right after the Acquisition Day ceremony to discover that my Magic had fled to the Mainland. I took my grandmother's boat to go after it."

"And what happened once you were on the Mainland?" asked the judge.

"I met a soldier boy who needed help finding his family. He's also a personal steward to Chancellor Cudek." Wren fought the urge to sit on her hands, as they were starting to clench at the thought of Shenli's face.

"Yes, your father told us of this . . . warning message." Judge Finlar's bushy dark eyebrows drew together. "Just to confirm his testimony: You opened magical communication . . . with a Mainlander?" asked Judge Finlar as a series of gasps pierced the air.

Wren nodded. "I did."

"Then we can officially add *that* to your lengthy list of infractions," said the judge.

Wren cringed as Judge Finlar scribbled something on a piece of paper and handed it to Elder Drenric, who sat directly behind him.

"The boy has proved to be a helpful informant, sir." Wren kept her voice steady, ignoring the terror in her thumping heart. "As my dad told you, Shenli warned me that Cudek wants our Meraki crystals."

There was a slight murmur from those sitting behind her.

"The Meraki crystals no longer contain magic," said Finlar, arching an eyebrow. "Cudek couldn't possibly have use for them."

"He must think they're still full of magic," said Wren, taking a steady breath. This next part was crucial. "Judge Finlar, at this very moment, the chancellor is preparing to go to war with our people."

Wren's words echoed through the chamber before settling on the stunned Meraki. The Elders, who'd received this information the night before, shared hushed whispers with one another. Judge Finlar held up a hand to silence them.

Did they believe her?

Judge Finlar leaned back in his chair, his eyes flicking upward to the colorful crystals shining through the glass ceiling. "You actually believe this Mainlander boy, Wren?"

Wren had spent all night running it over in her mind. There was much she was still unsure of with Shenli, but she knew how hard it must've been for him to use magic. He'd given up a lot in order to warn her. Plus, her Magic had affirmed him.

Maybe, just maybe, she could trust him.

"Yes, I believe him," she said finally, hoping to the Fates she was right.

"But how can you?" Judge Finlar pressed. "He is our enemy."

Wren frowned. She'd gotten really sick of that word. "Why?" she challenged. "Because of wars that happened hundreds of years ago?"

Finlar's silver eyes narrowed. "There's a *reason* the peace treaty was necessary, Miss Barrow. History proves that the Mainlanders are a foolish and dangerous people—not to be trusted. Declaration Day is but one example. They came to us with lies—blaming *us* for their own troubles—then they turned back around to build an army against us!"

Wren dug her fingernails into her palms in frustration. "But I've seen things for myself! It's the chancellor you have to worry about, not the Mainlander people."

The judge scoffed. "And you've come to such a *confident* conclusion after just a few days on the Mainland?"

"That's more days than *you've* spent on the Mainland, isn't it?" Wren shot back.

Judge Finlar's cheeks darkened. "Watch it, young lady," he warned.

Wren's Magic let out a low growl.

Wren inhaled slowly, trying to tame her temper. Challenging the judge wasn't the way to win this. She had to make the Council understand the whole picture.

"There's something else," she told them. "Cudek has found a way to put the Mainland dragons to sleep—permanently. It's only a matter of time before they're all incapacitated. Think of what the chancellor could do then—with no dragons to stop him!"

A new chorus of gasps echoed through the courtroom, and Judge Finlar stood up. His face was livid. "Enough!" he boomed, slamming down his gavel on the podium. "Wren, your falsehoods are out of line!"

"I . . . thought my father already told you this?"

"He did nothing of the sort."

Wren's heart thudded in her ears. She knew her father had wanted to make contact with one of the Riders on the Mainland in order to confirm the sleeping gas, but she'd assumed he'd at least given the Council a heads-up. How could he not have told them!

Fists clenched, Wren stood and turned to face the people behind her. Hundreds of eyes stared back, some anxious, some sympathetic. "I have no reason to lie!" she told them.

"It wouldn't be the first time a child lied to get out of trouble," said Finlar. It was impossible to miss the smugness in his voice.

"Shenli saw one of the sleeping dragons himself!" Wren said through gritted teeth. "I'm *not* making this up."

"What you claim is completely absurd," said Finlar, waving a dismissive hand. "We monitor all dragons of the Northern Realm. If they were in danger, we would know. Your *father* would know."

Wren stiffened, the absence of her father looming even larger in the room.

"The Dragon Riders would've notified us of trouble," Finlar went on, his voice now calm as he settled back down in his chair.

"But what if the Riders have been captured or put to sleep too?" said Wren. "They'd have no way to contact us."

Another wave of silence seeped through the room. Judge Finlar glared down on Wren for a long while as a flitting of whispers passed through the Council members.

"Miss Barrow," Finlar said at last. His voice had softened some. "You have been through a great ordeal these past years with the loss of your mother, and for that, I am sorry. But the accusations you are making are preposterous. I understand you are afraid, but you do yourself no favors by spinning stories."

A terrible dread settled on Wren's chest.

"They're *not* stories," said Wren, shooting a desperate look at Granmama. "What I'm telling you is *true*!"

Judge Finlar sighed. "You've always been a . . . unique girl, Wren. We are all well aware of your overactive imagination. Our people have treated your . . . *oddities* with kindness in the wake of your mother's tragic passing. But the fact remains that you committed treason."

Wren swallowed hard. "I understand. But the Mainlanders are *coming*. We have to prepare."

Would *none* of them listen to her? Granmama sat solemnly, her eyes unreadable.

"Your imagination has taken you too far this time," Finlar continued.

The crowd murmured their agreement. Wren rose from her chair, terror burning white-hot from her face to her fingertips. They *all* thought she was making it up! The fools! They were so out of touch with the realities of the Mainland, they couldn't see reason.

Judge Finlar stood. "I think we've heard enough, child. Members of the Council, would you please render your verdict?"

"No—no, please!" Wren begged as two guards came to stand on either side of her. This wasn't how things were supposed to go. Surely *this* couldn't be the story she was meant to be a part of.

Elder Poppy Drenric rose, her face grim. She handed the judge a slip of paper without a single glance at Wren. Judge Finlar read the paper slowly and blew out a long breath.

"Wren Barrow," said the judge, "the Council members—all but one"—he shot an annoyed look at Granmama, who countered with a scathing scowl—"have determined that your actions prove your serious lack of judgment. It is clear that neither you nor your Magic"—Wren's Magic snarled from her wrist—"can be trusted. You know the Meraki creed. Order. Preservation. Tradition. As it is, your reckless behavior indicates you have no place in our society. That is why you are both hereby exiled from Meraki Island."

All the air left Wren's lungs.

"You will be relocated to the Midland Isle of the north until further notice."

The Midland Isle was where all the worst Meraki prisoners were held, hundreds of miles north of Meraki Island. Rumor had it all the prisoners lived in tree-house cages and ate nothing but rotten fish and bananas.

This couldn't be happening.

"The Meraki are a people of order and civility," Finlar continued. "And you, Wren Barrow, are something else entirely." His eyes grew cold with certainty. "Something . . . *lesser.*"

At the judge's words, Wren's Magic unhooked itself from her wrist and shot up into the air. The periwinkle cloud grew in size and darkened to a dull charcoal. It let out a deep growl, echoing all around the chamber.

"Wren Barrow!" Finlar roared, his eyes wide. "Get ahold of your Magic this instant!"

Wren watched helplessly as her Magic inched toward the judge, whose confidence from moments before was leaking out of him faster than water from an overturned jug. Small crackles of energy surged through her Magic now, like tiny purply-blue lightning bolts. And there was a beeping sound coming from somewhere inside it.

"What's that?" someone asked from behind Wren.

Beep.

"Sounds like a timer?" someone guessed.

Beep.

"A timer? Like . . . for a bomb?"

Beep.

Wren gasped, realization hitting her as her Magic trembled violently right in front of Judge Finlar's face.

Beep.

Then her Magic let out a wild scream like an angry panther. All at once, pulses of violet and blue light shot forth from her Magic in every direction. Wren felt the blast of air against her face as the judge and all the Council members—except Granmama—were knocked out of their chairs.

For a moment, no one moved. Wren looked around in bewilderment. Every single person in the chamber except her grandmother now lay sprawled on the floor, their various-colored Magics hovering over them. Thankfully, no one seemed to be hurt.

Wren's Magic let out a satisfied huff and shrank back to its normal size. Then it floated back to Wren and secured itself innocently around her wrist. It inflated and deflated steadily, like a human out of breath.

"Well now," said Granmama, standing and tapping her cane in satisfaction. "That's one way to get rid of nonsense talk."

Slowly, people pushed themselves to their feet. Everyone's hair was blown back like they'd taken a wild ride on the back of a dragon.

Or a magnificent, time-bending fox.

"*WREN BARROW!*" Judge Finlar roared, pulling himself back into his chair behind the podium. His once-swooped hair now stood straight up on end. "Just *what* do you have to say for yourself!" He pointed his gavel shakily at Wren, and her Magic snarled in warning. "Of all the petulant *tantrums*—"

But the judge didn't get to finish. At that precise moment, the chamber doors burst open. Wren's father charged into the room with his Magic racing along behind him, glowing a brighter shade of honey gold than usual.

"Cudek has taken out the dragons! We have lost communication with our Riders on the Mainland—all but two!" Jarum looked clearly out of breath as he pushed his way through the crowd until he stood next to Wren, facing the Council.

Her heart soared in silent relief.

"Moments ago, I finally made contact with Hugo and Raeku, our remaining Riders in the Char District. They're in hiding with their dragon, Dallon. The other six Mainland dragons are in a deep sleep— I've confirmed it. The other Riders have all been abducted by Cudek's soldiers." Jarum put a hand on Wren's shoulder and squeezed. "Wren informed me yesterday, but it has taken me all night and morning to confirm it. It is just as my daughter has told us—Cudek is readying for war."

A great commotion rose through the crowd all at once. Judge Finlar stood slowly, bringing a hand to his mouth. Several moments of shocked silence settled over the room before the judge found his voice.

"The Council . . . is to proceed at once to the war room," he announced. "Everyone else, return to your homes immediately. We will inform you with updates as we have them."

Everyone stood abruptly, shuffling their way hastily out of the courtroom.

Judge Finlar turned to Wren. "Don't think you're off the hook here, Miss Barrow. You and your Magic will both serve your sentences." His eyes flicked to Granmama, who shot him a withering look. "But first it seems we have more pressing matters to attend to."

"May the Fates help us," Granmama breathed, giving her cane a solid thump. "The dreaded darkness is finally upon us. And I fear we most certainly will be overtaken."

PART V

SAVING
DRAGONS

50.

*T*here is a stirring in the realms.
　　Can you feel it?

*A Hunger or a Devil or a Devastation—I cannot tell which. I do
not have the gift of Sight, like some. But I can hear the whispers in the
place between dreams and wakefulness. We would do well to remember the old song, dear kit.*

I cannot promise you a happy ending, child.

But that doesn't mean we stop hoping for one.

The song is a warning:

NIGHT WILL FALL AND THE DARKNESS RISE
PEOPLE OF PEACE RECOUNT THEIR LIES
CONFRONT THE SHADOWS
AS DRAGONS SLEEP
THE CHILDREN FALL, THEIR MOTHERS WEEP

THE FATES TURN AWAY, THEIR SORROW WOKE
THE BEAST OF FIRE—THE ONLY HOPE
THE GIRL FROM THE MOUNTAINS WILL ENDURE
A FORGOTTEN SONG TO CLAIM THE CURE

51.

IN WHICH CUDEK
PREPARES FOR WAR

The Char District lay at the northernmost tip of the Mainland. A cluster of scraggly black mountains swept across the landscape, clawing toward the sky like angry arrows. Most of the land had become uninhabitable when its single volcano had erupted centuries prior. After that, Mainlanders considered the place bad luck and steered clear.

Shenli now stood waiting to meet Chancellor Cudek on the far side of the Char Mountains, where a large military base had been covertly constructed. Apparently, Cudek had been busy. Five enormous black-hulled ships towered before Shenli, docked and near-ready to deploy; rows of shiny cannons decorated each ship's perimeter. From atop each crow's nest, a crimson flag flapped in the breeze. A handful of cadets ran about, making repairs and loading supplies as Shenli waited.

He pulled at the collar of his new military uniform, the smell of volcanic ash clinging to the air. At last, the chancellor emerged, walking down the gangplank of the nearest ship, followed by a group of his military generals and commanders. Shenli stood a little straighter.

Commander Alizah spotted him and gave him a nod before she and the others walked on, leaving Cudek and Shenli alone, gazing at Cudek's impressive nautical fleet.

"I've never seen anything as grand as these ships, sir," said Shenli, falling in step with the chancellor as they walked the dock perimeter. He'd learned early on that a bit of well-timed flattery went a long way with Cudek. "We could fit all the people in my home village on one of these things."

"There's enough room to hold a thousand soldiers each."

Shenli recoiled. "You're sending *five thousand* soldiers?"

"Indeed. Let's show those magic fools what we're made of."

Shenli held back a grimace as he gazed at the five ships once more. Five thousand soldiers was *half* the military! So many lives at risk. And all for what—some magical gemstones? He hoped to the Fates Wren had been able to warn her people by now.

"The Meraki won't stand a chance," said Cudek.

"Won't they see us coming?" Shenli asked. Cudek's ships were mighty, but they were nothing the fire from the island dragons couldn't take care of.

"In fact, they won't see a thing," said Cudek. He held up his left palm and a wisp of maroon smoke shot out.

Shenli's mouth fell open, his eyes glued to the cloud. "You . . . have a Magic companion?"

The smoke cloud hovered at the front of the ship until the wooden hull began to disappear, like someone was erasing a drawing.

"Oh, I'm full of surprises. I've been planning this attack for decades."

Shenli stood dumbfounded as the entire ship vanished. Cudek grinned, flicking his hand upward. The little cloud flew back toward the chancellor, tucking itself into Cudek's coat sleeve.

"With this kind of magic cloaking, not even the dragons will detect us. We will surround the island and take the Meraki completely by surprise."

"Won't the ships crash into each other if they're all invisible?"

Cudek raised an eyebrow. "I appreciate your attention to detail, Zhao. But not to worry. I have it taken care of."

"Do the generals and commanders know about your Magic?" Shenli asked quietly.

"They do now." Cudek's mouth pulled into a grim line. "They will learn to adapt."

Shenli couldn't imagine they'd taken the news well, but he didn't dare mention it.

"What about the cannons, sir?" asked Shenli, nodding to the array of polished black cannons lining the ship's hull. They reminded Shenli of creepy spider legs. "Why so many?"

"I like to be prepared."

Shenli's wrist itched. He had to warn Wren. "When do we sail?"

"We're only waiting on the last dragon to fall. I've just been informed we've lost track of the Char District dragon." He muttered a few choice words under his breath.

Shenli hoped this meant Wren had been able to warn her people and the dragon was hiding somewhere safely.

"We can't move forward with the attack until that final dragon is found and sedated. But we have a solid lead, and I'm confident the firebreather will be dealt with shortly."

Well, that wasn't good news. Still, Shenli reactivated his *impressed* face. He had to keep Cudek talking. The more he learned, the more he could share with Wren.

"It's quite a remarkable feat, sir. Putting the dragons to sleep, I mean. I didn't know it was even possible."

"No one understands the opportunity that awaits us—if only we are audacious enough to seize it. All it takes is patience and preparation."

Shenli's *impressed* face faltered a bit as he caught the gleam in Cudek's eye.

"Like stealing the Meraki crystals?"

"My plan is much greater than crystals, Zhao. I'm talking about opportunity on a grander scale."

"What opportunity, sir?" Shenli whispered.

"Revenge, my boy. *Proper* revenge."

Shenli wondered if there was such a thing as *improper* revenge but didn't dare ask.

"You'll be a part of it too, you know. A chance to regain your family's honor."

That got Shenli's attention.

"Why do you think I brought you here today? Why do you think I'm telling you all this? You will be crucial to the final phase of our attack."

"Why me, sir?" Surely there were thousands of experienced soldiers who could do the job better.

Cudek tore his eyes from the ships, giving Shenli a once-over. "Let's call it another unpaid debt from your father."

Before Shenli could respond, Cudek thrust a finger into his chest.

"I'm taking an incredible gamble on you. And if you let me down—even for a *moment*—your mother and sisters will be the ones to pay." Cudek's eyes flashed dangerously. "Do we have an understanding?"

A deep shiver worked through Shenli's bones, and he forced himself to nod. "Yes, sir."

"Now come along," said Cudek, backing away from Shenli. "The decks need a good scrubbing."

Shenli, still shaken, followed Cudek up the nearest ship's gang-plank to the deck, where a mop and bucket awaited. As soon as Cudek was out of sight, Shenli slid two fingers to the underside of his left wrist, hidden beneath Mama's scarf, and sent Wren his message:

> *5,000 soldiers. A fleet of cloaked ships. And he's got a*
> *Magic companion!*

The message he *didn't* send but that his heart was screaming out in certainty was:

> *Cudek is too powerful.*
> *I'm so sorry.*
> *But the Meraki are going to lose.*

52.

IN WHICH THE DRAGONS PREPARE FOR WAR

It had been nearly two weeks since Blue's arrival at Meraki Island, and he'd spent every moment preparing for a war he didn't understand. In a body he still wasn't used to. The closest thing he knew to battle had been watching the sword drills of the royal knights, who were always ready to face a possible attack from dragons. But they'd never known *war*. Much like the kingdom knights, the younger island dragons were filled to bursting with honorable tenacity. And zero real-world experience.

If any of the older dragons felt afraid, they didn't show it. So Blue hid his fear tucked away someplace deep inside. He was a dragon too, after all—even if he didn't entirely want to be. More than anything, he wished he were still a human boy, small enough to hide in the stable rafters. No one had looked to Blue the stable boy to save anyone from war. Blue the human could spend his days peacefully cleaning out stalls, brushing Cedar's coat, and falling asleep to the sounds of crickets and horsey snores.

Life was so simple back then.

And Blue ached for it.

But he had little time to feel sorry for himself. The Meraki people were counting on him. So early each morning, Blue, River, and the other island dragons—Kado, Pydin, Argon, and Ikor—sat listening to Jarum and Xayndra tell stories of the wars of old. Kado the elder dragon always settled himself on the other side of Jarum, his purple scales gleaming in the dawn light, while Pydin, Argon, and Ikor sat solemnly with their Riders.

"War is a senseless horror," Xayndra told the dragons while Blue translated to the Riders and their Magics. "A swift victory is the best we can hope for. And perhaps we dragons might put an early stop to things, before they escalate."

"We've known many years of peacetime," said Jarum, gesturing to the vast sea. The dark waters lapped with a sense of foreboding. "But now we must prepare for what is to come. First, here is what we *know:* The Mainland dragons have been rendered unconscious, save one. Dear Dallon, as far as we know, is still safe, along with his two Riders. My daughter has also informed us, by means of her Mainlander soldier confidant, that Cudek has acquired a Magic companion for himself."

A cry of shocked horror rang through the group—from humans, dragons, and Magics alike.

"We don't know how he attained it," Jarum continued as his own Magic let out a growl of disgust. "But with it, Cudek plans to approach our islands in cloaked ships, which could happen any day now. It is very likely you won't be able to see, hear, or even smell the Mainlanders coming."

"Not even Smell their emotions, you mean?" asked Blue.

"Exactly," said Jarum, running his hands through his dark hair. "I imagine if the ships *do* get past us at sea and arrive on our shores, Cudek will not be able to manage continual cloaking, at which point, the fleet will be visible."

"And once the soldiers come," said Blue, the next words sticking in his throat, "are we supposed to . . . kill them?"

The dragons stared into the morning campfire, not daring to look at one another. The stench of Fear and Sorrow in the air enveloped them. Xayndra cleared her throat, signaling to Jarum her desire to answer the question first.

"May I remind you, dear ones, we want to end this war with as little loss of human life as possible—and that includes the lives of Mainlanders. They might be our enemy in wartime. But many of those soldiers are *children,* forced to fight for the cause of a tyrant. They will be frightened. Try to scare them into retreating, and attack only when you absolutely must. Is that understood?"

Blue nodded along with the rest of the dragons, even though he really understood very little.

After the sun hit the dragon caves each morning, the dragons trained. First, all the dragons practiced their mind-speak from various distances. Later they split up. The oldest three—Xayndra, Kado, and Pydin—honed their fire-breathing skills, working with targets along the mountainside in various attack scenarios. Blue, Ikor, and Argon worked on their flying skills. They practiced speed, agility, and soaring in formation. They flew until Blue's wings ached and his muscles struggled to obey him. In the afternoon, the Meraki children came to train with the dragons. Every day, the children took turns riding each of the six dragons in small groups.

"The children will be barricaded in our strongest buildings," Jarum told the dragons, helping a little girl down from Blue's back. "But even still, we want to be prepared for the worst. They've seen you around the island, but now they need to get to know you and trust you on a new level."

As the days went on, the reality of Blue's dragon duties weighed on him heavily. He did his best to treat each child gently to keep them in good spirits. Since he was the only dragon they could talk to, the children gravitated to him at the end of each training day, laying on a myriad of questions.

"Why do you have feathers?" asked one.

"Are dragons scared of the war?"

"My mama said you used to be a king—is that true?"

"How old are you?"

"Why are your eyes blue instead of yellow?"

A little girl with big brown eyes then leaned in close. "Will you keep me safe, Blue? I don't want to die."

Blue's heart nearly ripped into two as he lowered his face to the child's. Blue didn't know how to keep anyone safe. But maybe he could make her feel better anyway. "What's your name?" he asked.

"Lillian," she breathed, her voice barely a whisper.

"Of course I will keep you safe, Lillian." An ache burrowed deeper in his chest as he gave his best toothy grin. Lillian returned the smile, and it washed over Blue like sunshine. And with the promise of a dragon in her heart, the little girl skipped away with a fresh waft of Joy rising in the air.

After a full day of training, the children returned home and the dragons and Riders collapsed in their caves and tents in exhaustion. As Blue drifted off to sleep every night, he dreamed of golden threads and burning fields and each Meraki child's face and scent. In his dreams, he was large enough to carry them all on his back, soaring so far into the distance not even war could reach them.

53.

IN WHICH RIVER SINGS
AN IMPOSSIBLY OLD SONG

As all the Meraki Harvesters and Healers were called to the medical ward to prepare extra healing elixirs, River volunteered her evenings to help sort through the various plants in the greenhouse, gathering medicinal ingredients that might prove useful.

Once war found them.

After a full day training with Blue, River worked the night shift. She helped alongside Shahin, one of the greenhouse assistants. Exhausted as River was, the only solace she found in all the chaos of battle preparations was the welcoming scent of plants and soil. She now dug her hands into an old planter box, the cool dirt running through her fingers. She felt the familiar call of the earth.

Home, home, home, it called to her.

I miss you, I miss you, I miss you, River called back.

Shahin had a very calming demeanor, reminding River of her nana. As the days wore on, the two girls became loyal confidantes, almost like they were old friends, which was a new feeling for River. She was especially fascinated by the slight shimmer of Shoya on Shahin's hands as they worked under the moonlight filtering in through the glass ceiling. They talked all things gardening to pass the time, sifting through a myriad of greenhouse cupboards and pots and planter boxes with the help of Shahin's basil-colored Magic.

"My grandmother helped run the hospital unit in the last Great War," said Shahin as her Magic helped her organize the sprouted sage. "She specialized in magical plants with medicinal properties and was in charge of overseeing all the medicine prescribed to the wounded. I studied her old journals in the Academy." She shook her head sadly and tugged at her long dark braid. "I never thought I'd be putting her practices to use."

"Well, I think we've done brilliant work so far," said River, nodding to the crates of ingredients they'd collected already. "That's well enough for a hundred more healing elixirs." She hated to think what all those elixirs would be used *for*, and kept her worries to herself. She sighed. Ever since she and Blue had touched down on Meraki Island, every moment had been spent with people enveloped in fear. People hurried from attending meetings to building barricades to training for combat duty, and it was almost busy enough for River to forget about home.

Almost.

After loading some hazel creeper into a crate, River headed to the far side of the greenhouse, carrying a few empty jars. Cabinets of every size and color lined the back wall. She made her way slowly through each one, sorting the small bottles of liquids and powders. After stashing a hearty collection of barberry juice in jars, she opened the doors to a small red cabinet to find the shelves lined with hundreds of bottles of sparkling white dust. She gasped.

"Stardust," breathed River. It took the Dragon Growers *years* to grind the fallen stars into proper fine powder. Very few possessed the knack at the pestle with the ability to grate without sifting out the natural magic.

"It's beautiful to look at," said Shahin, joining her. Her Magic let out an impressed whistle.

"I've never seen so much at one time," said River, brushing one of the jars gently with her fingertips.

"It's prepared by our Magics," said Shahin, wiping some dirt from her forehead as her Magic bounced contentedly on her shoulder. "Though I imagine your people have to go about preparing it by hand, yes?" She shook her head. "It's so strange the Dragon Growers don't have companion Magics."

"The Offering Tree wasn't grown yet," River reminded her. "That happened after my people migrated to the mountain."

River gently removed one of the lids and wafted the smell toward her nose. The familiar scent of burned charcoal lifted her spirits. Oh, how many nights had she snuck out of the house and into the apothecary workshop to sit in the smell of burning stars.

River closed her eyes. "There was an old song my nana used to sing:

> "THE MOON WAKES TO SIFT OUR DREAMS
> AS THE STARS SHAKE DOWN THEIR DUST
> TAKE CARE TO REAP THE GIFT, MY DEARS
> GENTLE HANDLING IS A MUST"

Shahin smiled. "Aren't songs from grandmothers the best?"

"Nana used to sing all the time. But the songs of stardust were always her favorite."

"I can't say what we ever use it for, to be honest," said Shahin. "A shame too. It is stunning."

"The Dragon Growers use it in the dragon hibernation elixir," said River, remembering the Elders sprinkling the dust over the cauldron at Blue's hibernation ceremony. It seemed like so very long ago.

"It must be difficult work growing everything by hand."

"I suppose so," admitted River. "But that's what I love about it. I like getting my hands dirty."

"Ooh, then maybe you can help me with *these*," said Shahin, leading River to a small planter box in the corner. Several silver and red shoots sprouted from the soil. "Someone clearly mixed fire ginger seeds with the drake ginger seeds." She sighed. "We could use the drake ginger roots for healing elixirs, but I can't tell the two apart."

River nodded. "They are nearly identical," she said, rolling up her sleeves. "The key is to look at the patterning on the roots. It's faint, but if you look closely, the drake has straight lines and the fire root has swirls. See?" She held up two different roots.

"That's brilliant!"

"Another lesson from Nana." River laughed, tossing the drake ginger root into her crate. "Because you definitely don't want to get it *wrong*."

"I imagine the fire ginger would do a number on the digestive tract, yeah?" asked Shahin, raising an eyebrow. Her Magic snickered.

"Definitely *not* a fun way to clear out your bowels," said River. "Happened to one of our Elders once. A Harvester apprentice served him the wrong root juice and the poor man spent the entire next week on the toilet."

The girls giggled, then went back to work sorting roots. River sighed, a wave of homesickness rising in her chest. "Fire ginger works wonders for replenishing sick magical plants, though," she said, still halfway dreaming of home. "Kind of acts as an adrenaline shot. Saved a batch of my nana's moonberry bushes once."

"You are clearly a talented Harvester," said Shahin, inspecting the patterns of the root in her palm. "I can't imagine you ever allowing your plants to get sick."

River grinned. "Not so much, no. But in *theory*, fire ginger would do the trick."

A low gong sounded, signaling shift rotation.

"Guess these roots can keep until tomorrow," said Shahin, wiping her brow with the back of her hand. "I promised my parents I'd come along right at the gong."

River nodded, her own parents' faces settling into her thoughts. "I'm just going to finish sorting this last pile. Then I'll take my sleep shift."

Shahin nodded. "See you tomorrow."

"Tomorrow," River agreed, and they both wondered if it was true . . . or if the Mainlanders would finally be upon them. The girls waved their goodbyes and River closed her eyes, trying to remember another old song Nana used to sing.

GINGER IS A TRICKY ROOT
THE PATTERN OF VEIN PROVES TRUE
THE DRAKE RUNS STRAIGHT AS A SHOOT
WHILE THE FIRE ROOT SWIRLS IN VIEW

River clutched her chest, her tears splashing into the soil. Back at home, she knew her place, her *purpose.* Could she really be just as useful here? She'd been able to help Blue with his broken wing, so that was something. And she'd started to get the hang of flying on his back during training. She was still afraid of heights, but she was getting braver and learning to trust Blue more. But Madam Madera said River and Blue were part of some bigger story to help bring peace. Xayndra had even called them *Heroes.* River desperately wanted to believe it. That she'd been forced to abandon her home and everything she loved for a reason.

During training, she watched all the other Riders and their dragons working seamlessly together. But River and Blue weren't like that. They fumbled about, incredibly clumsy and inexperienced. Even though she and Blue were getting along better these days, River was still convinced Blue had made a mistake in choosing her. They hadn't even made it to the island in time to help Jarum scout the Mainland. Their first official mission had been a failure before it had even started. And here, alone in this room, so far from her parents and the little baby growing in her mama's belly? Sadness and fear welled up inside River, threatening to drown her.

She wiped her eyes on her sleeve and winced—the sleeve was full of dirt. She took a determined breath and tossed another drake ginger root into her crate. She stuck her hands into the planter box, searching for another root, then gasped.

The soil.

It trembled.

And she *knew.*

Just like she knew when the starlight shone too dimly, or the exact moment to harvest moonberries. She knew the soil trembled *in fear.* And she could hear the words it whispered to her, in its restless ache:

They are coming.

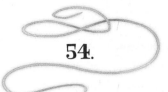

54.

IN WHICH WREN BECOMES A WARRIOR

Ultimately, the Council decided to temporarily postpone Wren's banishment. The day after the trial, Judge Finlar had approached her, somewhat abashedly, and admitted—with much reluctance—that her Magic's "unique" abilities, while "brazen and reckless," might ultimately prove useful in battle. Therefore, the Council would allow Wren and her unruly Magic to fight.

It had taken everything in Wren not to unleash a firestorm of verbal fury at the judge. At the trial, Finlar had called her *lesser*. Did he think she'd forgotten? Now he had the audacity to turn around and ask Wren and her Magic to risk their lives? It was beyond infuriating. The only reason she'd agreed was because her people needed all the help they could get. But then what would happen? If Wren and her Magic made it through to the other side of battle, would the Council still banish them to the Midland Isle? Everywhere Wren looked, things seemed hopeless. And the uncertainty of her future piled on angrily, like she was wearing a weighted backpack.

In a matter of days, the beauty of Wren's entire island transformed around her. There were the physical signs: landscaping left untended, the upkeep no longer a priority. Everyone ran where they needed to go, as there was little time to waste on walking. All around the island, Wren's world twisted upside down, painted in layers of preparation. The library turned into a second medical ward—Wren could hardly stand to think why such a vast space would soon be needed.

The Academy grounds were used for Magical Combat classes. Wren and her classmates were called to train with their young Magics alongside some of the adults. With Cephas spending his afternoons training with dragons and Granmama sealed away in Council meetings all day, Wren felt utterly alone, apart from her Magic. But she didn't have time for loneliness, so she shoved it down into the hidden places and focused on her training.

Elder Poppy Drenric, in charge of Magical Self-Defense, now stood before her group of fifty young pupils, who had been given the name Squadron Three just that morning.

"We will leave the fighting to the adults, especially those who have already known war," Elder Drenric told them, her pine-colored Magic hovering over her outstretched palm. "Those of you under the age of eighteen, I will teach you and your Magics to shield and defend."

And so they trained. The youngest of the Meraki warriors learned how to call their Magics to bend and form a protective shield. Each companion pair had to work as a team—the humans spoke their instructions and encouragement while the young Magics carried out orders. The Meraki teenagers had to exude patience and give precise direction in order for their Magics to be successful. Each human also had to know their Magic's limits, so as not to tire it out. As an added obstacle, connecting to Magics so intimately was draining for the human companions. They shared a sort of physical bond, so as one's stamina wore out, so did the other's.

Wren strained and struggled along with the rest, maintaining her shield for only a few minutes before she and her Magic became exhausted. When at last Elder Drenric allowed the students a break to rehydrate, Wren collapsed onto the grass. Her Magic called her water bottle to her, and Wren nodded her thanks.

"You're doing very well," Wren praised her Magic as it settled on the grass beside her. It made a few beeping sounds, and Wren laughed. "Yes, your explosion technique is especially impressive. Let's not use that again unless necessary, though."

Wren shivered, thinking of the Mainlanders who could be on their way at any moment. Shenli's last message still haunted her. *Five thousand soldiers.* The entire Meraki population barely reached that number, including all the Meraki who were too old or too young to fight.

Wren exhaled and pushed herself back up to her feet, her Magic hovering next to her. She took another drink of water, her gaze falling to the sea. Past the hastily constructed barricade wall, she could feel the Mainland out in the distance. The barricade caused the wind to reroute, sending the northwestern breeze across the lawn, the smell of apple pie settling into Wren's nose from the Memory Trees.

The old memory stirred: her mother baking apple pie late into the night, waiting for Father to get home from work. She'd sliced a piece for Wren as baby Cephas lay asleep in her lap. Together they watched the sunset.

"Did you know that no sunset is ever the same? Sunsets never get tired of creating something new," Wren's mother told her, kissing her on each temple. "And so it is I can never tire of telling you how much I love you, my sweet dolphin girl."

Elder Drenric called everyone back, and Wren shook the memory away, losing herself once more in her training. Squadron Three worked well past dinnertime, until the moon hung high overhead and at last Elder Drenric dismissed them for a few hours of sleep.

By the time Wren reached her bedroom, she could hardly stand. She kissed a sleeping Cephas's forehead—he'd pushed his bed into her room last week. She fell into her own bed, exhausted, every muscle screaming. Her Magic settled onto her pillow next to her, just as weary as she was. Wren's eyelids had barely drooped to a close when she felt a tingling on the underside of her wrist. Her eyes shot open, and she held out her wrist in the moonlight to read Shenli's update.

Just got word. The last dragon has fallen asleep.
    This is it.
    We sail at dawn.

55.

IN WHICH CUDEK
REVEALS A SURPRISE

Shenli stood next to Chancellor Cudek at the bow of the *Dregs'
Revenge I* with a thousand soldiers holding their breath behind him. After a full two days of sailing, Meraki Island now swept
out before them, the sun slowly creeping over the horizon. Beyond
the beach, Shenli could see heaps of green trees behind hastily
constructed barricades. He sighed at the stone blocks piled high,
stretched across the sand. A decent effort, but it would do little
against Cudek's cannons.

A seagull called in the distance, and Shenli tugged at the sleeve of
his uniform. His most recent message from Wren still inked across
his wrist, hidden beneath his mother's scarf.

Please stay safe.

Shenli inhaled deeply, trying to steady his nerves. He'd always
wondered what it would be like to get a closer look at the mysterious
island, but he'd never imagined he would do it as a soldier heading
into battle. Beyond the barricades, the island was stunningly beautiful. Tall palm trees lined the beach, surrounded by gardens filled

with every flower imaginable. The water was so crystal clear he could see the fish and coral on the ocean floor. It looked like paradise. He wondered if his grandfather had thought the same thing when he'd traveled to the island to ask the Meraki for help after the hurricane. The beachy coastline also reminded him of his dreams. All these years, he'd dreamed of Wren Barrow asking for his help. Now here he was, helping to destroy her island.

"You ready for this?"

Cudek's gruff voice snapped Shenli to attention. "Yes, sir," Shenli lied.

According to Cudek, their ship was the last to reach the island, though it was impossible to tell since all the other ships remained cloaked. Shenli glanced up at the strange maroon glow that surrounded their ship like a bubble. Apparently, Cudek's Magic had maintained their invisibility perfectly. When Shenli had asked how the other four ships were cloaked, the chancellor had grinned and made a veiled comment about having help from the borrowed Magics of some *unlucky incapacitated Dragon Riders.*

At Cudek's signal, one of the cadets dropped anchor. Very quietly, soldiers aimed the ship's twelve cannons toward land. All was silent, as if the island itself held its breath. Fear and anticipation wrestled inside Shenli's belly like two hungry monsters. He reminded himself he was doing this for his family.

The chancellor let out a satisfied exhale. "Remember where we're headed."

It was the first part of their surprise mission, which Cudek had shared with Shenli the night before. He'd forced Shenli to study a map of Meraki Island until he'd memorized it. Today, Shenli and the chancellor were supposed to go to the Offering Tree in the middle of the island. Shenli still didn't know what was supposed to happen next. That was the second part of Cudek's surprise, apparently.

"You said I could trust you. Now's the chance to prove yourself."

Shenli nodded, praying his churning insides wouldn't betray him.

Cudek let out a low whistle. At once, the cannons were lit; the sound of wicks burning tickled Shenli's ears in terrible anticipation. The crimson bubble dissipated and the Magic cloud floated downward, securing itself around Cudek's wrist like a wispy bracelet.

Shenli looked over the beautiful island one last time. The cannons fired, their thunder tearing across the sky. Moments later, a chorus of cannons from the other ships fired in response. But instead of flames, green smoke filled the air.

Shenli gasped, his pulse quickening.

Dreamshade.

Enough to cover the entire island.

"Surprise," said Cudek with a chuckle. "Let's see how the Meraki do without the protection of their dragons."

Shenli sucked in a terrified breath as he sent a hurried message to Wren, knowing it would do little good now.

Dreamshade! Dragons sleep!

"Let's get moving before the Meraki have time to recover." Cudek turned to the troops behind them. "Move out!" he called. The soldiers all saluted in unison, then filed down rope ladders and loaded into dinghies, swords at the ready. Shenli watched the small boats fill up and head to the shore.

"I'll race you to the tree." Cudek grinned, his smile cold.

Shenli managed an obedient nod and trudged after Cudek as a new pit of fear settled into his stomach.

Cudek hadn't warned Shenli about the dreamshade.

So what else hadn't the chancellor told him?

56.

IN WHICH THE DRAGONS
GO TO SLEEP

The thunder breaking open the sky rattled in Blue's ears. All around him, the Meraki children screamed. He, River, and Wren stood guard with twenty other Meraki teenagers in the greenhouse—the only building with an opening large enough for Blue to fit through. They formed a circle around the fifty-five Meraki children in their charge, projecting a wispy shield of Magics around them.

"Where'd that blast come from?" whispered Cephas, holding on to his sister's hand.

"There!" said River, pointing upward.

Blue followed her gaze through the large glass ceiling. The sky exploded with green puffs of smoke, until a thick layer formed. The smoke hovered for a moment, blocking out the morning sun. Then it began to drift downward, casting an emerald haze over everything.

"What is it?" asked one of the children.

"Maybe it's poison!" whispered another.

Blue tried to get a whiff, but all he could smell was the immense Fear saturating the air around him. The green haze continued to descend until it touched the ground, covering every inch of the earth like a creepy emerald blanket. The Meraki held their shield of Magics around everyone like a dome, but even still, the green smoke seeped under doorways like a persistent ghost. Blue could smell the fumes before anyone else.

"Are we going to die?" asked Cephas, breathing into his shirt collar. Blue looked down at the boy, his own terror reflected in Cephas's wide eyes. Before Blue could respond, Cephas swayed on his feet. He coughed; then his eyes rolled back in his head just before he collapsed to the floor.

"Cephas!" Wren screamed, breaking her shield and dropping to her brother's side. One by one, each child around the room fell to the ground with a sickening thud.

"What's happened to them?" shouted Rewa, one of the Meraki teenagers. Her hands shook, causing parts of the shield to shudder. Several Magics forming the shield let out low whimpers. "Is it only affecting the little kids?" asked Rewa, her electric-blue eyes wide. She held her hands out firmly to steady her own Magic, though they all knew their shield made little difference now. She looked around. "It looks like it's knocked out anyone too young to have a Magic."

Blue sniffed Cephas and the little girl on the ground next to him. He breathed a sigh of relief at her steady pulse. "They're still breathing," he said, and Wren let out a grateful sob. Her Magic swirled around Cephas's chest.

"I don't understand," said River, cradling the small girl, Lillian, who stayed limp in her arms. "Why use a gas that only affects the children?"

"And how is that even possible?" asked Minnow, one of the older girls. Her magenta braids were pulled tight in a high ponytail. Her lime-green Magic chittered loudly, echoing Minnow's concern.

"Also, if they're only sleeping," said Blue, shaking his head in confusion, "why go to the trouble?"

River gasped, turning to Blue. "Wait, they're only *sleeping*. Blue, it's almost like—"

The ground shook. Outside the window, Ikor soared overhead, his descent erratic, until he crashed against the Academy building midflight, his black scales dull in the green haze.

"Ikor!" Blue called, rising off the ground to get a better view. Ikor's yellow eyes flickered, and his head flopped to the side. Then he fell from the sky with a resounding crash. Blue called out to Ikor through mind-speak, but he got no reply.

"Is he . . . ?" River's hands went to her mouth.

Ikor's down! Blue called through his thoughts to any dragon who could hear him. Only silence came in return.

"Mercy of the Fates," breathed Wren. "They've taken out our dragons."

Qez, one of the youngest Meraki teenagers, gaped at Ikor's crumpled form. "But without the dragons protecting us, do we even stand a chance?" he asked, his cinnamon-colored eyes wide.

"It's the dreamshade—Shenli's just told me," whispered Wren, running a thumb over her wrist. Her eyes flicked to River. "That's what you started to tell us earlier, wasn't it?"

River nodded, her face pale.

"Dreamshade?" asked Blue. "Like what happened to the Mainland dragons?"

Wren's Magic shot up into the air, bursting outward into the shape of a large tree.

"That's . . . the Offering Tree," said Wren, puzzled. "But why—"

"There's Kado!" cried Qez, his tawny face pressed up against a window. Sure enough, off in distance, Kado's huge purple body crashed into the Meraki town square fountain. He flopped to the ground, where he lay unmoving.

"Why hasn't the gas affected you, Blue?" asked River.

"I don't know. Maybe because I'm not a full-grown dragon? Or because part of me is still human?"

"Well, now what do we do?" asked Minnow, her face ashen.

Blue frowned. Minnow was surely the oldest person in the room, and she was asking *him*. In fact, all the Meraki teenagers were looking at him for direction. Cripes, just because he was technically *bigger* didn't mean he knew any more than they did! He was still just a kid. But they were counting on him. Inhaling deeply, he summoned the bravery of the Gerbera knights and stood a little taller. Could he play the dragony role they needed him to?

"I'm going out there to see if I can help," Blue said, trying to keep his voice steady. "You all should stay here and keep your shields up. The children still need protecting."

"You can't go out there!" Wren told Blue as she scooped her Magic into a hug. "You saw what happened to Ikor and Kado."

"But the gas hasn't affected me," Blue pointed out. "And besides, if I'm the only dragon left, then I have a sworn duty to protect your people."

"I'm coming with you," said River, throwing a heap of ingredients into her shoulder bag. "I'm your Rider. I belong with you."

"I think I need to come too, then," said Wren, stroking her brother's hair one last time and pushing herself to her feet. "I know the island best, and I might be able to help."

Wren's Magic raced from her shoulder and expanded into a huge tree shape again, this time glowing white. It let out a low whine.

"I—I think it's confused," said Wren, her brow knitting in concern.

The large tree-cloud bounced up and down emphatically.

Blue eyed Wren's Magic sadly. It wasn't the only one who was confused. He didn't have the heart to tell the girls he didn't actually have a plan. That he was about to fly off into the heart of battle without any idea what to do next. He only knew it was his *duty*. He lowered his belly for River and Wren to climb onto his back; then he pushed off from the ground.

"Watch over my brother!" Wren called as Blue soared outside through the large double doors, wails piercing the morning air.

Blue circled around toward the back of the greenhouse, rising swiftly. The green fog had mostly settled onto the ground, and from his altitude, he could see the entire island. He nearly froze at the sight of it. As grown Meraki wept for their children, the five other dragons lay scattered in various locations. And they weren't moving.

But that wasn't even the worst of it.

Five massive ships had come ashore. Blue watched in horror as thousands of uniformed soldiers poured from small boats on the beach, like a swarm of sword-wielding locusts.

"Mercy," whispered Wren. "We are done for, aren't we?"

Just then, Wren's Magic let out a shriek and bolted forward. It hovered for a moment and started expanding in size. It shifted into the Offering Tree again, but this time it was glowing crimson.

"Why does it keep showing us the tree?" asked Blue as the Magic's hue darkened to a stormy gray. The Magic made a sound like a growling whimper.

"Maybe it's a warning," Wren realized. "Something must be wrong with the tree."

Her Magic huffed loudly, its image of the tree turning an even darker shade of charcoal.

"There are a *hundred* things wrong right now," River pointed out, gesturing to the mob of soldiers below. "No offense to your Magic, but we need to go find your father and see how we can help."

"My Magic wouldn't be showing us the tree if it weren't urgent," said Wren firmly. "This is the third time it's happened."

"Your father might be the only one who knows how to help the dragons!" River shot back, amped up to peak frustration. "Without the dragons, we can't hold back the Mainlanders!"

Wren narrowed her eyes. "We need to trust my Magic."

River let out a frustrated sigh and adjusted her grip on Blue's saddle horn. "I guess it's up to you, Blue."

Blue hesitated, smelling a great concentration of earthy leather in the wind. The Anger crackled hotly in the air between River, Wren, and her Magic. Wren's Magic resumed its shape as a smoky periwinkle cloud and hovered inches from Blue's snout. It let out a low, shuddering whine. A cry of desperation. Blue could feel something pulling in his gut, willing him to listen.

"Okay," Blue told it. "We'll go to the tree."

"You're sure?" asked River.

"I'm sure." Blue nodded.

River put a hand on his feathery neck. "After what happened back in the creepy shadow forest, I'm going to trust your instincts."

"You . . . are?" Blue blinked. River hadn't trusted him with anything before.

"We're a team," River told him. "I figure that means I have to let you take the lead sometimes."

Blue's heart swelled.

He hoped he was making the right choice.

"Head south, just past the gardens," Wren told him. "The Offering Tree is in the middle of the valley."

Blue could feel Wren's body trembling as he took off toward the tree. And he knew the same terrible truth pierced her heart as well as his own as they watched the swarms of Mainlanders flood deeper into the island below them. Without the help of the other dragons, there was no way for the Meraki to win this war.

57.

IN WHICH SHENLI PAINTS HIMSELF INTO TROUBLE

Shenli stumbled after Cudek as fast as his legs could keep up, his sword bouncing uncomfortably against his hip as he ran. In less than an hour, Cudek's soldiers had pinpointed the Offering Tree's location and reported it back to the chancellor. Most of the battle gravitated to the Meraki buildings on the northern part of the island, where the Meraki crystals were. So getting to the magic tree, in the center of the island, was surprisingly uncomplicated.

The tree itself was enormous. It stood on a hill in the middle of a large meadow blanketed with wildflowers. It glittered pure white, like a thousand tiny stars woven together. Its leaves were see-through, shaped like large hearts, each one bigger than Shenli's hand. When he looked from the right angle, the sunbeams cast rainbows through the leaves.

It was the most beautiful thing Shenli had ever seen.

As he and Cudek neared the tree, he heard a soft fluttery sound coming from the trunk. Like music.

"Here it is," Cudek said with a chuckle, putting a hand on the trunk. "With not a single Meraki in sight."

Shenli glanced around nervously. Cudek was right. The wildflower meadow spread for hundreds of yards in every direction, and he and Cudek were the only ones around. "How'd you manage that, sir?"

Cudek raised an eyebrow. "It would appear the Meraki have gathered all their forces around their famous crystals. For some reason they seemed to think I was after them." He stared at Shenli for a long moment. Did Cudek know he'd sent messages to Wren? But how could he? Shenli had been so careful. Even worse, Shenli realized Cudek didn't seem concerned about the crystals at all.

"Well, that . . . of course . . . makes sense. . . ." Shenli fumbled his words, trying to not give anything away. "I mean, the crystals are full of magic, right? So they'd suspect you want them."

Cudek scoffed. "My interest in those crystals was only because I believed that was where the Meraki grew new Magics from. But your little friend taught me otherwise. And it's possible I wanted to throw *you* off the trail." He gave Shenli a sharp look. "Turns out my suspicions were correct."

Shenli's cheeks burned. So Cudek did know he'd warned Wren.

"It worked out in my favor anyway." Cudek nodded to the Offering Tree. "With the magic fools preoccupied guarding the crystals, I have complete access to this beauty."

Shenli shifted nervously at the greed flashing in Cudek's eyes. "What are you going to do to the tree?"

"I can't see how that's any of your business," Cudek shot back. "Just do exactly what I tell you."

"Y-yes, sir."

Cudek took the pack from his shoulders and pulled out a large glass jar filled with red goop Shenli didn't recognize.

"What is that?"

"Nightfang paste. My own special recipe." Cudek grinned. "Now take it, and cover the entire base of the tree."

Shenli frowned and took the jar. A thick crimson paste squelched around inside it. "You want me to . . . what?" Shenli shuddered, eyeing the paste uncertainly. Nightfang? That didn't sound . . . good.

"Is there a problem?"

"I . . . um, no, sir."

"Then stop wasting time! Cover the tree. Now!"

Shenli gulped. "What does the paste *do*, though? I mean . . . will it hurt the tree?"

Cudek sneered, taking a step toward Shenli until he towered over him. "Yes. It *will* hurt. Now do your job."

Shenli stumbled back in horror. He'd thought Cudek was only going to steal some Magics from the tree—not destroy the whole thing. Wren's people depended on this tree to grow Magics!

Cudek leaned in closer. "You want to cancel that debt or not?"

Shenli's heart fluttered in response as he thought of his family. But putting Cudek's creepy goo all over the sacred tree felt so . . . wrong. The two Mainlanders held each other's gaze for a long moment.

Destroying the tree *was* wrong.

But Shenli had no choice.

"Yes, sir," Shenli finally answered, his voice trembling. "I'll do it—of course I will."

"That's a good boy."

Shenli shuffled toward the tree, terror thumping in every heartbeat. He willed himself to shut out all emotions as he unscrewed the lid and dipped a hand into the jar. The red paste squished between his fingers like warm mud. Gritting his teeth, Shenli slapped the goo onto the tree. Instantly, the white bark started to glow like embers in a fire. Shenli winced as he smeared the paste around, then dipped his hands into the jar for more, guilt swirling in his gut.

He wasn't sure how much time passed as he painted the tree red.

Cudek paced nearby, talking to his Magic in hushed whispers. Every once in a while he would glance at Shenli to check his progress, until at last the job was finished.

The entire tree trunk, as high as Shenli could reach, glowed an eerie red against the hillside. Slowly, the crimson glow inched its way up the trunk and onto the branches, like slithering snakes, until the bark was covered with Cudek's terrible nightfang paste.

"Well done, Shenli."

Shenli stared down at his red hands. He felt he was going to be sick.

"You might want to clean up, boy. That stuff will start to burn if it hasn't already."

Cudek let out a low chuckle as Shenli fell to his knees and wiped his hands in the grass. Back and forth, staining the flowers red. Biting back a sob, Shenli wondered if he'd ever truly be able to wipe away the terrible thing he'd just done.

58.

IN WHICH RIVER
REMEMBERS HER ROOTS

Up in the air, River held fast to Blue's saddle, with Wren behind her, as Blue flew onward. Down below, charcoal uniforms swelled upon the Meraki barricades from every direction. It reminded River of a swarm of black ants finding a piece of dropped food. The Mainlander soldiers were everywhere. Still, all across the island, flashes of color pushed up against steel blades.

The Magics were fighting back.

River watched in fascination as someone's tangerine-colored Magic flashed brightly, causing a large group of Mainland soldiers to stumble back, blinded. A magenta Magic wrapped itself around a soldier's sword hilt until the blade turned orange. The soldier screamed in pain, dropping her now-melting sword in horror. A pair of yellow Magics flew up behind the Mainlander swarm, slicing at soldiers' legs and arms, clearly causing painful cuts.

River raised an eyebrow, impressed. She'd had no idea companion Magics could be so effective in battle. Still, even with all the Magics and Meraki fighting bravely, there was a concerning number of fallen Meraki below. She wondered if Wren could recognize anyone from this height but didn't dare ask.

"Can Magics get hurt?" River asked instead, watching the color wisps bloom outward like shields against the Mainlanders' swinging swords and arrows.

"Absolutely," Wren answered, and her Magic grunted. "Magics may not bleed as we do, but they can become damaged, even destroyed."

"They're impressive fighters," Blue noted.

River nodded her agreement and peeked again at the battle below. She could see Meraki guiding their Magics to slice through steel swords with gusto as they pushed back against uniformed soldiers. But for every Meraki and Magic duo, there were ten Mainlanders surrounding them. Wren's people were clearly outnumbered, if not outmatched.

"How much farther is the tree?" asked Blue.

River blew out a frustrated breath but kept her mouth shut. She'd already voiced her opinion, and she'd been outvoted. No use raising her concerns again.

"A few miles," Wren answered. "Not far."

The three flew over rows upon rows of houses and hills until a vast green meadow lay below them. A deep valley dipped downward with a single hill rising in the middle. An enormous tree stood at the center.

Blue's head jerked up in shock. "Wren . . . something's wrong with the tree."

They circled around, and as the rest of the Offering Tree came into view, River and Wren gasped. Its trunk glowed completely red. Its crimson-stained branches stretched out toward the sky, as if pleading for help.

River gasped, horrified. "It's . . . *burning.*"

"Hang on, there's someone down there," said Blue, sinking lower.

River spotted a uniformed boy with dirt on his face sprinting away from the tree.

"It's Shenli!" said Wren. "Blue, take us down."

Shenli stopped in his tracks, his face ashen, as Blue descended and hovered right above the boy's head. Then he spotted Wren and looked visibly relieved.

"What's he doing here?" River demanded with another agonized glance at the tree.

"I don't know," Wren whispered, one hand over her heart.

Blue touched down, and River tumbled to the ground with Wren right behind her. River gave the boy a once-over. His black hair stood straight on end, and his dark brown eyes shone wild with fear. He looked too young to be a soldier. Barely older than River, anyway.

"Wren, I'm so sorry!" said Shenli, hugging his arms to his chest.

Wren took a step backward. "You—*you* did this?"

"Cudek . . . forced me to. I—"

Wren clenched her fists. "Shenli, how *could* you!"

"H-he threatened to hurt my family." The soldier boy's shoulders drooped in defeat, and he swiped his palm—a red palm, River noticed—across his eyes. "I am desperately sorry—"

Wren shook her head slowly, her eyes glued to the burning tree. "I really, really wanted to trust you." Her Magic whined, settling onto her shoulder.

River stepped forward and took Wren's hand. Tears pooled at the corners of River's eyes. Such a *beautiful* tree, now oozing with a terrible crimson glow like the smoldering coals of a campfire. It was clearly dying, and the Harvesting knack within River ached deeply. To destroy such a sacred tree was beyond tragic—it was evil.

She threw a withering look at Shenli, who rubbed the back of his neck and shifted his stance. "I . . . I don't think it's burning, exactly. Only glowing. Some kind of spell Cudek is doing."

River's eyes narrowed. "Cudek's Magic can do *spells*?"

"I thought Cudek was after those crystals," said Blue, the strange red glow of the Offering Tree reflecting in his bright blue dragon eyes. "So what's he doing messing with this tree?"

Shenli stumbled a few steps back, clearly in shock at Blue's voice.

"Well—answer him!" River barked at Shenli. "What's Cudek up to?"

Shenli eyed Blue warily. "Cudek told me he was after the crystals, but then he led me here. I only thought he'd try to steal some Magics from the tree. I didn't realize he was going to destroy it. And now he's disappeared." Shenli looked at Wren. "Can you stop the spell?"

Wren shook her head slowly, not meeting Shenli's eye. "There's no way my Magic is strong enough for that kind of counterspell." Her Magic grunted in response and flew toward the tree. "No, wait!" she called after it. But the periwinkle blur raced ahead and grew large enough to cover the entire tree.

"You'll hurt yourself!" cried Wren, running after it. The purply-blue shield-bubble quivered around the tree. For a moment, the tree's red glow seemed to lessen. Then the Magic yelped and shot back toward Wren as if it had been flicked away like a rubber band.

Wren cradled the whimpering cloud to her chest. "That was *very* foolish!" she scolded. Then her face softened. "It was also *very* brave. I'm proud of you for trying."

Her Magic cooed in response.

River turned back toward the tree, the beginnings of an idea fluttering through her. The tree was still a good forty yards away, but if they could get closer— She whirled around, grabbing Wren by the shoulders.

"What's the tree made of?" River asked her.

"It's grown from stardust."

River tore open her medical bag, digging through jars of chopped dream leaves and juniper paste, until she found what she was looking for. At the bottom of the bag, she pulled free two plants. "Fire ginger roots!" she said, showing the roots to Wren. "If the tree is grown from natural magic, then fire ginger will counteract the damage. I don't know if it can stop Cudek's spell completely, but it should help."

"What do we need to do?" asked Blue.

River bit her lip, considering. She pulled a bottle of buxbane elixir from her bag and dipped the fire ginger roots inside. "We need to get these roots to the tree. The buxbane will enhance their abilities. It could be enough to reverse the corruptive spell."

"Cudek's bound to be around here somewhere," Shenli reminded them, giving his hair a nervous ruffle.

"You'd better sort out whose side you're on, then!" River shot back. She didn't trust this shifty Mainlander boy. Not one bit. "We need to get closer," she said to Wren. "Can your Magic help us get these roots to the tree?"

"I don't know," Wren admitted, looking at her quivering Magic. "It didn't exactly go well last time."

Her Magic rose into the air with a huff.

"You're sure?" Wren asked, hands on her hips. Her Magic bounced up and down eagerly. Wren turned to River. "All right. Let's do this."

River nodded and held the purple roots out toward the periwinkle cloud. "Okay, I need these ground up and scattered on the tree roots. That should—"

Wren's Magic suddenly let out a low growl.

There was a faint shimmer next to the tree. A moment later, a man flickered into view, standing before them in a dark green military uniform.

The uniform of the Mainland chancellor.

"Why, Shenli." The man smiled wickedly. "You've brought company."

59.

IN WHICH BRAVERY
HAS CONSEQUENCES

Cudek stepped from the tree's shadow. With his flat golden hair parted neatly at the side and his impeccably clean uniform, he looked more ready for a fancy party than a battlefield. The chancellor was much younger than Wren had guessed—hadn't her history books taught that he'd been in charge of the Mainland for at least half a century? Didn't Mainlander men get gray hair and wrinkles by the age of fifty? He was almost handsome, with his neatly trimmed beard and chiseled jaw. But the coldness in his icy blue eyes set Wren's teeth on edge.

He turned to Wren, a thin smile spread across his face. "So you're the one Shenli's so fond of." His eyes flicked to River and Blue before settling back on Wren. "I see you've found your Magic again. You'd do well to keep it away from the tree."

Wren said nothing. Her Magic quivered at her shoulder, its eagerness coursing through her. "Not yet," Wren whispered, hoping that for once her Magic would have the patience to listen. At this point, she was waiting on River to make the first move. River held the fire ginger roots in her hands behind her back. As soon as she gave the go-ahead, Wren and her Magic would be ready.

"I was hoping you could tell me more about this spectacular tree, dear," said Cudek, his steely eyes still on Wren. "I seem to be having the most difficult time getting it to cooperate."

"It cannot be destroyed," Wren fumed, hoping to the Fates she was right. "Least of all by a *stolen* Magic." She threw a fierce look at the maroon cloud hovering at the chancellor's shoulder.

"Stolen?" Cudek raised an eyebrow. "Don't presume to know everything."

"I know you're trying to destroy our tree! You're a monster!"

"Tell me—what's the tree made of?"

"I . . . I don't know," Wren lied.

"I don't believe you," Cudek sneered. "Let's try this again." The chancellor snapped his wrist outward, and a blinding blur of maroon flew toward Wren. Cudek pulled his hand back, and his Magic snapped across Wren's cheek like a whip. She brought her hand to her face in surprise, her fingertips now stamped with drops of blood. Wren's Magic growled and rose into the air. Wren gritted her teeth, furious. What a dirty thing to use a Magic for!

"Now, now." Cudek raised his hand in warning. "Let's not do anything we're going to regret. My Magic is much more advanced than yours, and if necessary, my next strike will be more . . . permanent." Cudek's gaze fell on Wren's Magic. "Understand?"

Wren's Magic snarled again but lowered itself back onto Wren's shoulder.

"I only want to know what the tree is made of."

"Just tell him, Wren," whispered Shenli, his eyes pleading.

"It's grown from magic," said Wren, her fists clenched. "But I don't really understand how it works."

Cudek cocked his head. "I'm afraid your half-truths are no good to me." He looked at Shenli. "She's proving to be far less valuable than I'd hoped."

Wren flicked a scathing look at Shenli, who took a step back.

"He's just looking for information," Shenli urged. "Then he'll let you all go."

River scoffed. "*Sure* he will." She turned to Shenli. "Like we'd really trust *you*—after what you did?"

Shenli cringed and his cheeks flushed a deep shade of crimson.

Cudek eyed River curiously. "You must be fresh off the training line, Dragon Rider. Be careful, girl. There's more than one way to put a dragon to sleep." His eyes flashed dangerously to Blue, who lowered his head.

Wren shifted slightly, glancing toward the tree. River said the fire ginger had to be ground up, then sprinkled all over the tree roots. She'd seen her Magic do as much with the enderberries. The question was, how long would it take? Her Magic needed to do it all before Cudek noticed. Could her Magic really work that quickly? She ran a thumb over it, and in response, her Magic hummed in anticipation. She gave it the smallest of nods. She trusted it. Now she only had to keep Cudek distracted long enough for River to hand over the roots. River was already moving them behind her back, toward Wren.

"It wasn't enough to attack my people—you had to destroy our tree as well?" Wren demanded. "Are you truly that evil?"

All smugness vanished from Cudek's face. "Do you think life is really that simple, Wren? A line drawn in the sand, dividing the heroes and villains?"

"This tree is sacred to us!" cried Wren. "What you've done makes you the villain!"

Wren saw Shenli's shoulders slump as Cudek took a step forward, his eyes zeroed in on Wren.

"You know *nothing* of what is sacred!" he snapped, his cheeks red with fury. "Your people hoard both natural magic and companion Magics like gluttons while Mainlanders starve. It's just like the hurricane, all those years ago. You could help, but you refuse."

Wren's heart stilled, her eyes locked with Cudek's. Was it truly anger she saw? That couldn't be. The deprivation of his people was *his* doing.

"Your people are *not* the heroes!" Cudek spat. "No matter what your biased history books tell you. Ask your Elders about *the Forgotten Ones*, girl. Then you will know which of us is evil."

"You're *lying*," Wren growled, but a sliver of doubt slithered through her.

"You can't be angry because the Meraki don't share Magics," said River, inching closer to Wren. "The Mainlanders had the chance to bind with Magics long ago, but they refused."

Wren kept her eyes on Cudek as she shifted her stance closer to River. Very carefully, River slipped Wren the fire ginger roots.

"The Meraki hide behind their laws, pretending to be morally superior." Cudek clenched and unclenched his fists. "But the truth is, they are the worst humans of us all."

"And you're here for revenge?" River guessed.

"Revenge is far more complex than you could imagine," said Cudek with a dismissive wave of his hand. "Besides, this fight was never really *mine* to win."

"Wait—what's that supposed to mean?" asked Wren, momentarily losing focus on her task. The roots pulsed in her palm as her Magic slowly lowered from her shoulder to her wrist.

Cudek grinned. "Foolish children, *this* is only the beginning."

The roots pulsed a few moments more, Cudek's terrible words settling into Wren's gut. Then her Magic took hold of the roots and raced toward the tree faster than Wren could blink. There was a loud *pop*, and in seconds, the roots were shredded into a fine powder.

Cudek spun back around, his face contorted in fury as Wren's Magic sprinkled the powder hastily around the tree in a purply-blue whirlwind. There was a sputtering sound from the Offering Tree—much like the sound of water being poured onto burning coals. The bottom of the trunk started to glow yellow where Wren's Magic had dropped the roots. Soon the honey glow spread outward like a beautiful net, covering the red.

"What's this!" Cudek roared, shooting a furious gaze at Shenli. "What have they *done*?" Shenli took a step back, his face ashen as Cudek raised his palm, the maroon Magic hovering. "Did you know about this?"

River turned to Blue as Cudek crept closer. "You need to help Shenli—now."

Blue's entire body tightened with terror. "B-but what can I do?"

"You're a *dragon*!" River hissed. "Protect him!"

Blue's ears flattened, his wide eyes now on Cudek. He took a hesitant step forward, then lowered his head. "I . . . I don't know what do!"

"What's she *done* to the tree, boy?" Cudek repeated. When Shenli didn't respond, the chancellor whipped around toward Wren, the anger on his face blazing wilder than the fading crimson glow of the Offering Tree. "You! You've ruined everything!"

"Blue!" River pleaded, trying to push Blue forward. "*Do* something!"

Blue stood frozen as Cudek's eyes flicked to each of them. Then Cudek thrust his hand outward, hurling his Magic toward Wren. Wren's Magic, coming back from the tree, raced toward her, trying to project a protective shield. But Cudek's Magic was faster. At the last moment, Shenli pushed Wren out of the way, and Cudek's Magic slammed into him, knocking him backward.

"Shenli!" Wren screamed, falling to his side. She watched in horror as a dark stain spread across his chest.

"Fool!" growled Cudek, his eyes falling on Shenli as his Magic returned to him. For a moment, the chancellor's face looked stricken. "You were supposed to be better than your worthless father!" He raised his palm once more, his eyes now locked on Wren. "This . . . is *your* fault—"

Wren's Magic rose into the air and expanded like a purple balloon with blue lightning inside, shielding Wren inside. Cudek grunted, his Magic crackling like maroon lightning in his palm. "Time to teach you *and* your meddlesome Magic a lesson."

"That is ENOUGH!" a voice boomed.

From behind the children, a cloud of purple fog shimmered into view. Then Granmama stepped forward, thumping her cane in the grass. Her violet Magic hovered next to her, dark clouds rippling through it. It let out a deep growl.

Cudek's face went pale.

"So you're attacking *children* now, Cudek? That's low—even for you."

Cudek's gaze flitted to Shenli's body, lying motionless on the ground. "They were foolish enough to get in my way."

"It appears we've underestimated you, Chancellor." Granmama glared at Cudek's Magic, now hovering behind him. "You've kept your secrets well, I see."

Cudek's laugh sounded more like a snarl. "It is *you* who have kept secrets, Madera!"

If Granmama was surprised Cudek knew her name, she didn't show it.

Cudek pointed a finger at the old woman. "I know what you did to the Forgotten Ones, Seer."

Granmama's mouth fell open. For a moment, no one spoke. The fear swirling in Granmama's eyes was enough to take Wren's breath away.

"That's right, old woman. I know where they are." Cudek's wicked grin sent chills down Wren's spine as he took a step forward. "And I'm going to set them free. They will have their revenge, at long last."

Granmama leaned on her cane and regarded Cudek for a long while. "You're no match for my Magic, Chancellor."

Cudek scoffed. "*That's* all you have to say for yourself?" He shook his head in a show of disgust. But he took a few steps backward, putting some distance between himself and Granmama. "I concede I am no worthy opponent against your Magic, Seer. But your warriors are also no match for my soldiers. Not without your dragons. Besides, I got what I came for." He waggled his eyebrows. "Well, *almost.*"

Cudek muttered something to his Magic. There was a bright shock of maroon light, bursting in all directions. Wren had to shield her eyes, the light intensifying behind her eyelids. There was a loud whooshing sound; then the light faded.

And apparently, so did Cudek.

When Wren opened her eyes, the chancellor was nowhere to be seen. In his place, a blue fire blazed, circling the tree. Wren gasped. "How'd he do that?"

Granmama sent her Magic forth, searching. After a few moments, she shook her head. "His Magic is more advanced than I realized. He's gone."

The blue flames rose higher, creeping across the grass, heading straight toward them. Granmama sent her Magic toward the flames, but it whined, jumping back, clearly unable to douse the fire.

That was when Wren realized.

Her own Magic was missing.

"Hang on, where's my Magic—does anyone see it?"

The others looked around, backing away from the crackling flames.

"We have to get out of here!" cried River, throwing a desperate glance at Blue.

Blue's ears pulled back. "I can't carry four people! I'd never get off the ground."

"My Magic!" Wren wailed. "We can't leave it here!"

"My dear." Granmama put a hand on Wren's shoulder. "I believe Cudek has stolen it."

"Wh-what?" Her Magic . . . stolen? Wren let out a sob. She put a shaky hand to Shenli's chest, where a dark stain remained across his tattered uniform. The panic in her heart tripled. Everything terrible was happening all at once. "He's hardly breathing."

"My Magic's strong enough to transport me and one other person," said Granmama. "I'll get Shenli to the medical ward." She gazed at Wren. "He doesn't look good, dear. I don't know if . . ." She shook her head and eyed the growing blue flames behind them. "One thing at a time. Blue, get the girls out of here now. Find Xayndra."

Blue lowered himself to the ground as River helped Wren up onto his saddle. The blue flames were inching dangerously close to them now.

"Xayndra?" Blue repeated. "But she's still asleep. How can she help?"

"She cannot—not without your help. You now have the most difficult job of all, Blue. One that even my Magic cannot manage."

"I do?" asked Blue, shaking out his wings, preparing for takeoff.

Granmama smiled sadly as her Magic wrapped around her and Shenli like a lavender bubble, readying for transport. "You must wake the other dragons and put an end to this war."

"But *how*?" Blue gasped, utterly baffled.

"I have no idea how. But you're the only dragon left, so it has to be you." Granmama's cool violet eyes locked with Blue's. "Do not let us down, my beautiful Dragonboy. Or else it will be the end of us all."

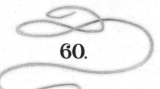

60.

IN WHICH BLUE ENTERS
THE DARKNESS

Blue took to the skies as poor Wren sobbed through the rising smoke, mourning her Magic. When Blue glanced behind him, he could see River patting Wren's back, both of their faces smeared with smoky ash. Below them, Cudek's fire raced across the wild-flower meadow.

"This is my fault!" Wren cried. "I'm the one who told Shenli about the tree."

River uttered a steady stream of encouragement as Blue took them higher into the air to get out of the smoke. His heart twisted with guilt. Everything had happened so quickly. But if anyone was to blame, it was *him*. River had begged him to protect Shenli, but he'd frozen in terror. He hadn't known how to fight Cudek's Magic, and in that moment, he'd felt so overwhelmed by his own in-decisiveness that it was as if all the air had been stolen from his lungs. And he ended up doing *nothing*. Everyone around him was being brave and fighting, but when Blue's moment came, he proved completely useless.

Some dragon he was.

The three traveled in heavy silence, heading north toward Xayndra, who'd fallen near the Academy buildings. Down below, the battle raged on. All over the island, thousands of arrows, shot by Mainlander archers, stuck out of the ground like a tiny forest. Fallen warriors on both sides were scattered as overwhelmed medics rushed to their aid. By now, the Mainlander soldiers had advanced deeper toward the northern part of the island, where a massive Meraki squadron surrounded the Council Chambers to protect the crystals.

Blue snorted. It was all for nothing. And Cudek was right. Without the help of the other dragons, the Meraki couldn't possibly get all the Mainlander soldiers to retreat. But Blue couldn't breathe fire, let alone scare away five thousand soldiers on his own. So what was he supposed to do, exactly? *It has to be you*, Madam Madera had told him.

But she was wrong.

He couldn't do this.

"Maybe you can try something with mind-speak," said River.

"I've already tried that," Blue pointed out. "I can't hear any of them." He grunted in helpless frustration, catching sight of one of the Meraki barricades below. A swarm of black uniforms attempted to shoot arrows through the sandbag walls as a flurry of Magics swirled around them. The Magics appeared to disorient the soldiers enough to make them stagger sideways. The Meraki seemed to be holding their own—for now.

"Granmama believes you can do it," Wren told Blue.

"I believe it too," River added.

Blue tried to allow the girls' encouragement to seep into him, but all he could think about was how he'd let everyone down back at the tree. And how he was just as likely to do the same with Xayndra. Because there were some things that hadn't changed since he'd become a dragon. Underneath the shiny scales and fluffy feathers, he was still just a stable boy. Raised for grooming horses and shoveling hay.

Not saving the world.

"You *can* do this, Blue," said River, her voice whipping through the wind. He wondered if she could sense his despair. "I'm certain you can." She patted his neck. "I have a knack for knowing things, remember?"

He wanted to believe her. And to think—if he *could* wake the dragons, maybe it would all be worth it. Losing his humanness in order to become a dragon. The old Elder had told him his dragon life would matter, and his duty as a dragon was to protect the people. Maybe *this* was Blue's part of the story. Everything came down to this moment.

At last, the Academy campus came into view. Poor Xayndra still lay on her side next to the school entrance, her enormous golden body rising and falling steadily with sedated breath. Blue sank lower, where an invisible cloud of Fear hung more saturated near the ground, closer to all the humans. He dropped down and lowered himself for River and Wren to dismount, then stepped forward, nudging Xayndra's neck with his snout.

"I wonder what this dreamshade is made of," said River, stroking the top of Xayndra's head. "She looks so much like a dragon in hibernation."

"I still don't have a clue how to wake her," Blue admitted.

"There has to be a way for you to enter Xayndra's mind," said Wren, putting a hand on the great dragon's golden belly.

"I've only been doing mind-speak training for a few weeks," said Blue. "And the other dragons weren't unconscious then."

Wren frowned, clutching the amulet hanging from her neck. Her brow knitted as she eyed Blue curiously. "How did you wake so early from your hibernation, Blue?"

"Oh. Um. I really don't know, honestly."

Wren tapped her lips thoughtfully. "Well, if you could wake up early from your own hibernation, then maybe you can wake the other dragons from theirs."

Blue shared a look with River. He'd never thought about it like that. But he hadn't purposely done anything to wake himself.

Or had he?

It was . . .

"A dream," he remembered. "I woke because of a dream."

"Some dream," said River, holding different bottled elixirs to Xayndra's nose to see if the dragon would stir. "Do you remember what it was about?"

Blue closed his eyes, sifting through memories: The fox in the forest. Meeting River at Dragon Mountain. His dragon cave, where he'd gone to sleep. Oh! Yes! He remembered riding on a lion to the endless meadow, where he'd seen himself standing on a hill.

"There was a dragon shadow," said Blue, searching the memory. "It burned everything. The village. The sky. I couldn't stop it. And then . . . a golden thread." His eyes shot open. "The same gold thread we saw right before we crashed! It appeared in my dream. I pulled it, and the next thing I remember is waking in my cave. River was waiting for me."

"The thread can visit *dreams*?" Wren wondered aloud.

"Even if that's true, how does that help us now?" said River, rubbing her temples.

"The thread must mean something significant," said Wren. "Maybe Blue can . . . I don't know . . . send them a golden thread in their minds—just like in his dream?"

Blue scrunched his snout in uncertainty. It sounded crazy. But he didn't have a better idea.

"It's worth a try, I guess," said Blue, closing his eyes. He lay down next to Xayndra and shut out the world around him, focusing on his own breathing, like he'd learned in his training. After a while, in the quietness of his mind, he saw darkness. He could feel Xayndra nearby. He reached out to her with his thoughts.

It's time to wake, he told her. *Xayndra, please. We need you.*

In the darkness, he followed her breathing. A green fog appeared, rising before him. It bubbled and swirled, filling the air. He coughed—did he cough in real life, or only in his mind? He wasn't sure, but the strange fog burning his eyes felt real enough.

It was dreamshade, he realized. The same fog covering the island. He pressed on and a rumbling sound shook the air around him. It sounded like . . . snoring. He walked onward through the fog in his mind and heard breathing coming from another direction. His right. No. He paused, shaking his head. Coming from his left. He turned. Now it was behind him.

Reveal yourself! he demanded, though he wasn't sure *who* he was challenging. At once, the fog cleared. Blue stood inside a golden circle etched into the ground. All around him, five golden lights stretched across the earth in different directions. A star. He was standing in the center. At the tip of each star point, one of the five island dragons slept. Beyond them, seven more dragons circled around the first five. The Mainland dragons! Of course. They were all asleep too.

Wake! he pleaded. *WAKE!*

But all twelve dragons snored on. A surge of doubt sliced through him. He tried to move toward the sleeping body of Ikor, but his feet wouldn't budge. The dragons couldn't hear him and he couldn't get any closer.

This wasn't working.

War blazes all around us like fire—can't you feel it?

Wake!

Please. I am all alone.

379

I need your help.

Hope sank in Blue's chest. None of the dragons stirred. He wasn't strong enough for this.

Then he remembered. The golden thread. But how could he make—

Just as he thought it, a golden thread weaved itself into the space above his head. The thread glittered in the darkness, a faint humming tickling his ears. The thread sat, waiting. Now what? How could he use it to wake the others?

Send the gold thread in their minds, Wren had said. Whatever that meant. Really, though, it wasn't all *that* much more absurd than him standing in some dreamworld with the other dragons, was it? If he could think the thread into existence, then why shouldn't he be able to move it?

Go, he commanded the thread. *Into their dreams. Wake them!*

He watched, dumbstruck, as the thread divided into fifths that raced outward, one to each point of the star—toward the slumbering dragons. Then seven more threads branched out toward the Mainland dragons.

Like a beautiful web, the threads extended onward. As he watched, Blue's vision clouded. He coughed and shook his head, trying to focus, as he started to stagger on his dream feet. He felt so unbelievably *tired* all of a sudden. He struggled to remain standing, watching desperately as each thread reached a sleeping dragon. One thread tapped Ikor on the head, then disappeared. The other threads did likewise, reaching their dragons, then evaporating.

Blue waited, as the world swayed and blurred. But all twelve dragons remained deep in slumber. His shoulders drooped. Absurd as it was, he'd thought the plan might work.

"Blue!"

River's voice?

He turned, and as he did, the darkness bubbled into daytime. He could smell the familiar Fear of the war swirling around him. He blinked. River knelt before him, her tiny hands on his cheeks.

"D-didn't w-work," he tried to say, but the words stuck in his throat.

"Blue, it's Xayndra!" said River. "She's waking."

Blue pushed himself to his feet. He gazed at Xayndra. The dragon's mouth twitched. Her golden eyelids fluttered.

"Xayndra?" whispered Blue, his heart leaping in his chest. He tried to ignore the ringing in his ears. The burning in his throat.

Xayndra's eyes opened one at a time. "Blue?" She blinked slowly. "I—I heard you. In my dream. You were there. And the golden thread—it called to me." She shook her head, her eyes still droopy. "I never knew such a thing was possible."

Blue's world tilted. Something . . . something was wrong. Something burned like a small coal just behind his forehead.

"Oh, Blue," said Xayndra with a grin. "You are *far* more powerful than you know, youngling."

He laughed. A sort of delirious giggle. *Powerful?* Hah! He wasn't powerful. He could hardly . . . keep . . . his eyes open.

"Blue—are you all right?" asked River.

Blue couldn't form his words to respond. He swayed sideways and crashed to the ground. Someone shouted his name.

His name.

Not really a name at all, was it?

More of a placeholder, given to him by the kitchen maid who found him swaddled in a blanket and abandoned on the castle steps as a newborn.

"There isn't even a note. Nobody wants to claim him," the maid had declared, gazing down at him. "Poor little one. But he's a survivor. Just look at those eyes. Like shining blue stars, they are."

Blue the Dragonboy breathed in the long-forgotten memory, tears falling down his dragon cheeks.

And then he remembered nothing at all.

61.

IN WHICH CUDEK'S SOLDIERS MAKE HASTE

The screams of Cudek's five thousand soldiers rang through the air as the five dragons woke all over the island, sending the Mainlanders back to their ships with flames licking at their freshly polished boots. Off in the distance, Kado the purple dragon, with the power to call on rain, sent a flood of water across the meadow, dousing Cudek's terrible fire.

A wave of relief washed through River.

The war was over.

Blue had *done* it.

But he still had not stirred.

Wren had left to check on Cephas, leaving River to keep Blue company. River stroked Blue's neck feathers gently and told him stories of the Dragon Growers as Meraki tended to their wounded all around her. She cupped the small dragon's snout, his cerulean scales matching those around her wrists. Blue had to pull through.

He *had* to.

"You are so brave," River whispered, believing he could hear her. "But I need you to be braver still. Please, *please* wake up."

To lose one's dragon is to lose one's self.

The fate of the Dragon Riders.

Weeks ago, she hadn't considered the emotional connection possible for herself. Now, the thought of losing Blue wrapped around her like ice—cold and terrible. Maybe she and Blue weren't a perfect team, but he was her partner.

Her friend.

To pass the time, River pulled arrows out of the ground, left over from the Mainlander archers. There must've been tens of thousands of arrows, sticking up out of the soil like little spears. It was the strangest thing. River didn't know much about war, but it was hard to imagine that the Mainlander soldiers were such bad shots as to leave this many arrows behind. And the way many of them were grouped together . . . It didn't seem natural.

River reached down toward yet another arrow shaft and gave a stiff pull. She held the arrow out into the sunlight. As with all the others, the arrow's tip was smeared with crimson.

"I mean, it's not blood, right?" River said to Blue, who still lay unconscious a few yards away. She talked to him in case he could hear her somehow. "Since it came from the ground . . . I mean, the *ground* can't be bleeding." She brought the arrow tip to her nose. "It smells . . . fruity. Like firefruit juice. I'd know that smell anywhere." She sniffed again. "But there's something else mixed in. Something I don't recognize. It's kind of a rotten, bitter smell." She gagged a bit. "Ugh. It's disgusting, whatever it is."

River sighed and threw the arrow onto the pile with the hundreds of others she'd unearthed. She swept her gaze around, peering at the thousands of arrows still stuck in the ground like creepy little monuments to the war. These arrows *meant* something, she just knew it. Something bad. But she couldn't put her finger on it.

"Poor Blue. He's a hero."

River turned to find Jarum Barrow coming up next to her, putting his hands on his hips. The man looked exhausted. River knew he'd been helping in the medical wards, tending to the Meraki's many wounded. She spotted the red stains on the Dragon Master's shirt and looked away quickly.

"He wouldn't want you to call him a hero," River told him. "Even if it is true." And of course it *was*. So many fallen around them, but because of Blue, so many more still *lived*.

"What happened?" asked Jarum, kneeling down next to Blue's head.

"He woke the other dragons through mind-speak. He met them in their dreams somehow." River shook her head. "I don't understand it. He was immune to the dreamshade. Then, as soon as Xayndra woke, he passed out."

Jarum rested his palm on Blue's neck. "His pulse is steady. A little weaker than I'd like, though. From what you told me, I think Blue absorbed the dreamshade from the other dragons through their dreams. That's what allowed them to wake."

River raised an eyebrow. "Is that possible?"

"Sounds absurd, I know." Jarum sighed, opening his medical bag. "I've heard the stories of dragons dream-walking in the ancient days. But I always thought they were silly legends." He pulled an oversized stethoscope from his bag and held the metal diaphragm to Blue's chest.

"Sounds amazing, actually," said River.

"Have you seen Wren?" Jarum asked, his voice laced with worry. "I haven't seen her since this morning—"

"She's all right," River promised. "She's just gone to check on Cephas."

Jarum raised an eyebrow. "And what about that Mainlander boy?"

River didn't miss the sudden gruffness in Jarum's tone. "Madera took him to the medical ward. He . . . saved Wren, you know." She wasn't sure it was her place to tell Jarum this news, but she figured it might be easier coming from her than Wren. River had many reasons to still be furious with Shenli, but the boy also deserved *some* credit. "Cudek sent some kind of cursed spell at Wren, and Shenli jumped in front to block her. It was really brave."

"He did that?" Jarum blew out a long breath and shook his head. "Madera told me that the boy was important. I didn't want to believe it—I still don't."

River nodded. "I get it." Shenli had made some major mistakes, but River would never forget the way he had courageously leaped in front of Wren to protect her.

"Any word on Cephas?" River asked, feeling like Jarum needed a subject change.

Jarum's shoulders slumped. "All the children remain unconscious. We can't make any sense of it. We'd hoped once the dragons woke, the children would as well." He stuffed the stethoscope back into his bag. "Especially since the dreamshade evaporated some time ago."

River frowned. "Do you know what dreamshade is made of?"

"I have my theories. Many centuries ago, the dragons were put to sleep temporarily in a similar fashion. It was"—his eyes drifted to Blue—"deemed necessary at the time. Back then, the main ingredients for the sleeping elixir were stardust and dream petals. I imagine Cudek used something similar, though I don't have any idea how he would've been privy to that information. Or where he acquired such rare magic ingredients."

River knitted her brow, deep in thought. "We use stardust for growing dragons. Along with moonberries and firefruit." Something tugged at her. If she could understand how dreamshade was created, perhaps she could find a way to counteract it. All magical elixirs were about stringing together the right quantity of ingredients, and every ingredient had an antidote. Nana had taught her that.

"Let's see." River considered, tapping a finger to her chin. "The moonberries act as a sleep aid for making dragons, much like the dream petals do for dreamshade. And the firefruit helps to slow down their heartbeats, just like an animal in hibernation. But the stardust . . . That's there to add to the *strength* of the spell. Stardust can magnify any spell." She gasped. "Even . . . a spell reversal."

"A spell reversal?" Jarum's mouth fell open a bit. "River, what are you saying?"

River ran through the idea in her head once more, praying to the Fates that she was right. "I'm saying . . . I think I know how we can reverse the effects of dreamshade on the children."

62.

IN WHICH SHENLI
IS LEFT BEHIND

Shenli heard an echoing of voices at first. Then the swirling speech separated into two voices. He still couldn't open his eyes, and his thoughts were all fuzzy, like bubbles underwater. Slowly, he recognized the feeling of a soft mattress underneath him. A *mattress*? Wasn't he on the ground? Cudek had just blasted him with that cursed Magic of his. Shenli's eyes blinked open. Wren and an older woman came into focus. The woman had long silver-white braids and strange purple eyes.

"Wh-where am I?" asked Shenli. His throat felt like gravel.

"You're in the medical ward," Wren told him. "You've been out for a few days."

Shenli winced, willing his brain to work faster. "I'm still on the island?"

"I'm afraid your ride up and left without you," said the old woman, tapping her cane against the floor. "So I suppose you're stuck with us for a while. I'm Madera Starling. Wren's grandmother."

"But I—*arrghh!*" Shenli tried to sit up, and immediately his chest felt on fire.

"Whoa there, soldier," said Madera, gently pushing him to lie back down. "That was a full blast of Magic to the chest, child. You may be feeling a little better, but you are by no means ready to be *going* anywhere. You have a long road of recovery ahead of you."

Shenli winced. Then it all came back to him.

Cudek firing his Magic at Wren, next to the glowing tree.

The tree Shenli helped destroy.

All of this was his fault.

Tears pooled in Shenli's eyes as he forced himself to look at Wren. "Wren, I'm so, *so* sorry—" He blinked hard and shook his head slowly. *Sorry* wasn't enough, not nearly enough, for what he'd done.

Wren cast a glance at her grandmother before meeting Shenli's gaze.

"What you did was horrible." Wren crossed her arms. "I can't imagine ever forgiving you for it."

Wren's words burned white-hot in Shenli's chest. But he couldn't blame her. "Is the tree . . . dead?"

"Nearly," Madera told him, her face stern. "But it's worse than that. That strange glowing red paste was a preparation potion—a means of preparing an object for physical transport."

Shenli frowned.

"It means Cudek wasn't trying to kill the tree," Wren muttered. "He was trying to steal it—to transport it to the Mainland."

Shenli gasped. "Was he successful?"

Wren and her grandmother shared a pained look.

"Yes and no," Madera told him. "Half of the tree is gone. And what's left . . . Well, the Offering Tree will likely never be able to grow new Magics again."

Shenli let out a shuddering breath as he closed his eyes. He couldn't fight back images of his hands painting the tree red.

He had done this.

Someone took his hand. He opened his eyes to find Madera looking at him intently.

"I know what it means to make a grave mistake, child," Madera whispered, her violet eyes awash with pain. "What matters most is what you choose to do after the mistake is made." She squeezed his hand. "Do not let one terrible decision define who you are, Shenli Zhao."

Shenli tried to hold her gaze, but his vision blurred with tears. "I feel like a monster."

"You were scared for your family, so you made a choice. A seemingly impossible choice that ended with dire consequences." Madera cupped Shenli's cheek. "But you also saved my granddaughter's life. And that counts for something."

Shenli blinked, letting the tears flow.

"Not to mention, that brave choice has consequences too." Madera nodded to Shenli's chest, which still ached dreadfully. "You are lucky to be alive, child. Though I fear you will always carry a scar."

Shenli touched his chest gently where the Magic had crashed into him, and a sharp pain shot through his entire body. His mind spun with all that had happened in the past few days. He'd not only helped ruin the sacred magical tree of the Meraki but also completely blown his chance to cancel his debt and get answers about his father from Cudek. All his horrible work on the tree had been for nothing.

And then there were his mom and sisters.

Fates.

"My family! Cudek's going to—" Shenli couldn't bear to say it aloud.

"He thinks you're dead," Madera pointed out. "Seems like he'd have very little reason to bother your family now."

Shenli winced. Cudek didn't need a reason to *bother* anyone. And after what Shenli had done, he'd probably triple the years of Zhao family debt—if not more. Was Meili supposed to take it all on now? She was only ten! He thought of the promise he'd made to Mama that he'd make everything better. He'd ended up making things worse.

"Also, I imagine your chancellor is far too busy with that new tree of his to worry about any dead soldier's family debt," said Madera, as if reading his mind.

"Cudek's grudges don't just go away," said Shenli. "Though you're probably right about the tree keeping him busy."

But how long before the chancellor's thoughts wandered to Shenli's family? A day? A week? Longer? Shenli had to get back and— then what? Beg for Cudek's forgiveness? What choice did he have? He couldn't stay here with the Meraki forever. Surely they all knew what he'd done.

"You have been through a great ordeal," said Madera as her swirl of purple Magic settled on Shenli's chest. At once, a wave of calm passed through him, and his racing heart slowed. The old woman smiled, tapping a finger on the scarf around Shenli's wrist.

"That's a fancy accessory for a soldier," she said.

"It's my mother's."

"It is lovely. Though I am a bit surprised you wore it into battle." Madera arched an eyebrow.

"It's more of a . . . um . . . *practical* accessory," he admitted. "I got to visit her before I left the Mainland. She was in prison with my little sisters. She spotted Wren's message on my wrist and covered it up with this. I thought it was clever, so I kept it."

And also because it smelled like Mama. But he couldn't bring himself to admit *that*.

Madera looked like she was going to say something but then thought better of it. She smiled. "I think your mother might be full of surprises, young man. And I have a feeling she's going to take care of herself and those little girls just fine."

Shenli gave a reluctant nod, thinking of the wooden dragon tied to his ankle, and his eyelids started to droop. He felt so tired all of a sudden. Madera's Magic purred soothingly against his chest, reminding him of his cat, Whiskers.

"For now, you need to rest," said Madera, brushing the hair from Shenli's eyes. "The best thing you can do for your mama is to get better—understood?"

Shenli nodded. He couldn't help Mama and his sisters if he was too tired to even get out of bed. Wren stepped forward then. There was something off about her, something . . . missing. But Shenli suddenly felt too sleepy to sort out what it was.

"Feel better," Wren whispered. A smile flickered at the corner of her mouth, then disappeared. There was little warmth in her eyes.

As Shenli drifted off to sleep, he wondered if Wren would ever forgive him. He definitely didn't deserve it. In the past weeks, he'd managed to betray both the Meraki and the Mainlanders, so what did that make him?

Shenli didn't know who he was anymore.

63.

IN WHICH A TREE
IS MOURNED

The next several days were spent cleaning up Meraki Island while Blue remained in a deep sleep. The footprints of five thousand Mainlander soldiers definitely left their marks. Gardens were trampled. Grassy walkways turned to mud. All the hastily built barricades lay in tatters across the shore, like shredded driftwood. While Blue slept, the other dragons helped carry the pieces to a designated spot where all the debris would be burned. Many buildings looked the worse for wear. Windows were shattered and walls torn away in places where the Mainlander soldiers tried to breach an entrance. There was fire damage to much of the Council Chambers exterior. Surprisingly, the seven Meraki crystals lay untouched. They still shone brightly atop the glass roof.

The only flicker of hope during these dark days was when River and Shahin developed a remedy to reverse the dreamshade effects on the children. After swallowing the elixir, each child woke in a droopy daze. By the end of the week, all the children were back to their normal selves. Which is to say that they woke to find their beloved island very much in sad disarray.

On the seventh day after the battle, the Meraki held a memorial service around the ruined Offering Tree to mourn their loss as a community. The humans stood in a circle around the tree with their Magics while the dragons sat behind them. Madera had also transported Blue's body next to the tree, where he remained in a dismal slumber. Thanks to the efforts of River's roots and Wren's Magic, Cudek had been successful in transporting only half of the tree. But the half that remained was a devastating sight. Charred black from Cudek's fire, it looked like it had been sliced jaggedly down the middle, with its bare scraggly branches reaching to the sky.

Shenli stood on the far outskirts of the Gathering Place, watching the Meraki from a distance, his chest wrapped in thick bandages under his tunic. He nearly hadn't come to the ceremony. After the Meraki Healers said he was strong enough to get out of bed, he'd kept to himself, living in an extra Dragon Rider tent at the very edge of Meraki Island. With all the dirty looks Shenli was getting from the magic folk, he was certain they all knew by now he'd helped Cudek steal and destroy their beloved tree. Still, despite their withering glares, he'd wanted to come today. He felt gutted about having a part in the tree's destruction, and he felt he owed it to the tree to pay his respects.

Shenli caught sight of Wren in the crowd in front of him, but she never looked his direction. He squeezed his eyes shut, wondering if the terrible guilt lodged in his chest would ever go away. "Forgive me," Shenli whispered.

To Wren.

To the tree.

To his family.

River stood next to Wren in the crowd. She'd spent all her waking hours mixing different elixirs—both to try to heal the tree and to try to wake Blue. But she'd had zero luck with either. There were moments, as River sang to the tree and applied a variety of homemade elixirs, when she thought she heard whispers coming from the trunk. But then she'd shake her head and hear only silence. She wasn't going to give up—she'd promised as much to the Meraki Council. But truthfully, River was starting to lose hope that the tree would ever be healed. As for Blue, the Healers had told her that since he'd likely absorbed the dreamshade from all the other dragons in order to wake them, there was no telling what the side effects would be. With every day that passed, it seemed less and less likely that her dragon companion would ever wake.

Among all the gathered Meraki, it was Wren Barrow who grieved more than anyone. The loss of her stolen Magic had carved out a haunting ache inside her. Like part of her soul was missing, and she didn't know who she was without it. To make matters worse, she still had the Council to deal with. Would they carry out their sentence and banish her, after all she and her Magic had risked and done? Were they really that heartless? And then there was Cudek's strange, ominous secret about Granmama's connection to the Forgotten Ones— whoever they were. In fact, Wren had tried confronting her several days ago. After a long afternoon of Council meetings, Granmama had been pruning her sage flower bushes when Wren found her.

"So, Cudek implied this whole battle had something to do with the Forgotten Ones," Wren had said, wringing her hands nervously. "Please tell me who they are."

Her grandmother had closed her eyes for several long moments before finally giving Wren a measured look. "Some things are truly better left buried in the past."

Wren's heart had stuttered. Her grandmother had always been honest with her. She hadn't expected Granmama to dodge the question. Had Cudek been right? Was the Meraki Council truly hiding something horrible about their past?

Wren had tried again. "But Cudek said he's going to set them free to have their revenge. Don't we have a right to know—"

Something dangerous had flashed in Granmama's eyes then. Something Wren had never seen before. A kind of fury. And fear. "Child, I'm asking you to leave it alone. Understood?"

Wren had nodded, even though she understood very little. It was like a coldness had wrapped itself around Madera Starling. Since their talk, Wren couldn't help but feel like Granmama had been avoiding her, and that realization cut almost as deeply and painfully as the loss of her Magic.

Wren shivered, and River noticed. The Dragon Rider frowned and gave Wren's shoulder a gentle squeeze. Wren tried to smile her thanks. River had been a good friend to Wren during these terrible times. The two girls had spent many nights sitting with Blue at the Offering Tree, swapping stories. Or not talking at all. River seemed perfectly at ease with Wren's grieving silence. It was a strange thing to have a friendship grow through shared sorrow. But somehow, for Wren and River, it seemed fitting.

At exactly the seventh hour of the seventh morning after the battle, the sound of a conch shell being blown rose over the ocean, and the Meraki looked at one another apprehensively. The Mainlander call to military training drills had not ceased a single day as they'd toiled over their island cleanup.

As if on cue, the Meraki Elders joined hands, encircled Blue and the tree, and began singing the Songs of Mourning. Then Judge Finlar told the story of the Offering Tree.

"When the First Magics originally visited our world, they initially made their home with the Sodi tribe of the Parch District, in the place that has now become the Wastelands. Wherever the First Magics touched the earth, a new tree grew. From this was born an entire forest of Offering Trees, which would eventually produce a new generation of Magics."

Judge Finlar spoke softly to the crowd while his silver Magic slumped low on his broad shoulder. "After a long while, the forest was burned down by magic-hating humans, and this unforgivable atrocity led to the Third War. All the trees were thought to have been destroyed. But unbeknownst to the nonmagic humans, one little sapling was secretly rescued. And when our people relocated to this island, that resilient little sapling was planted. With much patience and care, the last Offering Tree grew, and with it, new Magic companions were born to our people once more." Finlar paused, giving a mournful glance at the charred trunk. "Today, our pain is great, and our enemy even greater." Finlar's eyes found Shenli off in the distance, and several Meraki spun around to glare at him.

Shenli wanted to turn and slink away, but instead, he stood firm. The judge wasn't wrong, after all.

Madam Madera took a step forward. She leaned on her cane, her ancient eyes scanning the crowd carefully. "Dear Ones, may you commemorate all that has passed between us these last few weeks. More than anything else, we must remember who we are—through the stories we tell." Madera paused, allowing the significance of the moment to build between each human and dragon.

"Remember, Meraki, how we banded together honorably to fight an enemy who outnumbered us. We also remember, of course, the greedy chancellor who took so much from us. But, my dears, our story is so much more than darkness. Our story is one of hope. Because we *also* remember the heroic children and the courageous Magics who bravely risked everything to keep the darkness at bay."

In the crowd, Wren felt her breath shudder, and River linked arms with her for support.

Madera steeled her gaze, her violet eyes shining in the dawn. "We remember our Healers, who've worked tirelessly to bring us back to health and bring our children back from their long slumber. We remember our countless Meraki soldiers, and their Magics, who fought valiantly, without ceasing." Her voice hitched, and everyone in the crowd stood a little taller, many of them still nursing battle wounds. "But above all else, my dears, we must remember the stories of the Awaited One, who binds our hope together and keeps it grounded." Madera's gaze turned to Blue, his feathery chest rising and falling steadily. "A small blue dragon with eyes like the sea."

Many people clapped and cried, though the sleeping dragon paid them no attention.

At that moment, the sky exploded.

Dark clouds gathered overhead, casting a shadow across the Meraki and dragons, who stared up wide-eyed with fear. All the Magics growled in trepidation. Red lightning crackled across the sky; then an enormous maroon cloud lowered. It shifted its shape until it resembled . . . a face.

"That's Cudek!" Wren yelled. All at once, shouts and cries rang from the Meraki as they clutched one another in terror. The cloud face chuckled, deep and gravelly, causing Shenli's arm hairs to stand on end.

"Good day, wretched magic folk. Just wanted to stop by and see how all your children are doing." Cudek's cloud face chuckled once more. "I imagine by now that meddlesome Dragon Rider has helped you find the remedy."

River lifted her chin and glared back at the Cudek cloud while Wren squeezed her hand.

"Yes, I'm told I also have her to thank for meddling with my transportation spell." The cloud face scowled.

"Told?" repeated Wren. "Who's *telling* him?"

"I still can't seem to erase the stench of fire ginger roots from my uniform," cloud-Cudek growled. "Next time you will not be so lucky, Dragon Rider."

River steeled her jaw.

And several people in the crowd murmured, *"Next time?"*

The Cudek cloud lowered. "I wonder, have you all discovered my little surprise yet? If not, you will before long."

Wren clenched her fists.

Shenli's chest wound throbbed painfully.

Blue snored away, dreadfully unaware.

And River whispered something that sounded like *the arrows . . .* but no one heard her.

"Though I'm not the only one with surprises and secrets—am I, Madera?" Cloud Cudek winked. "And on *that* note, I bid you farewell, Meraki. Rest assured, I will be seeing you all very soon."

With that, the crimson cloud flickered and dissipated, taking with it the last slivers of hope within each Meraki and dragon, until Cudek's face was nothing more than a burning image in everyone's minds.

64.

*A*nd so it has begun, kit.
Now we wait.

We watch.

We listen.

Above all else, we hope.

Yes! We will carry the Great Hope in our bellies until all goodness has been restored. Listen, young one, to the rest of the Havensong, and hide its hope in your heart:

THE TYRANT THWARTED, HIS ARMIES RETREAT
BUT THE TYRANT LIES—AND DEATH WILL CHEAT
LOYALTIES FALTER
THE GREAT TREE IS LOST
THE FOUR HEROES WILL SURELY COUNT THE COST

THE ENEMY WILL RISE, O PEOPLE OF PEACE
A NEW DARKNESS STIRS, BENEATH THE DEEP
SECRETS UNFOLD, A CAUSE TO AVENGE
THE FORGOTTEN ONES WILL HAVE THEIR REVENGE

But sleep soundly now, as peace allows
Prayers of comfort steepled in ancient vows
For there is One who can make amends—
With the aid of three Unlikely Friends

ACKNOWLEDGMENTS

When it comes to slaying dragons (or transforming into one!), having an awesome team by your side is of the utmost importance. To Team Havensong: I couldn't have done it without all of you. This story started as mine, but then it grew. To anyone who believed in Blue and his three Unlikely Friends and shared their story, thank you.

To the incomparably brilliant Joanna Volpe: I am beyond blessed to have you as my agent. I am forever grateful for your guidance and encouragement. Thank you for helping me get unstuck from the Weeds of Revision—you are a brainstorming wizard! I am so proud and honored to be one of your leaves!

Thank you to the entire New Leaf Literary team for the passion you put into bringing amazing books to the world. Jordan Hill, thank you for answering my newbie client questions with such kindness and making me feel welcome. Jenniea Carter, assistant extraordinaire, thanks for having my back. Kate Sullivan, I'll never forget how you helped me find Shenli's voice and the kind words you said about Blue's farewell scene to the Gerberan knights. To Team World Domination: you are rock stars! Thank you for all of your hard work in sending Heroes of Havensong overseas!

To Liesa Abrams: Editors are the mages of the book world, and you never cease to help bring the Story Magic. I am so grateful I get to work with you. You've helped me understand my characters more deeply and recognize what the best kind of conflict looks like. Thank you for helping me shape my story into the greatest version of itself. You were right—it was worth all those rounds of revisions! ☺

To the extraordinary Labyrinth Road team and the amazing people at Random House Children's Books who made my story an *actual* Book-Shaped Thing: Thank you for your warm welcoming of my book. Your hard work and enthusiasm mean the world to me. Emily Harburg, thanks for all your kindness, humor, and encouragement. Thank you to the proofreaders and copy editors. (From you I learned how often I like my characters to widen their eyes and cross their arms!) Thanks also to the sales and marketing teams for your support. Sylvia Bi and April Ward, you did a stellar job with my cover design—it looks amazing! An extra-big thank-you to the extraordinarily talented Ilse Gort for illustrating my *stunning* cover—you captured the essence of my story beautifully and exceeded my expectations. And a very special shout-out to Abby Fritz, who took the time to read early drafts and helped brainstorm fantastic ideas like Blue and River crash-landing—you truly helped make this story better. And your love of Wren's Magic was inspirational.

To Sveta Dorosheva, you have my whole heart of gratitude for the gorgeous map of Haven. You are so wonderfully talented, and it was an honor to work with you.

A huge thank-you to Christa Adell Kile for your phenomenal work on the educator guide—at this point you know my words better than I do, and I am so grateful for your skill, creativity, and enthusiasm.

To my Pitch Wars mentor, Stacey Trombley, you were the first one to see potential in my writing. Juliana Brandt, thank you for connecting me to my first CPs and for always being so supportive. Big hugs to my critique partners who have helped me craft better stories: Mel Stephenson, Stacy Hackney, Gabrielle Byrne, Hilary Harwell, Victoria Piontek, and Aubrey Schoenfeld. Special thanks go to Audrey Fae Dion (*cue: throwing of confetti*). Your brilliant feedback helped shape the draft that found its way to my agent. I will forever be grateful. Taryn Albright, you were my first real editor, all those years ago, who showed me the ropes of revision. Someday you'll teach me how you can write twenty books a year. To Naomi Hughes, your encouraging edit letters kept me going through some tough years. Esme Symes-Smith, my Labyrinth Road sibling: Thank you for being so gracious with your time as we walk this road together. Cat Bakewell, I'm so happy to have found you! Your optimism is contagious and much appreciated. Jenna DeVillier, you've been a constant support all these years. Chiara Beth Colombi, it's so great to have an agency sibling to navigate this road with! Matt McMann, thank you for your patient and thoughtful responses—both about writing and about faith. Also a big shout-out to my writing communities: #MGin23, #MGBookHub, #2023Debuts, and #MGremlins: I'm grateful to have y'all to collaborate (and commiserate) with.

To the authors who welcomed me in ways big and small, thank you for lighting the path for me to follow: Allison Brennan, Lindsay Currie, A. J. Sass, Lorelei Savaryn, and Tracey West. Lisa McMann, thanks for helping me learn the ropes of publishing (and also your reminder to *breathe*). To the agents who made me feel *seen*—and not like just another author in the slush pile: Fiona Kenshole, your lovely workshops were a much-needed creative spark, and your never-ending enthusiasm is quite magical. Danielle Chiotti, you were always so kind in our correspondence; thank you for your encouragement over the years. Saba Sulaiman: I'll never forget how you gave me such detailed and personalized feedback after a submission. Truly, it was the kindest and most optimistic rejection letter I've ever received.

To the authors who fill me with inspiration: Jonathan Auxier, your creativity is astounding. Anne Ursu, no one layers emotional arcs like you do. Kelly Barnhill, your beautiful words and whimsical worlds helped me realize what kind of writer I want to be. Shannon Messenger, queen of cliff-hangers, you are the master of combining delicious dialogue, lovable characters, and high-stakes plot.

To Barbara Blank, my ninth-grade English teacher: You assigned our class to read *Ender's Game* and write a three-page science-fiction short story. My story—the first real story I ever attempted—was thirty-one pages long. I still have it. Crafting those words truly sparked my love of writing. I hope someday to thank you in person.

To my dearest Friend Squad, which has cheered me on over the years: Alice Issac, you have been a faithful, constant, joyful encouragement of a friend. Someday your life story needs to become a book! Brenda Miller, thank you for all your kind and caring guidance over the years. Laura Rettinger (*"This girl is on fire!"*), I will never forget the love and encouragement you gave me early on. It meant the world to me. Danielle Young, your "seven" enthusiasm for my writing journey has always been most welcome. Jenny Azevedo, you will always be a kindred spirit. You're my people. Heather Nunn, thanks for sticking with me through all the ups and downs. (You are the only one with video footage of me literally falling on my face.) You are braver than you know. Lindsey Williams, thank you for asking for book updates and giving this Enneagram 9 the space to gush about my work. I'm so happy to share life with you and your family.

And to Tabitha Howell, my bestie: Where would I be without you? I'm so thankful for our daily Marco Polo check-ins. You are my cheerleader, therapist, comic relief, and travel buddy. Thank you for always listening, encouraging me, talking me off the ledge, and making me laugh (*honk!*), and for lighting the fire whenever I need to be brave. I will forever be grateful for your friendship. May we always be planning our next BFF Disney Trip. (I'm lookin' at you, Paris!) ☺

To my parents: I love you both. This book wouldn't exist without all your love, encouragement, and support of my creative pursuits. To my mom, Susan Berndt, thanks for taking me to the library all those times as a kid. It was there, sitting on the floor in the children's book section, that I learned my love of dragons and magic. To my dad, William Berndt, thanks for driving me to countless soccer games and practices. It was on the soccer field that I learned teamwork, perseverance, and how to do hard things. To my sister, Michelle Berndt, who always has accepted me for who I am, weird quirks and all: I love you, and I can't wait to hear where you're traveling next.

To my goober boys: You spur on my imagination each and every day. Being your mom is my absolute greatest adventure. Mason, you show me how to have a kind and helpful heart. Parker, my little engineer, you inspire me to be creative in new ways. Joey, you remind me how to be silly and have fun. Elijah, you teach me to be brave and find joy in all things. I love you all to the moon and back.

And lastly, to my husband, Ric Reyes: Thank you for your ceaseless optimism. You were my first reader, editor, and fan. You've read every book I've written (sometimes twice). I remember when you read my very first manuscript and ever so gently suggested that *maybe I could read a book on the craft of writing?* (That was totes *smort.*) I will forever be grateful for the times you encouraged me to pursue writing not just as a hobby but as a career. Thank you for the countless hours you watched the kids so I could write—especially during my weekend writer retreats. You get the Dundie award for being an amazing husband-slash-genius. You have all my love and thanks. I owe you all the Oreos.

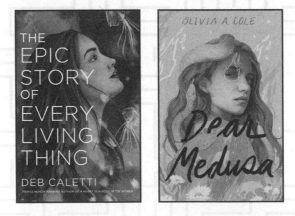